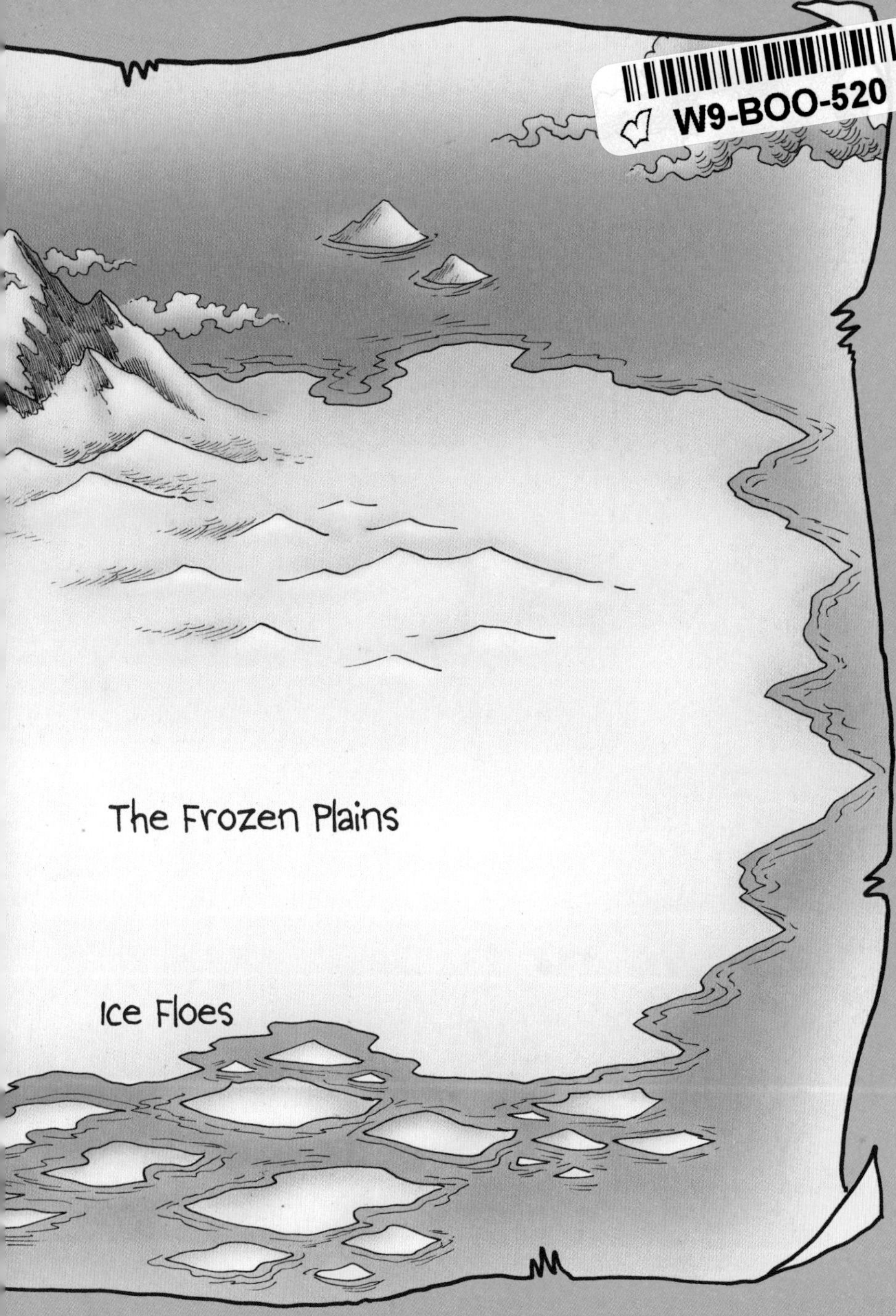
The Frozen Plains
Ice Floes

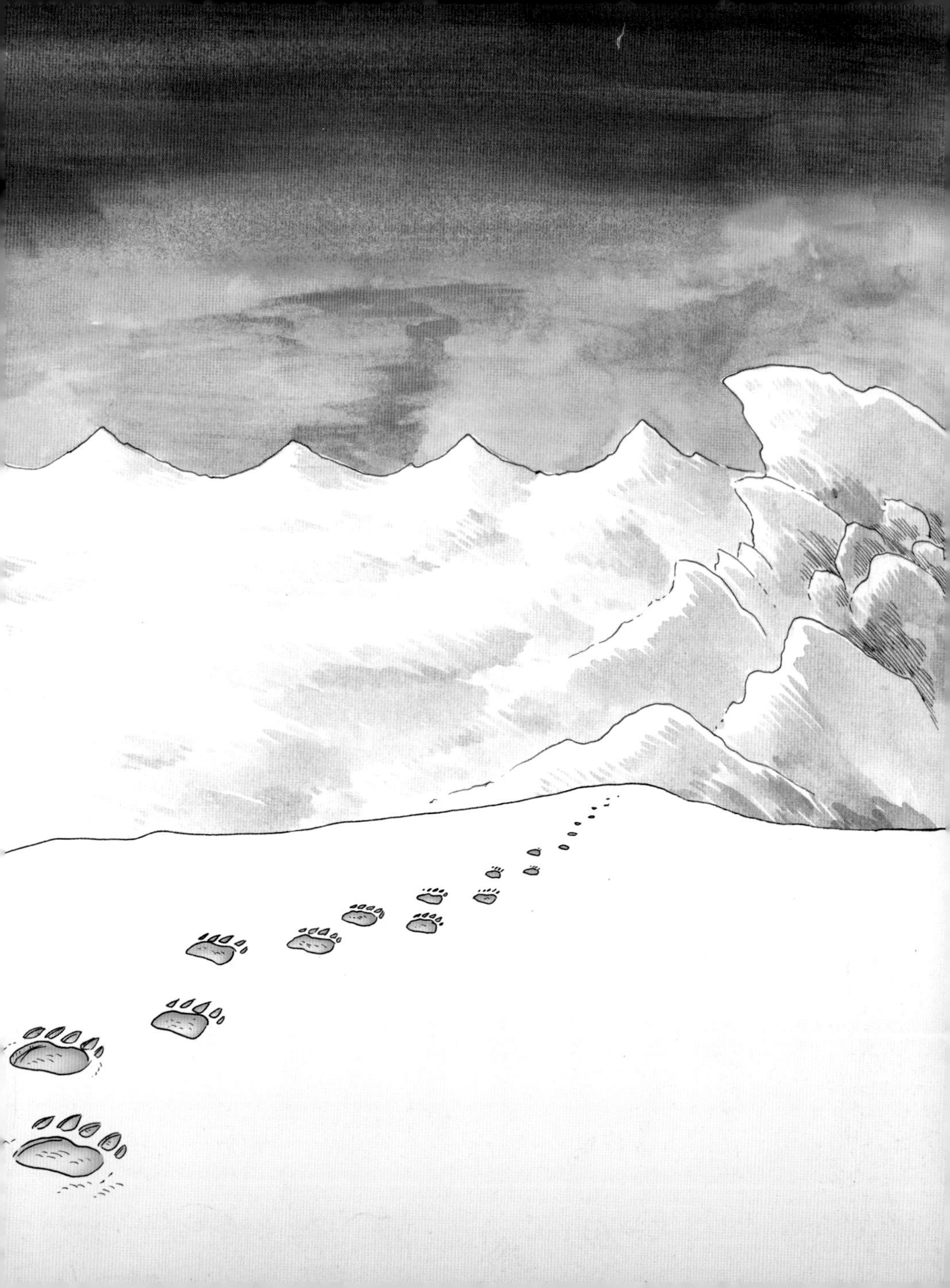

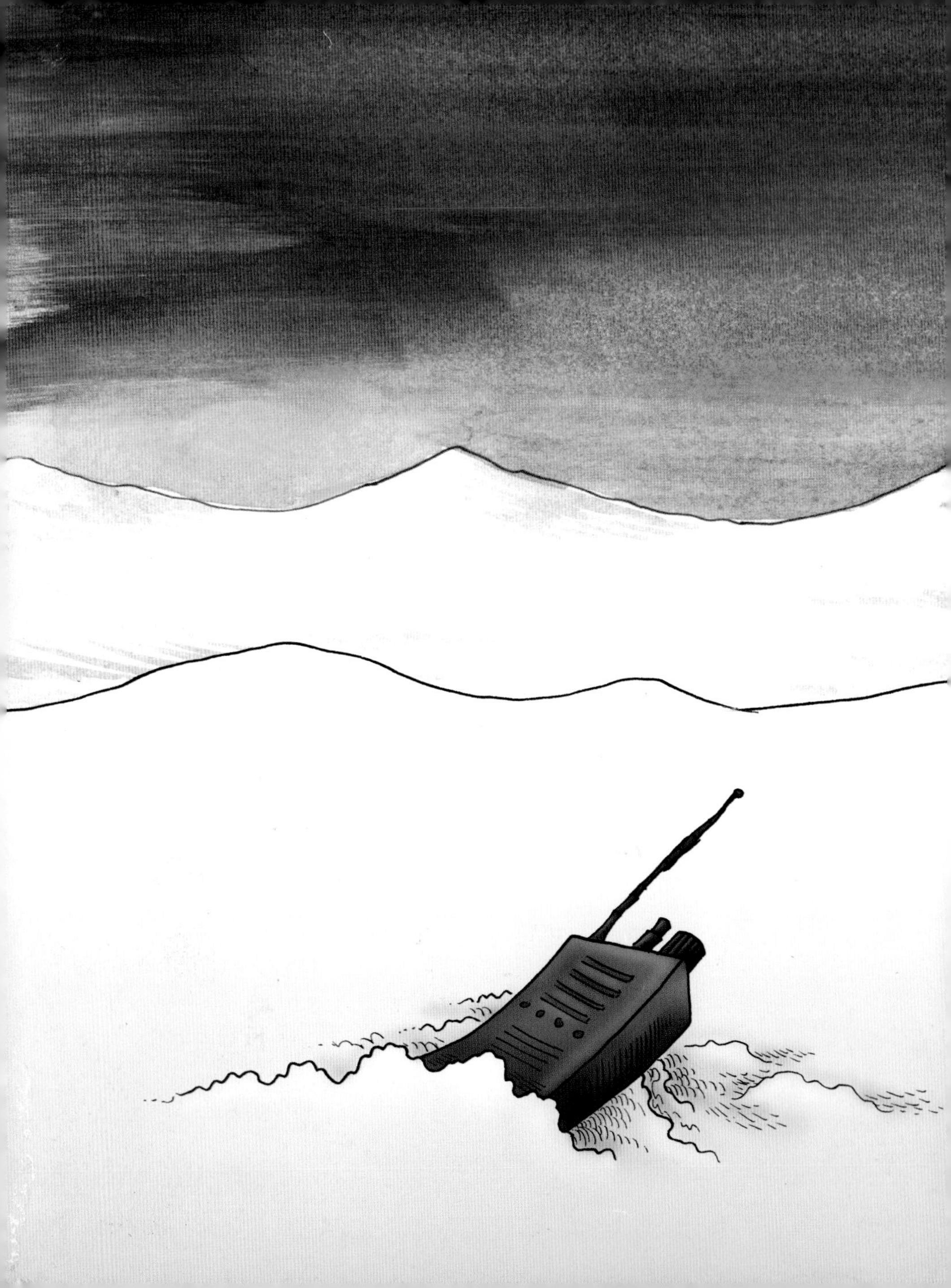

Poptropica ®²

T_{HE} LOST EXPEDITION

BY
MITCH KRPATA

ILLUSTRATED BY
KORY MERRITT

SERIES BASED ON
A CONCEPT
BY **JEFF KINNEY**

AMULET BOOKS
NEW YORK

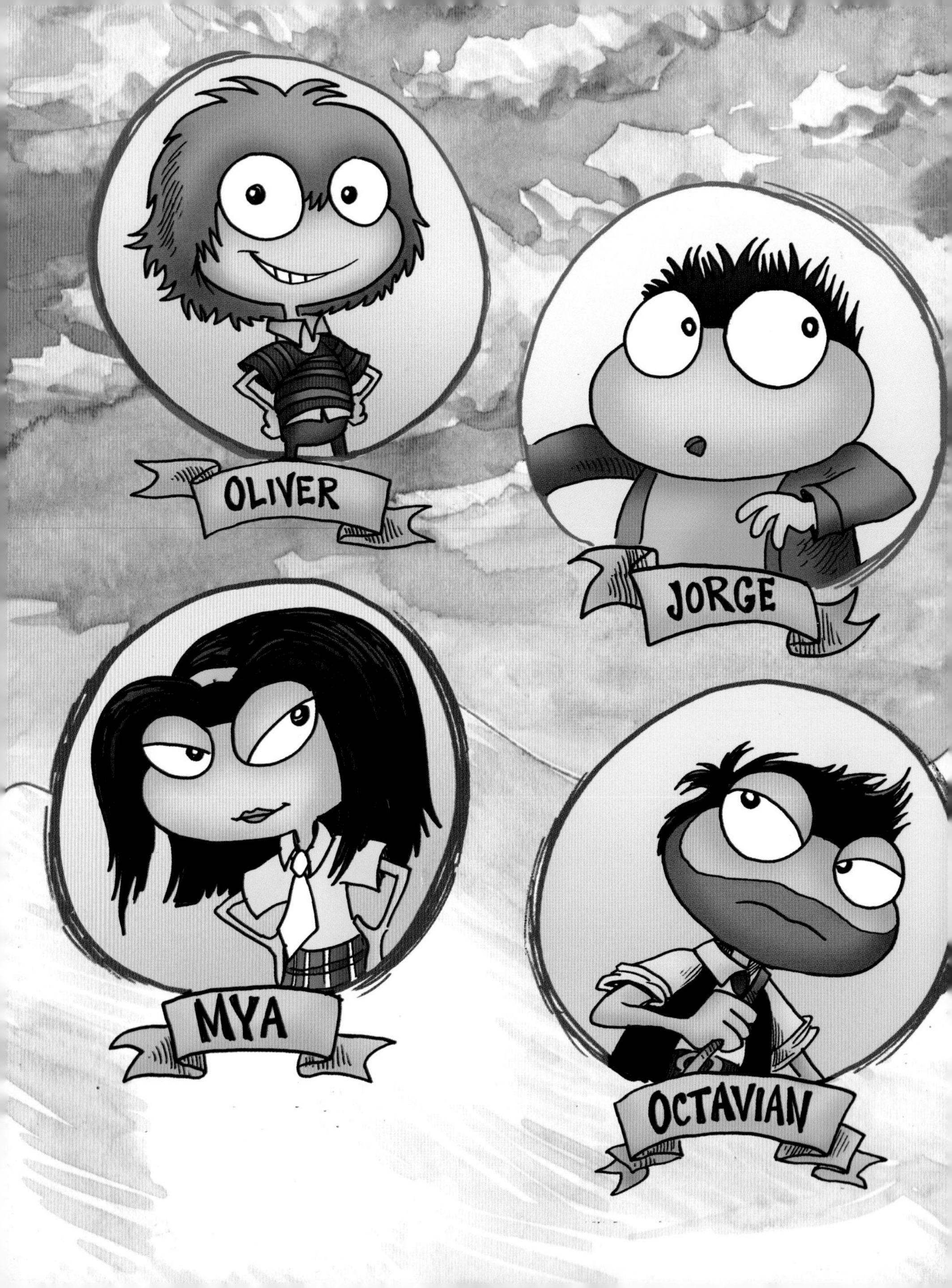
OLIVER
JORGE
MYA
OCTAVIAN

PREVIOUSLY ON

Poptropica®

Mya, Oliver, and Jorge were transported
to the mysterious islands of Poptropica
by the evil Octavian. After narrowly
escaping a band of Vikings, the kids have
taken to the seas. With the help of a
magical map, they now search for
a way home—but Octavian
is hot on their trail!

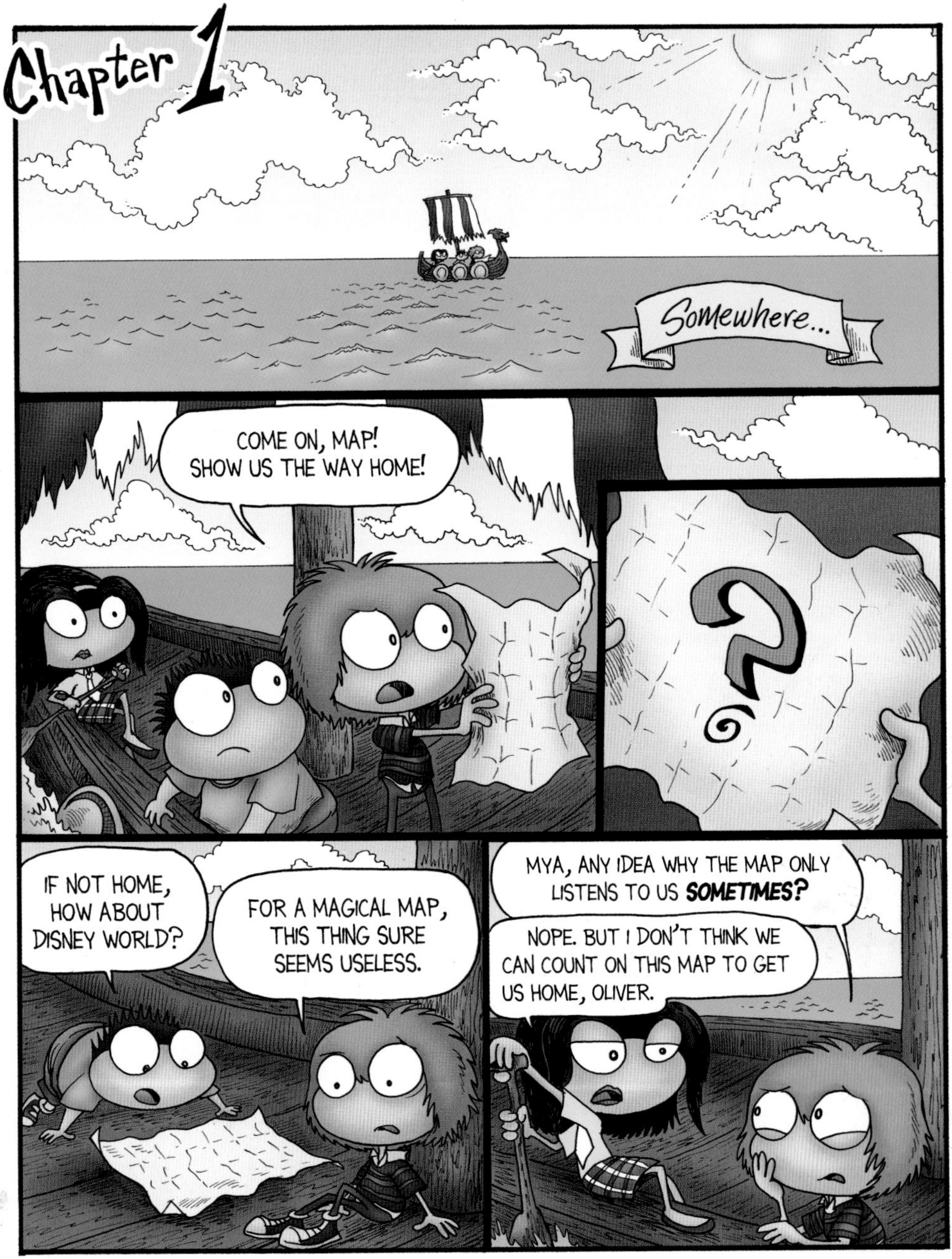
Chapter 1
Somewhere...
COME ON, MAP! SHOW US THE WAY HOME!
IF NOT HOME, HOW ABOUT DISNEY WORLD?
FOR A MAGICAL MAP, THIS THING SURE SEEMS USELESS.
MYA, ANY IDEA WHY THE MAP ONLY LISTENS TO US **SOMETIMES?**
NOPE. BUT I DON'T THINK WE CAN COUNT ON THIS MAP TO GET US HOME, OLIVER.

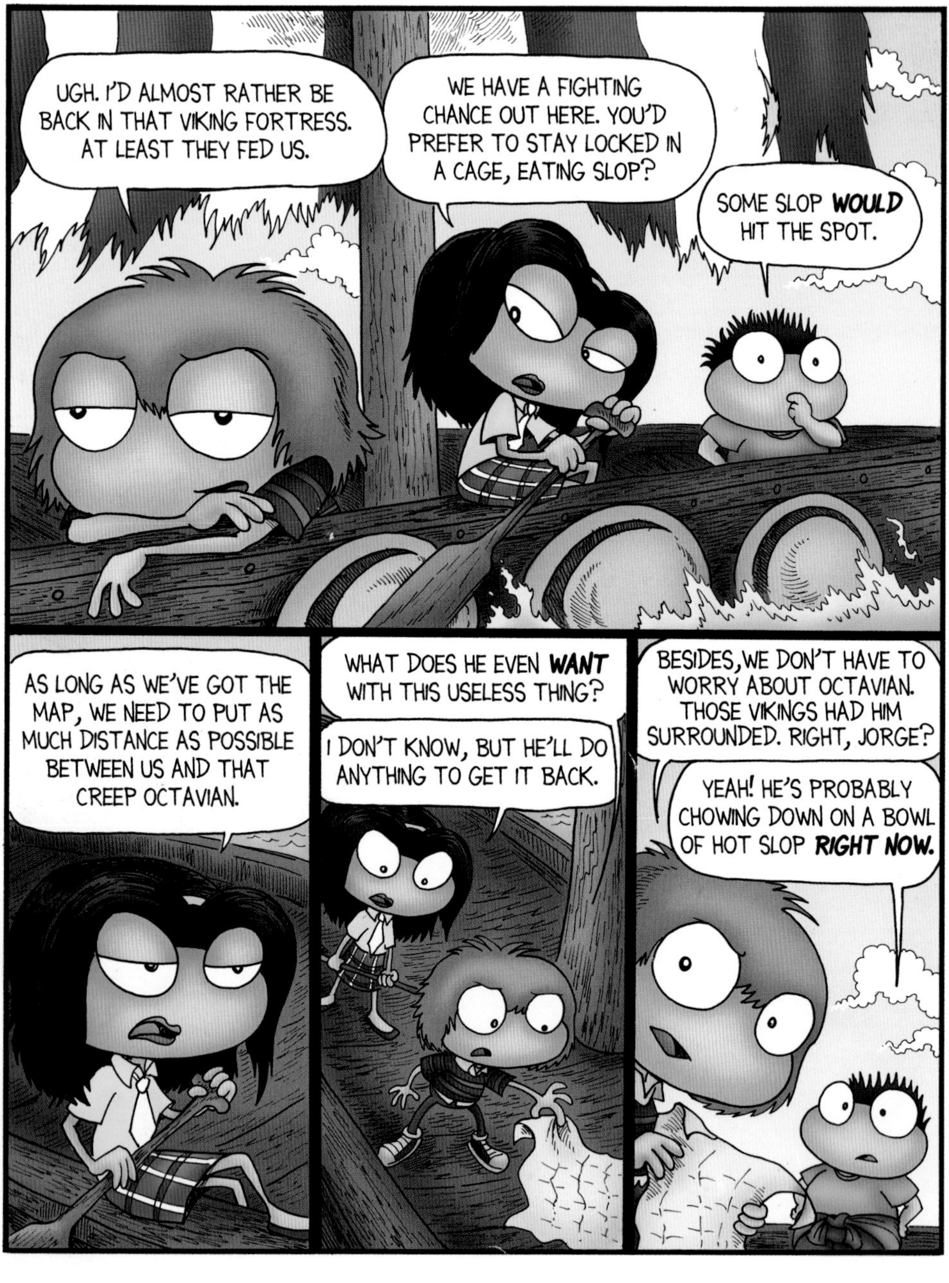
UGH. I'D ALMOST RATHER BE BACK IN THAT VIKING FORTRESS. AT LEAST THEY FED US.
WE HAVE A FIGHTING CHANCE OUT HERE. YOU'D PREFER TO STAY LOCKED IN A CAGE, EATING SLOP?
SOME SLOP **WOULD** HIT THE SPOT.
AS LONG AS WE'VE GOT THE MAP, WE NEED TO PUT AS MUCH DISTANCE AS POSSIBLE BETWEEN US AND THAT CREEP OCTAVIAN.
WHAT DOES HE EVEN **WANT** WITH THIS USELESS THING?
I DON'T KNOW, BUT HE'LL DO ANYTHING TO GET IT BACK.
BESIDES, WE DON'T HAVE TO WORRY ABOUT OCTAVIAN. THOSE VIKINGS HAD HIM SURROUNDED. RIGHT, JORGE?
YEAH! HE'S PROBABLY CHOWING DOWN ON A BOWL OF HOT SLOP **RIGHT NOW.**

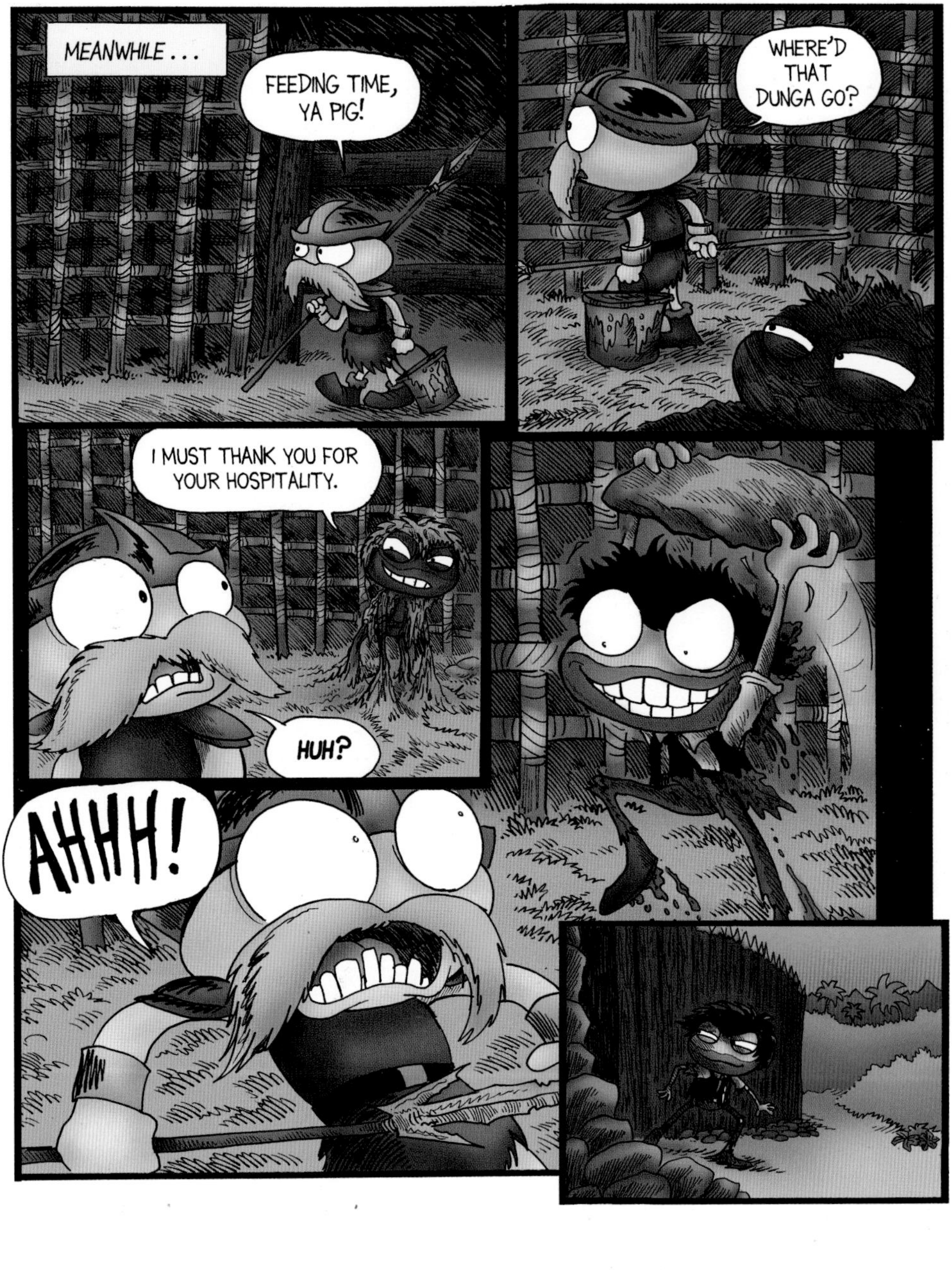
MEANWHILE . . .
FEEDING TIME, YA PIG!
WHERE'D THAT DUNGA GO?
I MUST THANK YOU FOR YOUR HOSPITALITY.
HUH?
AHHH!

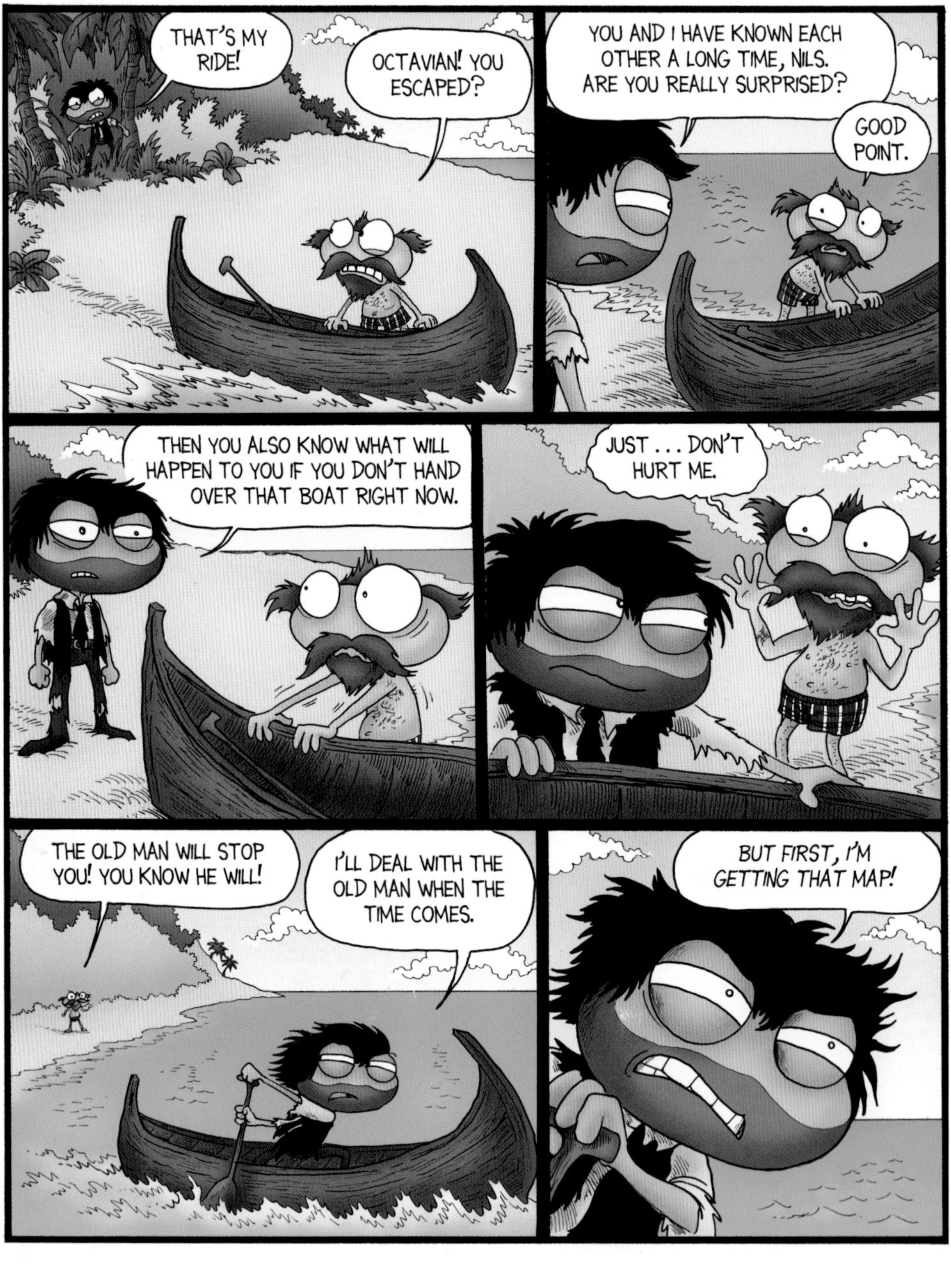
THAT'S MY RIDE!
OCTAVIAN! YOU ESCAPED?
YOU AND I HAVE KNOWN EACH OTHER A LONG TIME, NILS. ARE YOU REALLY SURPRISED?
GOOD POINT.
THEN YOU ALSO KNOW WHAT WILL HAPPEN TO YOU IF YOU DON'T HAND OVER THAT BOAT RIGHT NOW.
JUST . . . DON'T HURT ME.
THE OLD MAN WILL STOP YOU! YOU KNOW HE WILL!
I'LL DEAL WITH THE OLD MAN WHEN THE TIME COMES.
BUT FIRST, I'M GETTING THAT MAP!

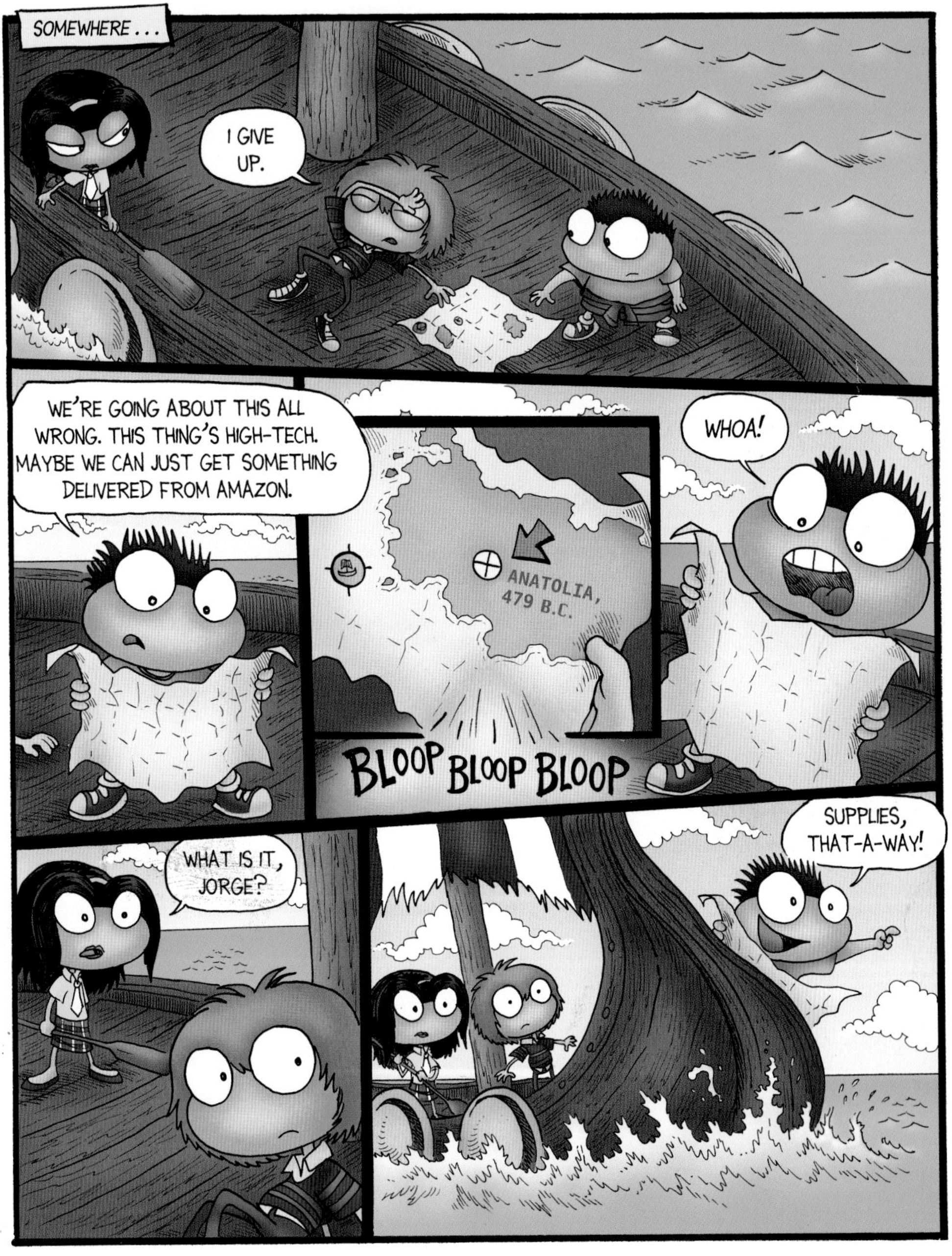
SOMEWHERE . . .
I GIVE UP.
WE'RE GOING ABOUT THIS ALL WRONG. THIS THING'S HIGH-TECH. MAYBE WE CAN JUST GET SOMETHING DELIVERED FROM AMAZON.
ANATOLIA, 479 B.C.
BLOOP BLOOP BLOOP
WHOA!
WHAT IS IT, JORGE?
SUPPLIES, THAT-A-WAY!

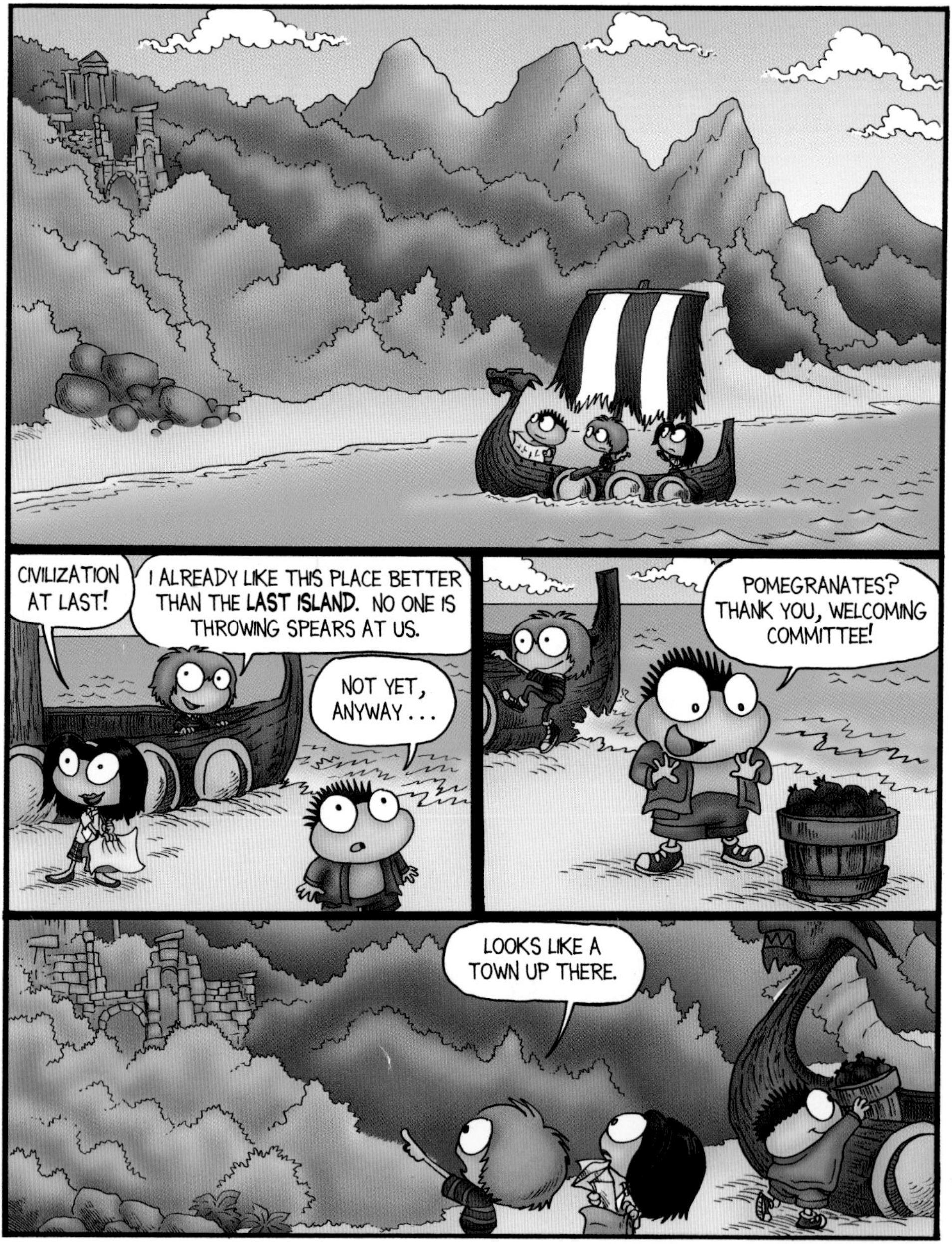
CIVILIZATION AT LAST!
I ALREADY LIKE THIS PLACE BETTER THAN THE LAST ISLAND. NO ONE IS THROWING SPEARS AT US.
NOT YET, ANYWAY . . .
POMEGRANATES? THANK YOU, WELCOMING COMMITTEE!
LOOKS LIKE A TOWN UP THERE.

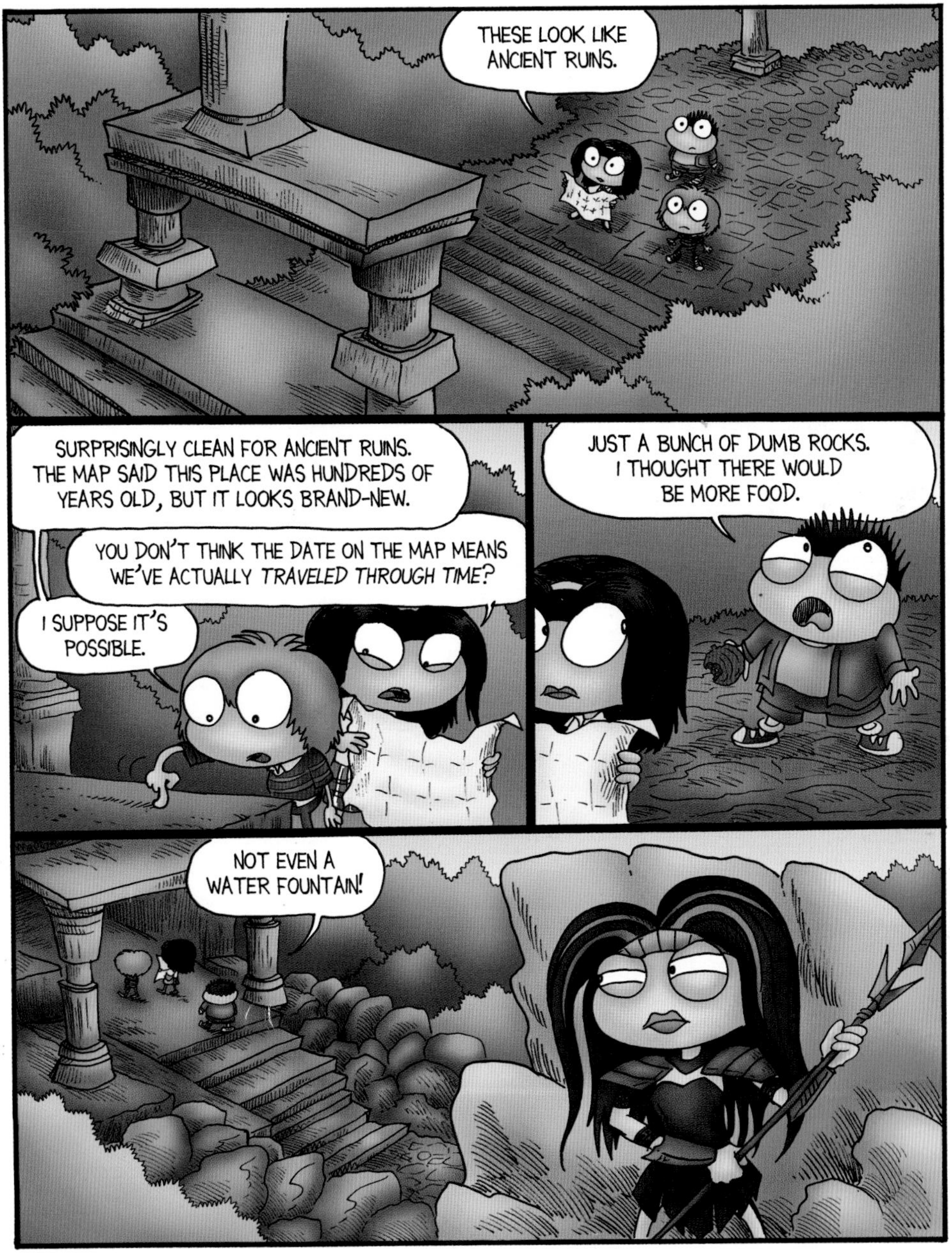

THESE LOOK LIKE ANCIENT RUINS.
SURPRISINGLY CLEAN FOR ANCIENT RUINS. THE MAP SAID THIS PLACE WAS HUNDREDS OF YEARS OLD, BUT IT LOOKS BRAND-NEW.
YOU DON'T THINK THE DATE ON THE MAP MEANS WE'VE ACTUALLY *TRAVELED THROUGH TIME*?
I SUPPOSE IT'S POSSIBLE.
JUST A BUNCH OF DUMB ROCKS. I THOUGHT THERE WOULD BE MORE FOOD.
NOT EVEN A WATER FOUNTAIN!

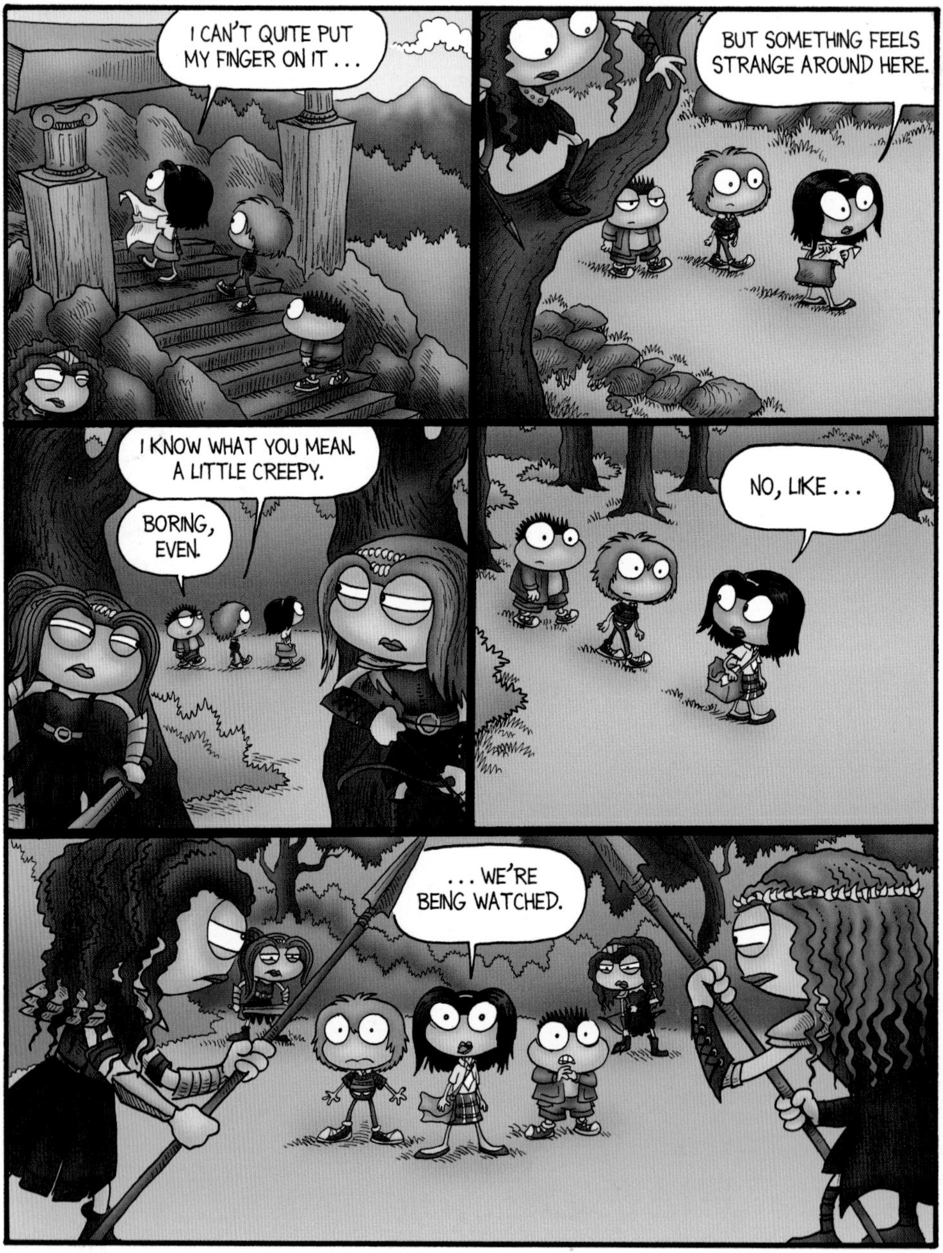

I CAN'T QUITE PUT MY FINGER ON IT . . .
BUT SOMETHING FEELS STRANGE AROUND HERE.
I KNOW WHAT YOU MEAN. A LITTLE CREEPY.
BORING, EVEN.
NO, LIKE . . .
. . . WE'RE BEING WATCHED.

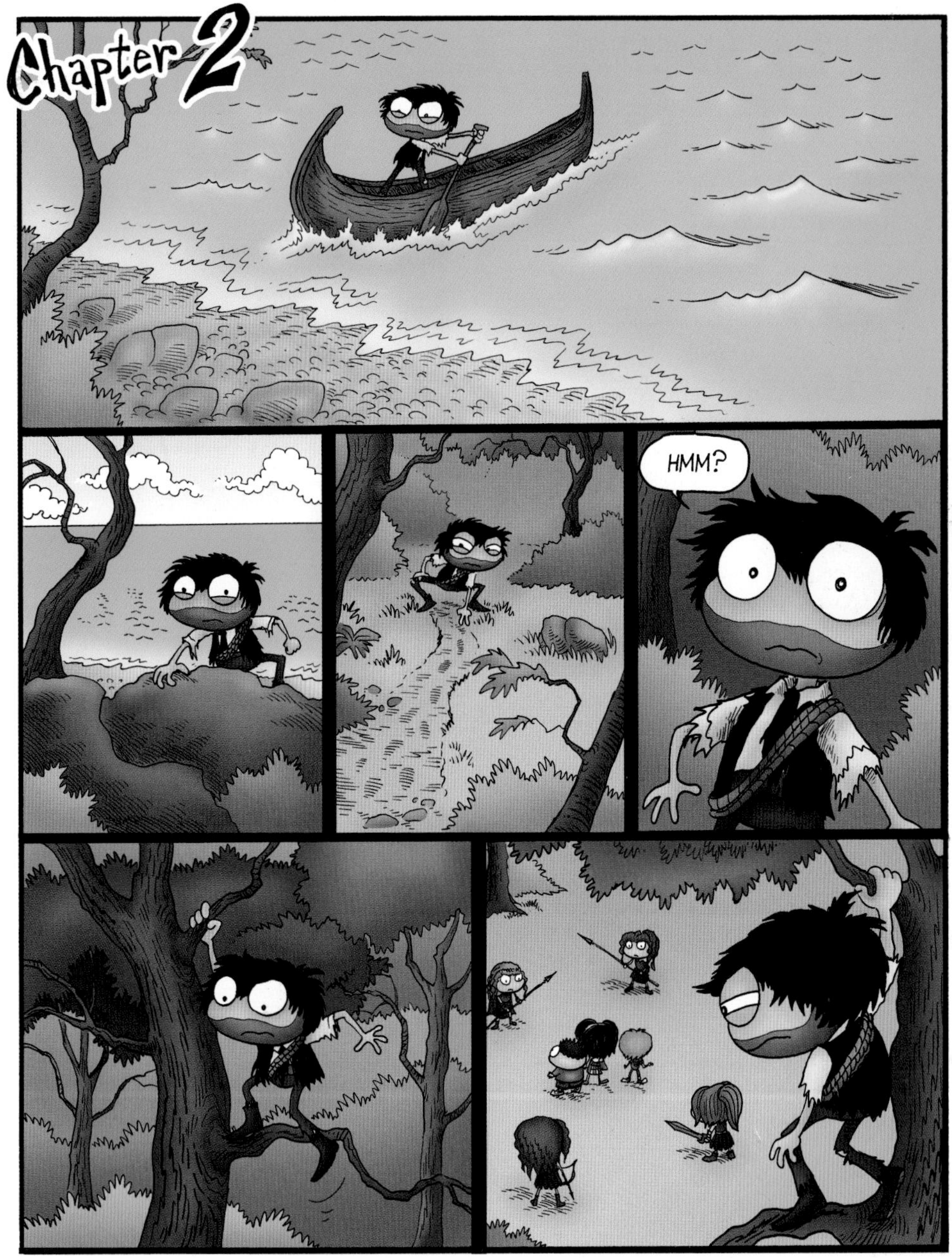
Chapter 2
HMM?

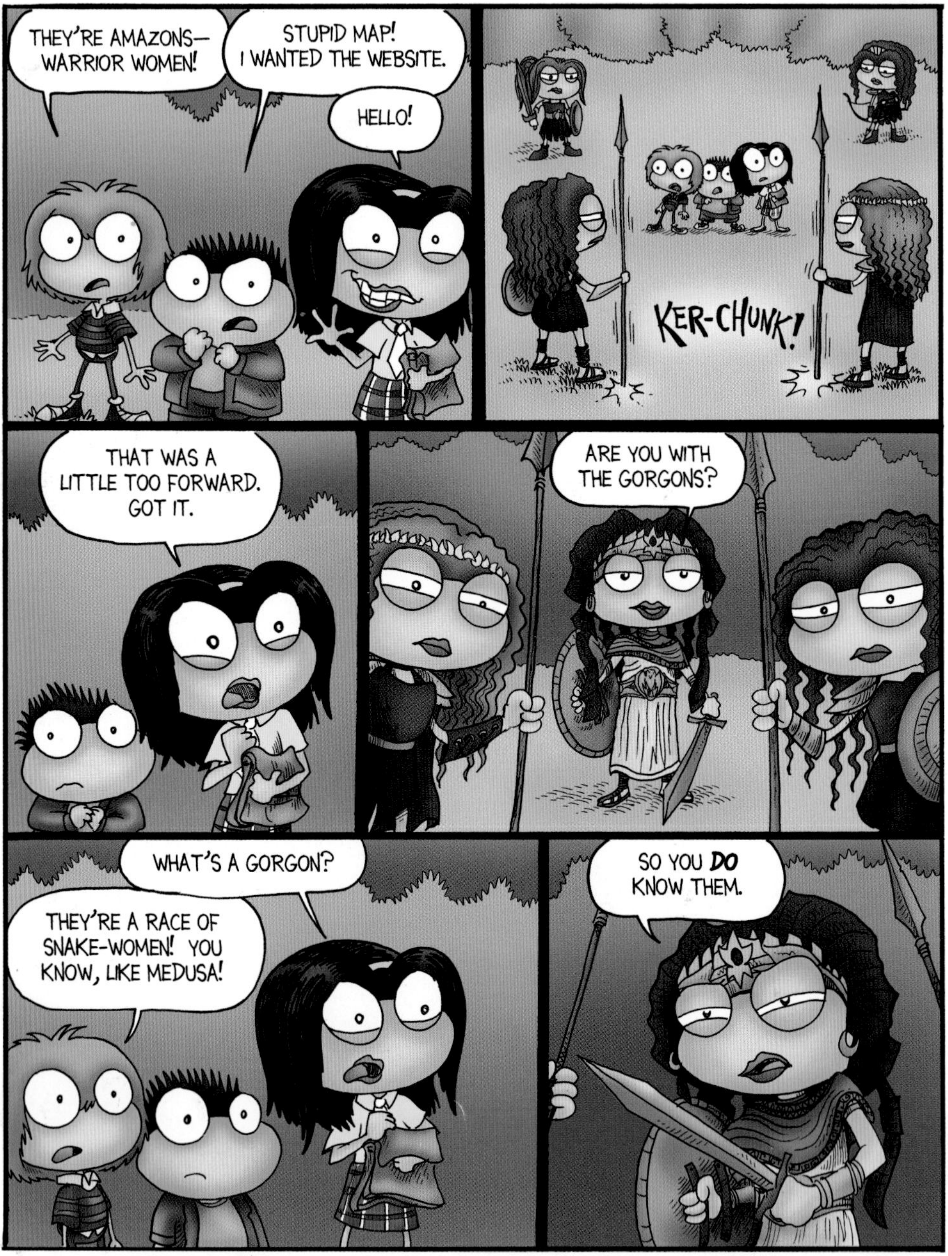
THEY'RE AMAZONS— WARRIOR WOMEN!
STUPID MAP! I WANTED THE WEBSITE.
HELLO!
KER-CHUNK!
THAT WAS A LITTLE TOO FORWARD. GOT IT.
ARE YOU WITH THE GORGONS?
WHAT'S A GORGON?
THEY'RE A RACE OF SNAKE-WOMEN! YOU KNOW, LIKE MEDUSA!
SO YOU **DO** KNOW THEM.

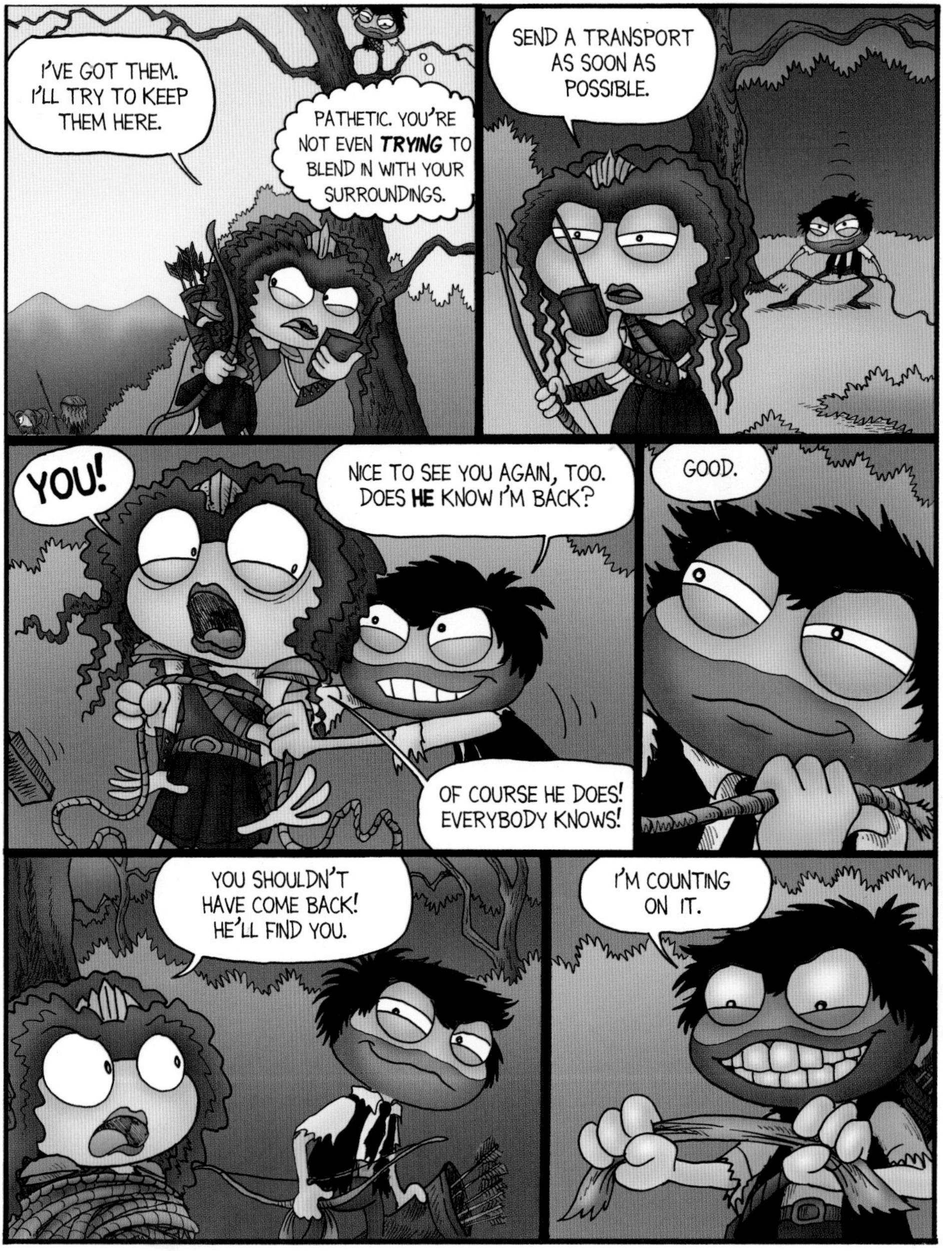
I'VE GOT THEM. I'LL TRY TO KEEP THEM HERE.
PATHETIC. YOU'RE NOT EVEN **TRYING** TO BLEND IN WITH YOUR SURROUNDINGS.
SEND A TRANSPORT AS SOON AS POSSIBLE.
YOU!
NICE TO SEE YOU AGAIN, TOO. DOES **HE** KNOW I'M BACK?
OF COURSE HE DOES! EVERYBODY KNOWS!
GOOD.
YOU SHOULDN'T HAVE COME BACK! HE'LL FIND YOU.
I'M COUNTING ON IT.

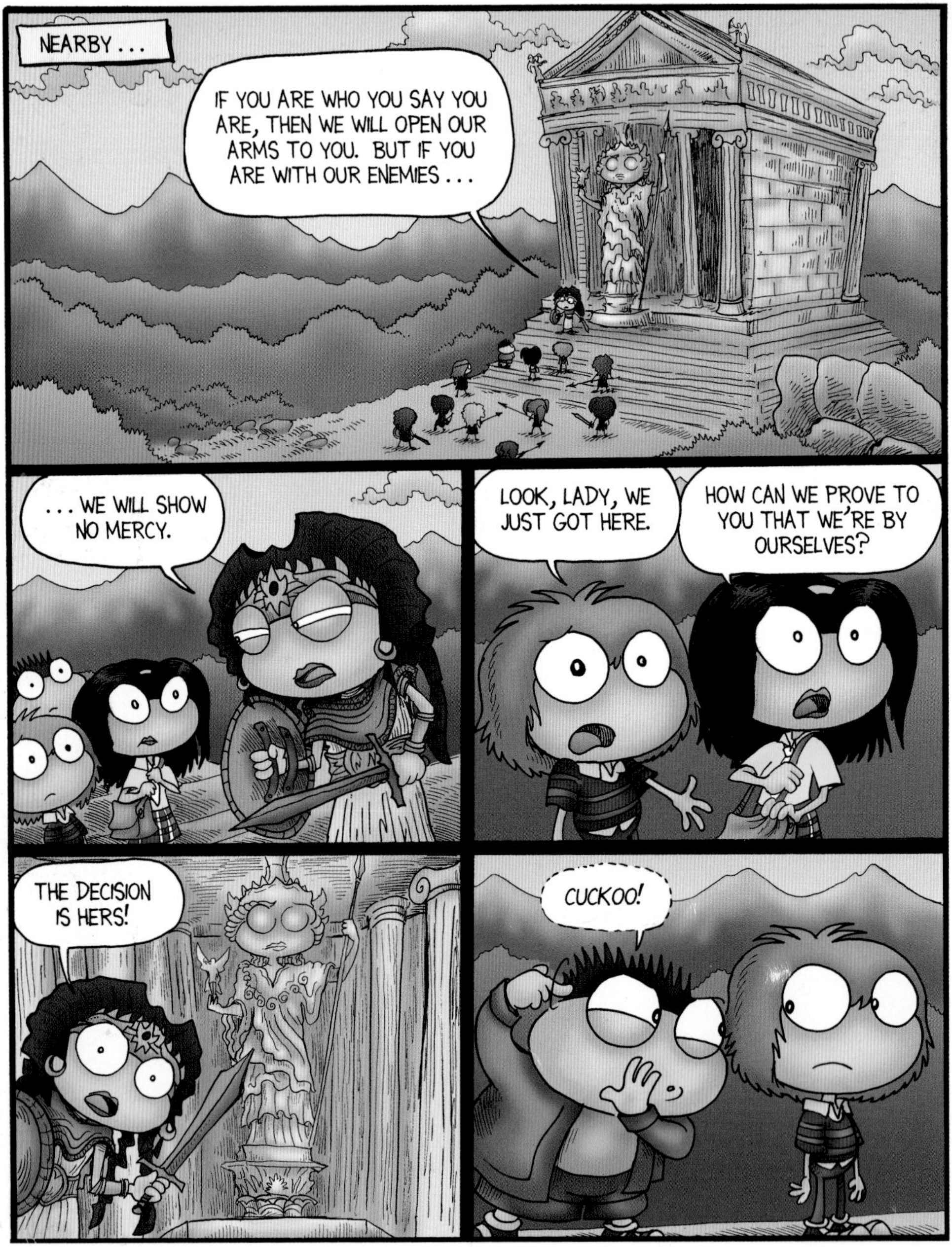
NEARBY . . .
IF YOU ARE WHO YOU SAY YOU ARE, THEN WE WILL OPEN OUR ARMS TO YOU. BUT IF YOU ARE WITH OUR ENEMIES . . .
. . . WE WILL SHOW NO MERCY.
LOOK, LADY, WE JUST GOT HERE.
HOW CAN WE PROVE TO YOU THAT WE'RE BY OURSELVES?
THE DECISION IS HERS!
CUCKOO!

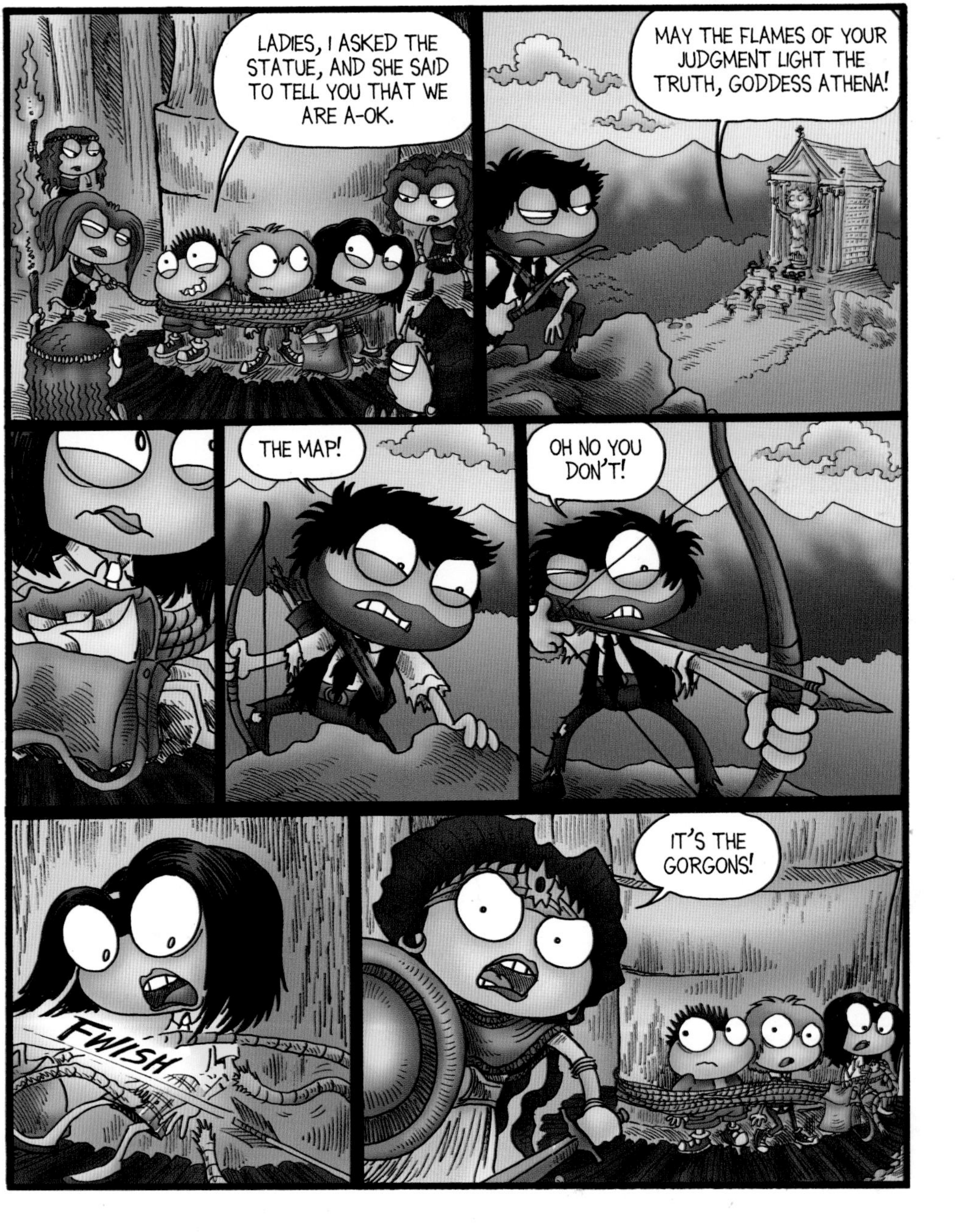
LADIES, I ASKED THE STATUE, AND SHE SAID TO TELL YOU THAT WE ARE A-OK.
MAY THE FLAMES OF YOUR JUDGMENT LIGHT THE TRUTH, GODDESS ATHENA!
THE MAP!
OH NO YOU DON'T!
FWISH
IT'S THE GORGONS!

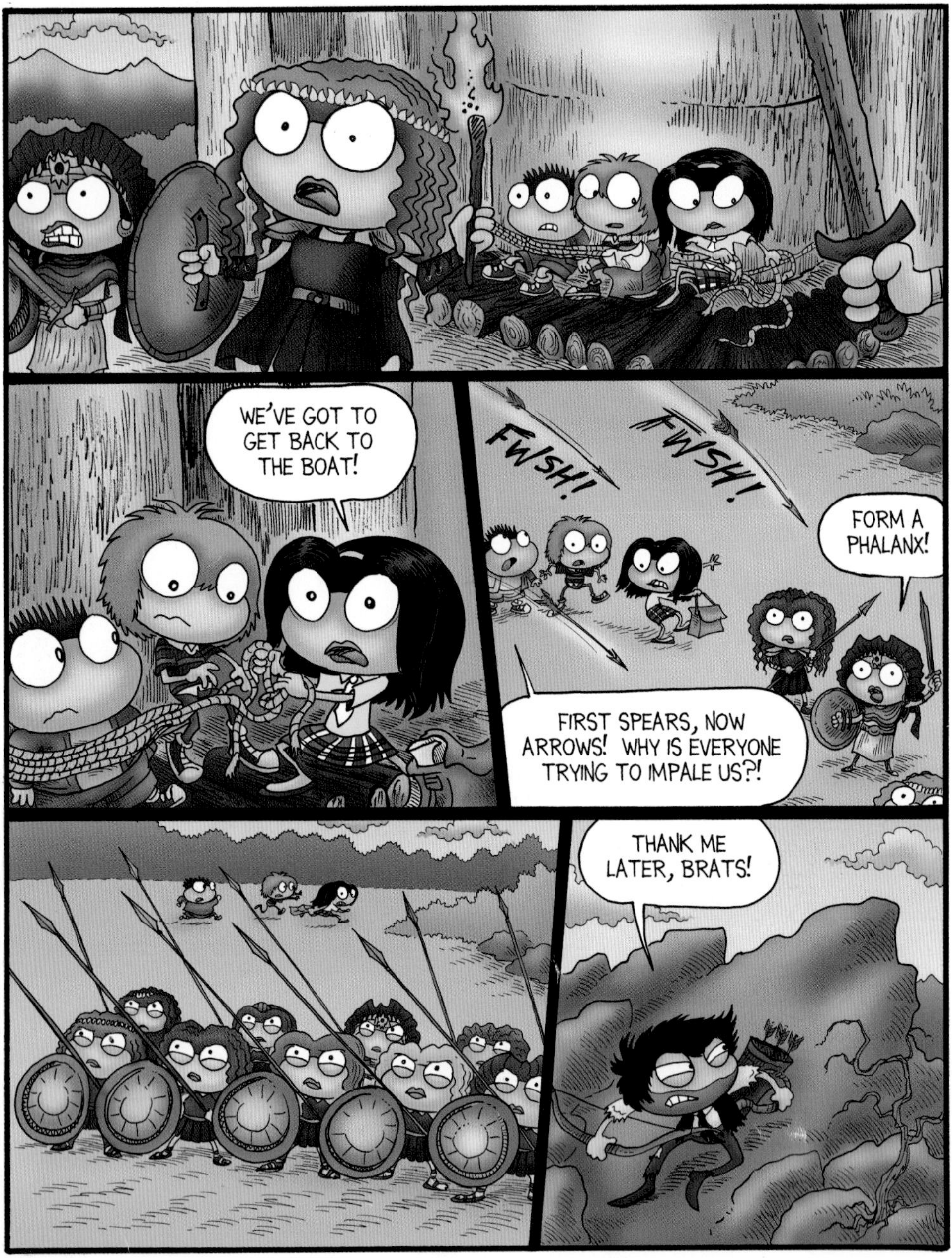
WE'VE GOT TO GET BACK TO THE BOAT!
FWSH!
FWSH!
FORM A PHALANX!
FIRST SPEARS, NOW ARROWS! WHY IS EVERYONE TRYING TO IMPALE US?!
THANK ME LATER, BRATS!

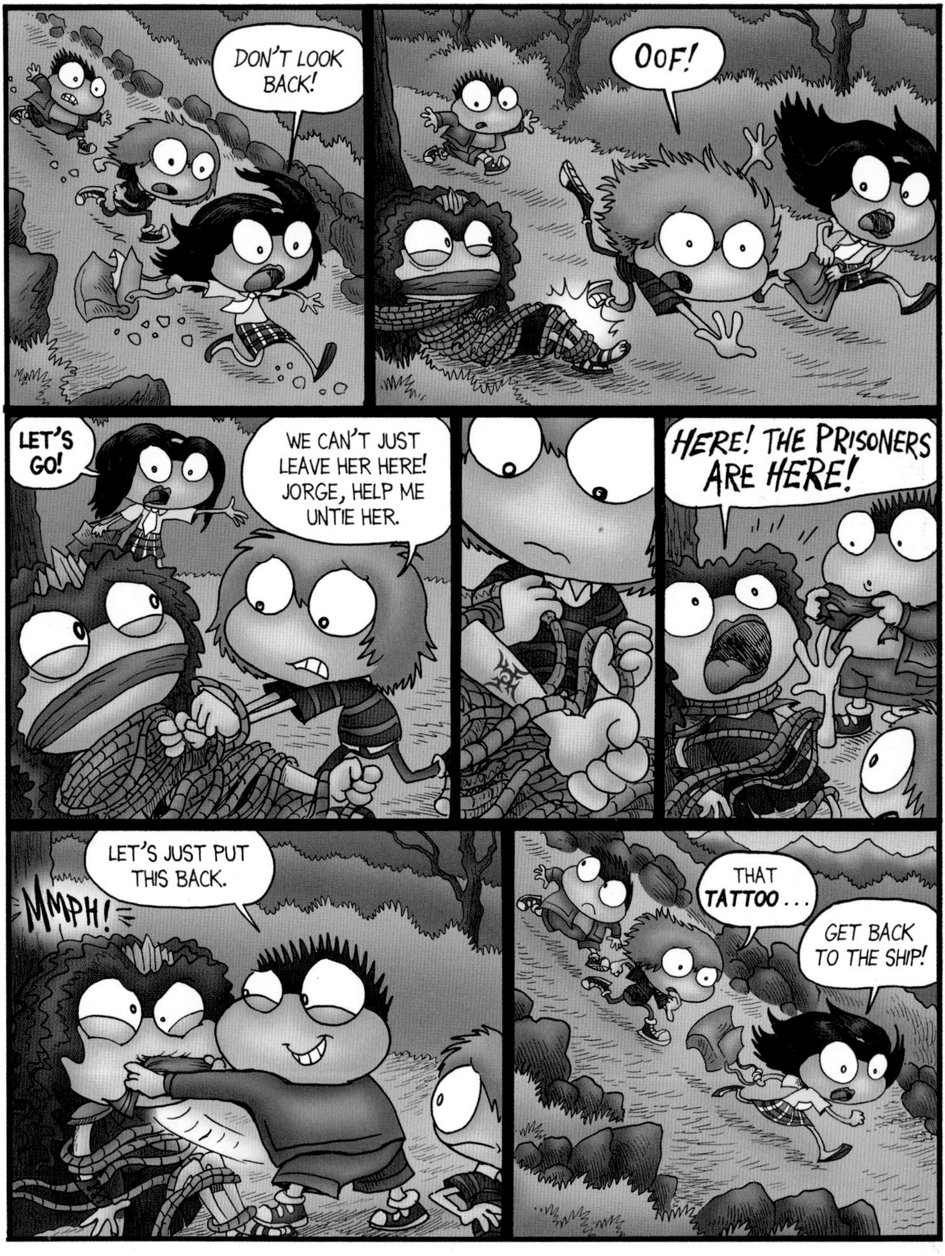
DON'T LOOK BACK!
OOF!
LET'S GO!
WE CAN'T JUST LEAVE HER HERE! JORGE, HELP ME UNTIE HER.
HERE! THE PRISONERS ARE HERE!
MMPH!
LET'S JUST PUT THIS BACK.
THAT TATTOO . . .
GET BACK TO THE SHIP!

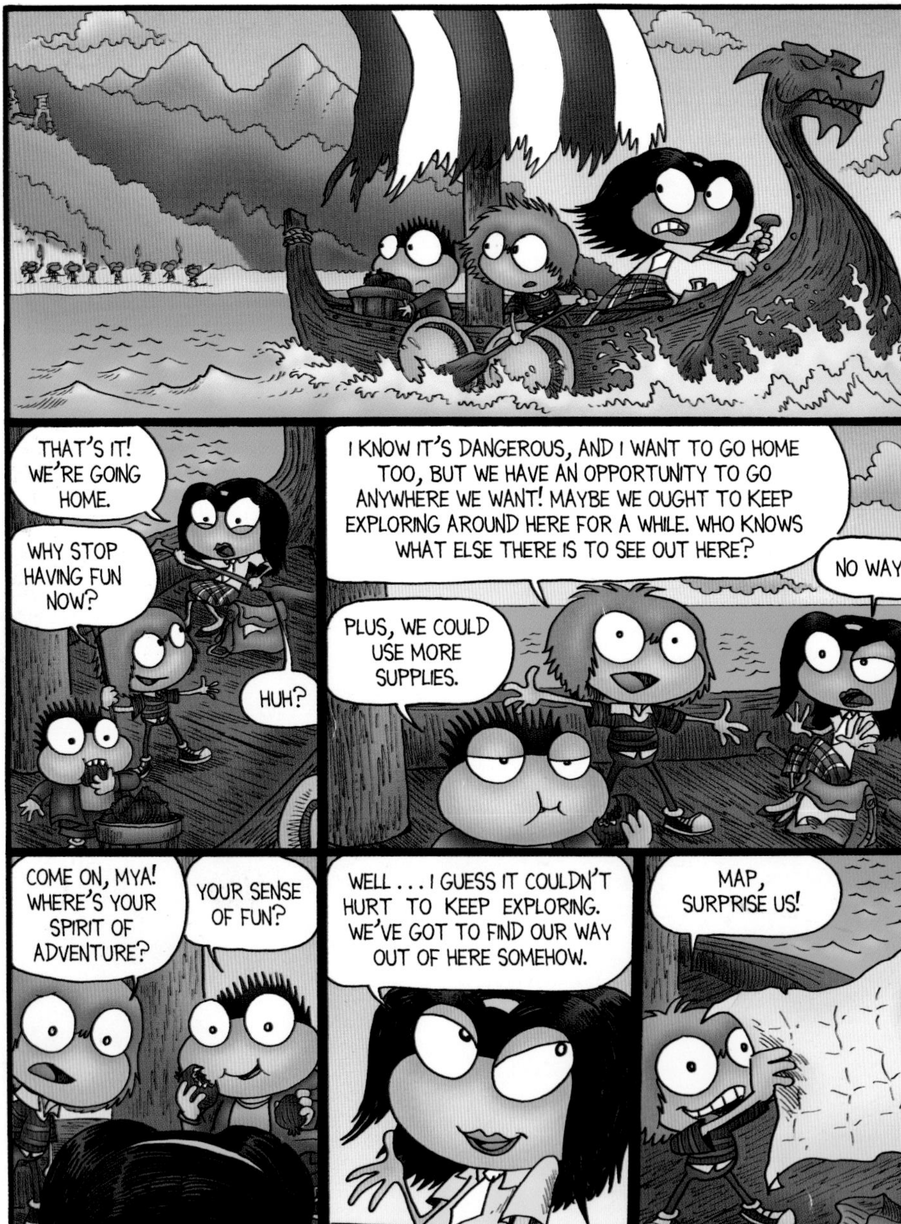
THAT'S IT! WE'RE GOING HOME.
WHY STOP HAVING FUN NOW?
HUH?
I KNOW IT'S DANGEROUS, AND I WANT TO GO HOME TOO, BUT WE HAVE AN OPPORTUNITY TO GO ANYWHERE WE WANT! MAYBE WE OUGHT TO KEEP EXPLORING AROUND HERE FOR A WHILE. WHO KNOWS WHAT ELSE THERE IS TO SEE OUT HERE?
NO WAY.
PLUS, WE COULD USE MORE SUPPLIES.
COME ON, MYA! WHERE'S YOUR SPIRIT OF ADVENTURE?
YOUR SENSE OF FUN?
WELL . . . I GUESS IT COULDN'T HURT TO KEEP EXPLORING. WE'VE GOT TO FIND OUR WAY OUT OF HERE SOMEHOW.
MAP, SURPRISE US!

Chapter 3

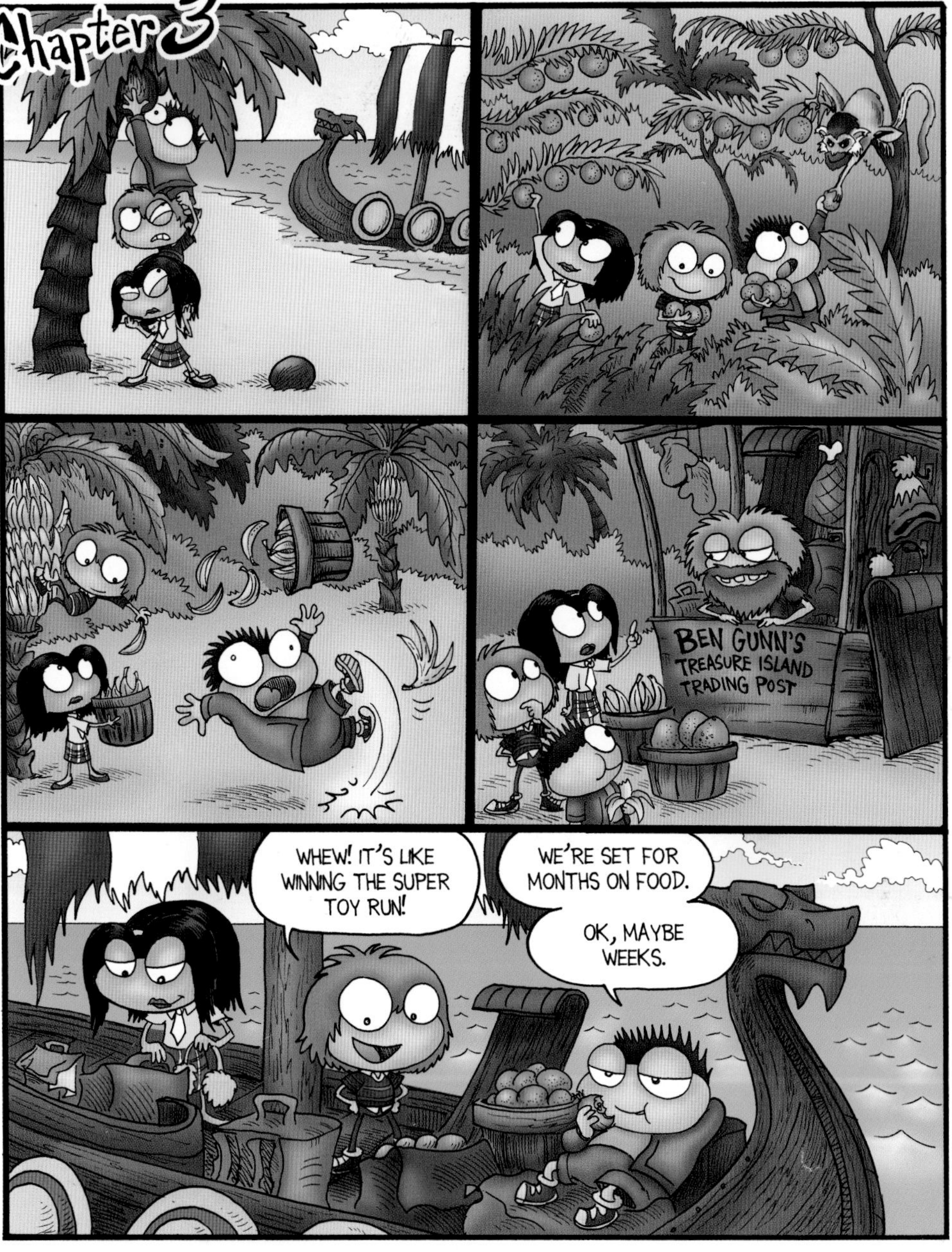
BEN GUNN'S TREASURE ISLAND TRADING POST
WHEW! IT'S LIKE WINNING THE SUPER TOY RUN!
WE'RE SET FOR MONTHS ON FOOD.
OK, MAYBE WEEKS.

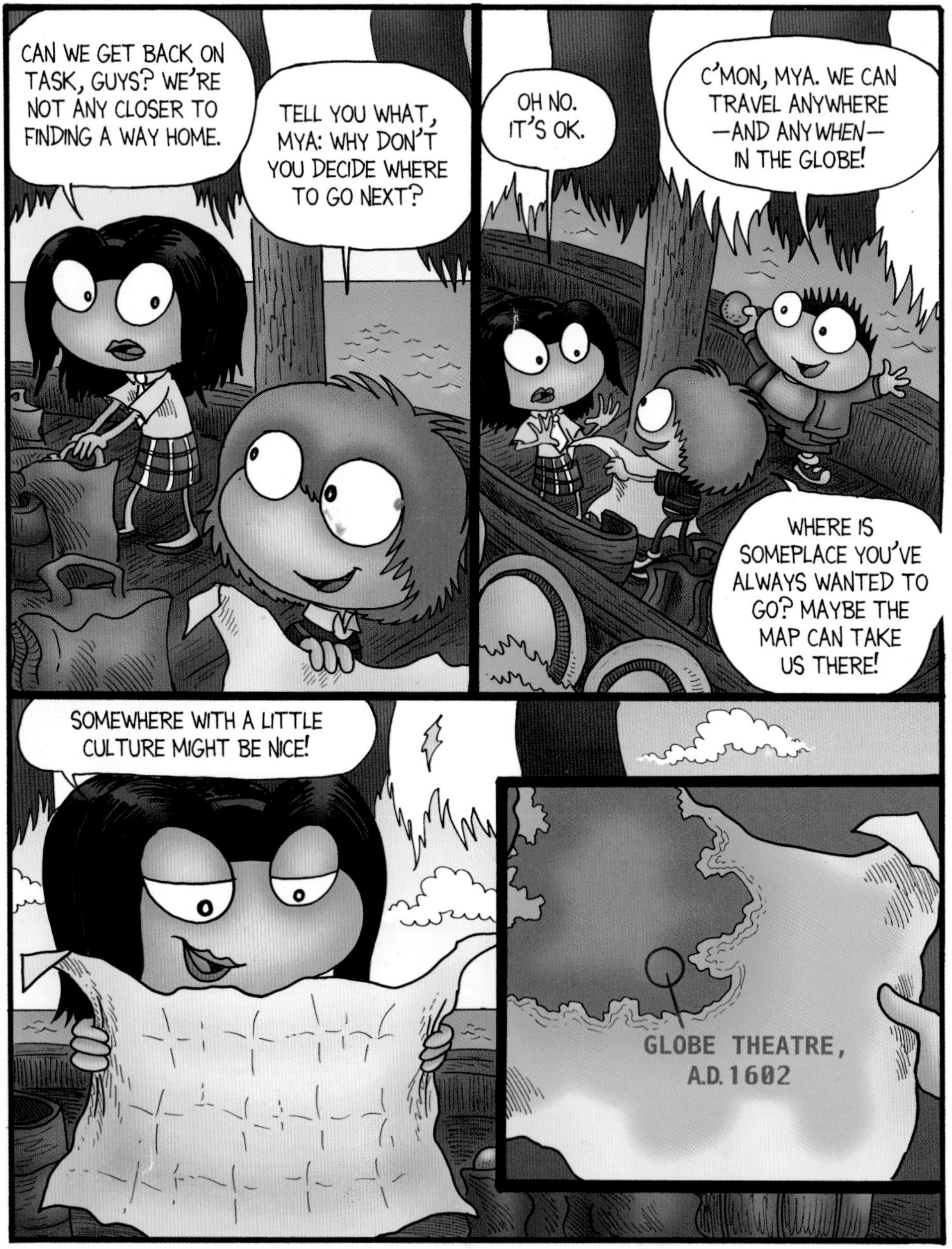
CAN WE GET BACK ON TASK, GUYS? WE'RE NOT ANY CLOSER TO FINDING A WAY HOME.
TELL YOU WHAT, MYA: WHY DON'T YOU DECIDE WHERE TO GO NEXT?
OH NO. IT'S OK.
C'MON, MYA. WE CAN TRAVEL ANYWHERE —AND ANYWHEN— IN THE GLOBE!
WHERE IS SOMEPLACE YOU'VE ALWAYS WANTED TO GO? MAYBE THE MAP CAN TAKE US THERE!
SOMEWHERE WITH A LITTLE CULTURE MIGHT BE NICE!
GLOBE THEATRE, A.D. 1602

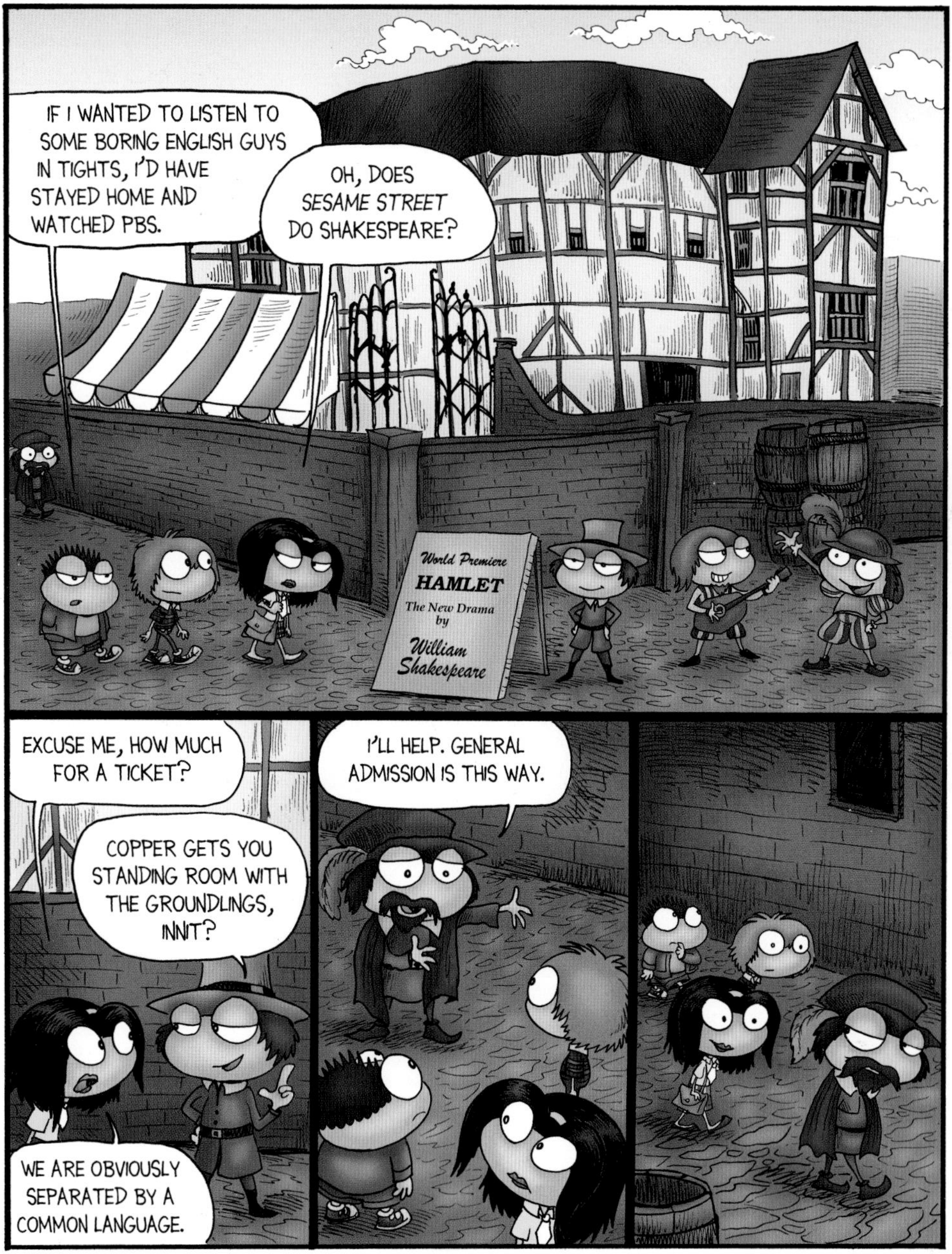
IF I WANTED TO LISTEN TO SOME BORING ENGLISH GUYS IN TIGHTS, I'D HAVE STAYED HOME AND WATCHED PBS.
OH, DOES SESAME STREET DO SHAKESPEARE?
World Premiere
HAMLET
The New Drama by
William Shakespeare
EXCUSE ME, HOW MUCH FOR A TICKET?
COPPER GETS YOU STANDING ROOM WITH THE GROUNDLINGS, INNIT?
WE ARE OBVIOUSLY SEPARATED BY A COMMON LANGUAGE.
I'LL HELP. GENERAL ADMISSION IS THIS WAY.

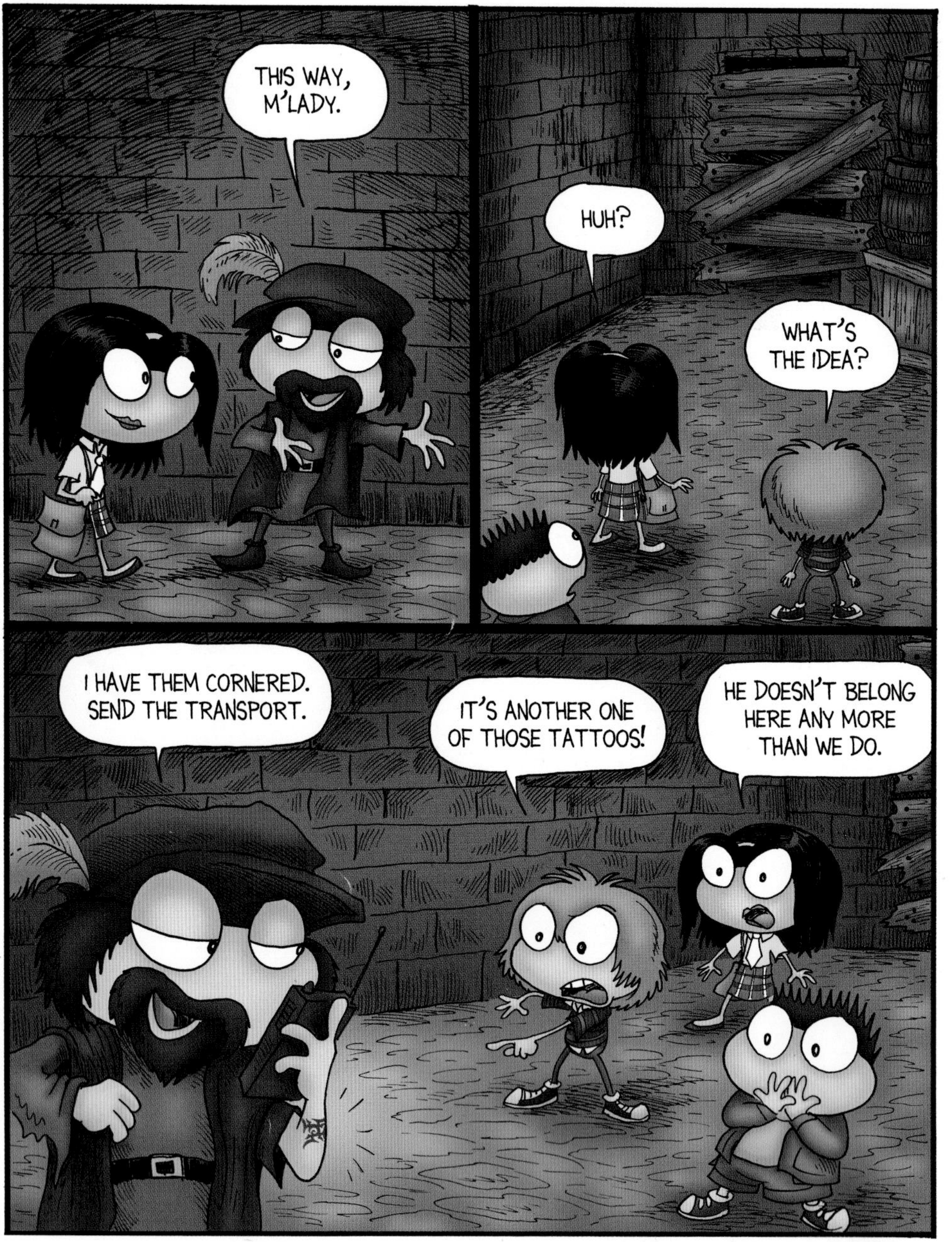
THIS WAY, M'LADY.
HUH?
WHAT'S THE IDEA?
I HAVE THEM CORNERED. SEND THE TRANSPORT.
IT'S ANOTHER ONE OF THOSE TATTOOS!
HE DOESN'T BELONG HERE ANY MORE THAN WE DO.

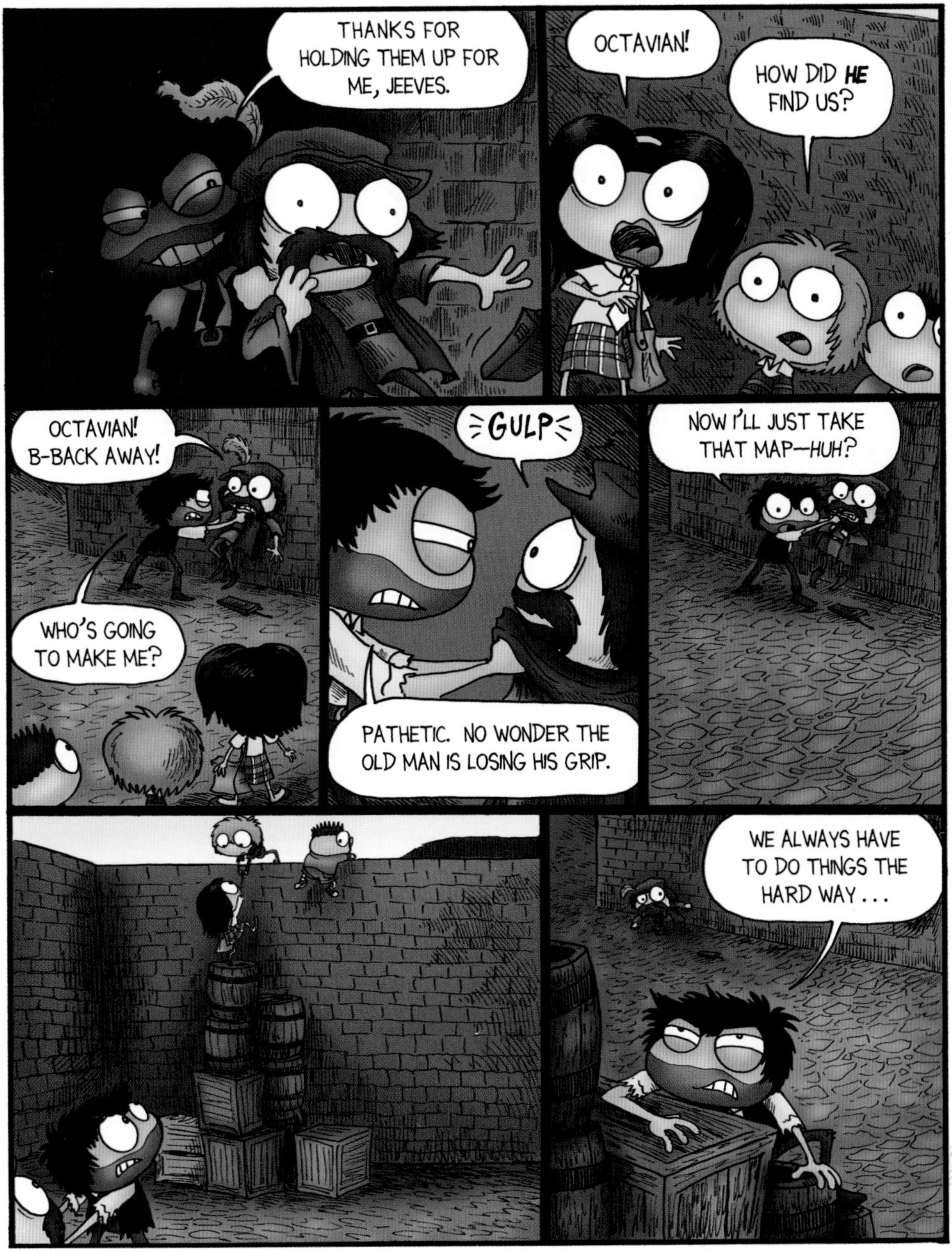
THANKS FOR HOLDING THEM UP FOR ME, JEEVES.
OCTAVIAN!
HOW DID **HE** FIND US?
OCTAVIAN! B-BACK AWAY!
WHO'S GOING TO MAKE ME?
GULP
PATHETIC. NO WONDER THE OLD MAN IS LOSING HIS GRIP.
NOW I'LL JUST TAKE THAT MAP—*HUH?*
WE ALWAYS HAVE TO DO THINGS THE HARD WAY . . .

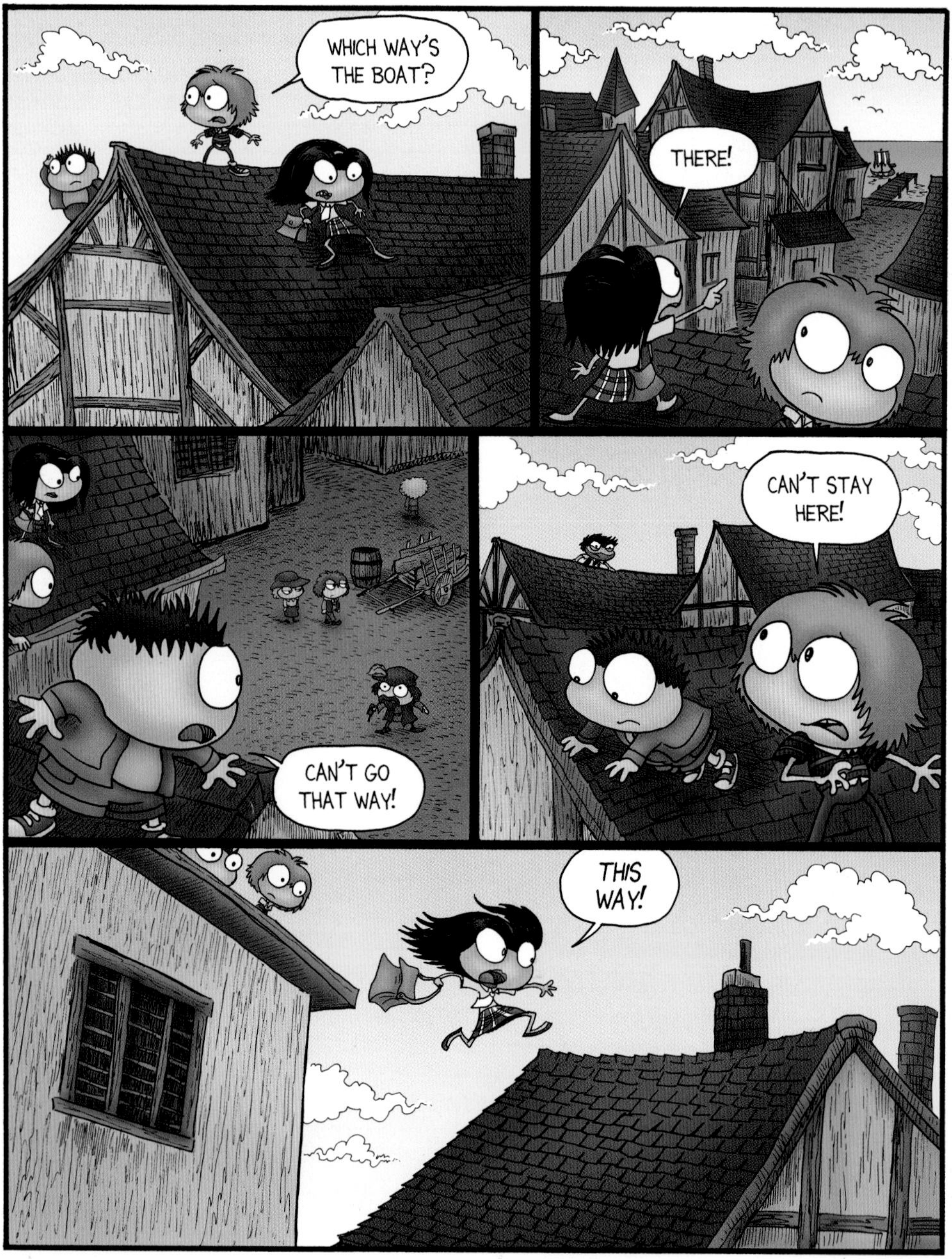
WHICH WAY'S THE BOAT?
THERE!
CAN'T GO THAT WAY!
CAN'T STAY HERE!
THIS WAY!

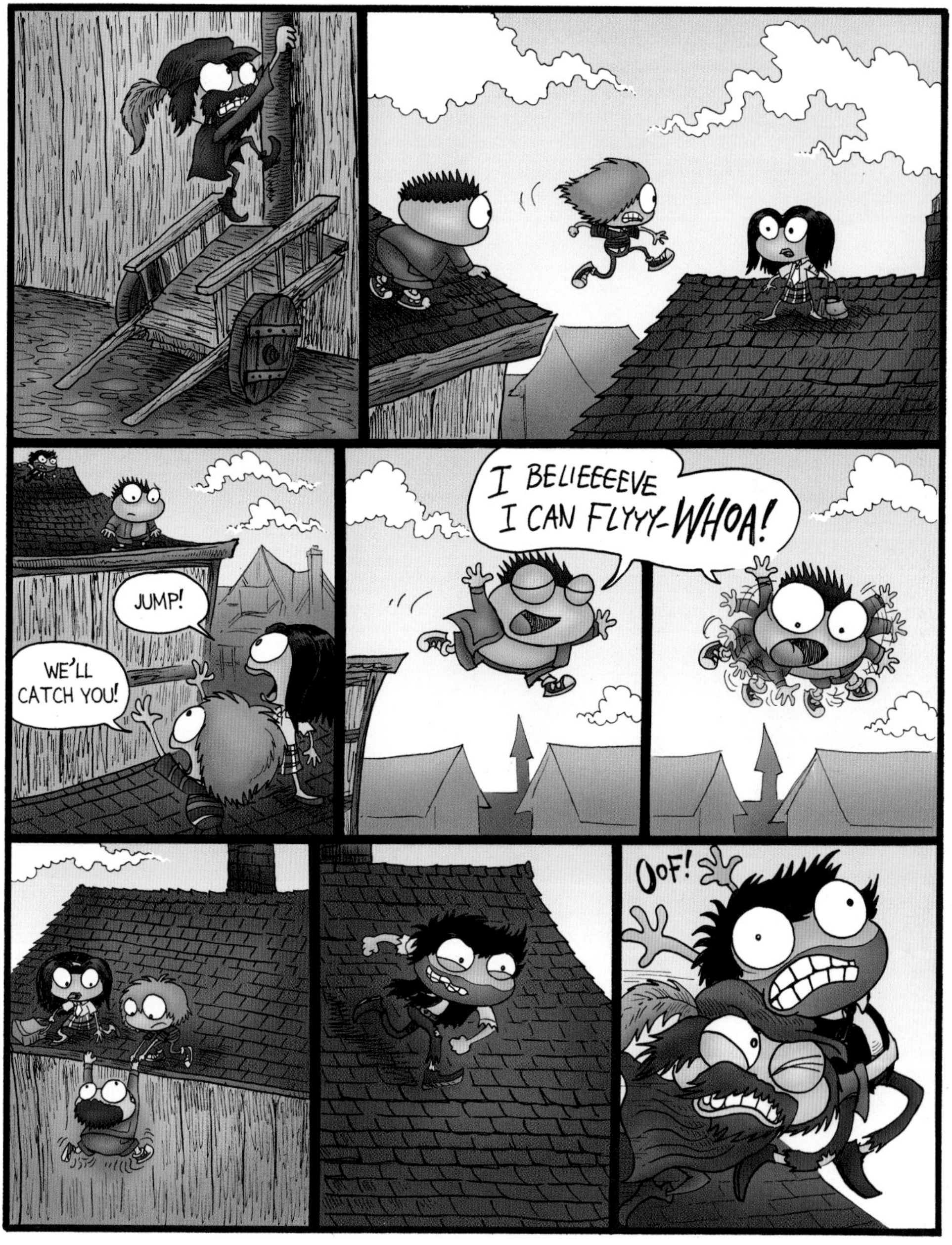
JUMP!
WE'LL CATCH YOU!
I BELIEEEEEVE I CAN FLYYY-WHOA!
OOF!

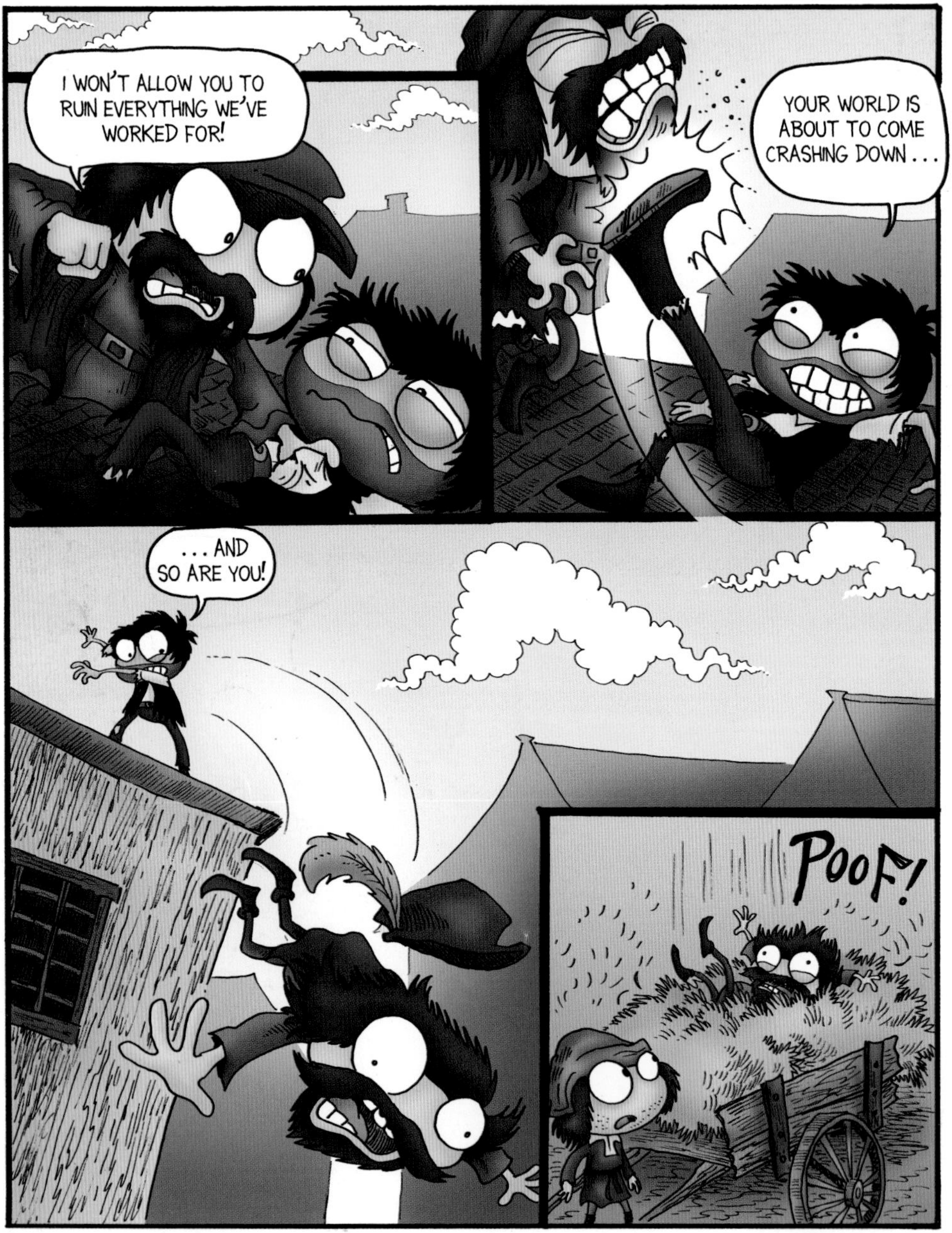
I WON'T ALLOW YOU TO RUIN EVERYTHING WE'VE WORKED FOR!
YOUR WORLD IS ABOUT TO COME CRASHING DOWN . . .
. . . AND SO ARE YOU!
POOF!

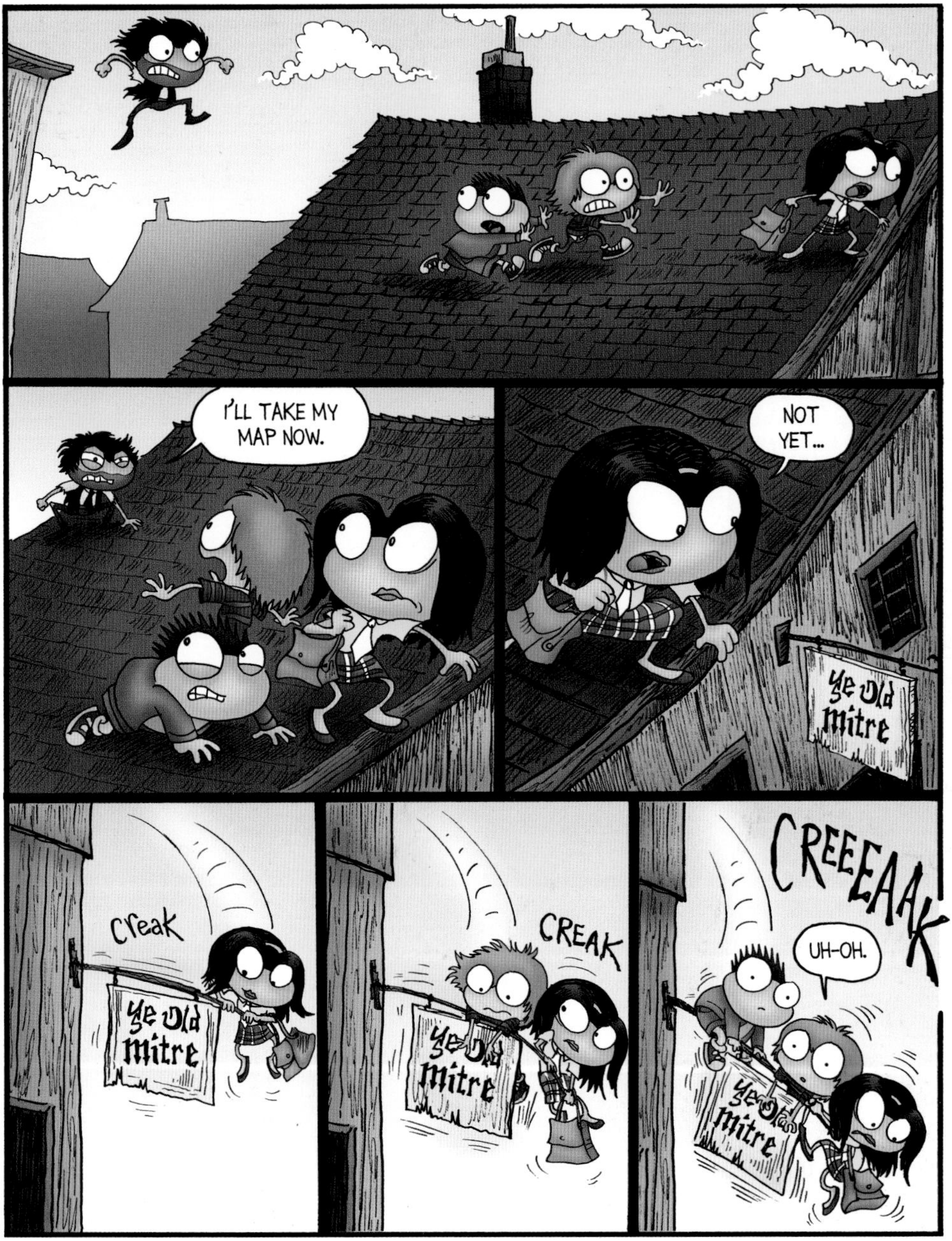
I'LL TAKE MY MAP NOW.
NOT YET...
ye Old mitre
Creak
ye Old mitre
CREAK
ye Old mitre
CREEEAAK
UH-OH.
ye Old mitre

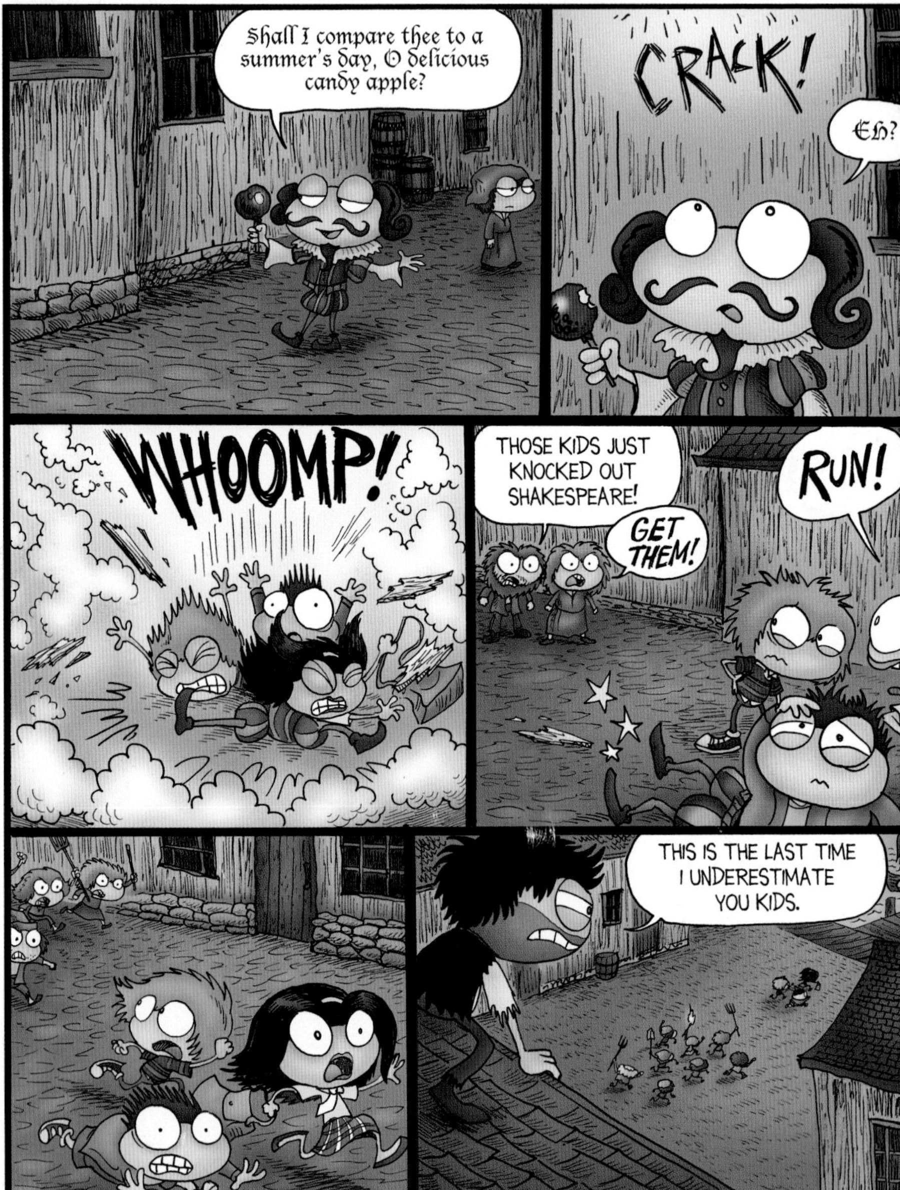
Shall I compare thee to a summer's day, O delicious candy apple?
CRACK!
Eh?
WHOOMP!
THOSE KIDS JUST KNOCKED OUT SHAKESPEARE!
GET THEM!
RUN!
THIS IS THE LAST TIME I UNDERESTIMATE YOU KIDS.

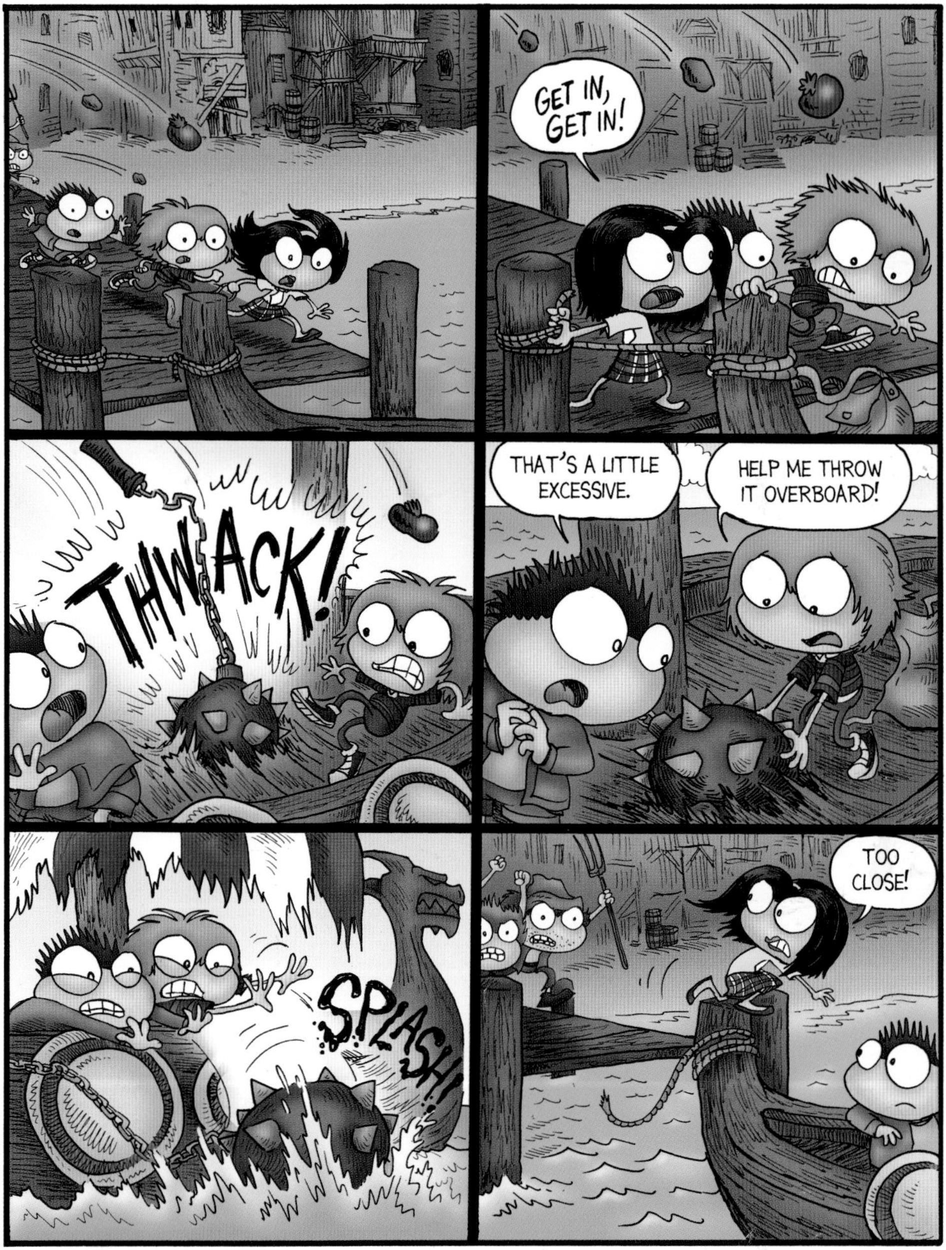
GET IN, GET IN!
THWACK!
THAT'S A LITTLE EXCESSIVE.
HELP ME THROW IT OVERBOARD!
SPLASH!
TOO CLOSE!

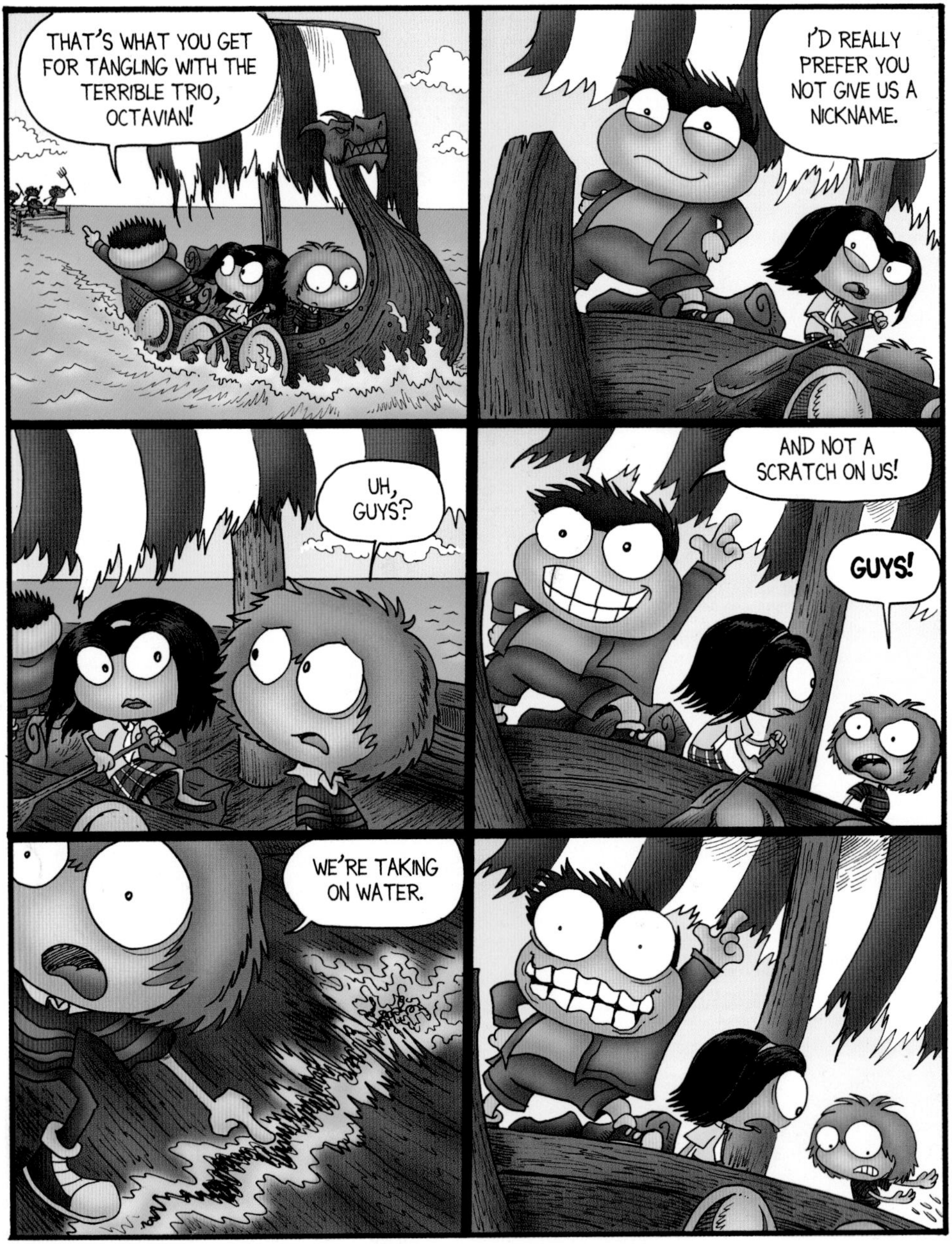
THAT'S WHAT YOU GET FOR TANGLING WITH THE TERRIBLE TRIO, OCTAVIAN!
I'D REALLY PREFER YOU NOT GIVE US A NICKNAME.
UH, GUYS?
AND NOT A SCRATCH ON US!
GUYS!
WE'RE TAKING ON WATER.

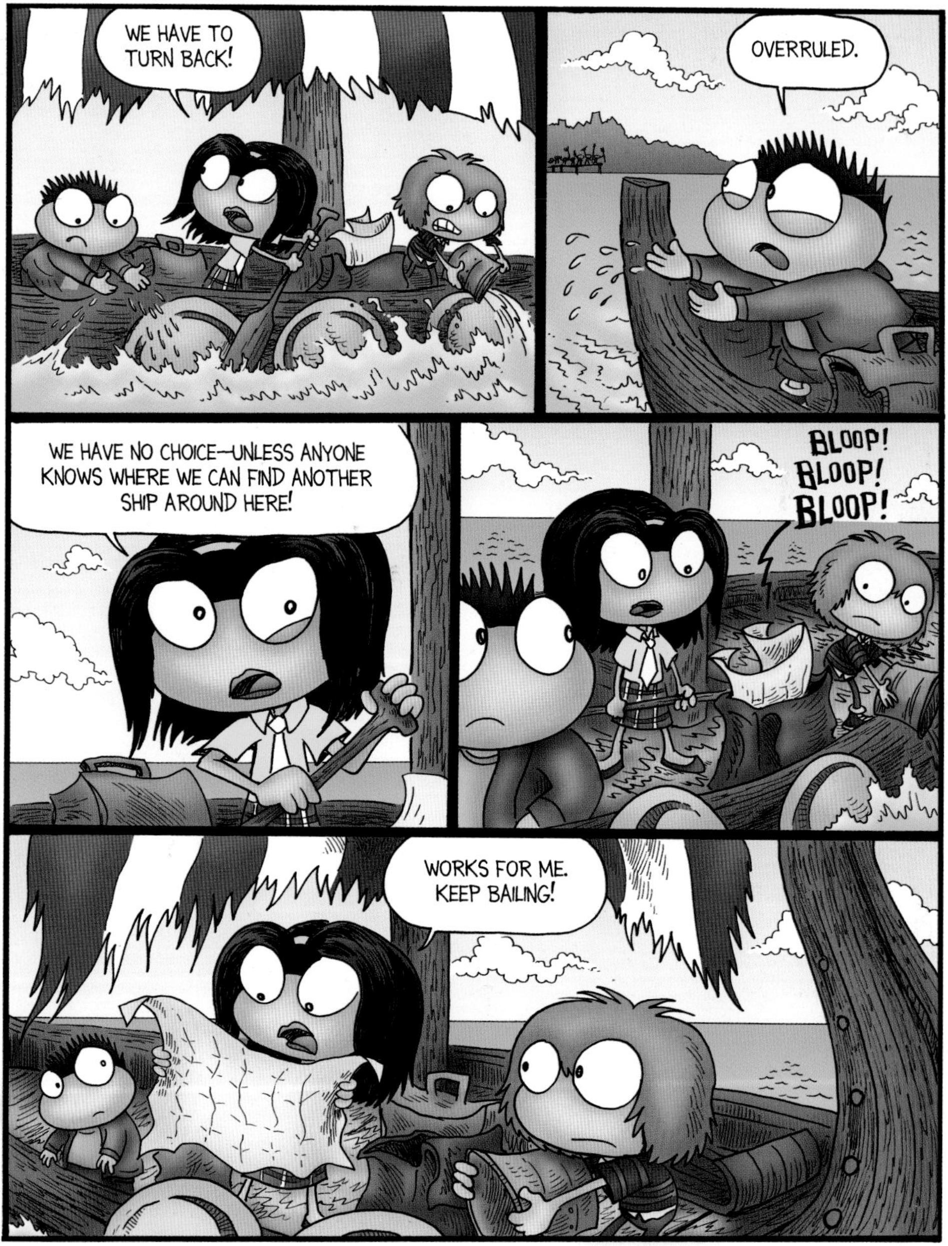
WE HAVE TO TURN BACK!
OVERRULED.
WE HAVE NO CHOICE--UNLESS ANYONE KNOWS WHERE WE CAN FIND ANOTHER SHIP AROUND HERE!
BLOOP! BLOOP! BLOOP!
WORKS FOR ME. KEEP BAILING!

Chapter 4

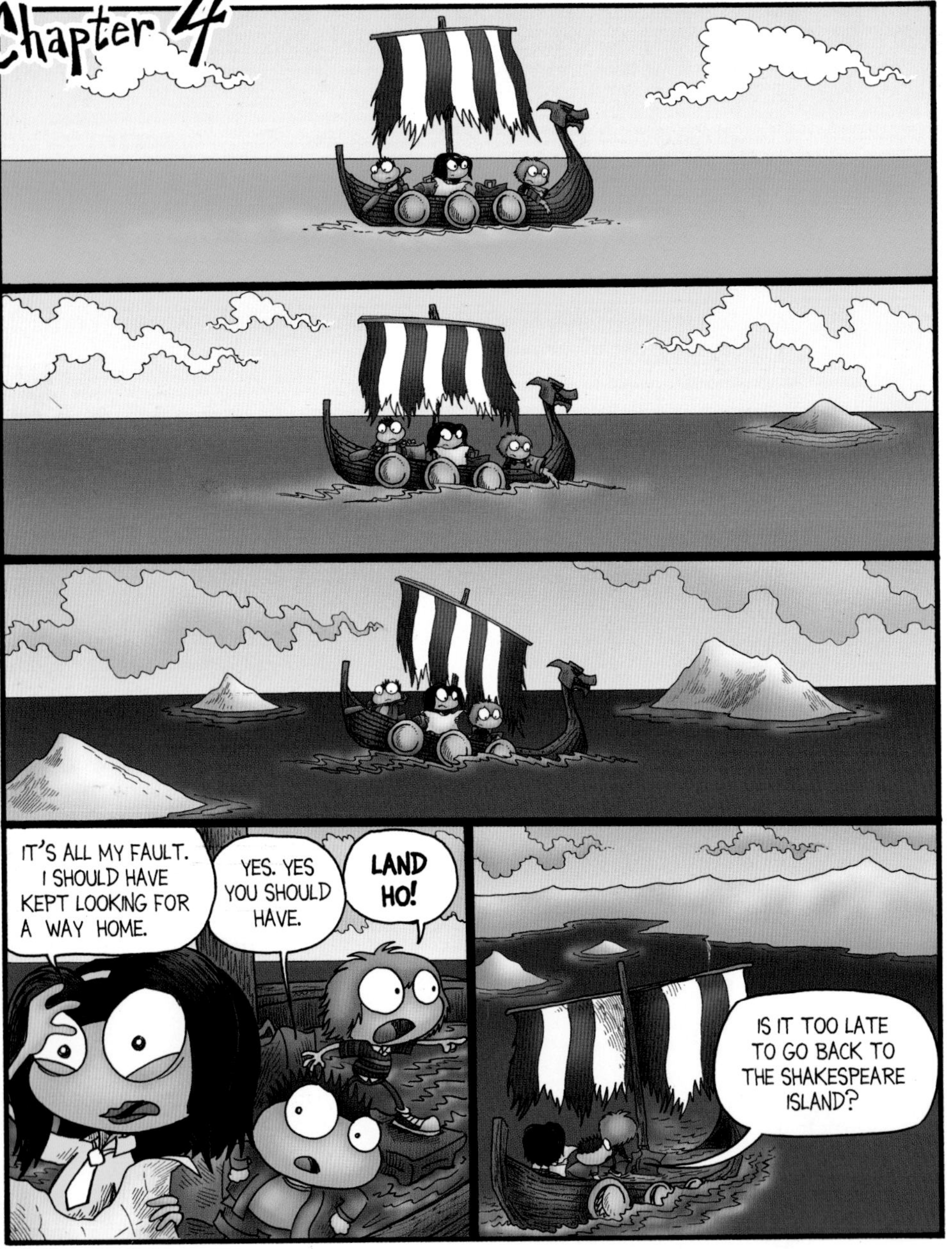

IT'S ALL MY FAULT. I SHOULD HAVE KEPT LOOKING FOR A WAY HOME.
YES. YES YOU SHOULD HAVE.
LAND HO!
IS IT TOO LATE TO GO BACK TO THE SHAKESPEARE ISLAND?

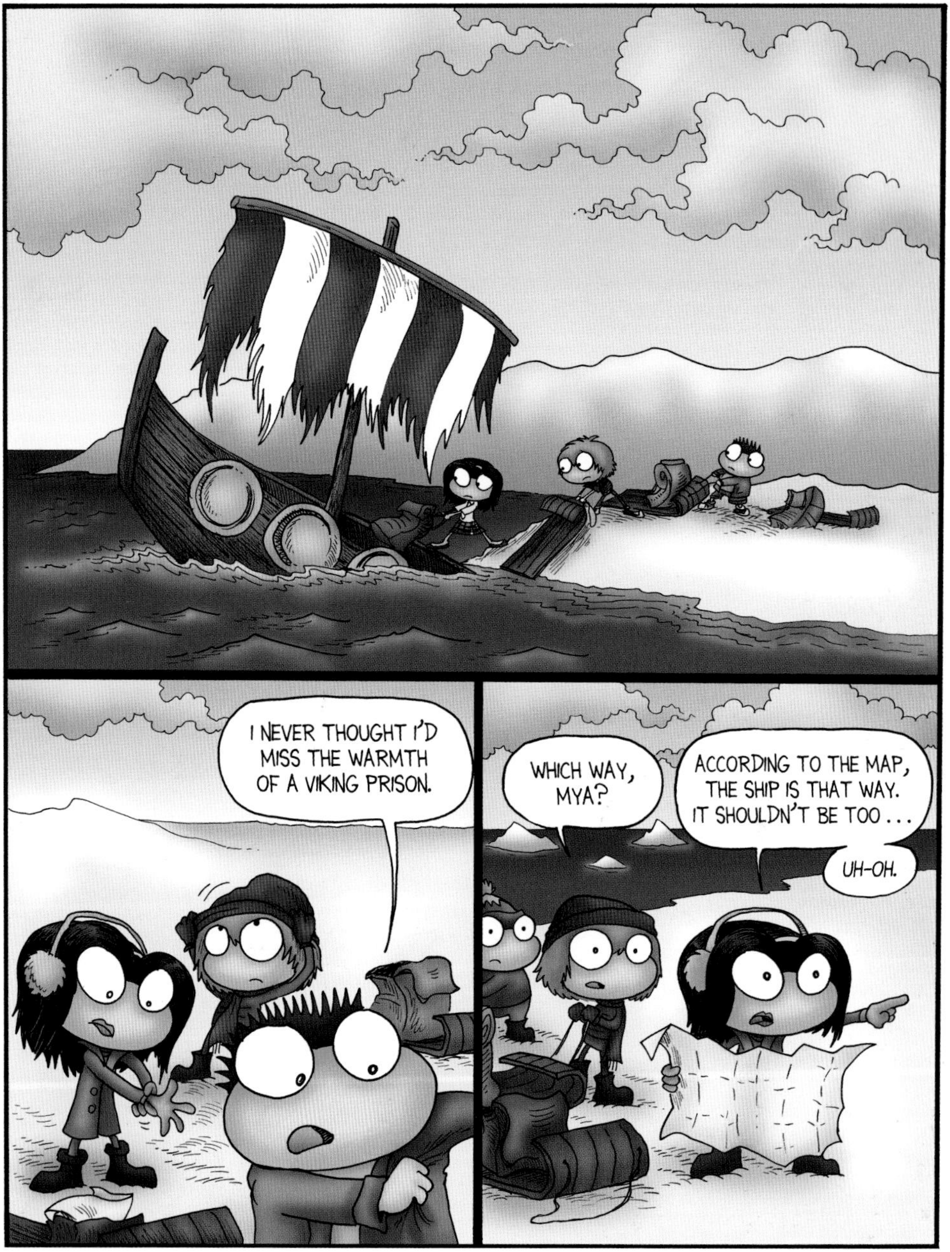

I NEVER THOUGHT I'D MISS THE WARMTH OF A VIKING PRISON.
WHICH WAY, MYA?
ACCORDING TO THE MAP, THE SHIP IS THAT WAY. IT SHOULDN'T BE TOO . . .
UH-OH.

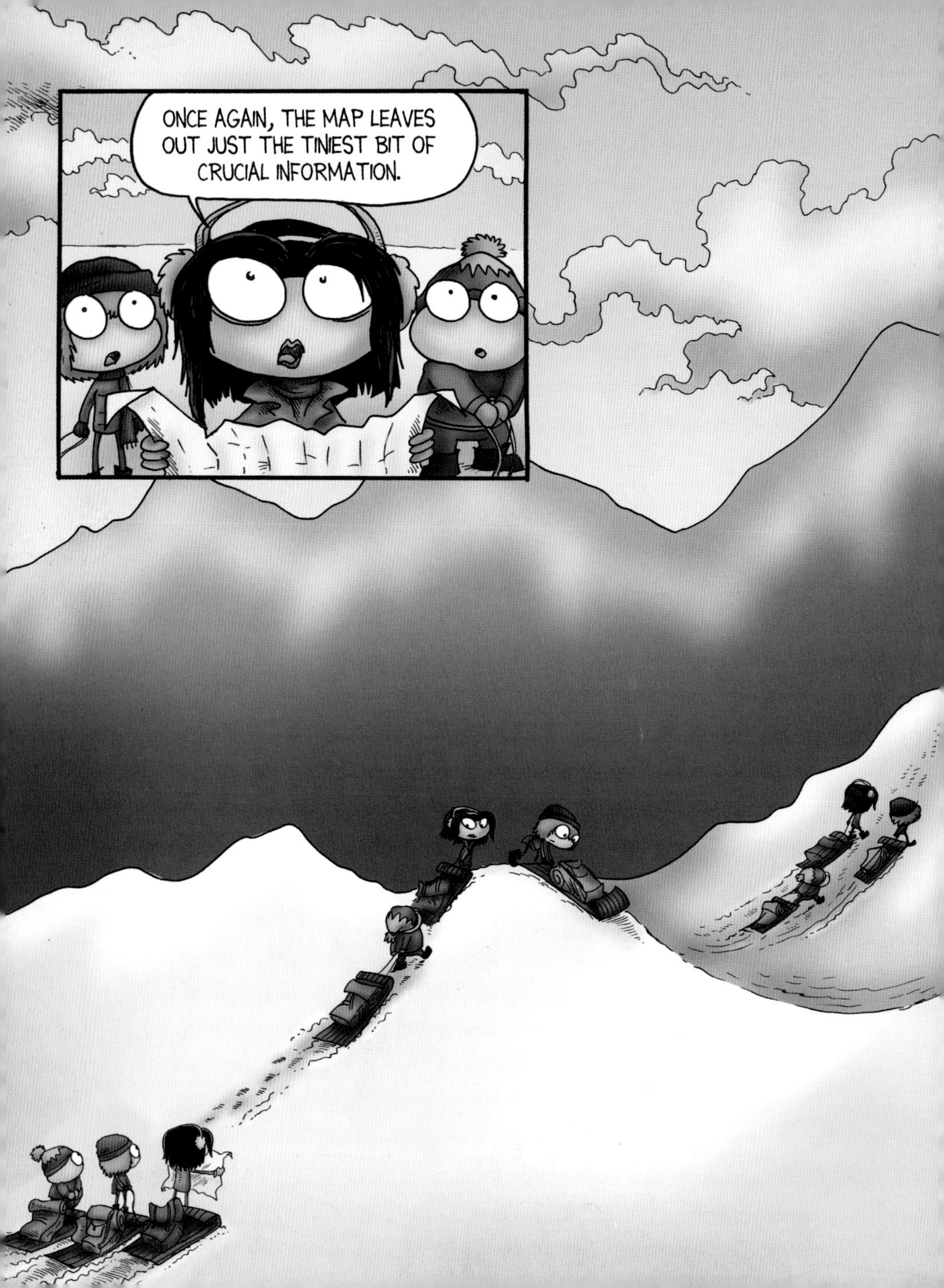
ONCE AGAIN, THE MAP LEAVES OUT JUST THE TINIEST BIT OF CRUCIAL INFORMATION.

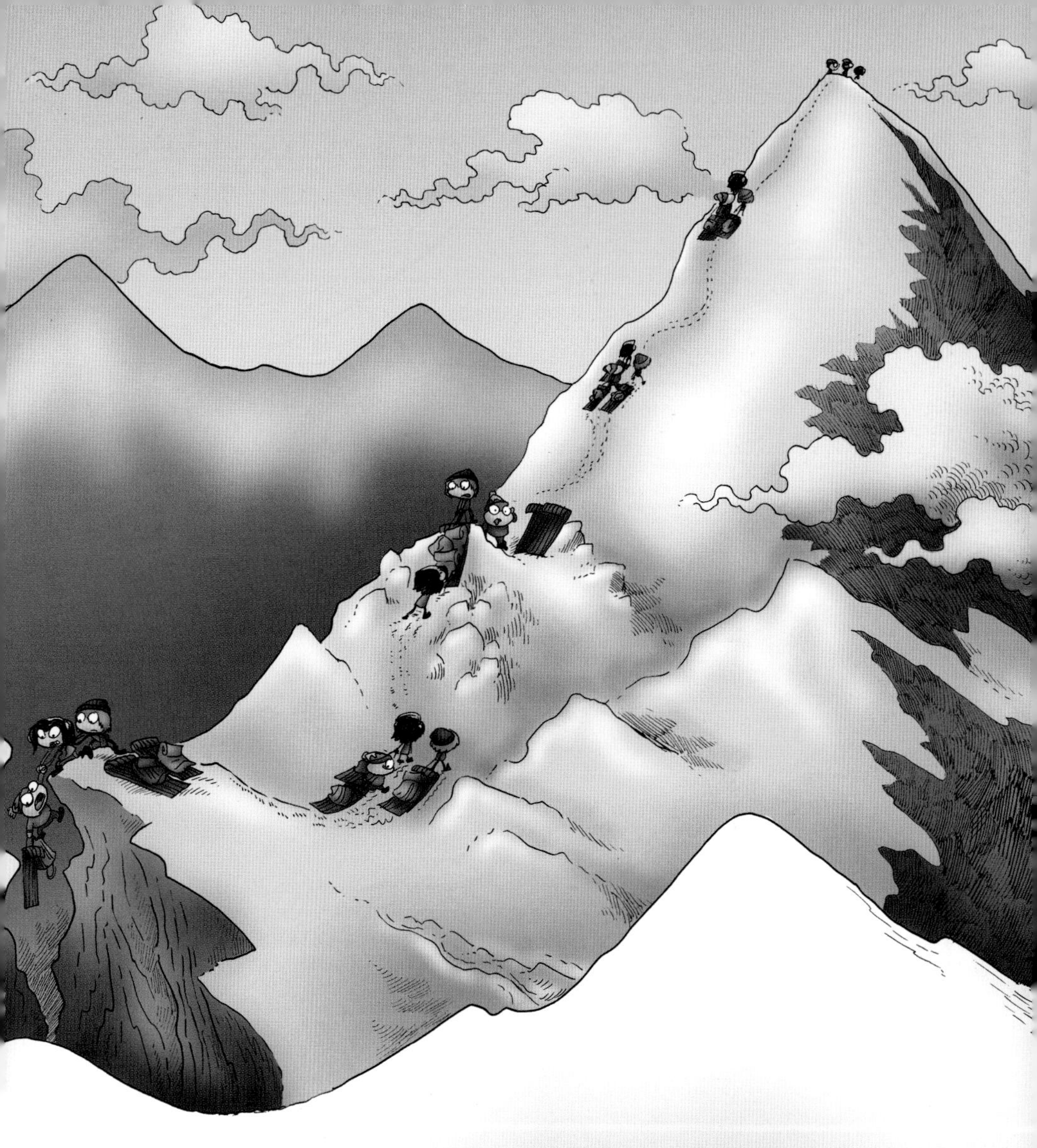

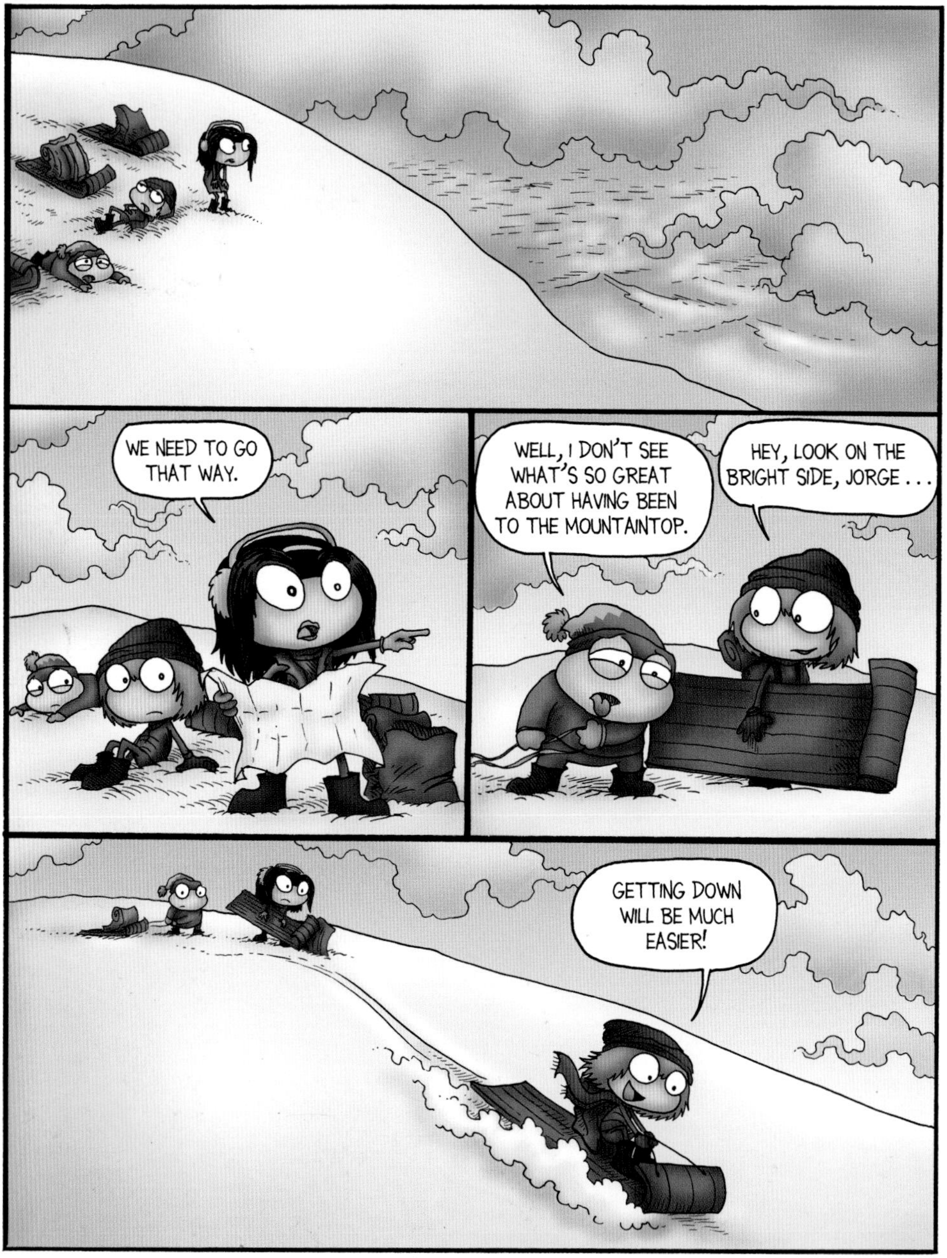
WE NEED TO GO THAT WAY.
WELL, I DON'T SEE WHAT'S SO GREAT ABOUT HAVING BEEN TO THE MOUNTAINTOP.
HEY, LOOK ON THE BRIGHT SIDE, JORGE . . .
GETTING DOWN WILL BE MUCH EASIER!

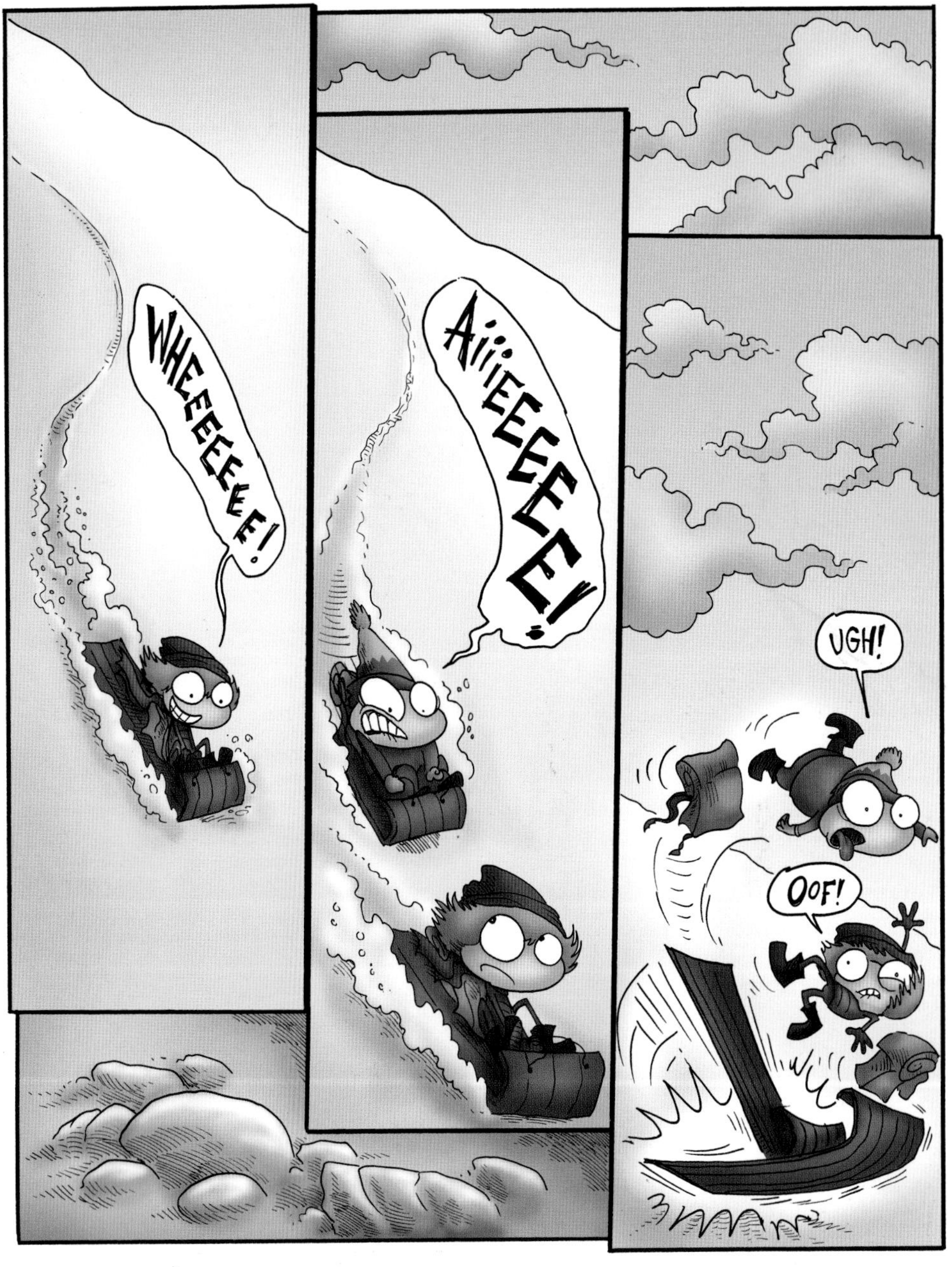
WHEEEEEEEE!
AiiiEEEEEEE!
UGH!
OOF!

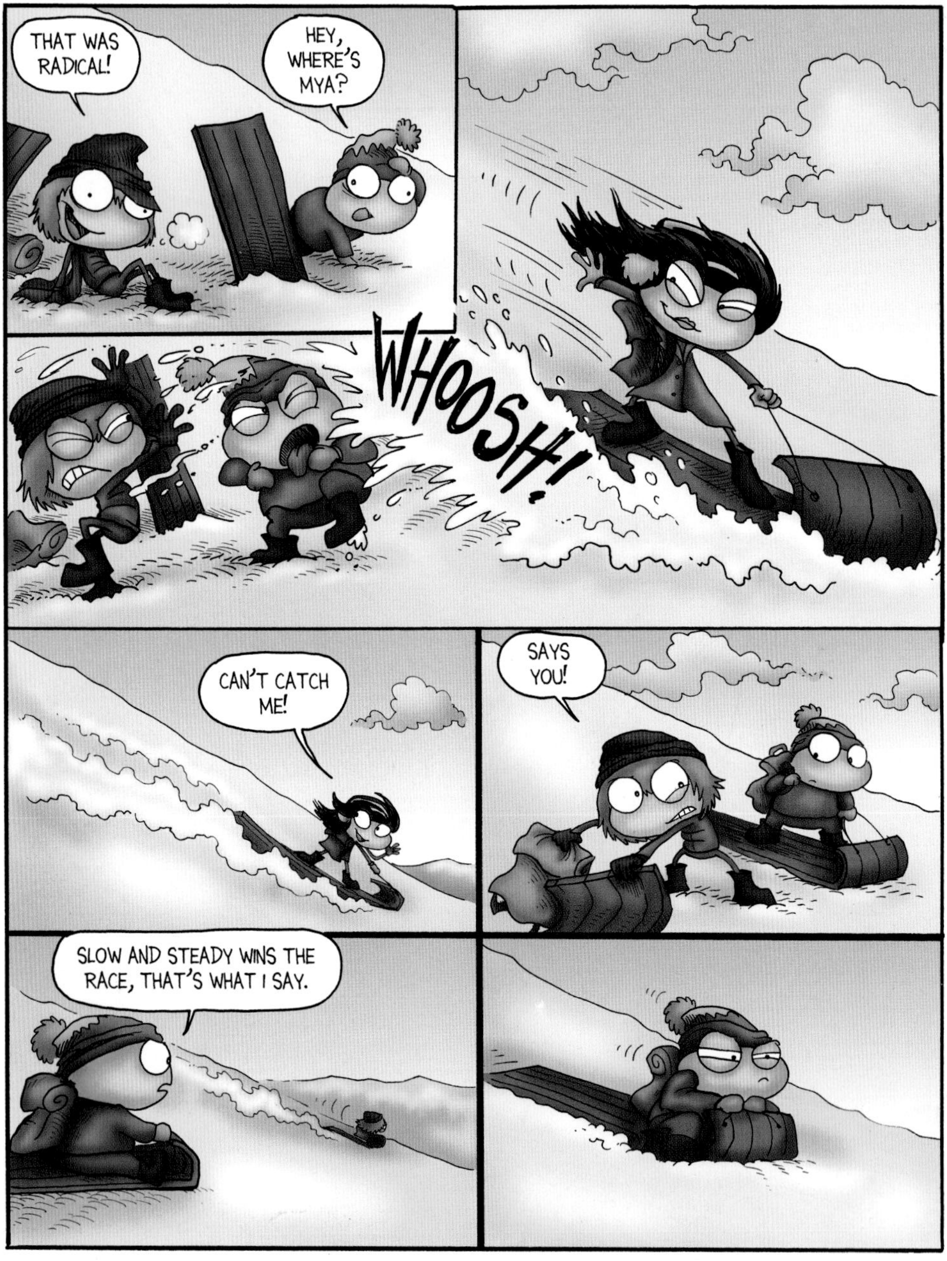
THAT WAS RADICAL!
HEY, WHERE'S MYA?
WHOOSH!
CAN'T CATCH ME!
SAYS YOU!
SLOW AND STEADY WINS THE RACE, THAT'S WHAT I SAY.

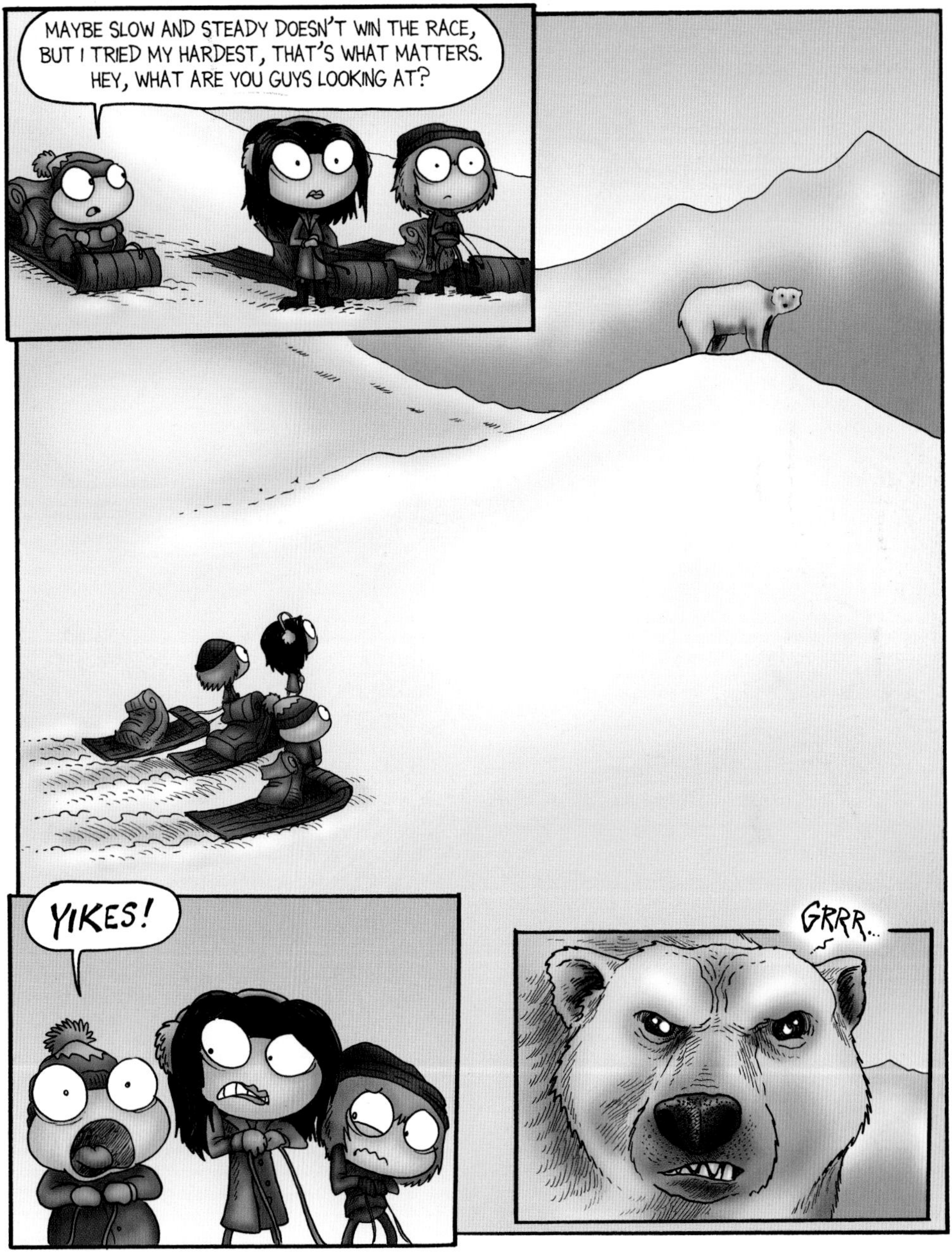
MAYBE SLOW AND STEADY DOESN'T WIN THE RACE, BUT I TRIED MY HARDEST, THAT'S WHAT MATTERS. HEY, WHAT ARE YOU GUYS LOOKING AT?
YIKES!
GRRR...

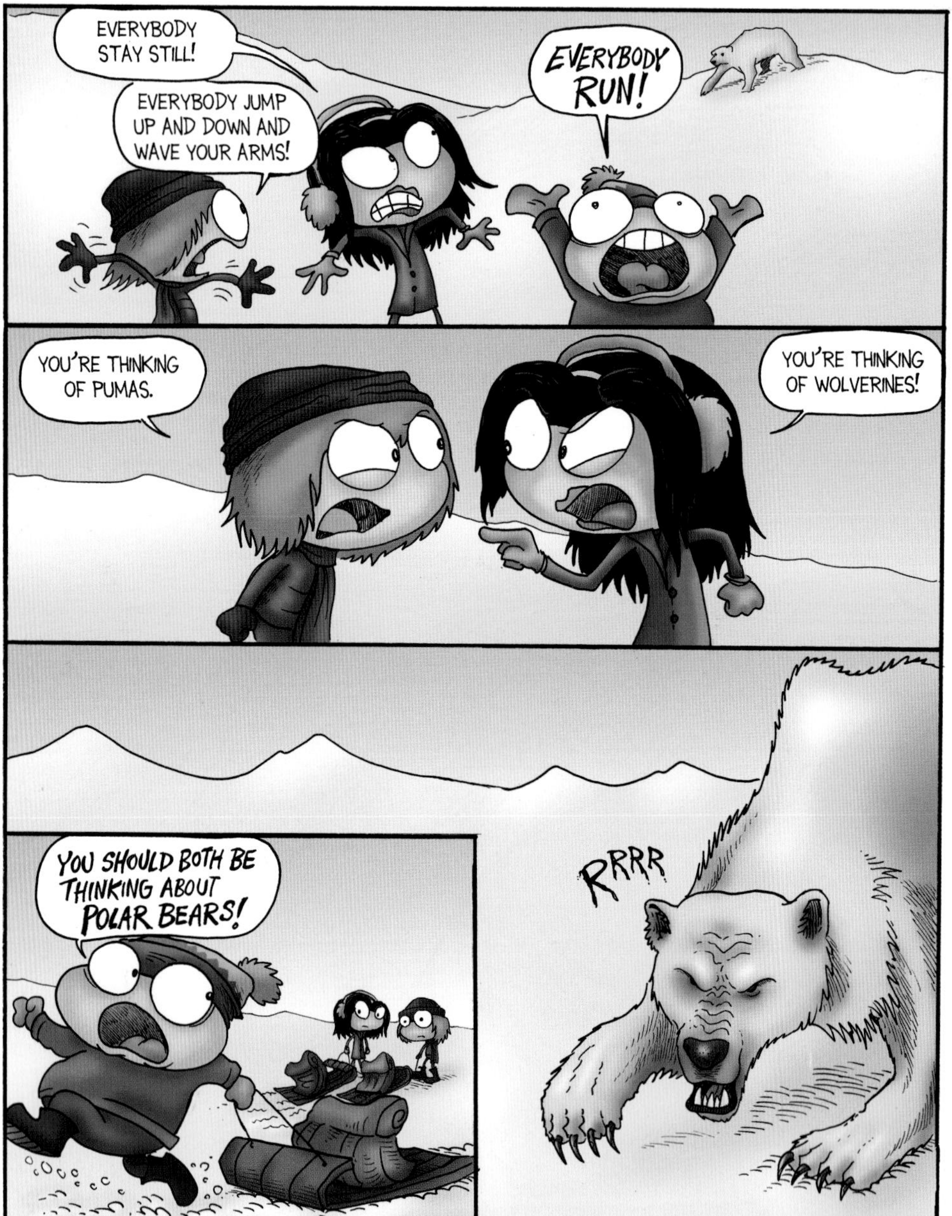
EVERYBODY STAY STILL!
EVERYBODY JUMP UP AND DOWN AND WAVE YOUR ARMS!
EVERYBODY RUN!
YOU'RE THINKING OF PUMAS.
YOU'RE THINKING OF WOLVERINES!
YOU SHOULD BOTH BE THINKING ABOUT POLAR BEARS!
RRRR

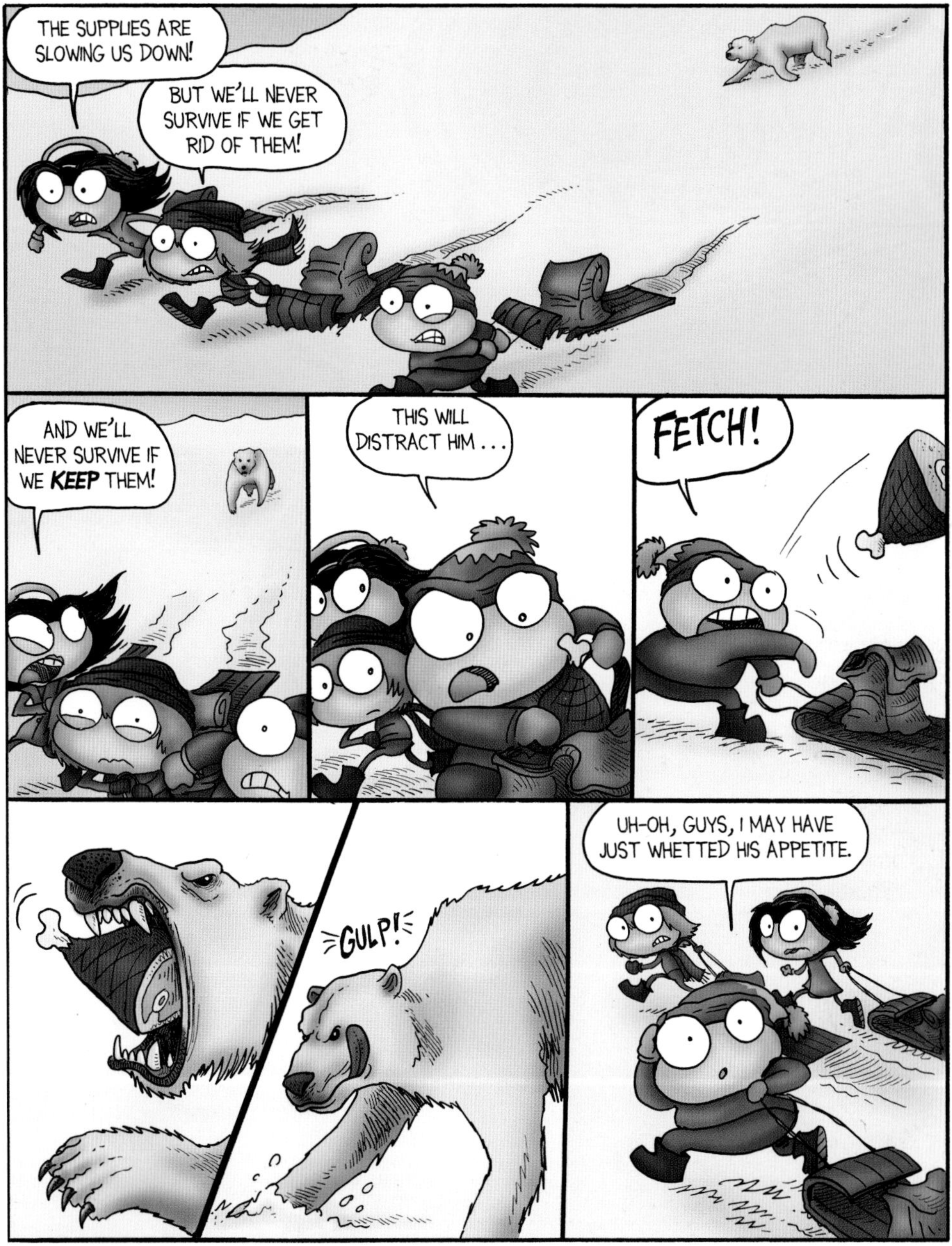
THE SUPPLIES ARE SLOWING US DOWN!
BUT WE'LL NEVER SURVIVE IF WE GET RID OF THEM!
AND WE'LL NEVER SURVIVE IF WE **KEEP** THEM!
THIS WILL DISTRACT HIM . . .
FETCH!
GULP!
UH-OH, GUYS, I MAY HAVE JUST WHETTED HIS APPETITE.

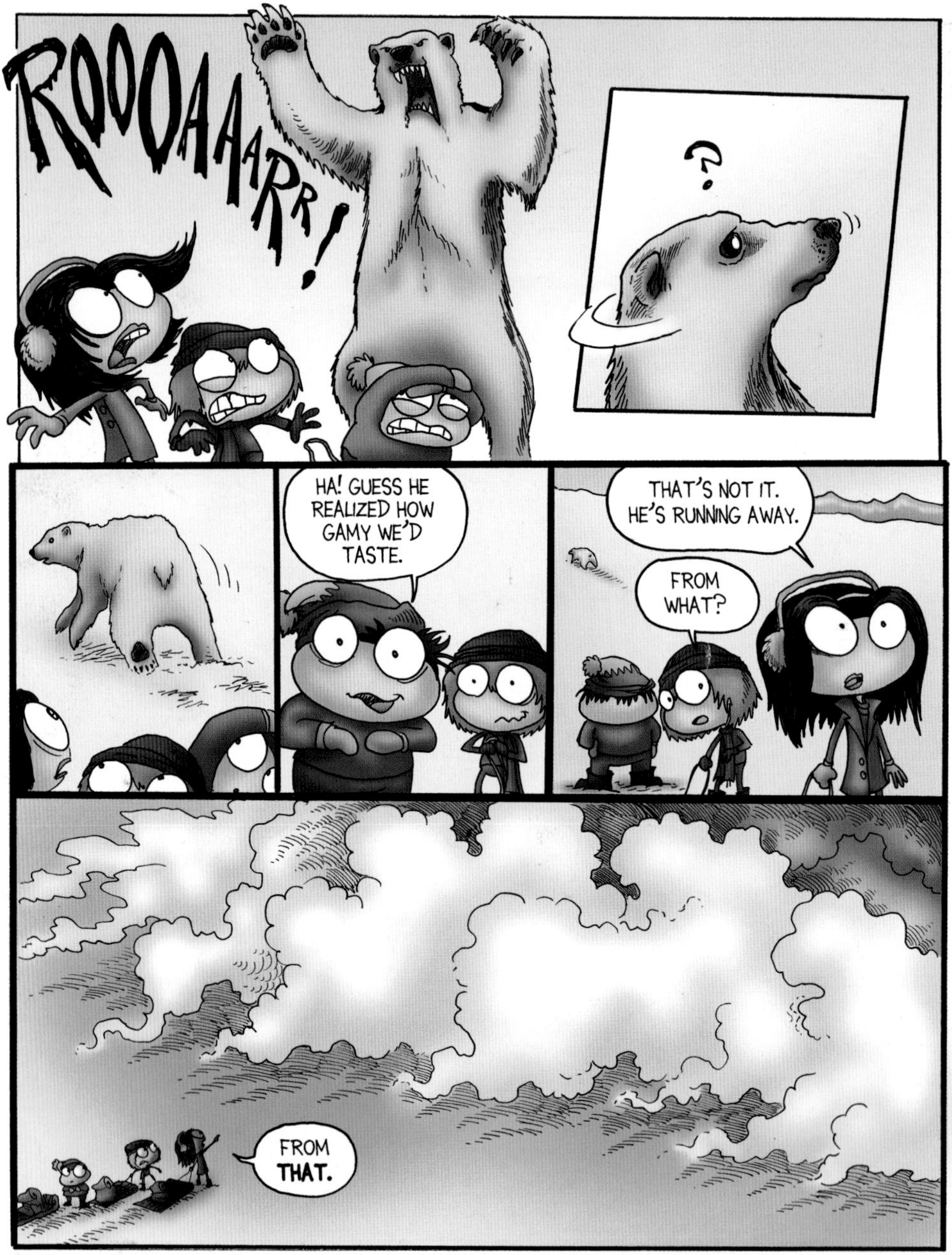
ROOOAAARR!
?
HA! GUESS HE REALIZED HOW GAMY WE'D TASTE.
THAT'S NOT IT. HE'S RUNNING AWAY.
FROM WHAT?
FROM **THAT.**

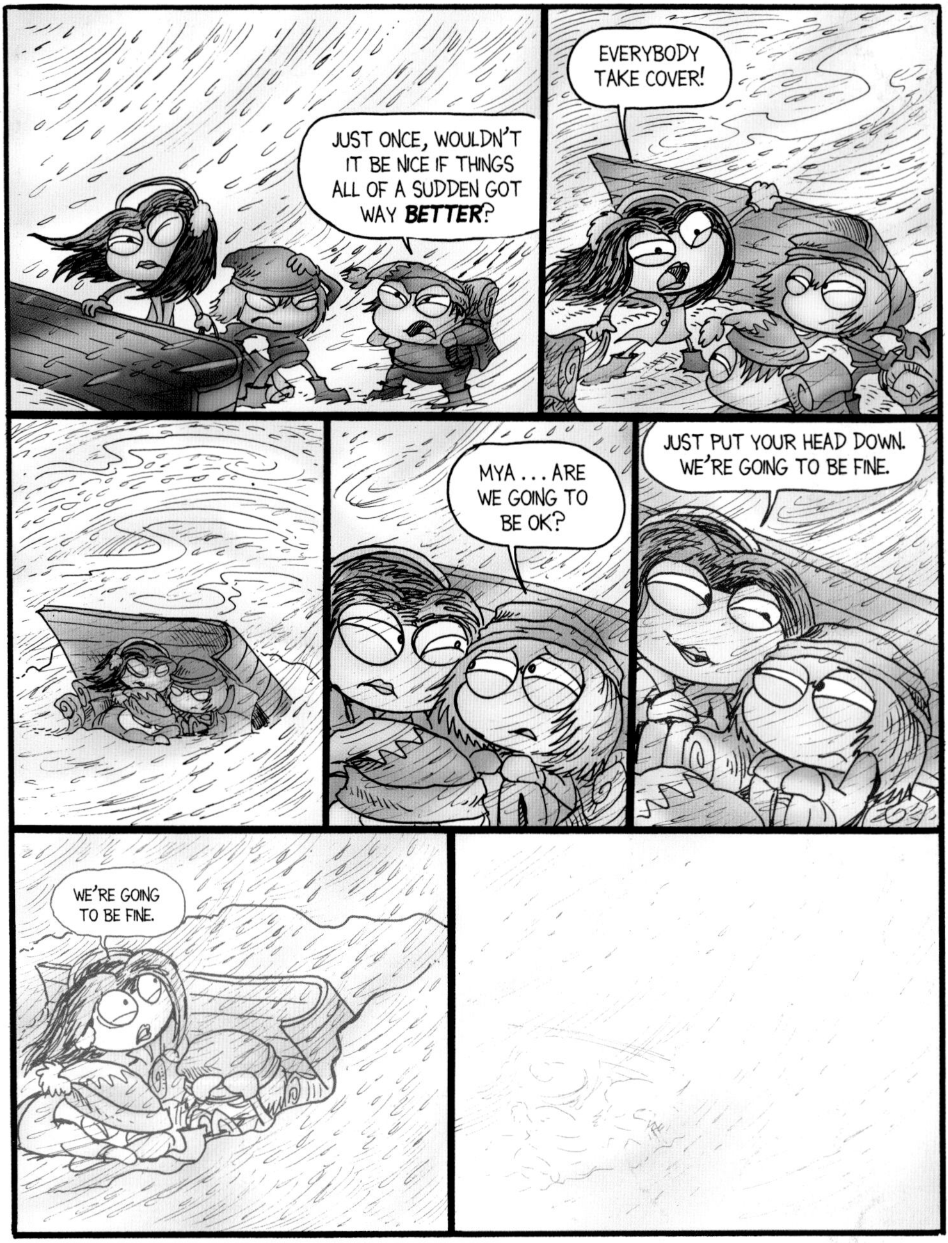
JUST ONCE, WOULDN'T IT BE NICE IF THINGS ALL OF A SUDDEN GOT WAY **BETTER**?
EVERYBODY TAKE COVER!
MYA . . . ARE WE GOING TO BE OK?
JUST PUT YOUR HEAD DOWN. WE'RE GOING TO BE FINE.
WE'RE GOING TO BE FINE.

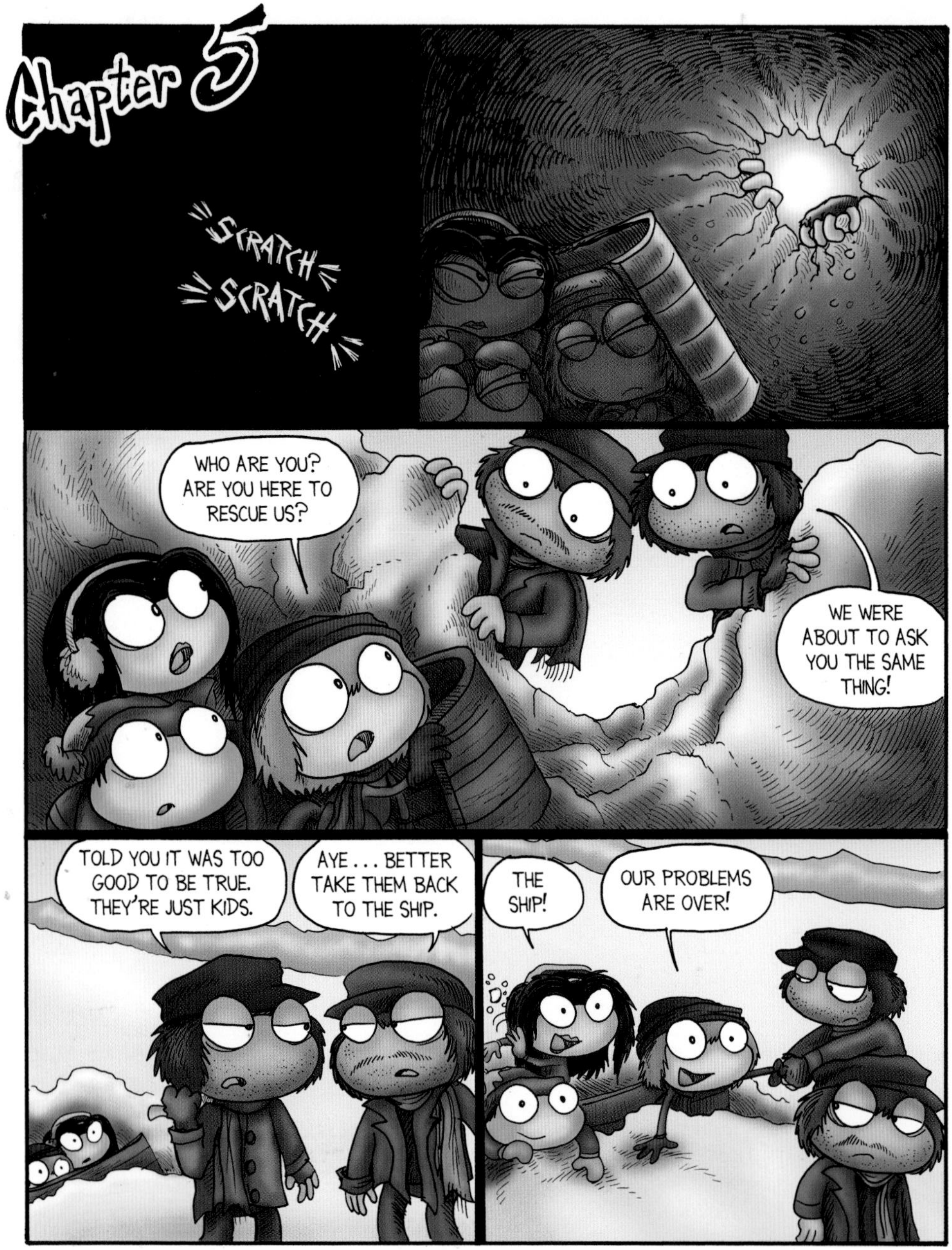
Chapter 5
SCRATCH
SCRATCH
WHO ARE YOU? ARE YOU HERE TO RESCUE US?
WE WERE ABOUT TO ASK YOU THE SAME THING!
TOLD YOU IT WAS TOO GOOD TO BE TRUE. THEY'RE JUST KIDS.
AYE . . . BETTER TAKE THEM BACK TO THE SHIP.
THE SHIP!
OUR PROBLEMS ARE OVER!

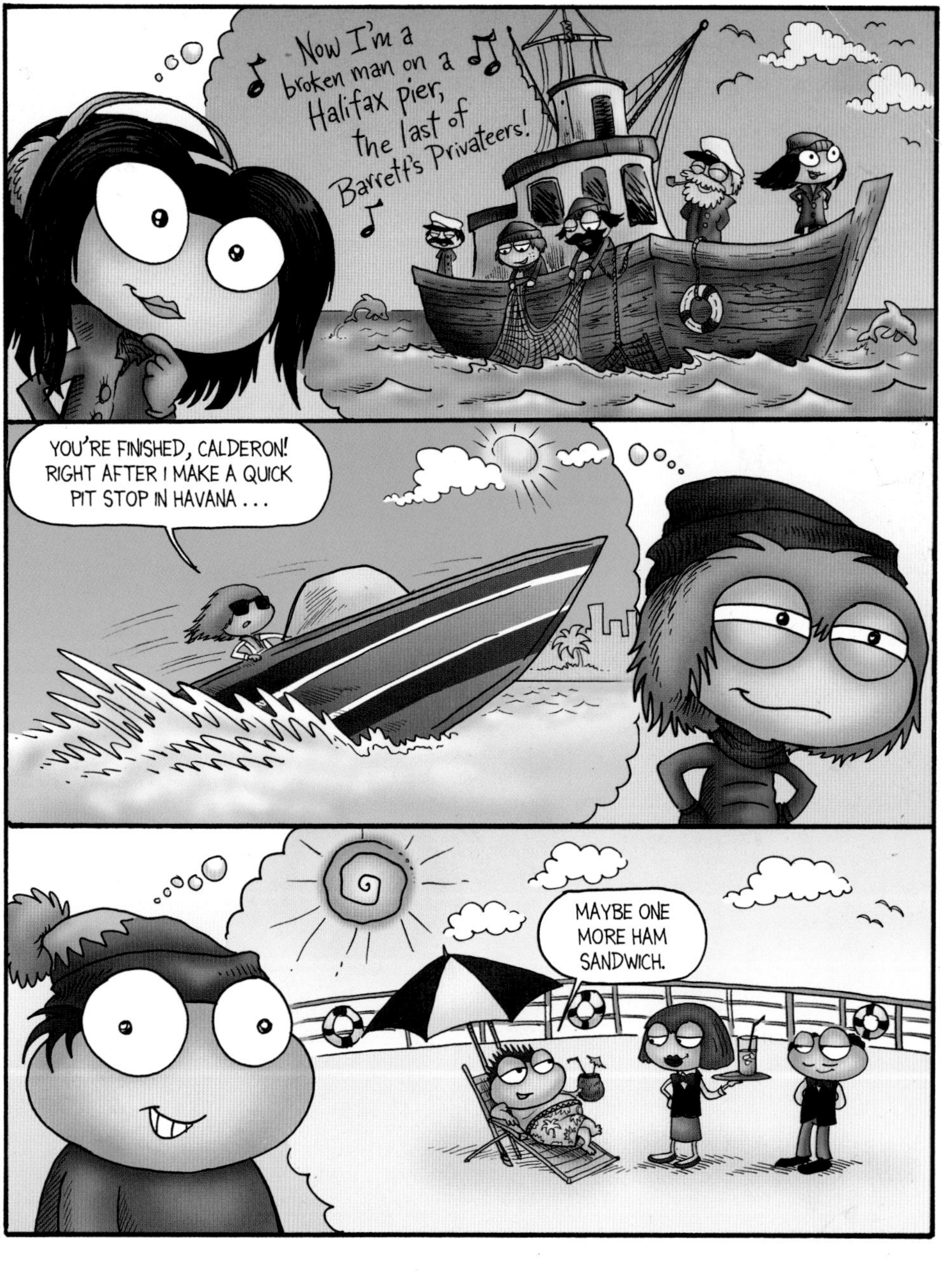

Now I'm a broken man on a Halifax pier, the last of Barrett's Privateers!
YOU'RE FINISHED, CALDERON! RIGHT AFTER I MAKE A QUICK PIT STOP IN HAVANA . . .
MAYBE ONE MORE HAM SANDWICH.

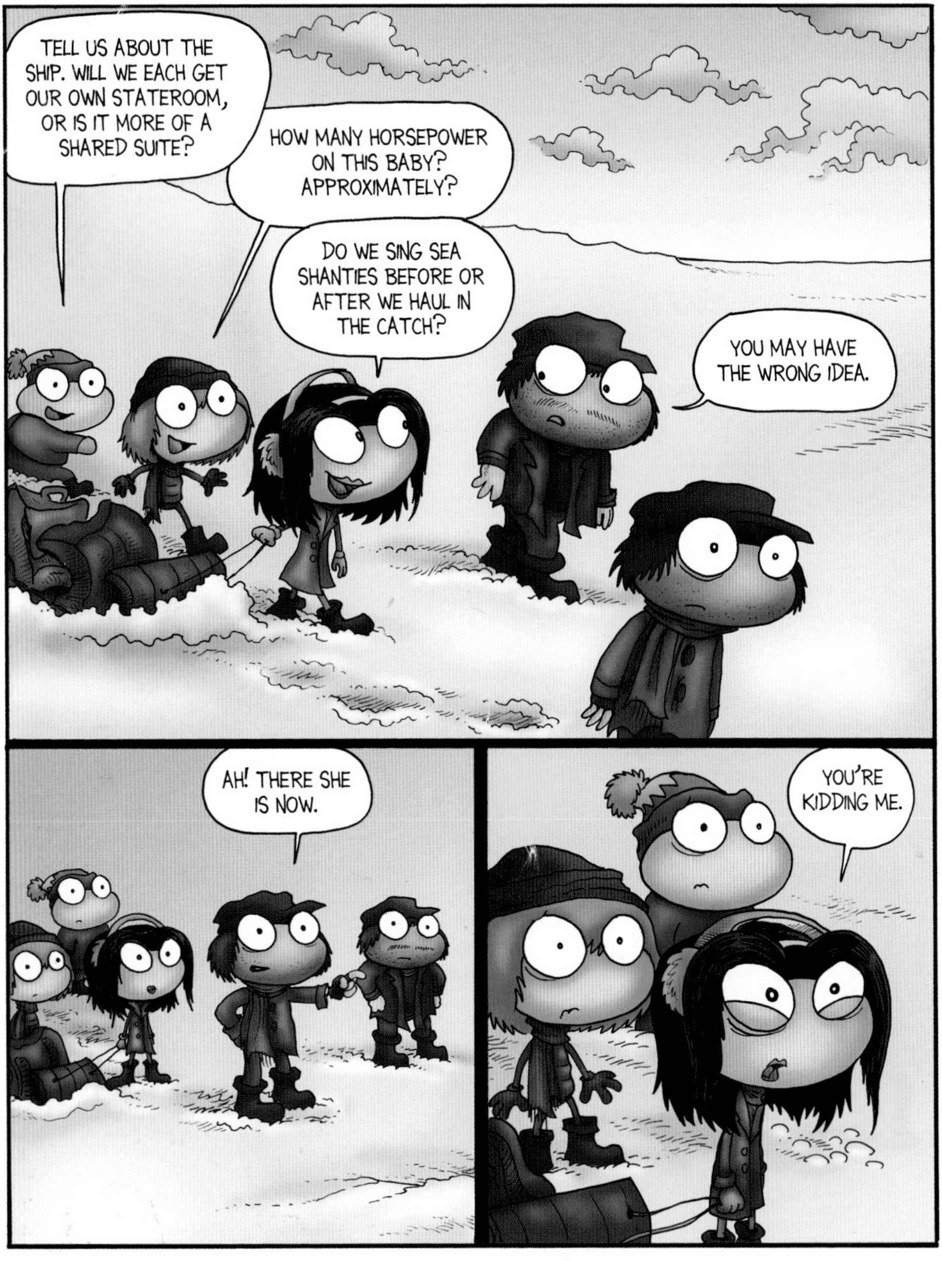
TELL US ABOUT THE SHIP. WILL WE EACH GET OUR OWN STATEROOM, OR IS IT MORE OF A SHARED SUITE?
HOW MANY HORSEPOWER ON THIS BABY? APPROXIMATELY?
DO WE SING SEA SHANTIES BEFORE OR AFTER WE HAUL IN THE CATCH?
YOU MAY HAVE THE WRONG IDEA.
AH! THERE SHE IS NOW.
YOU'RE KIDDING ME.

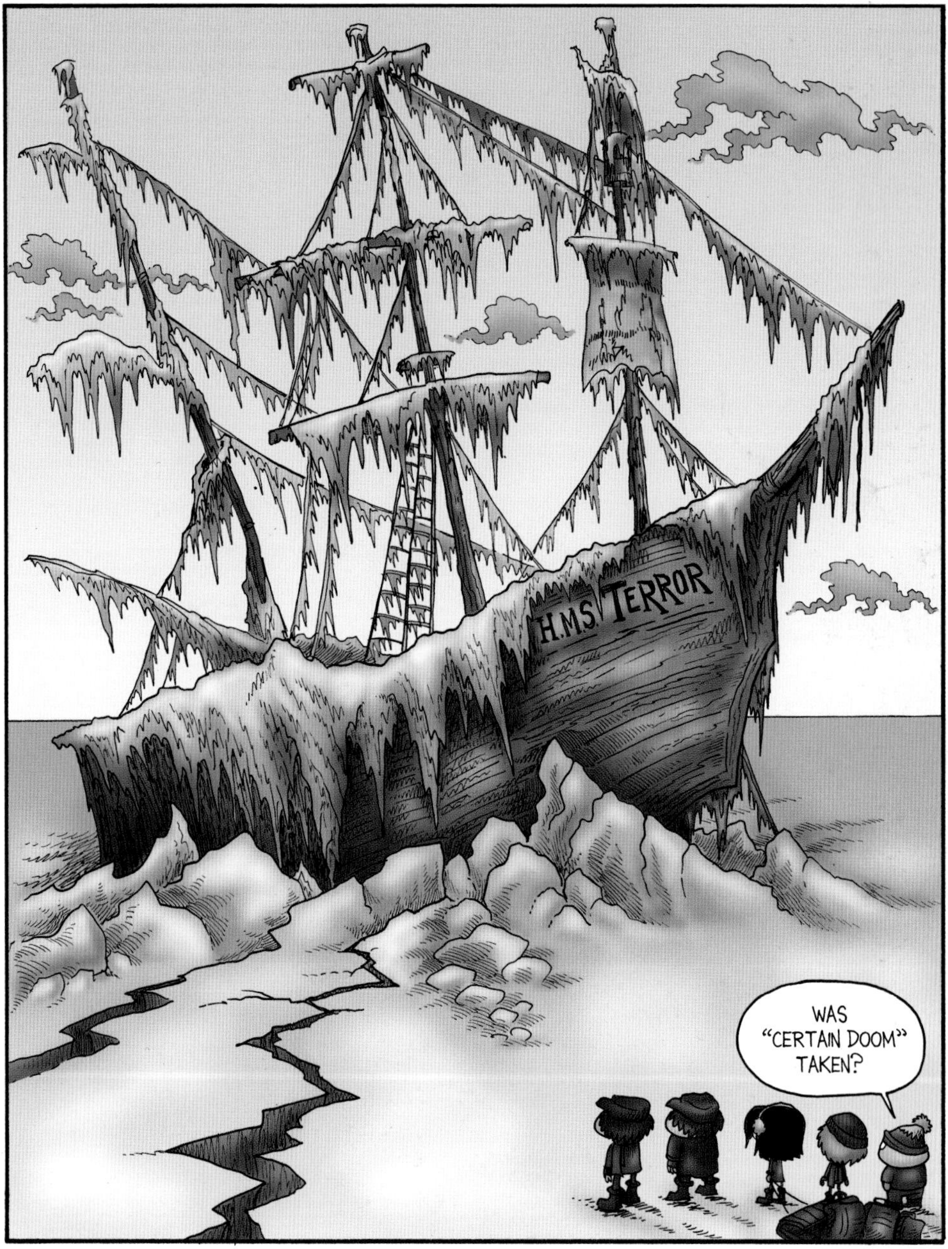
H.M.S. TERROR
WAS "CERTAIN DOOM" TAKEN?

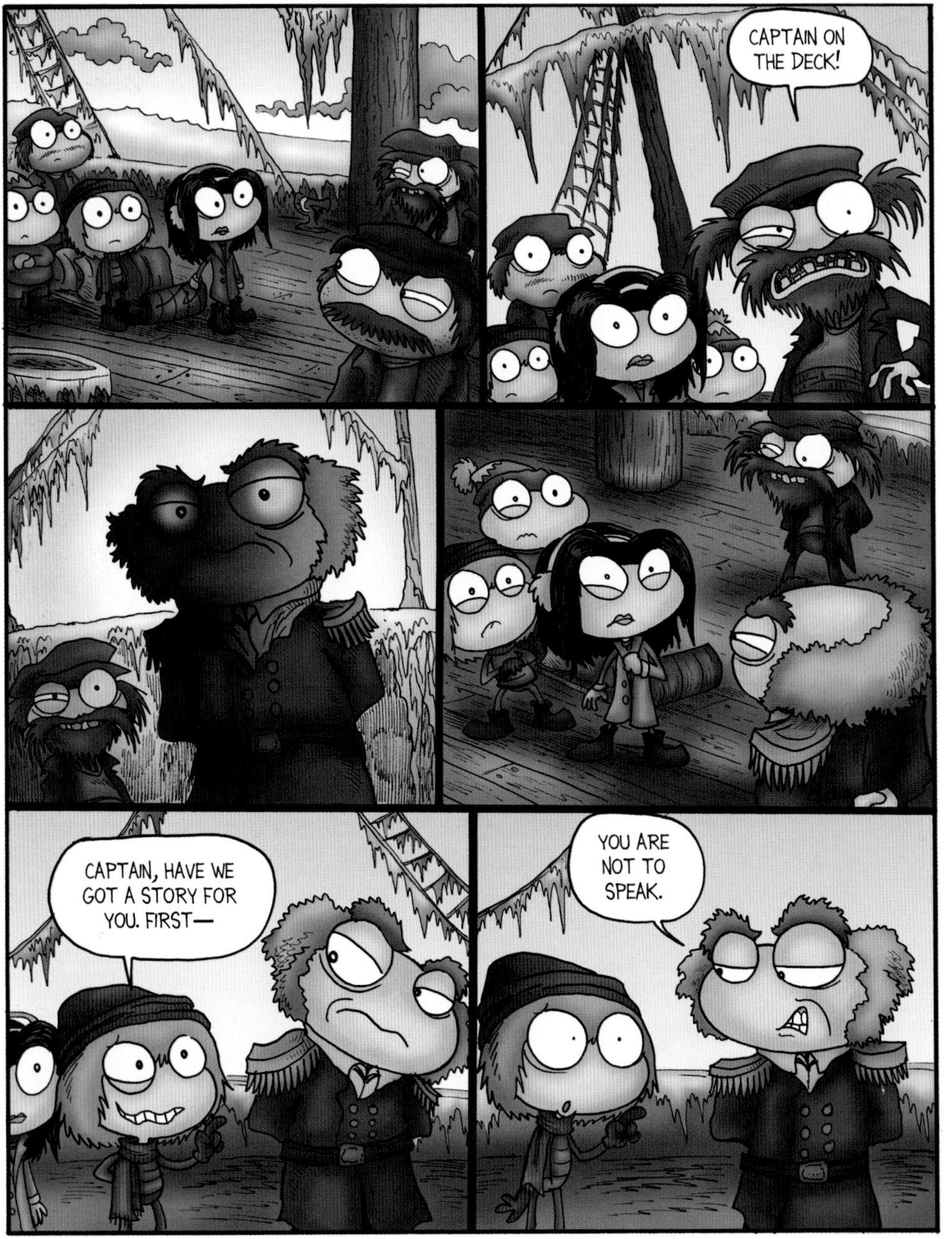
CAPTAIN ON THE DECK!
CAPTAIN, HAVE WE GOT A STORY FOR YOU. FIRST—
YOU ARE NOT TO SPEAK.

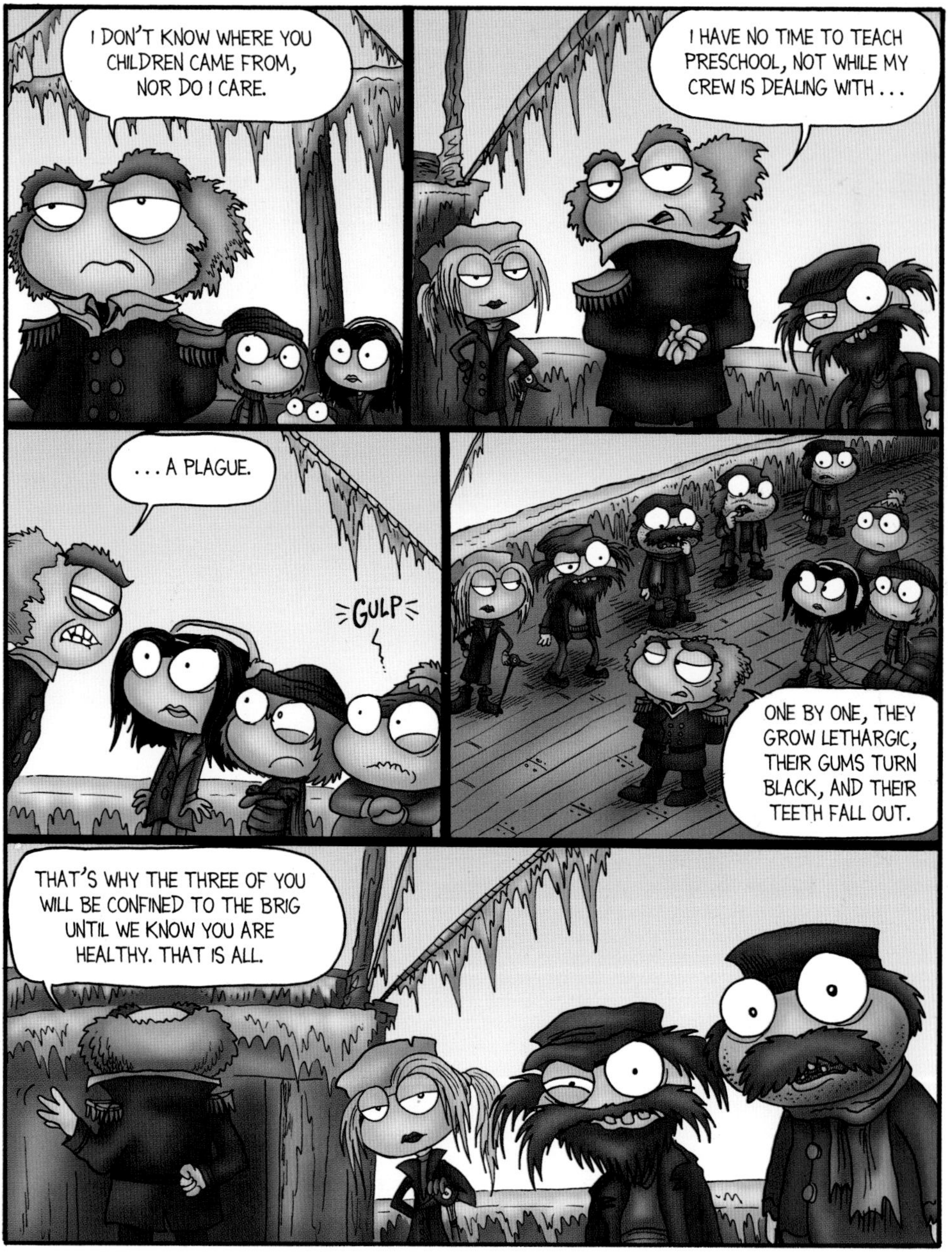
I DON'T KNOW WHERE YOU CHILDREN CAME FROM, NOR DO I CARE.
I HAVE NO TIME TO TEACH PRESCHOOL, NOT WHILE MY CREW IS DEALING WITH . . .
. . . A PLAGUE.
GULP
ONE BY ONE, THEY GROW LETHARGIC, THEIR GUMS TURN BLACK, AND THEIR TEETH FALL OUT.
THAT'S WHY THE THREE OF YOU WILL BE CONFINED TO THE BRIG UNTIL WE KNOW YOU ARE HEALTHY. THAT IS ALL.

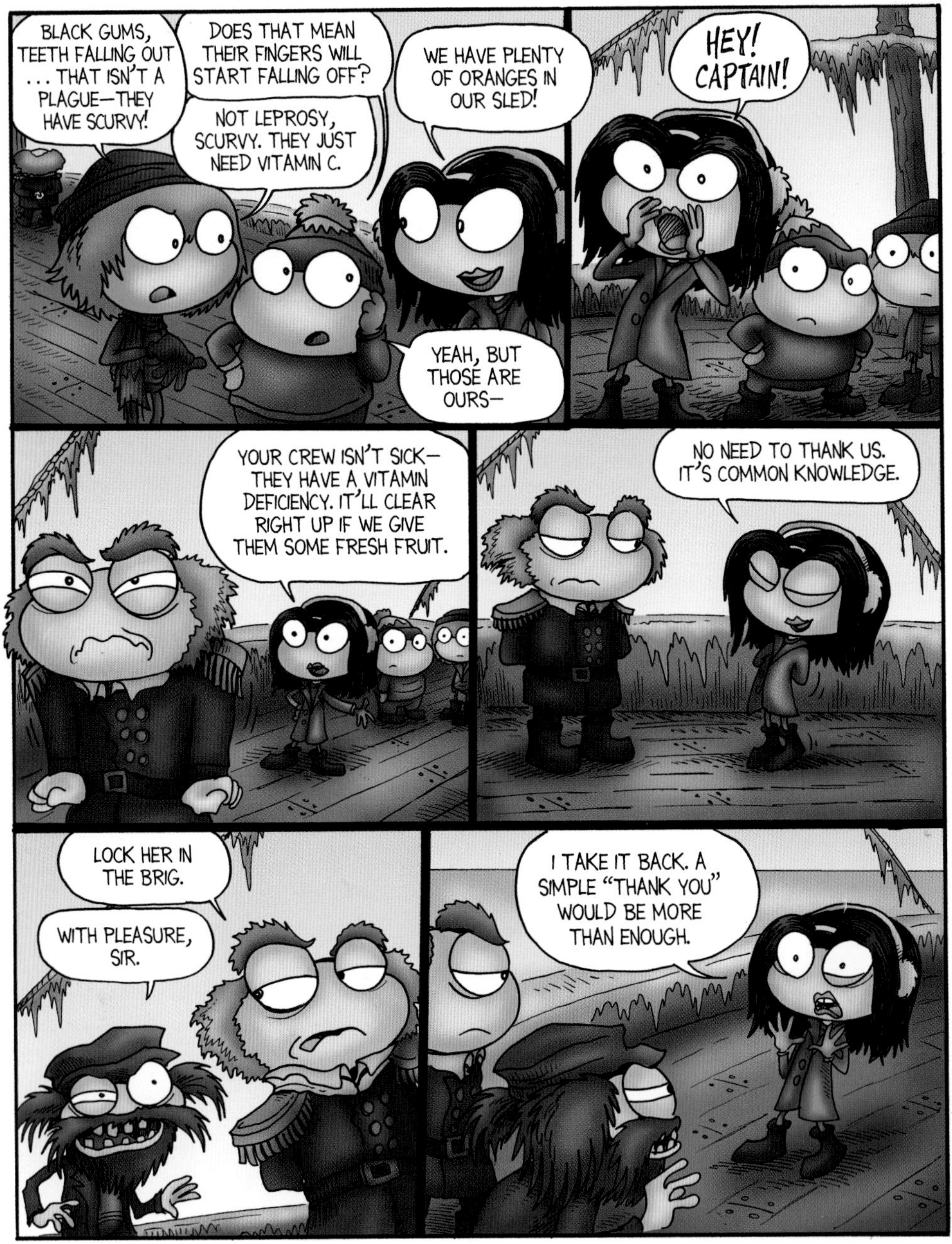
BLACK GUMS, TEETH FALLING OUT . . . THAT ISN'T A PLAGUE—THEY HAVE SCURVY!
DOES THAT MEAN THEIR FINGERS WILL START FALLING OFF?
NOT LEPROSY, SCURVY. THEY JUST NEED VITAMIN C.
WE HAVE PLENTY OF ORANGES IN OUR SLED!
YEAH, BUT THOSE ARE OURS—
HEY! CAPTAIN!
YOUR CREW ISN'T SICK—THEY HAVE A VITAMIN DEFICIENCY. IT'LL CLEAR RIGHT UP IF WE GIVE THEM SOME FRESH FRUIT.
NO NEED TO THANK US. IT'S COMMON KNOWLEDGE.
LOCK HER IN THE BRIG.
WITH PLEASURE, SIR.
I TAKE IT BACK. A SIMPLE "THANK YOU" WOULD BE MORE THAN ENOUGH.

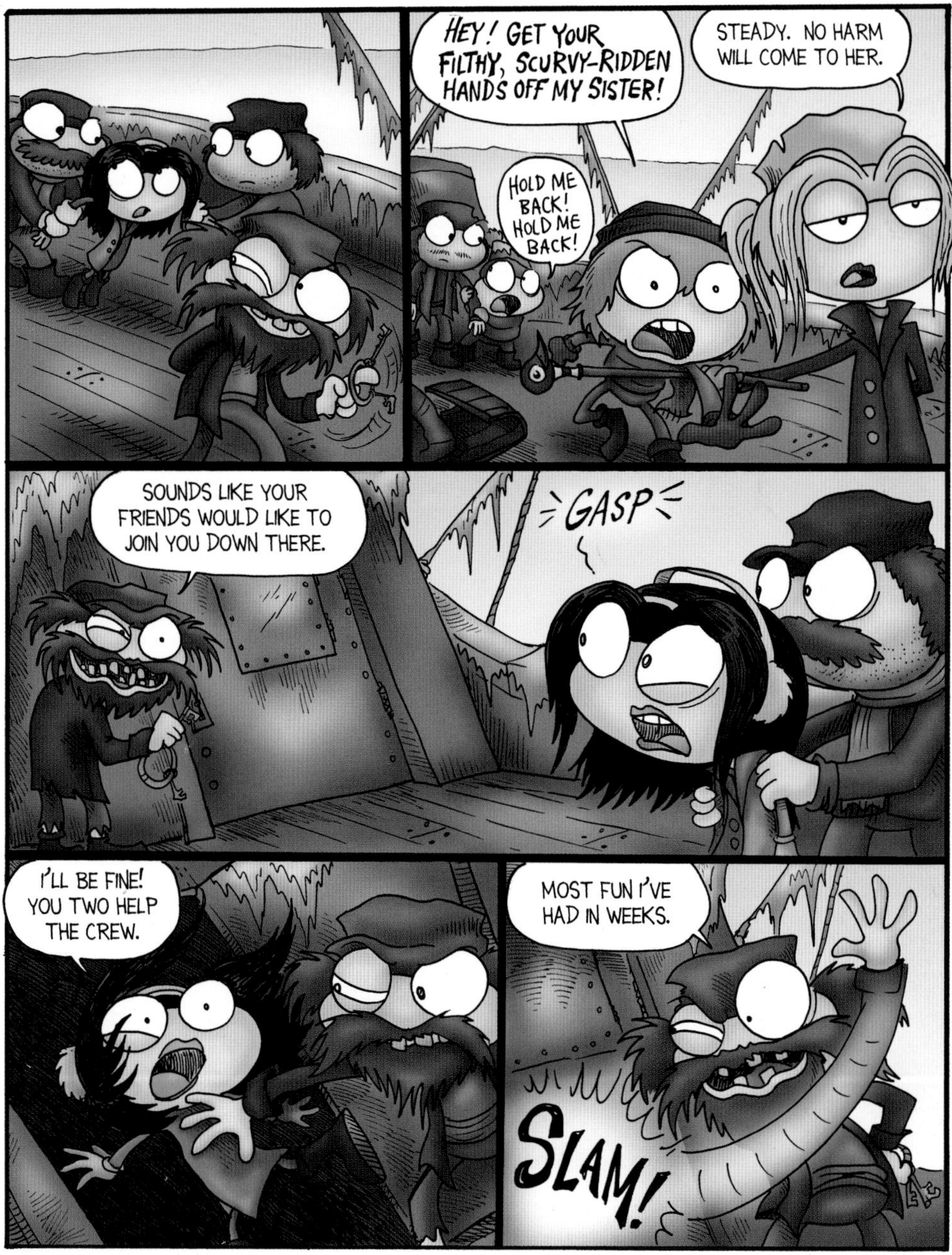
HEY! GET YOUR FILTHY, SCURVY-RIDDEN HANDS OFF MY SISTER!
STEADY. NO HARM WILL COME TO HER.
HOLD ME BACK! HOLD ME BACK!
SOUNDS LIKE YOUR FRIENDS WOULD LIKE TO JOIN YOU DOWN THERE.
GASP
I'LL BE FINE! YOU TWO HELP THE CREW.
MOST FUN I'VE HAD IN WEEKS.
SLAM!

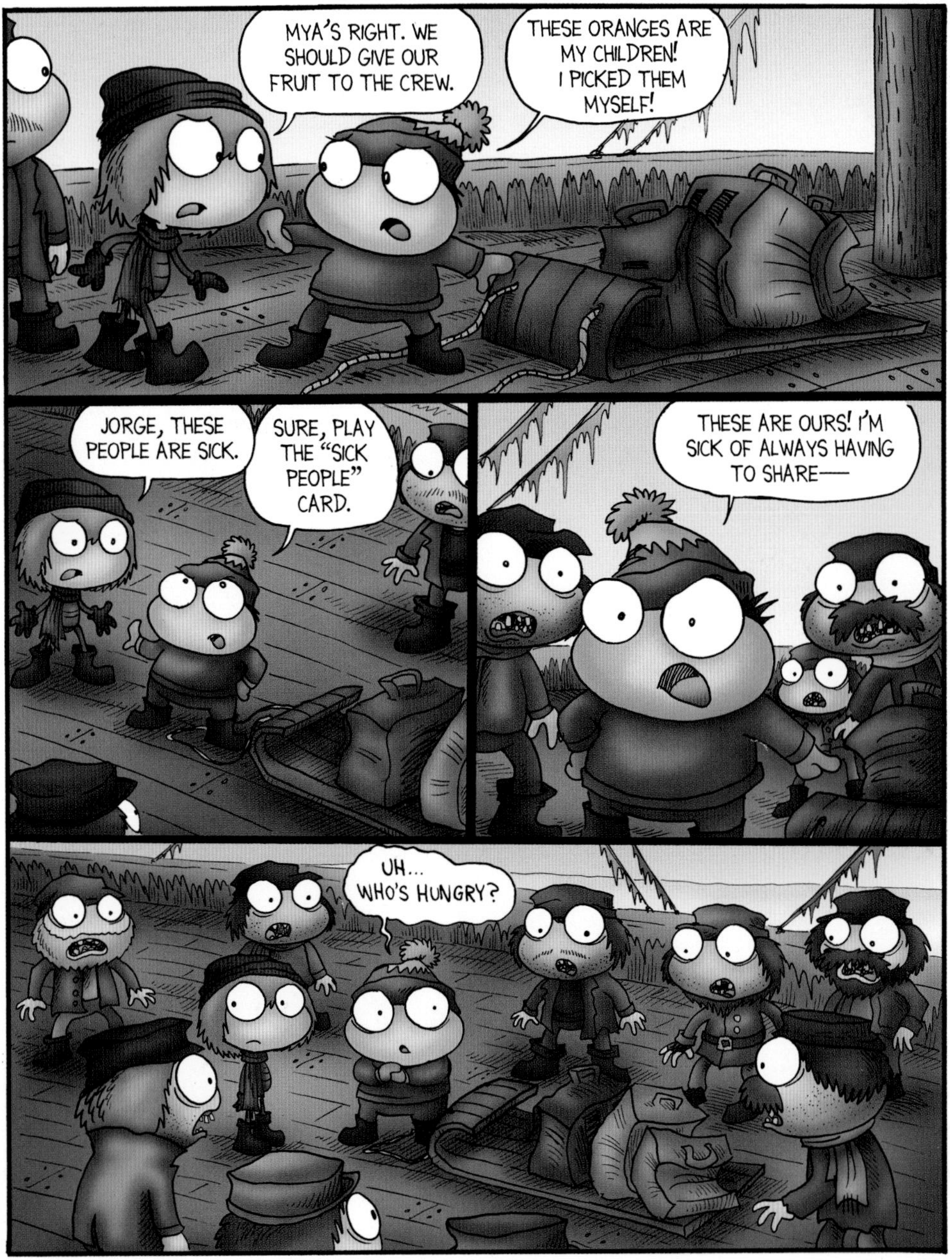
MYA'S RIGHT. WE SHOULD GIVE OUR FRUIT TO THE CREW.
THESE ORANGES ARE MY CHILDREN! I PICKED THEM MYSELF!
JORGE, THESE PEOPLE ARE SICK.
SURE, PLAY THE "SICK PEOPLE" CARD.
THESE ARE OURS! I'M SICK OF ALWAYS HAVING TO SHARE—
UH... WHO'S HUNGRY?

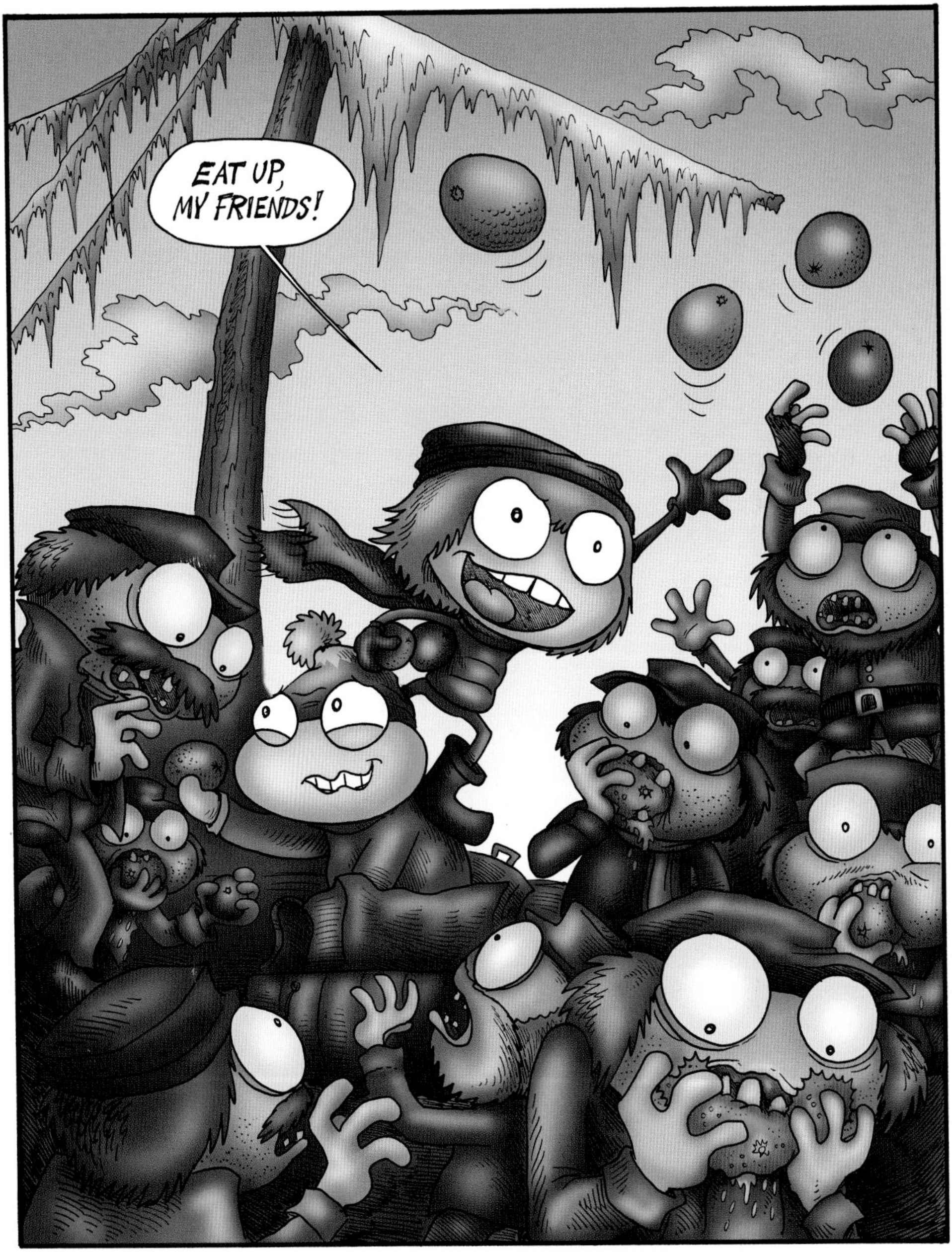
EAT UP, MY FRIENDS!

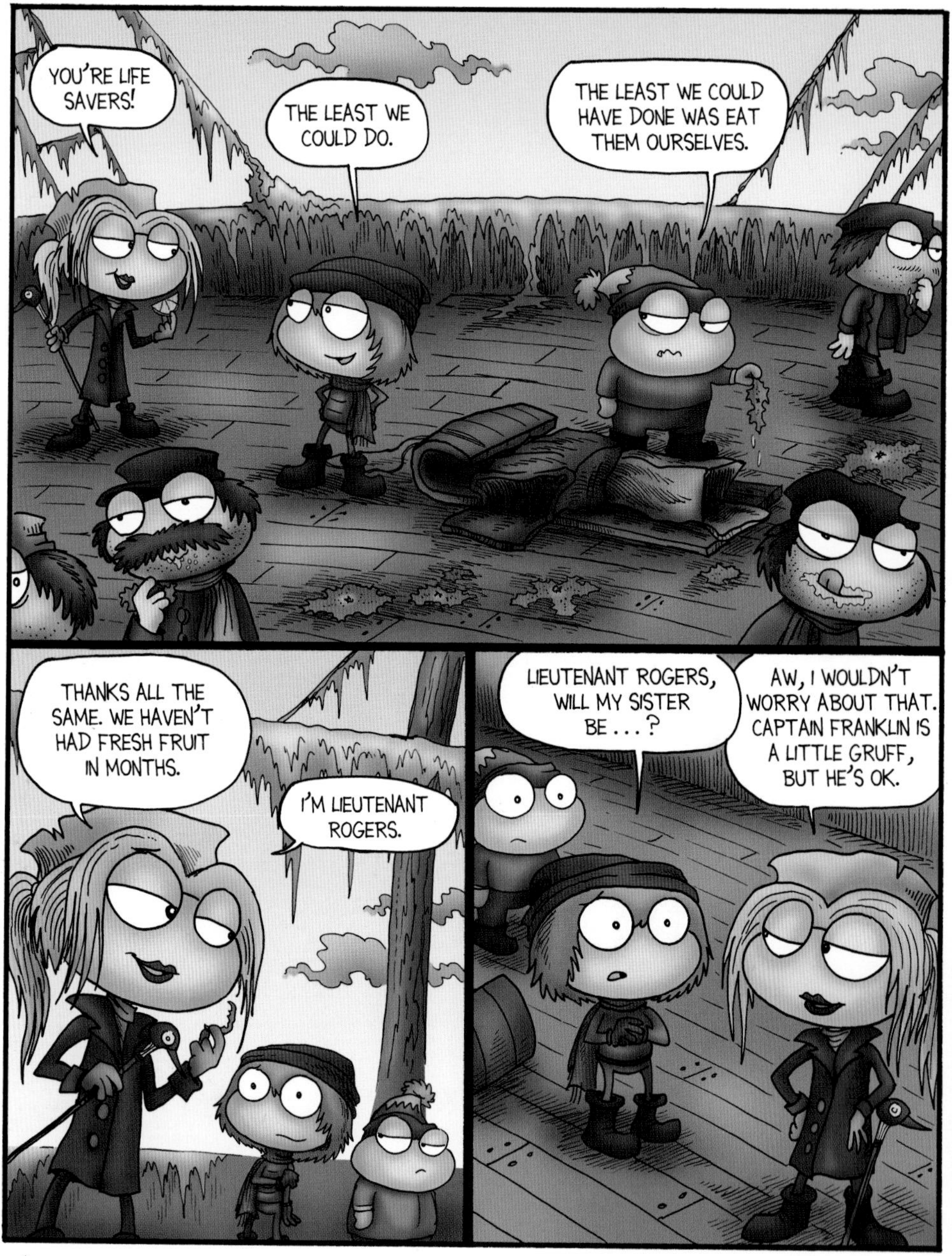
YOU'RE LIFE SAVERS!
THE LEAST WE COULD DO.
THE LEAST WE COULD HAVE DONE WAS EAT THEM OURSELVES.
THANKS ALL THE SAME. WE HAVEN'T HAD FRESH FRUIT IN MONTHS.
I'M LIEUTENANT ROGERS.
LIEUTENANT ROGERS, WILL MY SISTER BE . . . ?
AW, I WOULDN'T WORRY ABOUT THAT. CAPTAIN FRANKLIN IS A LITTLE GRUFF, BUT HE'S OK.

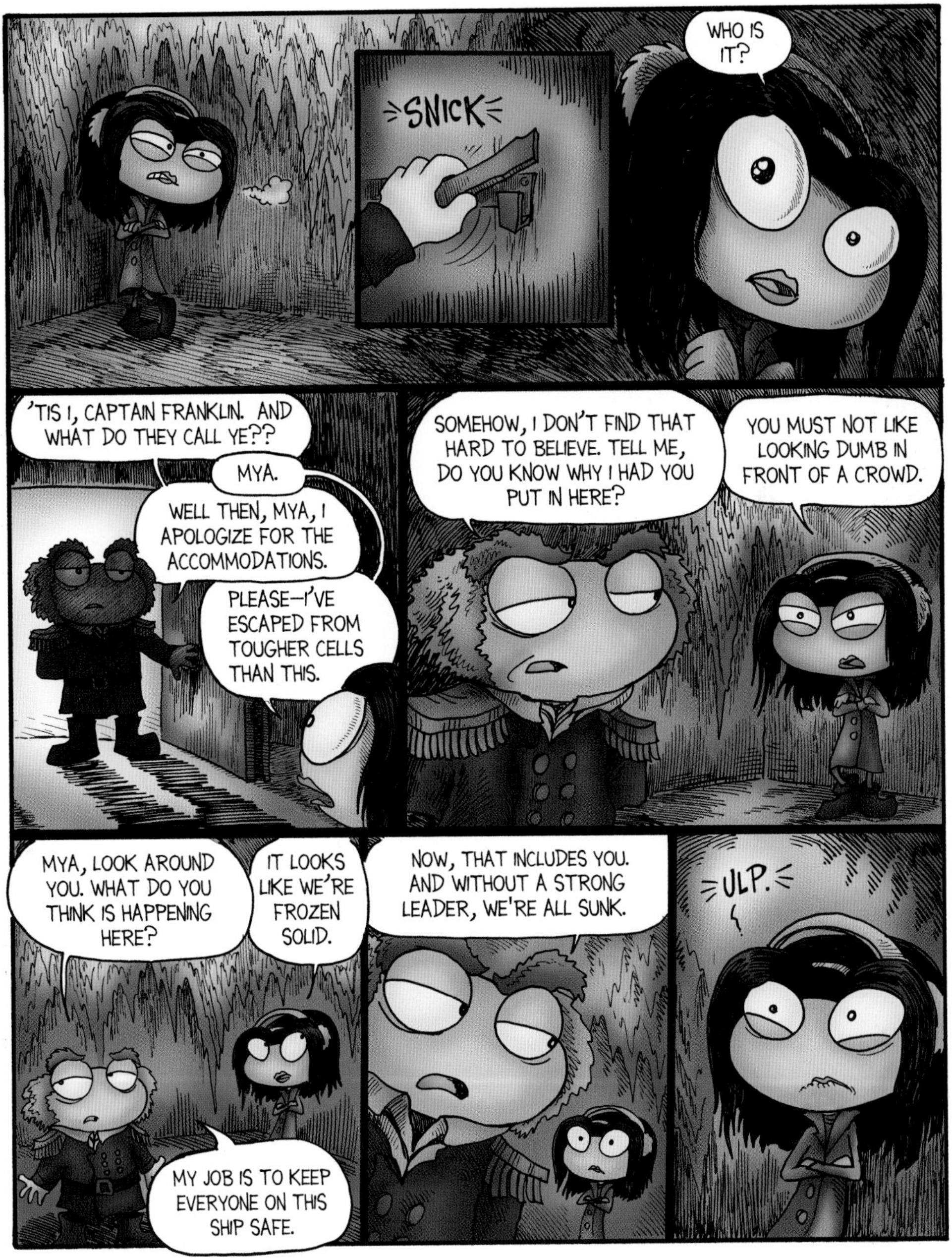
SNICK
WHO IS IT?
'TIS I, CAPTAIN FRANKLIN. AND WHAT DO THEY CALL YE??
MYA.
WELL THEN, MYA, I APOLOGIZE FOR THE ACCOMMODATIONS.
PLEASE—I'VE ESCAPED FROM TOUGHER CELLS THAN THIS.
SOMEHOW, I DON'T FIND THAT HARD TO BELIEVE. TELL ME, DO YOU KNOW WHY I HAD YOU PUT IN HERE?
YOU MUST NOT LIKE LOOKING DUMB IN FRONT OF A CROWD.
MYA, LOOK AROUND YOU. WHAT DO YOU THINK IS HAPPENING HERE?
IT LOOKS LIKE WE'RE FROZEN SOLID.
MY JOB IS TO KEEP EVERYONE ON THIS SHIP SAFE.
NOW, THAT INCLUDES YOU. AND WITHOUT A STRONG LEADER, WE'RE ALL SUNK.
ULP.

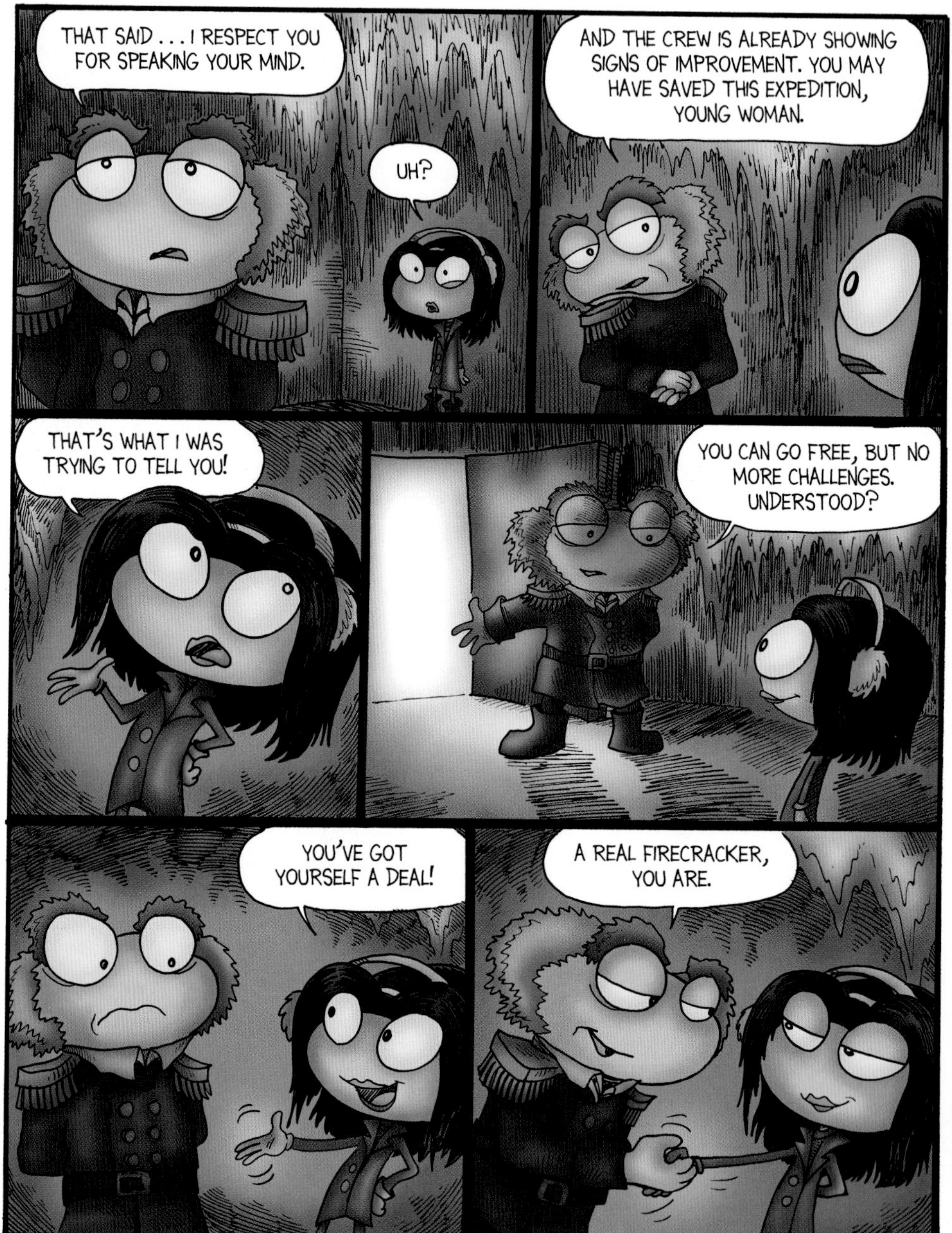
THAT SAID . . . I RESPECT YOU FOR SPEAKING YOUR MIND.
UH?
AND THE CREW IS ALREADY SHOWING SIGNS OF IMPROVEMENT. YOU MAY HAVE SAVED THIS EXPEDITION, YOUNG WOMAN.
THAT'S WHAT I WAS TRYING TO TELL YOU!
YOU CAN GO FREE, BUT NO MORE CHALLENGES. UNDERSTOOD?
YOU'VE GOT YOURSELF A DEAL!
A REAL FIRECRACKER, YOU ARE.

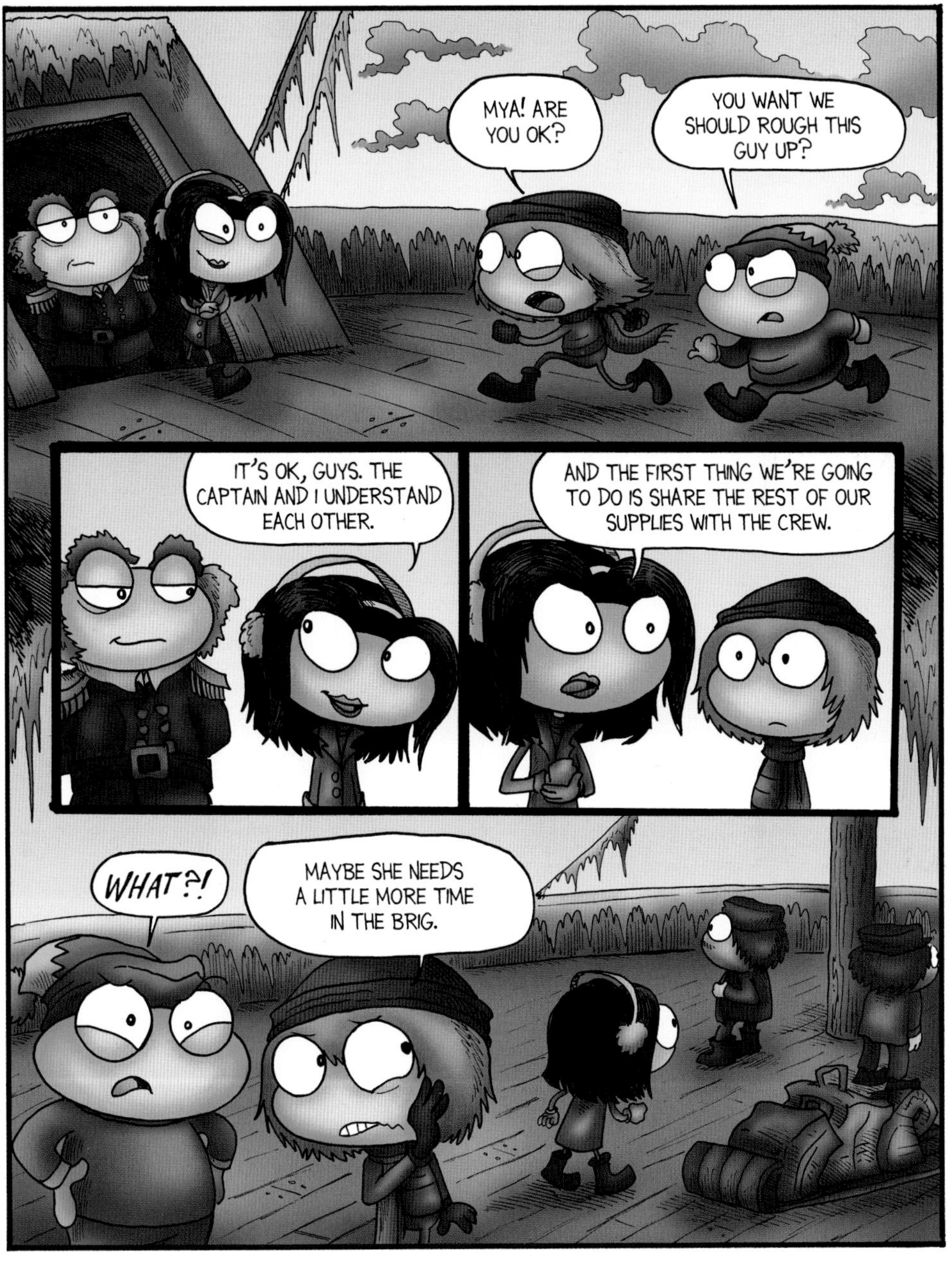
MYA! ARE YOU OK?
YOU WANT WE SHOULD ROUGH THIS GUY UP?
IT'S OK, GUYS. THE CAPTAIN AND I UNDERSTAND EACH OTHER.
AND THE FIRST THING WE'RE GOING TO DO IS SHARE THE REST OF OUR SUPPLIES WITH THE CREW.
WHAT?!
MAYBE SHE NEEDS A LITTLE MORE TIME IN THE BRIG.

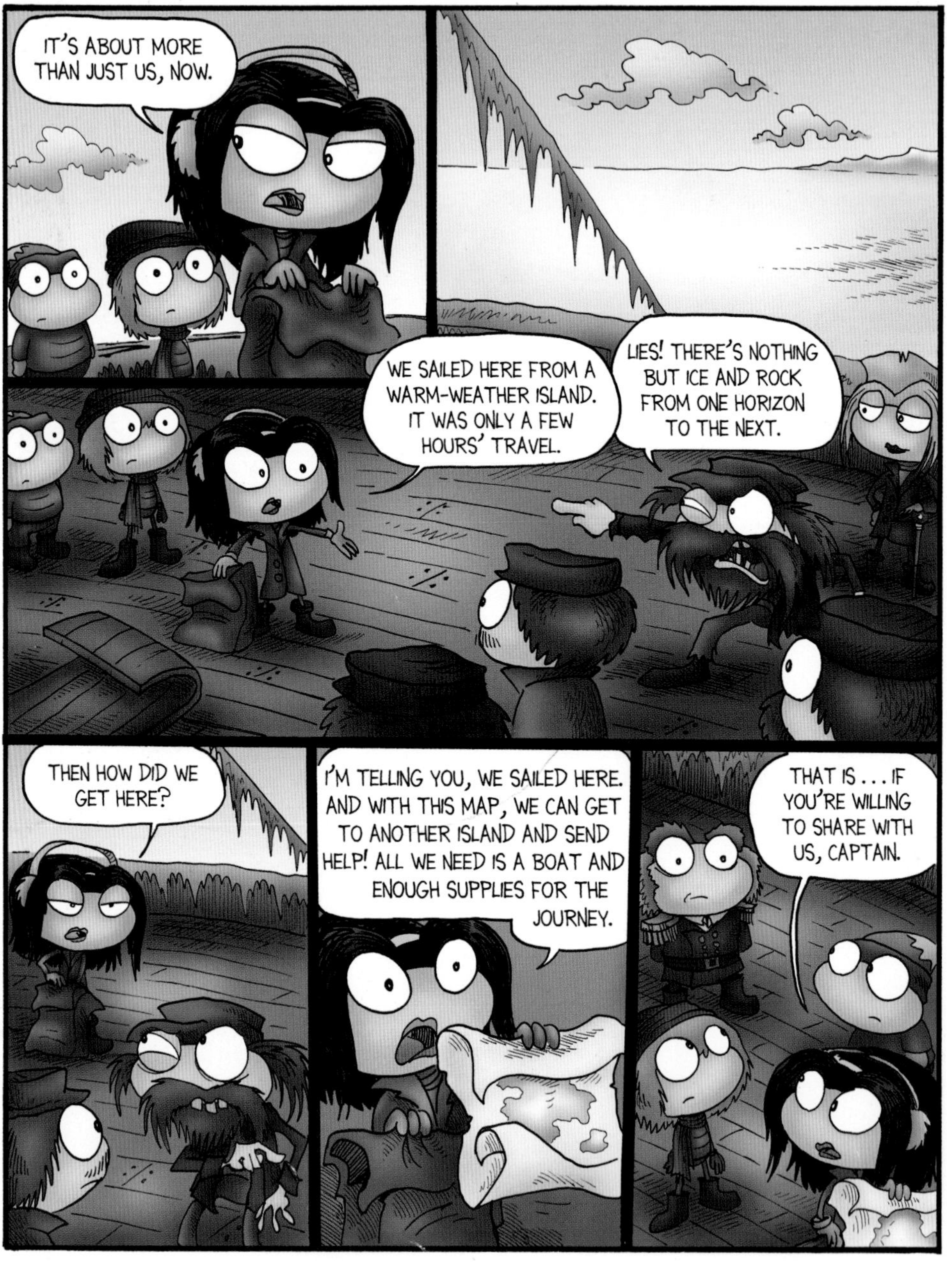
IT'S ABOUT MORE THAN JUST US, NOW.
WE SAILED HERE FROM A WARM-WEATHER ISLAND. IT WAS ONLY A FEW HOURS' TRAVEL.
LIES! THERE'S NOTHING BUT ICE AND ROCK FROM ONE HORIZON TO THE NEXT.
THEN HOW DID WE GET HERE?
I'M TELLING YOU, WE SAILED HERE. AND WITH THIS MAP, WE CAN GET TO ANOTHER ISLAND AND SEND HELP! ALL WE NEED IS A BOAT AND ENOUGH SUPPLIES FOR THE JOURNEY.
THAT IS . . . IF YOU'RE WILLING TO SHARE WITH US, CAPTAIN.

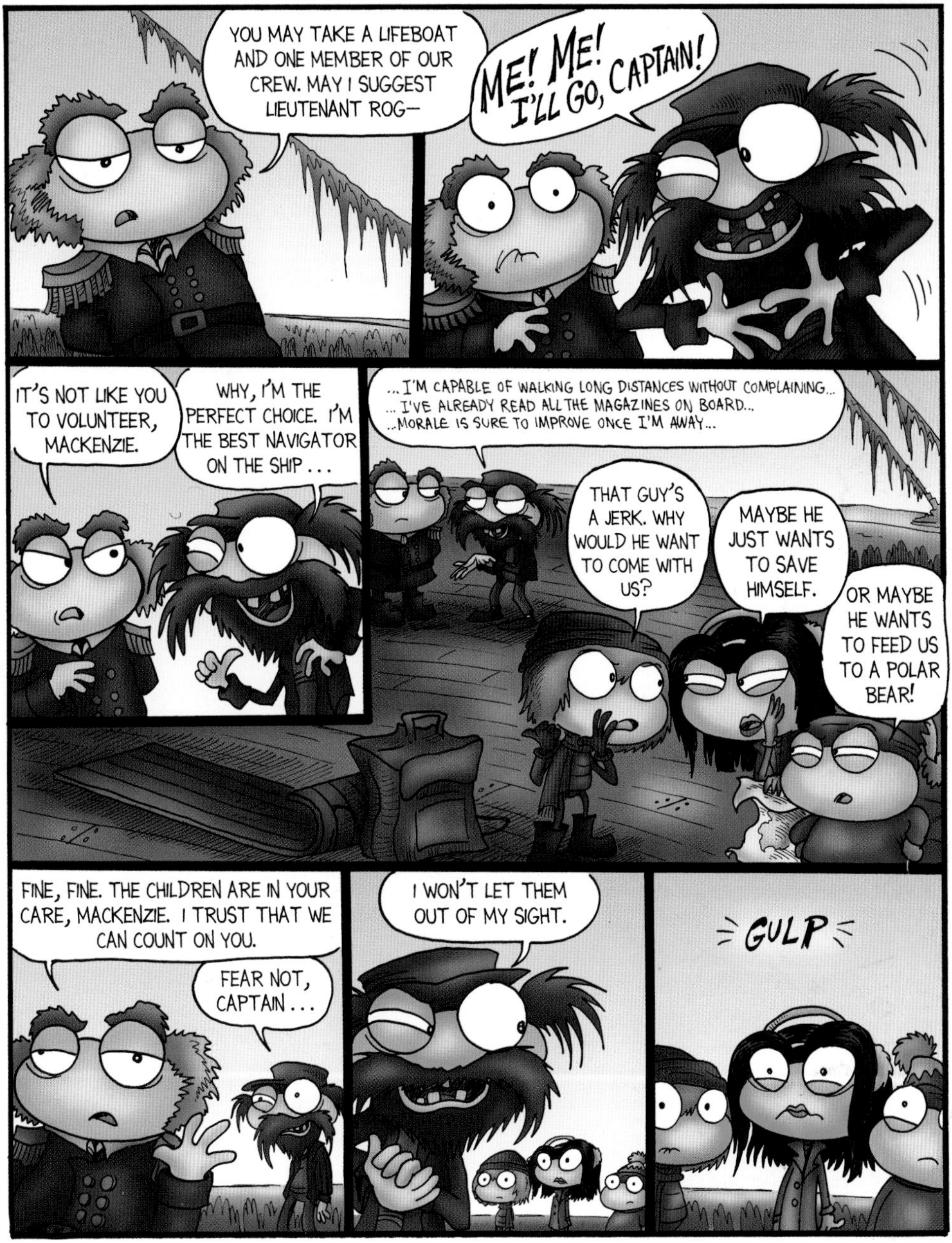

YOU MAY TAKE A LIFEBOAT AND ONE MEMBER OF OUR CREW. MAY I SUGGEST LIEUTENANT ROG—
ME! ME! I'LL GO, CAPTAIN!
IT'S NOT LIKE YOU TO VOLUNTEER, MACKENZIE.
WHY, I'M THE PERFECT CHOICE. I'M THE BEST NAVIGATOR ON THE SHIP . . .
... I'M CAPABLE OF WALKING LONG DISTANCES WITHOUT COMPLAINING... ... I'VE ALREADY READ ALL THE MAGAZINES ON BOARD... ..MORALE IS SURE TO IMPROVE ONCE I'M AWAY...
THAT GUY'S A JERK. WHY WOULD HE WANT TO COME WITH US?
MAYBE HE JUST WANTS TO SAVE HIMSELF.
OR MAYBE HE WANTS TO FEED US TO A POLAR BEAR!
FINE, FINE. THE CHILDREN ARE IN YOUR CARE, MACKENZIE. I TRUST THAT WE CAN COUNT ON YOU.
FEAR NOT, CAPTAIN . . .
I WON'T LET THEM OUT OF MY SIGHT.
GULP

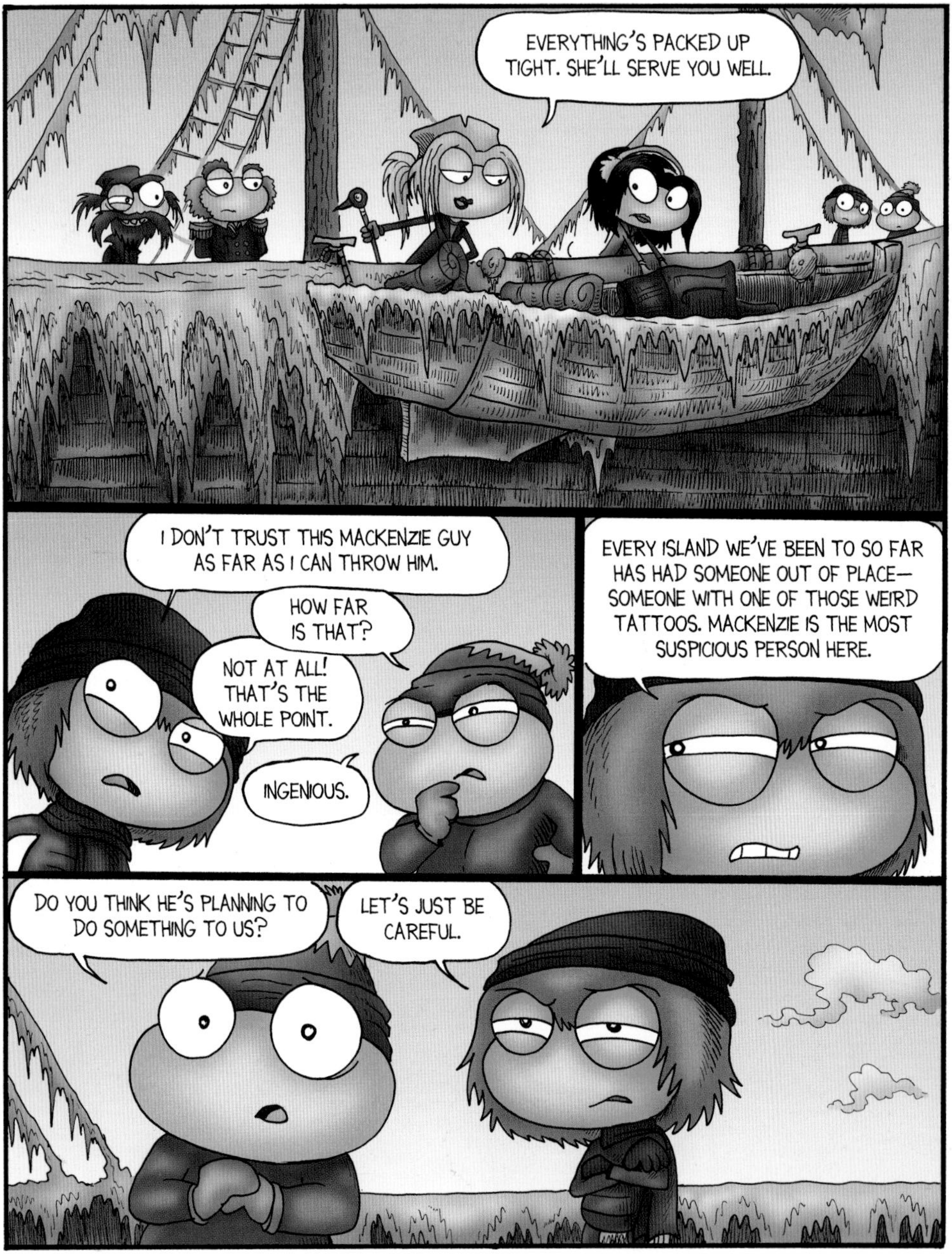
EVERYTHING'S PACKED UP TIGHT. SHE'LL SERVE YOU WELL.
I DON'T TRUST THIS MACKENZIE GUY AS FAR AS I CAN THROW HIM.
HOW FAR IS THAT?
NOT AT ALL! THAT'S THE WHOLE POINT.
INGENIOUS.
EVERY ISLAND WE'VE BEEN TO SO FAR HAS HAD SOMEONE OUT OF PLACE— SOMEONE WITH ONE OF THOSE WEIRD TATTOOS. MACKENZIE IS THE MOST SUSPICIOUS PERSON HERE.
DO YOU THINK HE'S PLANNING TO DO SOMETHING TO US?
LET'S JUST BE CAREFUL.

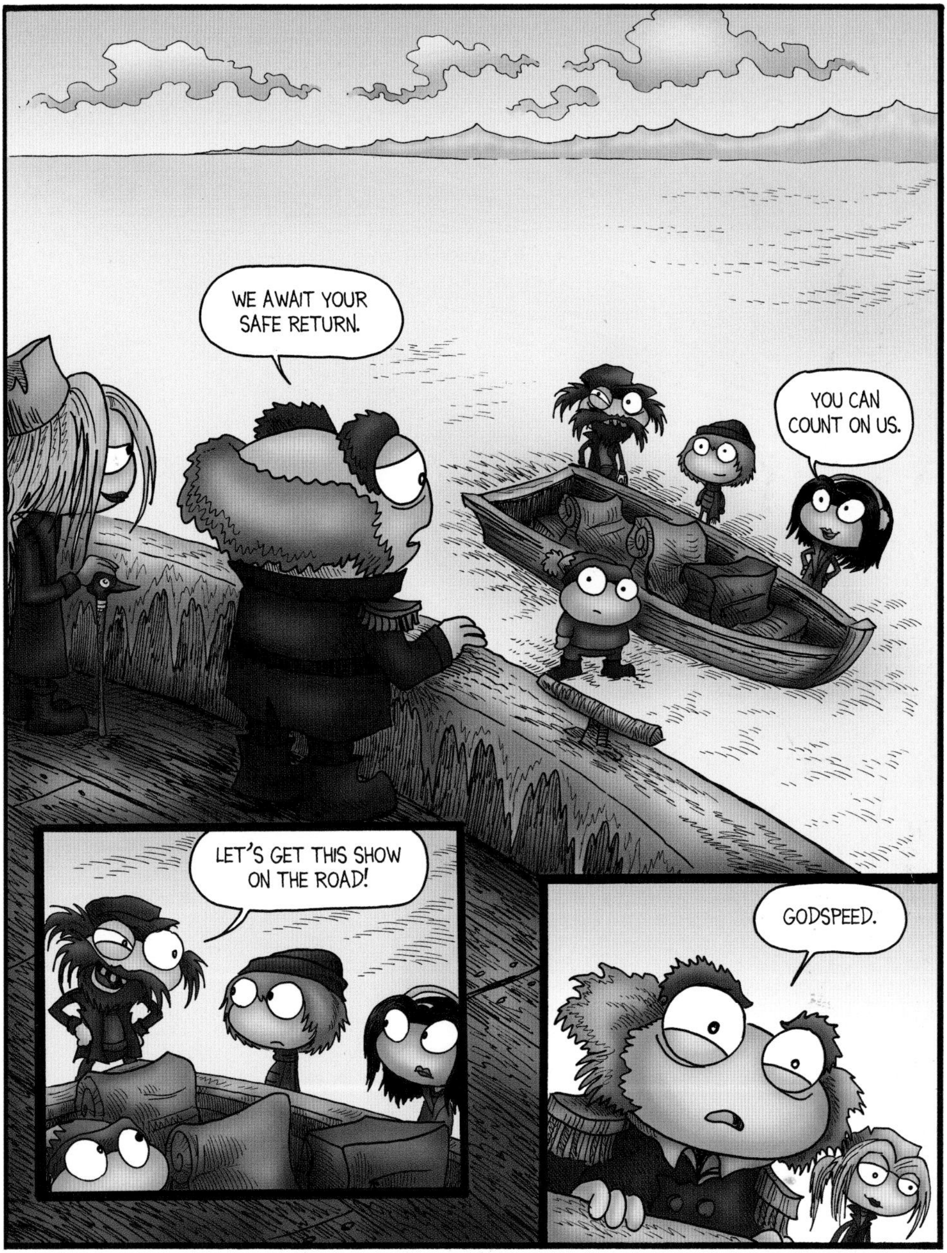
WE AWAIT YOUR SAFE RETURN.
YOU CAN COUNT ON US.
LET'S GET THIS SHOW ON THE ROAD!
GODSPEED.

Chapter 6

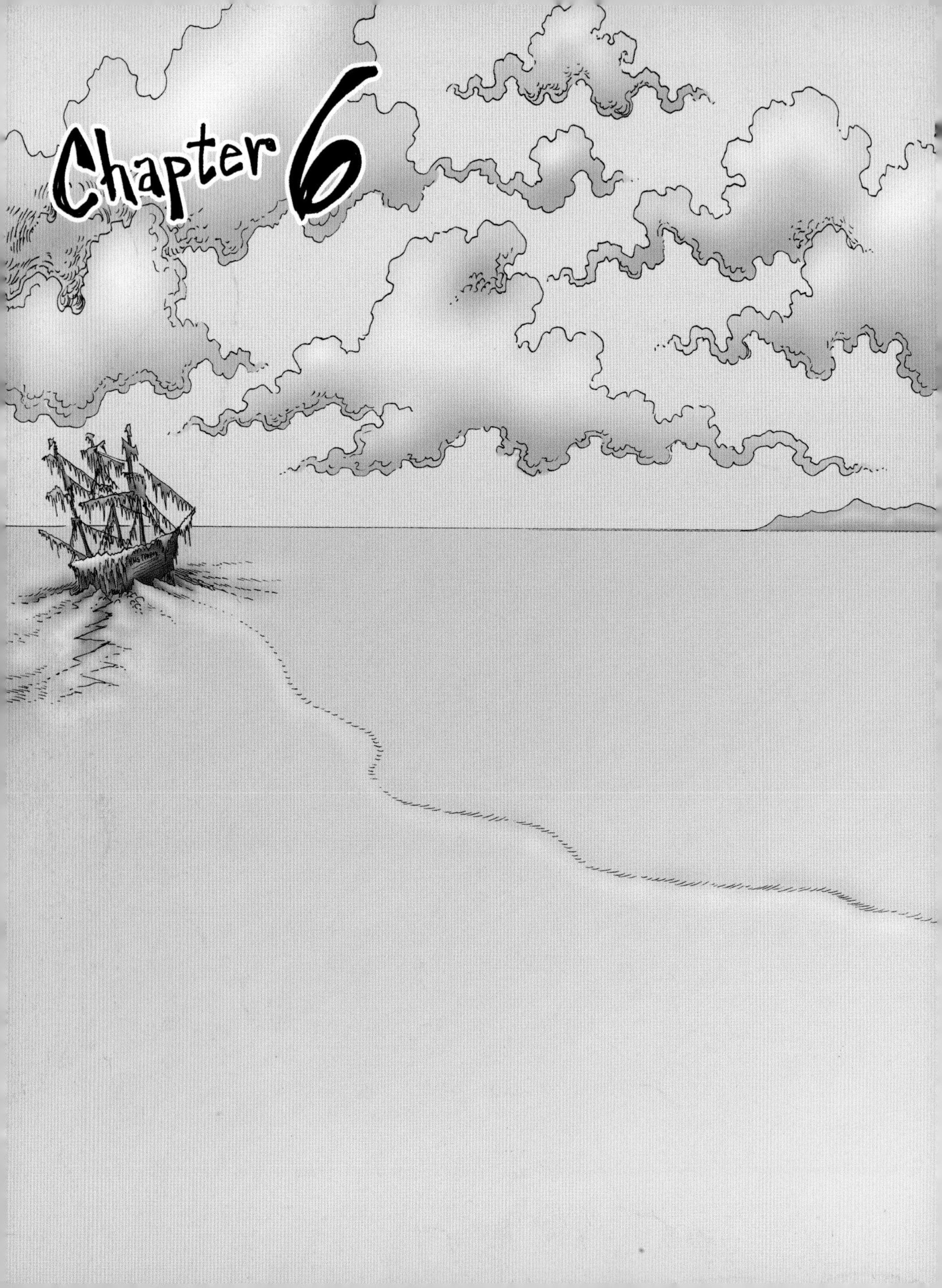

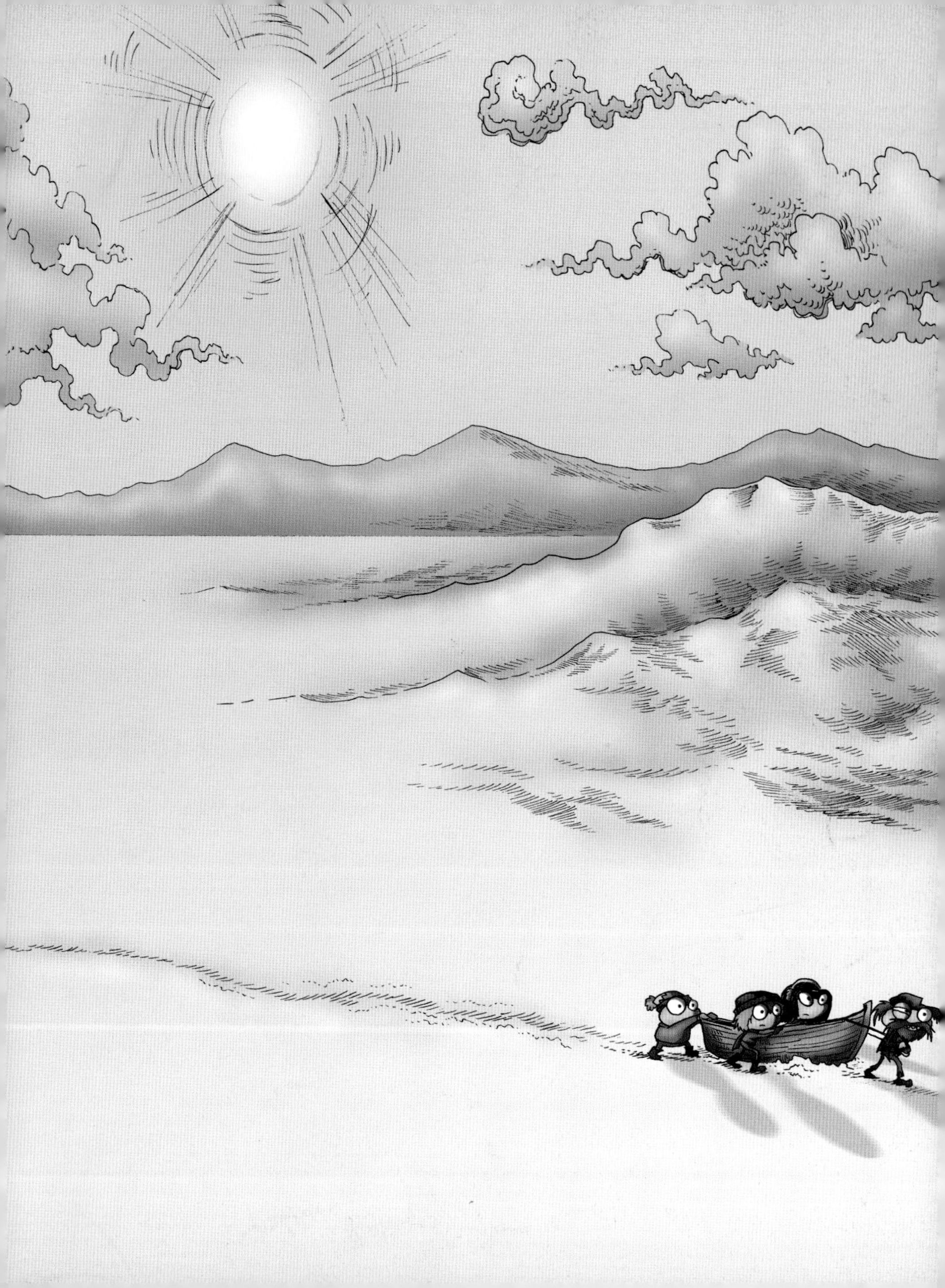

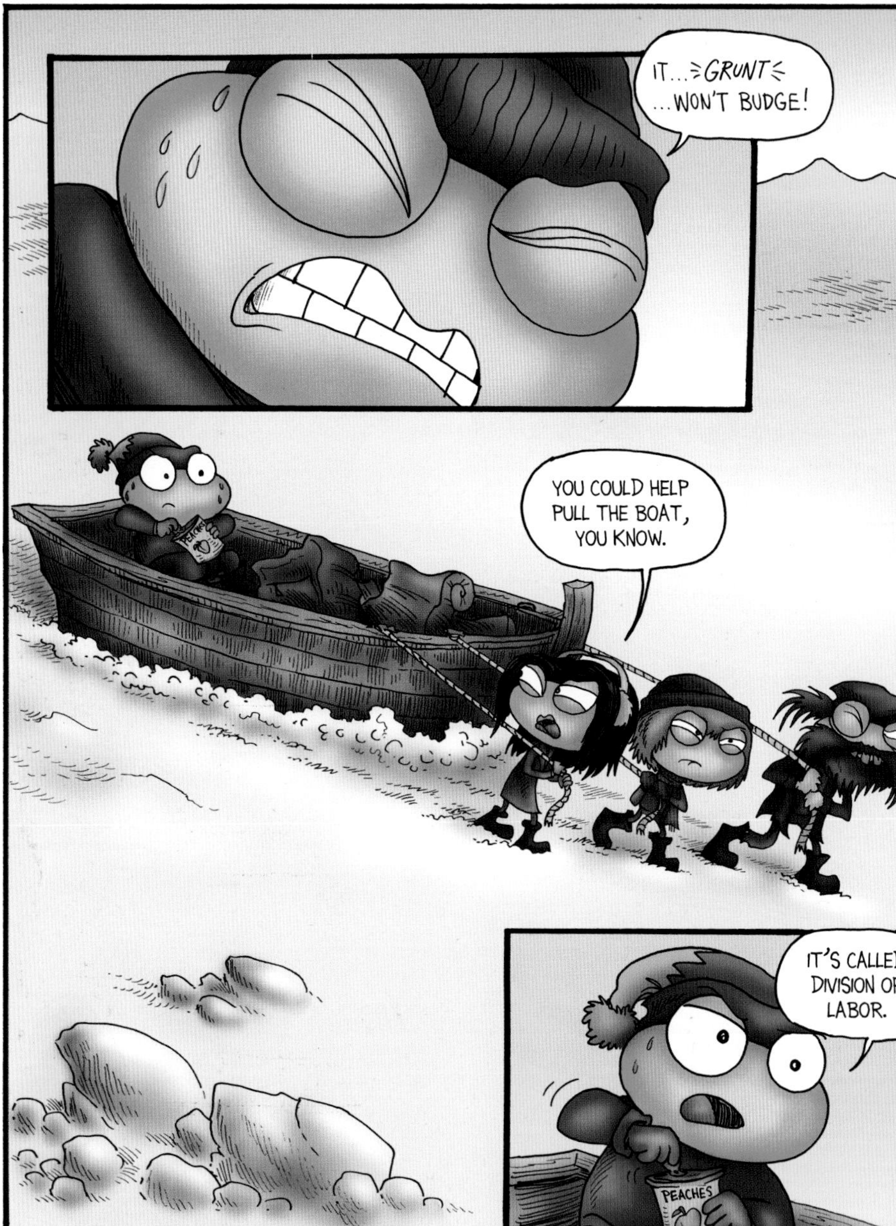
IT... GRUNT ...WON'T BUDGE!
YOU COULD HELP PULL THE BOAT, YOU KNOW.
PEACHES
IT'S CALLED DIVISION OF LABOR.
PEACHES

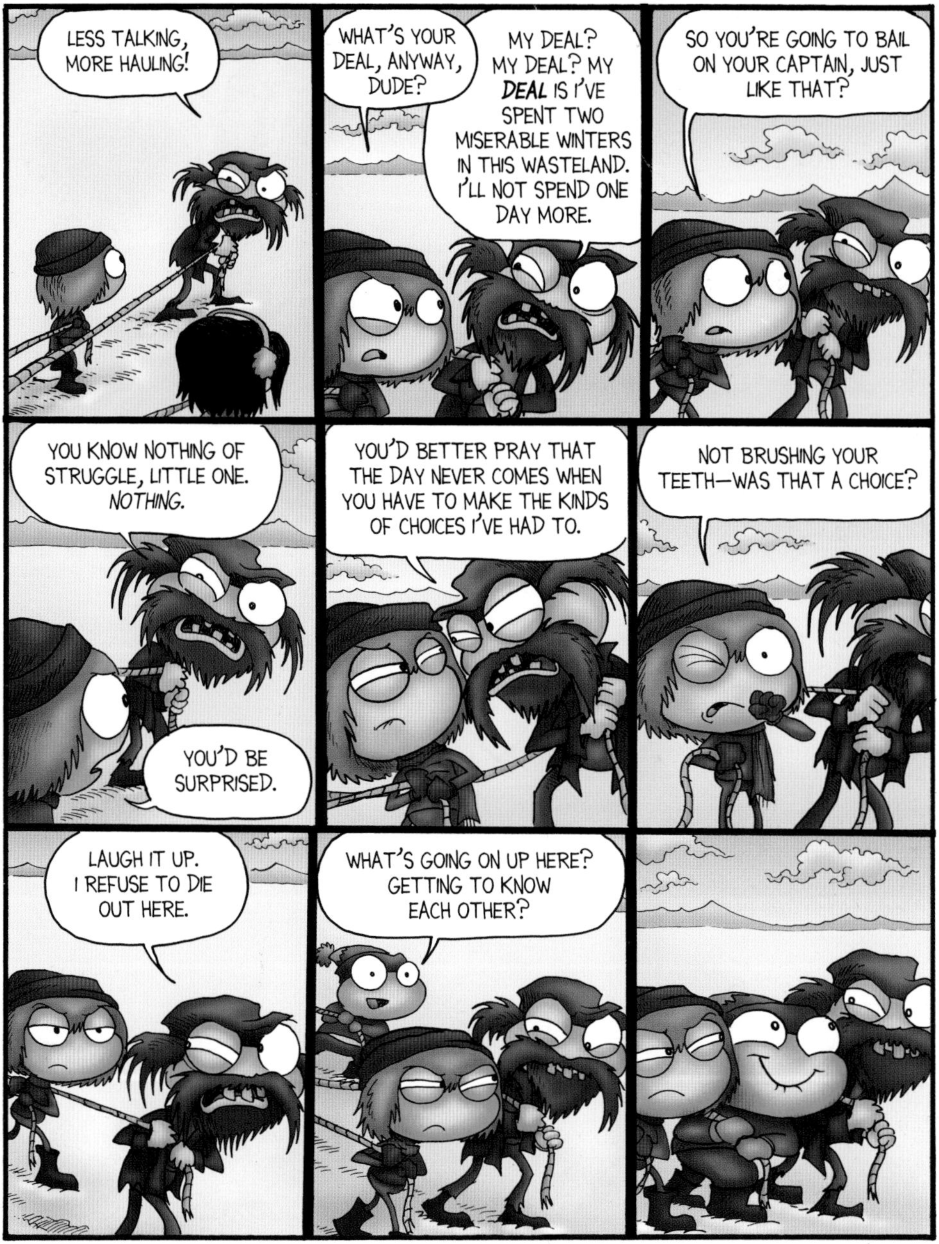
LESS TALKING, MORE HAULING!
WHAT'S YOUR DEAL, ANYWAY, DUDE?
MY DEAL? MY DEAL? MY DEAL IS I'VE SPENT TWO MISERABLE WINTERS IN THIS WASTELAND. I'LL NOT SPEND ONE DAY MORE.
SO YOU'RE GOING TO BAIL ON YOUR CAPTAIN, JUST LIKE THAT?
YOU KNOW NOTHING OF STRUGGLE, LITTLE ONE. NOTHING.
YOU'D BE SURPRISED.
YOU'D BETTER PRAY THAT THE DAY NEVER COMES WHEN YOU HAVE TO MAKE THE KINDS OF CHOICES I'VE HAD TO.
NOT BRUSHING YOUR TEETH—WAS THAT A CHOICE?
LAUGH IT UP. I REFUSE TO DIE OUT HERE.
WHAT'S GOING ON UP HERE? GETTING TO KNOW EACH OTHER?

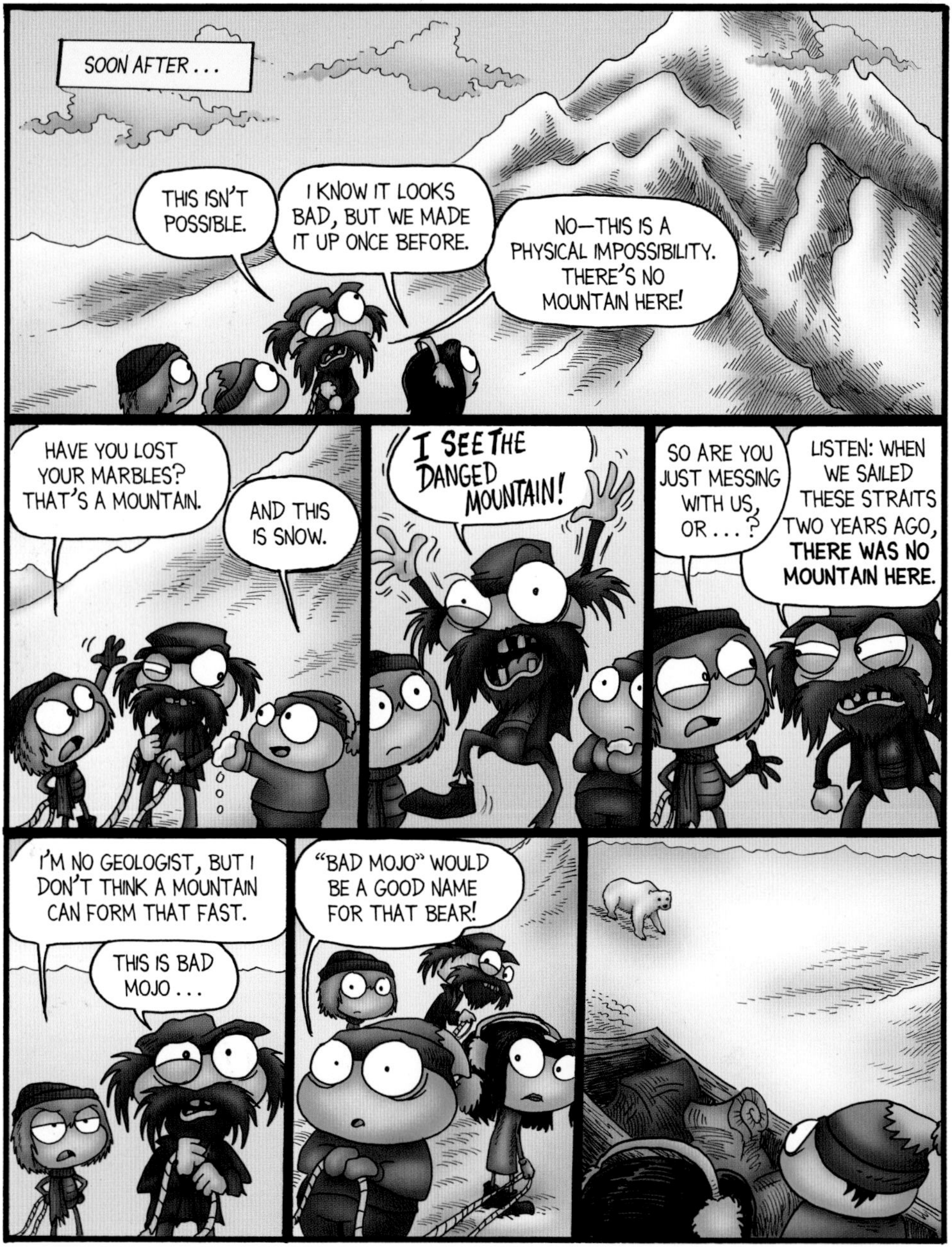
SOON AFTER . . .
THIS ISN'T POSSIBLE.
I KNOW IT LOOKS BAD, BUT WE MADE IT UP ONCE BEFORE.
NO—THIS IS A PHYSICAL IMPOSSIBILITY. THERE'S NO MOUNTAIN HERE!
HAVE YOU LOST YOUR MARBLES? THAT'S A MOUNTAIN.
AND THIS IS SNOW.
I SEE THE DANGED MOUNTAIN!
SO ARE YOU JUST MESSING WITH US, OR . . . ?
LISTEN: WHEN WE SAILED THESE STRAITS TWO YEARS AGO, THERE WAS NO MOUNTAIN HERE.
I'M NO GEOLOGIST, BUT I DON'T THINK A MOUNTAIN CAN FORM THAT FAST.
THIS IS BAD MOJO . . .
"BAD MOJO" WOULD BE A GOOD NAME FOR THAT BEAR!

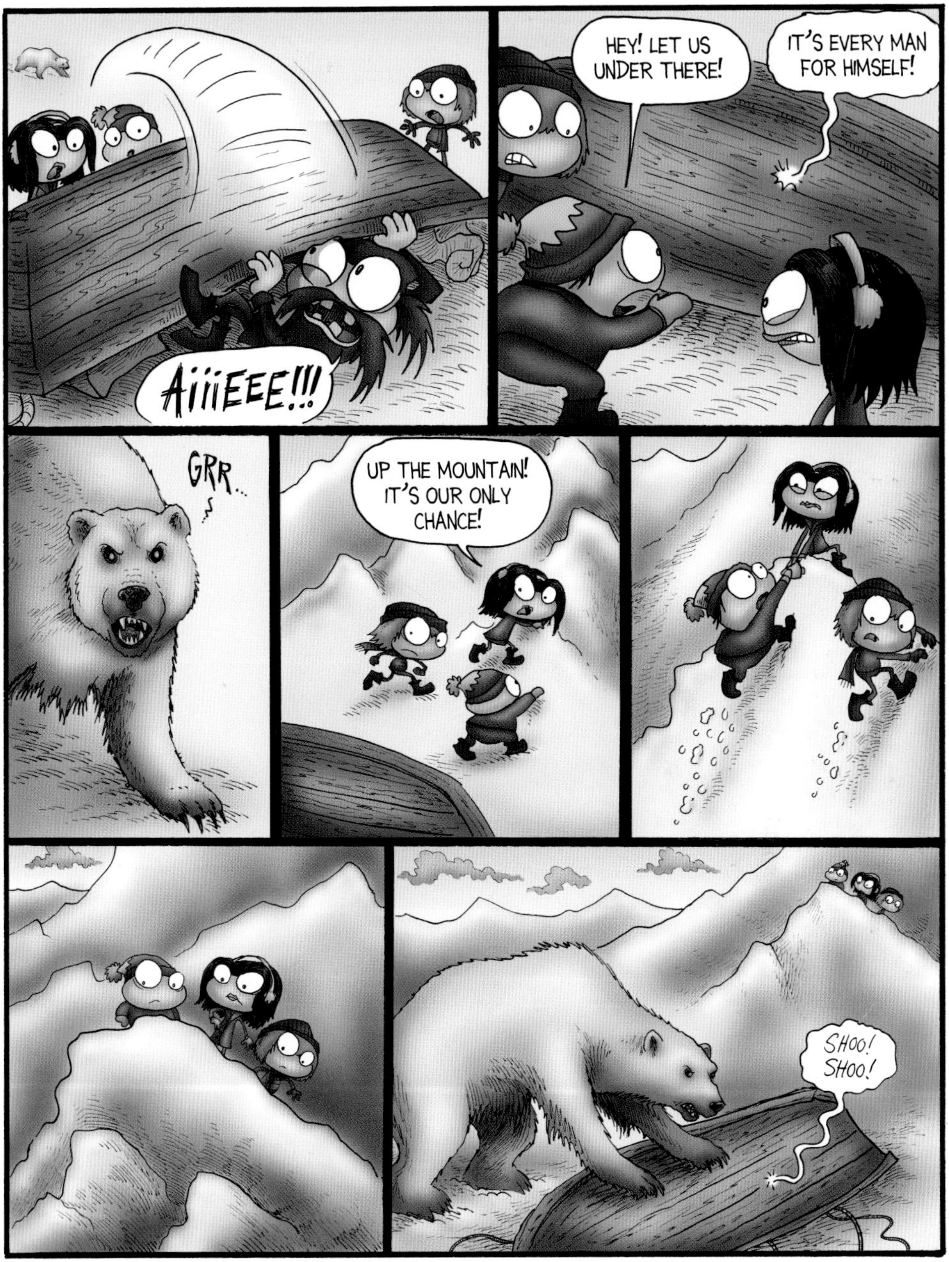
AiiiEEE!!!
HEY! LET US UNDER THERE!
IT'S EVERY MAN FOR HIMSELF!
GRR...
UP THE MOUNTAIN! IT'S OUR ONLY CHANCE!
SHOO! SHOO!

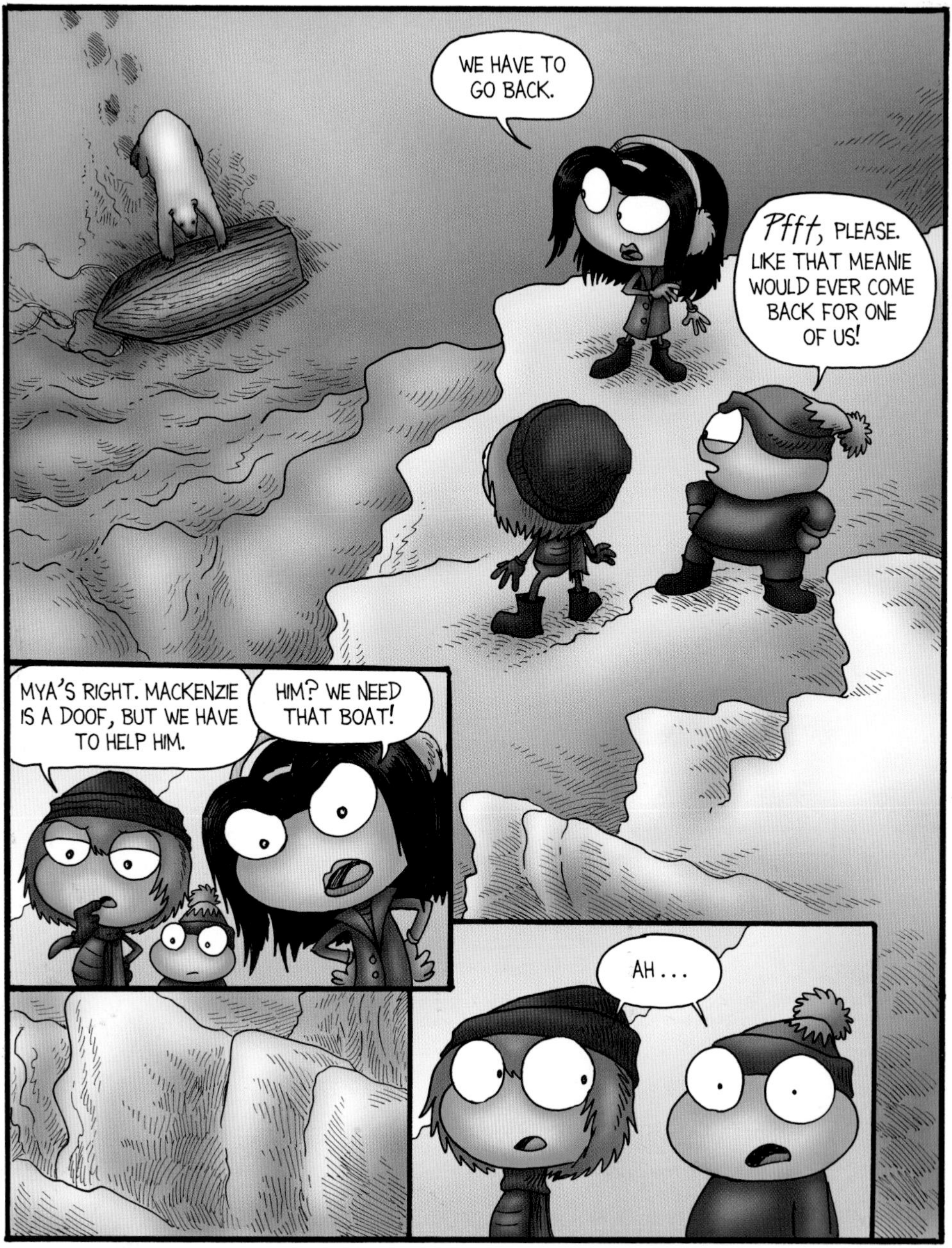
WE HAVE TO GO BACK.
Pfft, PLEASE. LIKE THAT MEANIE WOULD EVER COME BACK FOR ONE OF US!
MYA'S RIGHT. MACKENZIE IS A DOOF, BUT WE HAVE TO HELP HIM.
HIM? WE NEED THAT BOAT!
AH . . .

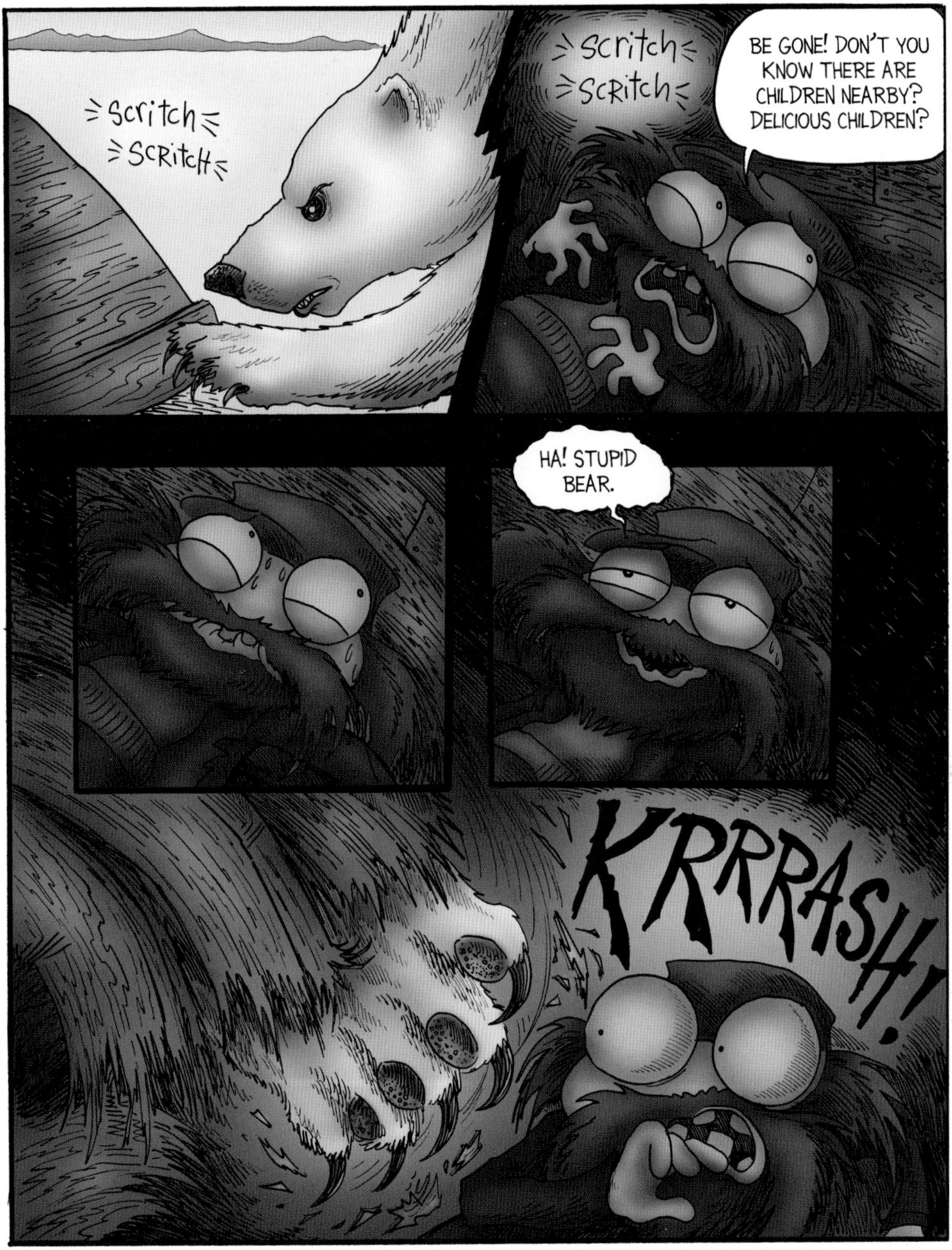
Scritch
Scritch
Scritch
Scritch
BE GONE! DON'T YOU KNOW THERE ARE CHILDREN NEARBY? DELICIOUS CHILDREN?
HA! STUPID BEAR.
KRRRASH!

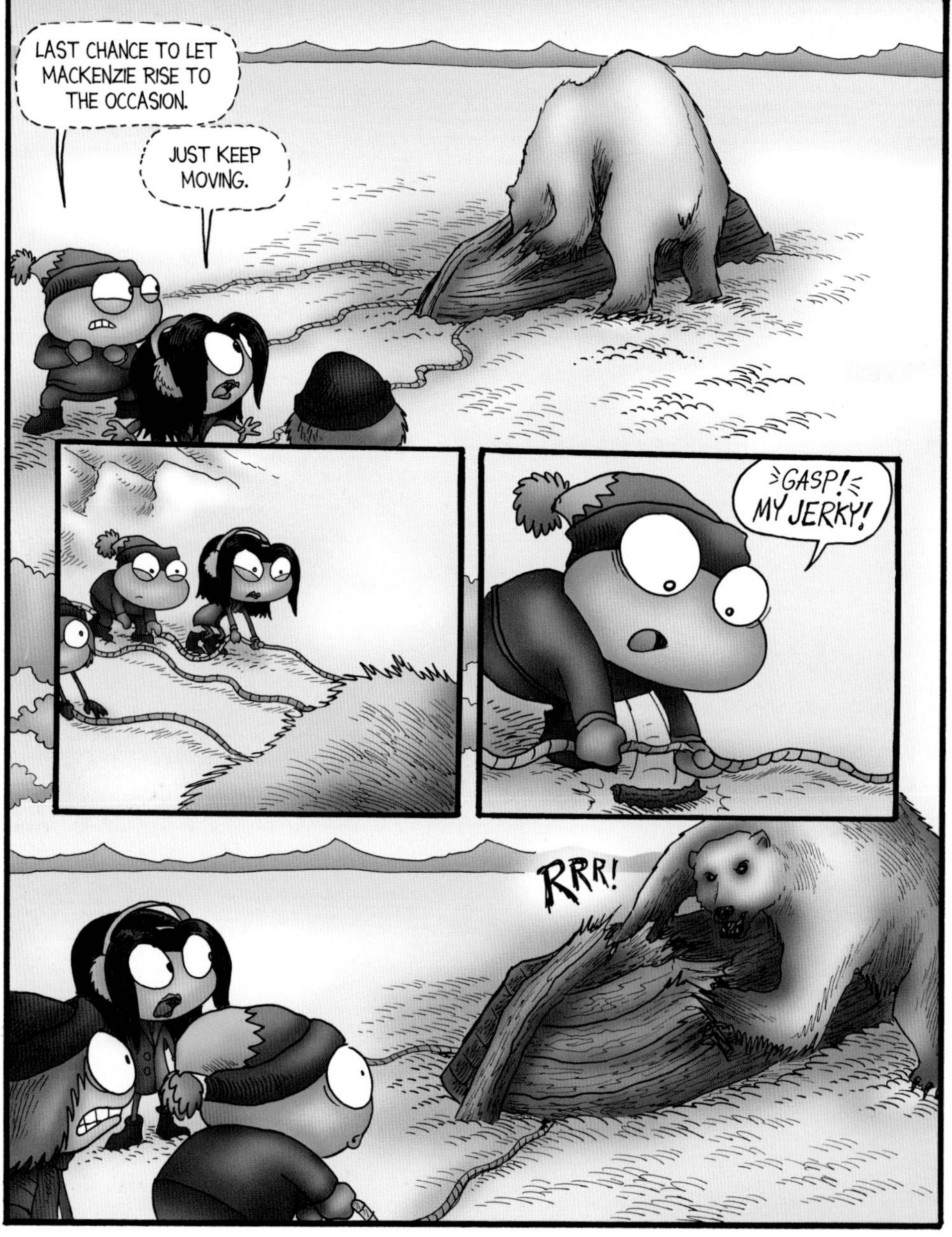
LAST CHANCE TO LET MACKENZIE RISE TO THE OCCASION.
JUST KEEP MOVING.
GASP! MY JERKY!
RRR!

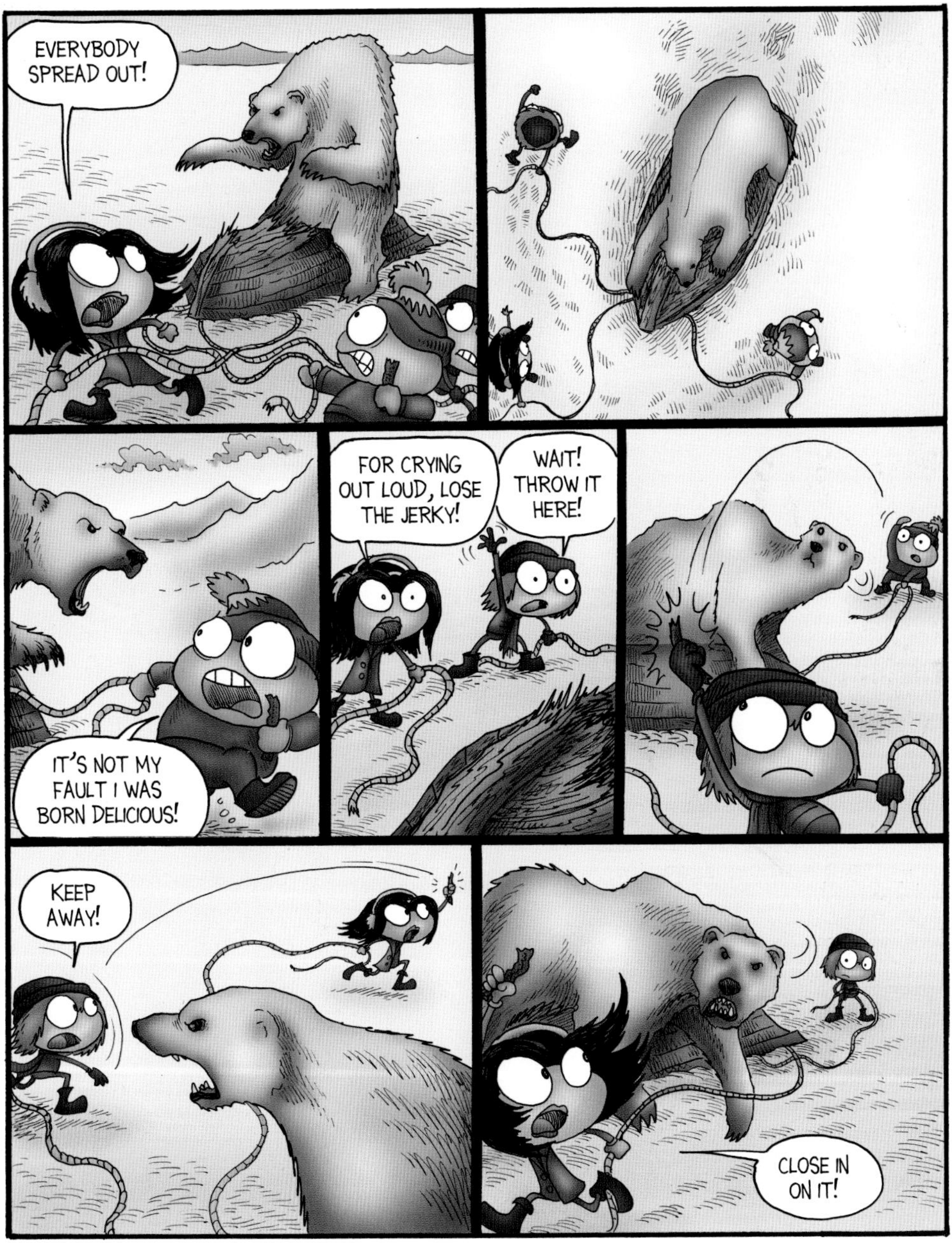
EVERYBODY SPREAD OUT!
IT'S NOT MY FAULT I WAS BORN DELICIOUS!
FOR CRYING OUT LOUD, LOSE THE JERKY!
WAIT! THROW IT HERE!
KEEP AWAY!
CLOSE IN ON IT!

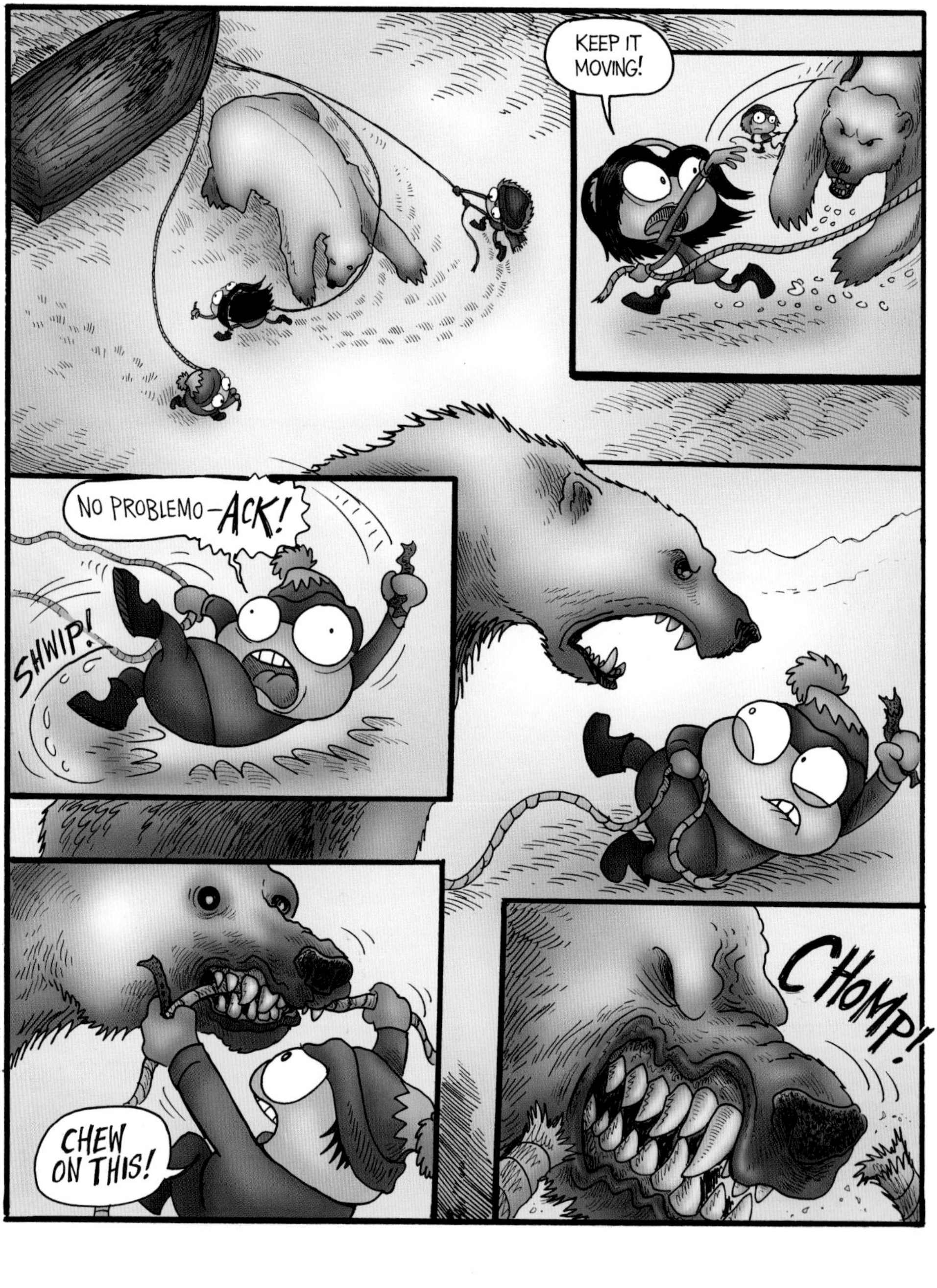
KEEP IT MOVING!
NO PROBLEMO—ACK!
SHWIP!
CHEW ON THIS!
CHOMP!

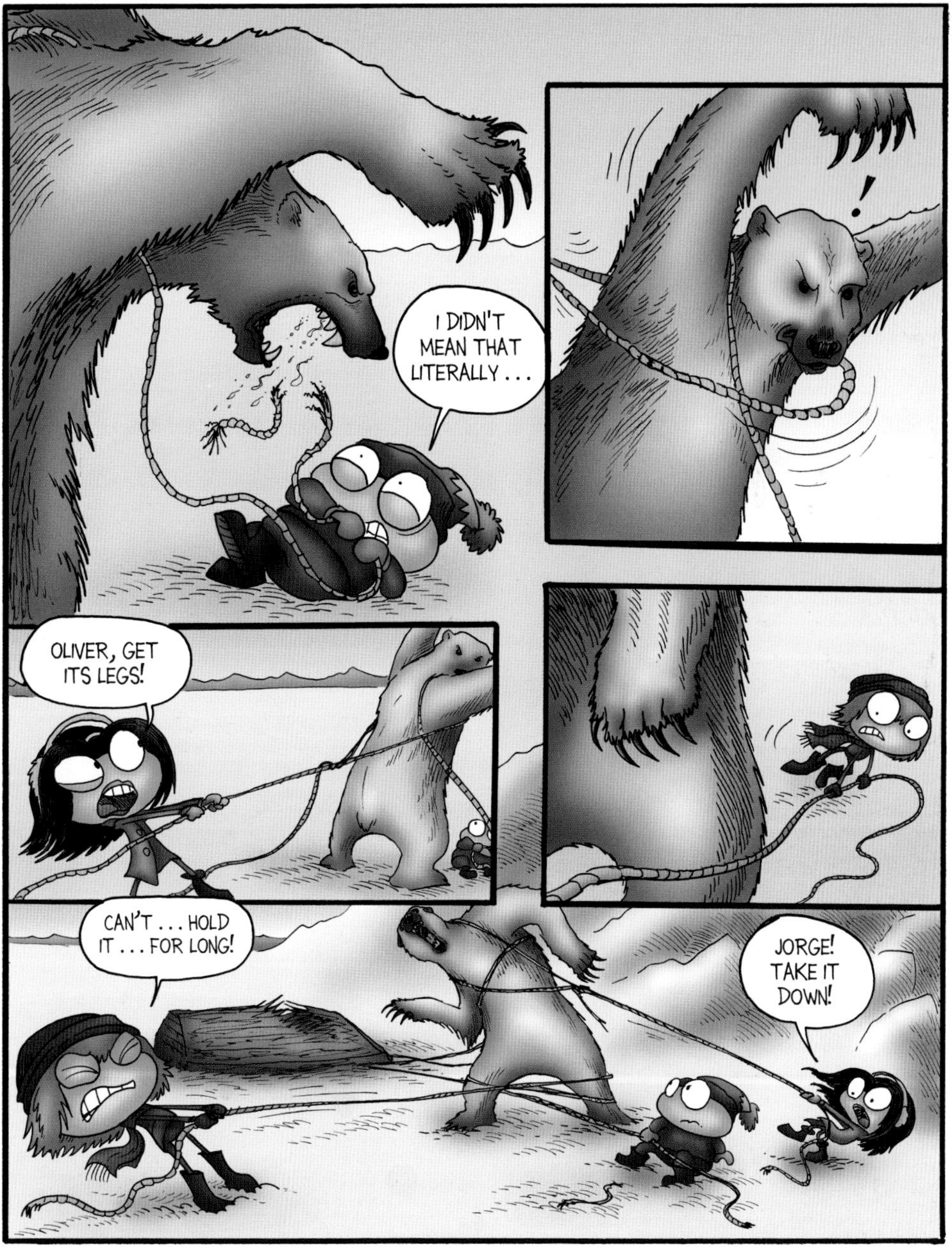
I DIDN'T MEAN THAT LITERALLY . . .
!
OLIVER, GET ITS LEGS!
CAN'T . . . HOLD IT . . . FOR LONG!
JORGE! TAKE IT DOWN!

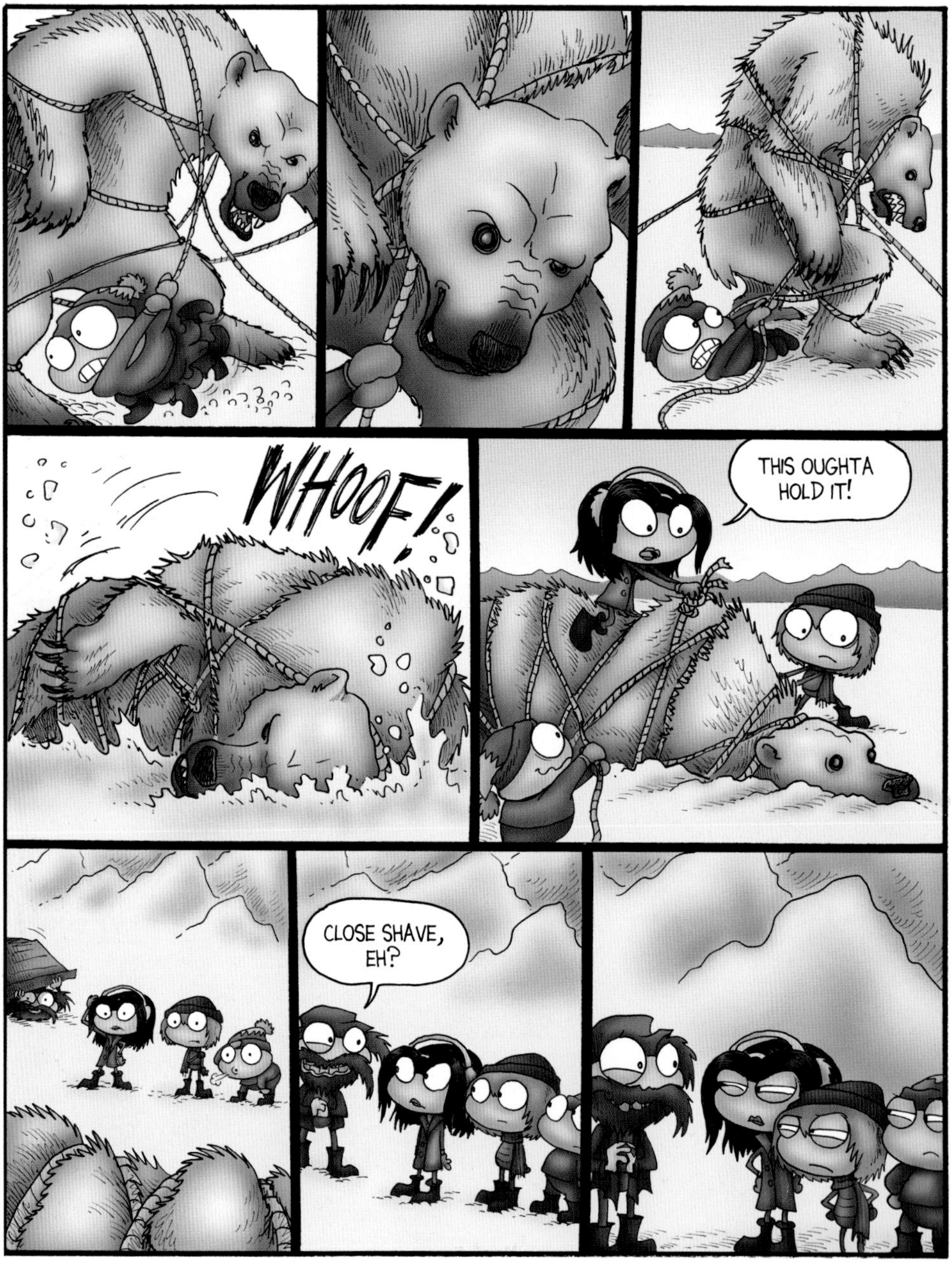
WHOOF!
THIS OUGHTA HOLD IT!
CLOSE SHAVE, EH?

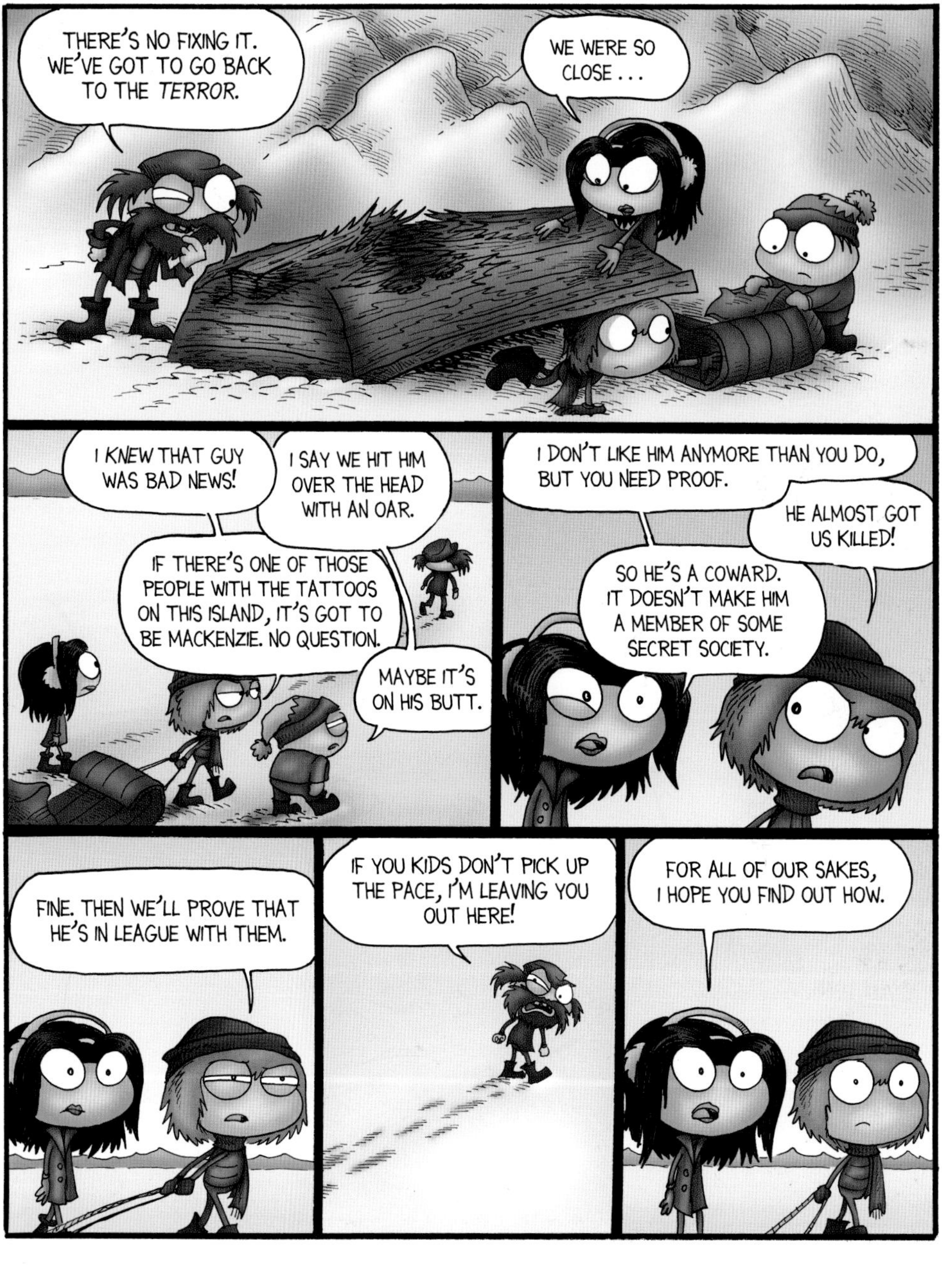

THERE'S NO FIXING IT. WE'VE GOT TO GO BACK TO THE *TERROR*.
WE WERE SO CLOSE . . .
I KNEW THAT GUY WAS BAD NEWS!
I SAY WE HIT HIM OVER THE HEAD WITH AN OAR.
IF THERE'S ONE OF THOSE PEOPLE WITH THE TATTOOS ON THIS ISLAND, IT'S GOT TO BE MACKENZIE. NO QUESTION.
MAYBE IT'S ON HIS BUTT.
I DON'T LIKE HIM ANYMORE THAN YOU DO, BUT YOU NEED PROOF.
HE ALMOST GOT US KILLED!
SO HE'S A COWARD. IT DOESN'T MAKE HIM A MEMBER OF SOME SECRET SOCIETY.
FINE. THEN WE'LL PROVE THAT HE'S IN LEAGUE WITH THEM.
IF YOU KIDS DON'T PICK UP THE PACE, I'M LEAVING YOU OUT HERE!
FOR ALL OF OUR SAKES, I HOPE YOU FIND OUT HOW.

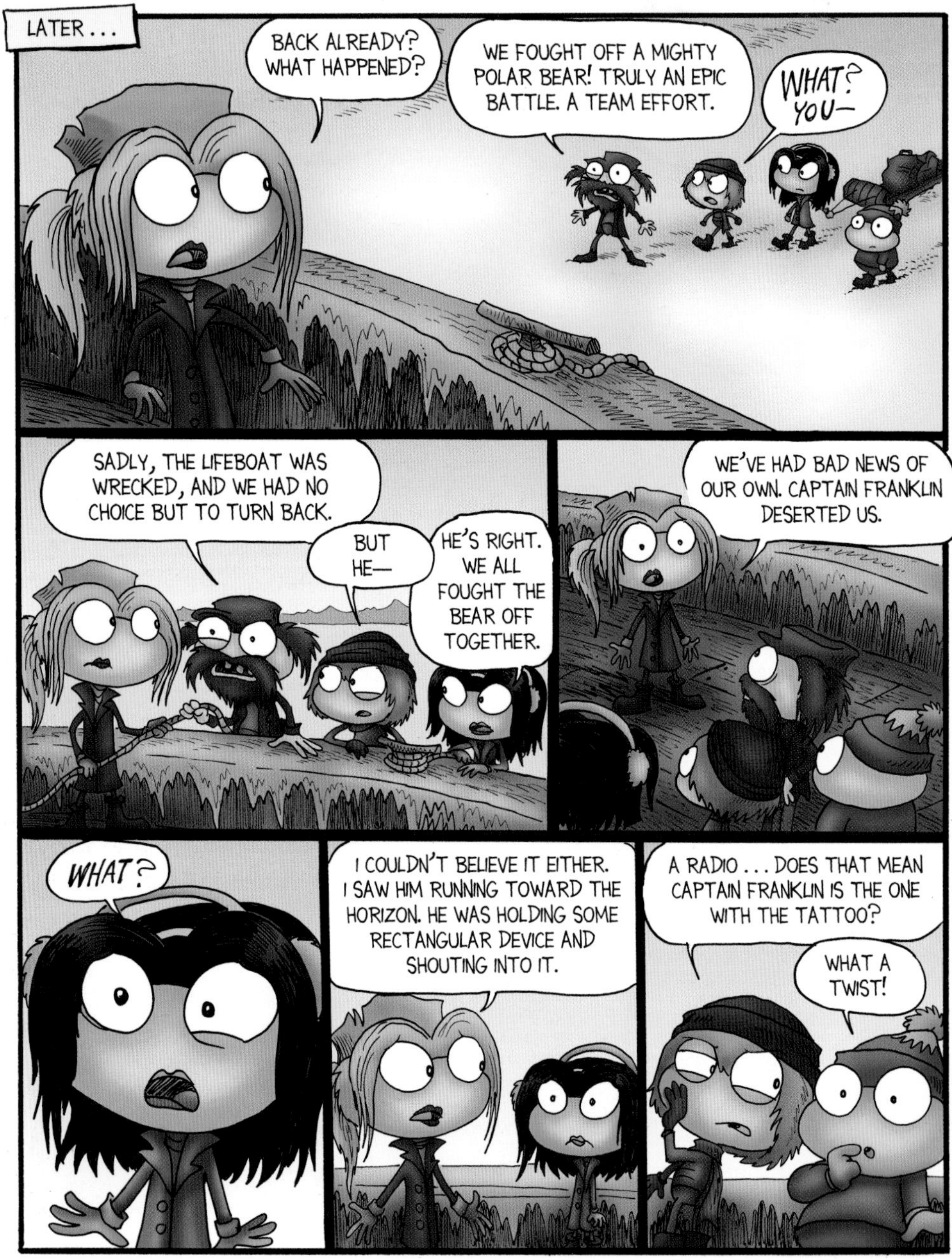
LATER . . .
BACK ALREADY? WHAT HAPPENED?
WE FOUGHT OFF A MIGHTY POLAR BEAR! TRULY AN EPIC BATTLE. A TEAM EFFORT.
WHAT? YOU—
SADLY, THE LIFEBOAT WAS WRECKED, AND WE HAD NO CHOICE BUT TO TURN BACK.
BUT HE—
HE'S RIGHT. WE ALL FOUGHT THE BEAR OFF TOGETHER.
WE'VE HAD BAD NEWS OF OUR OWN. CAPTAIN FRANKLIN DESERTED US.
WHAT?
I COULDN'T BELIEVE IT EITHER. I SAW HIM RUNNING TOWARD THE HORIZON. HE WAS HOLDING SOME RECTANGULAR DEVICE AND SHOUTING INTO IT.
A RADIO . . . DOES THAT MEAN CAPTAIN FRANKLIN IS THE ONE WITH THE TATTOO?
WHAT A TWIST!

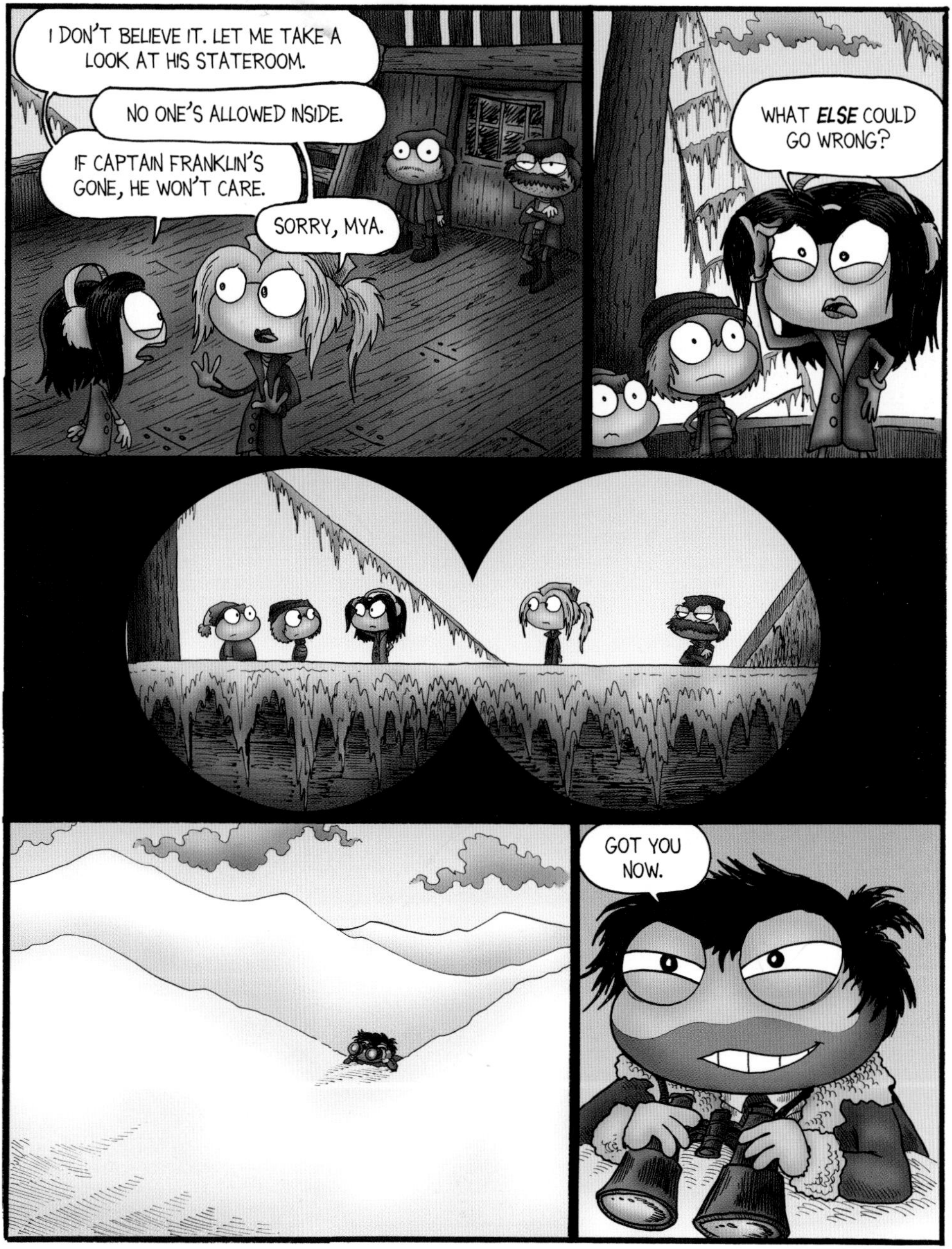
I DON'T BELIEVE IT. LET ME TAKE A LOOK AT HIS STATEROOM.
NO ONE'S ALLOWED INSIDE.
IF CAPTAIN FRANKLIN'S GONE, HE WON'T CARE.
SORRY, MYA.
WHAT *ELSE* COULD GO WRONG?
GOT YOU NOW.

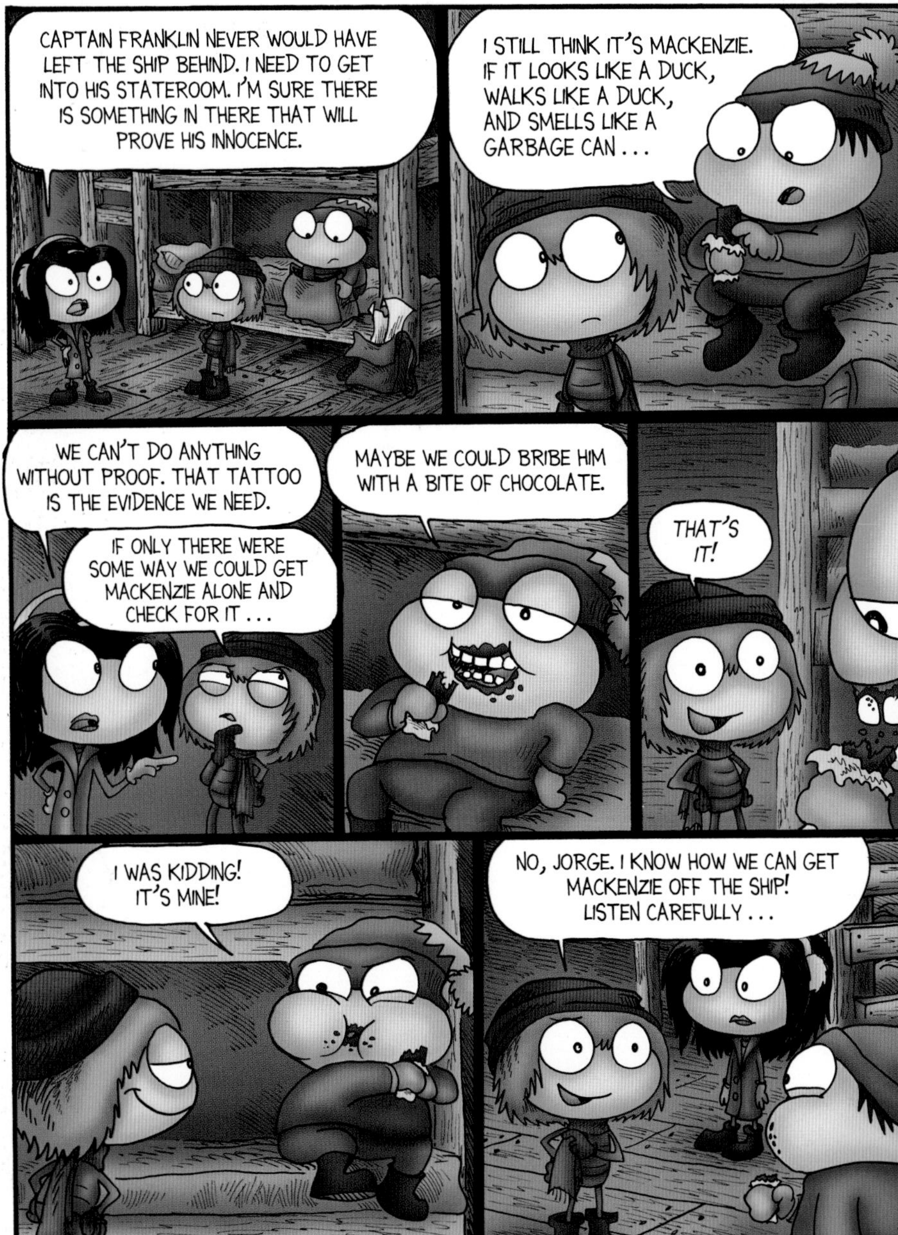
CAPTAIN FRANKLIN NEVER WOULD HAVE LEFT THE SHIP BEHIND. I NEED TO GET INTO HIS STATEROOM. I'M SURE THERE IS SOMETHING IN THERE THAT WILL PROVE HIS INNOCENCE.
I STILL THINK IT'S MACKENZIE. IF IT LOOKS LIKE A DUCK, WALKS LIKE A DUCK, AND SMELLS LIKE A GARBAGE CAN . . .
WE CAN'T DO ANYTHING WITHOUT PROOF. THAT TATTOO IS THE EVIDENCE WE NEED.
IF ONLY THERE WERE SOME WAY WE COULD GET MACKENZIE ALONE AND CHECK FOR IT . . .
MAYBE WE COULD BRIBE HIM WITH A BITE OF CHOCOLATE.
THAT'S IT!
I WAS KIDDING! IT'S MINE!
NO, JORGE. I KNOW HOW WE CAN GET MACKENZIE OFF THE SHIP! LISTEN CAREFULLY . . .

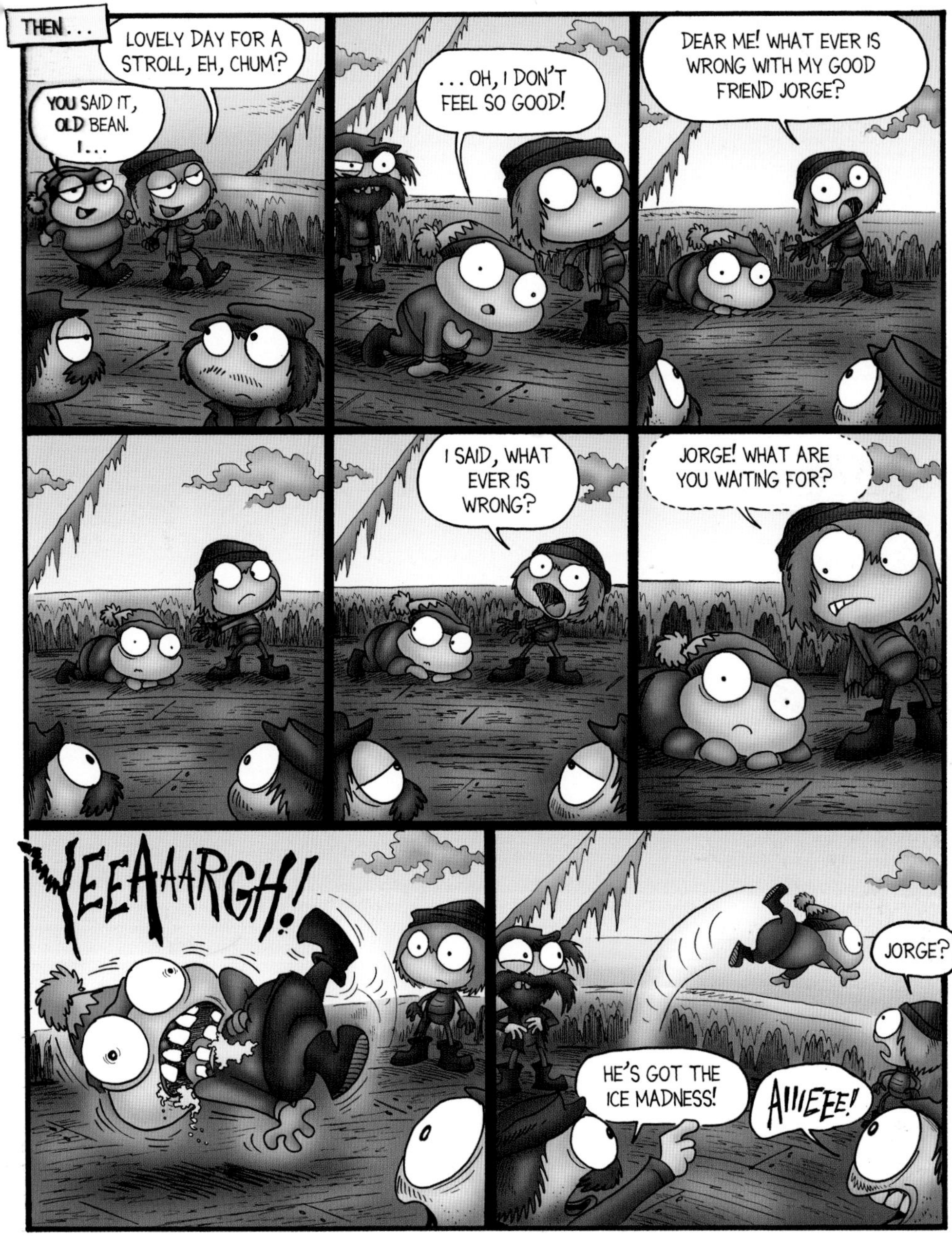
THEN . . .
LOVELY DAY FOR A STROLL, EH, CHUM?
YOU SAID IT, OLD BEAN. I . . .
. . . OH, I DON'T FEEL SO GOOD!
DEAR ME! WHAT EVER IS WRONG WITH MY GOOD FRIEND JORGE?
I SAID, WHAT EVER IS WRONG?
JORGE! WHAT ARE YOU WAITING FOR?
YEEAAARGH!
JORGE?
HE'S GOT THE ICE MADNESS!
AIIIEEE!

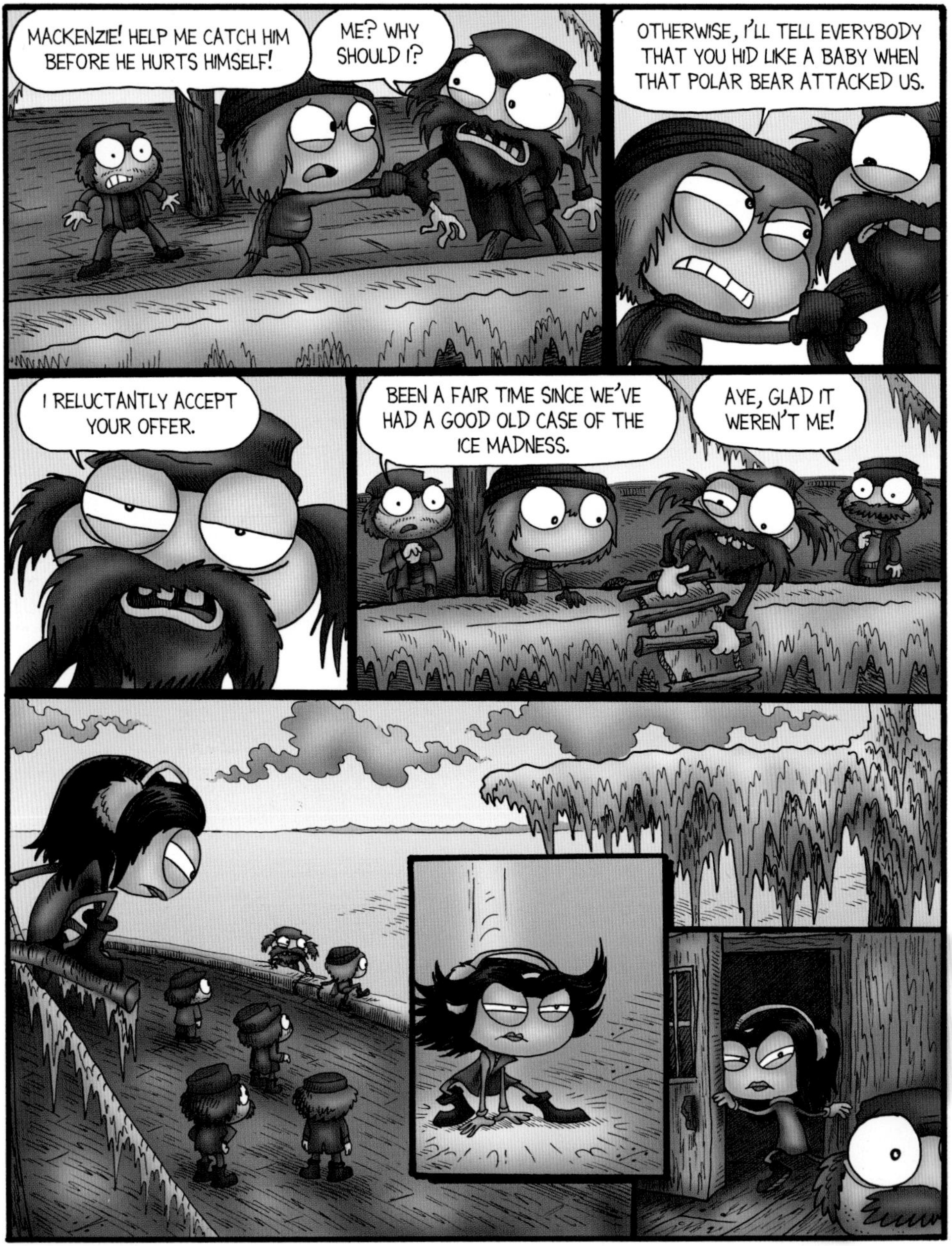
MACKENZIE! HELP ME CATCH HIM BEFORE HE HURTS HIMSELF!
ME? WHY SHOULD I?
OTHERWISE, I'LL TELL EVERYBODY THAT YOU HID LIKE A BABY WHEN THAT POLAR BEAR ATTACKED US.
I RELUCTANTLY ACCEPT YOUR OFFER.
BEEN A FAIR TIME SINCE WE'VE HAD A GOOD OLD CASE OF THE ICE MADNESS.
AYE, GLAD IT WEREN'T ME!

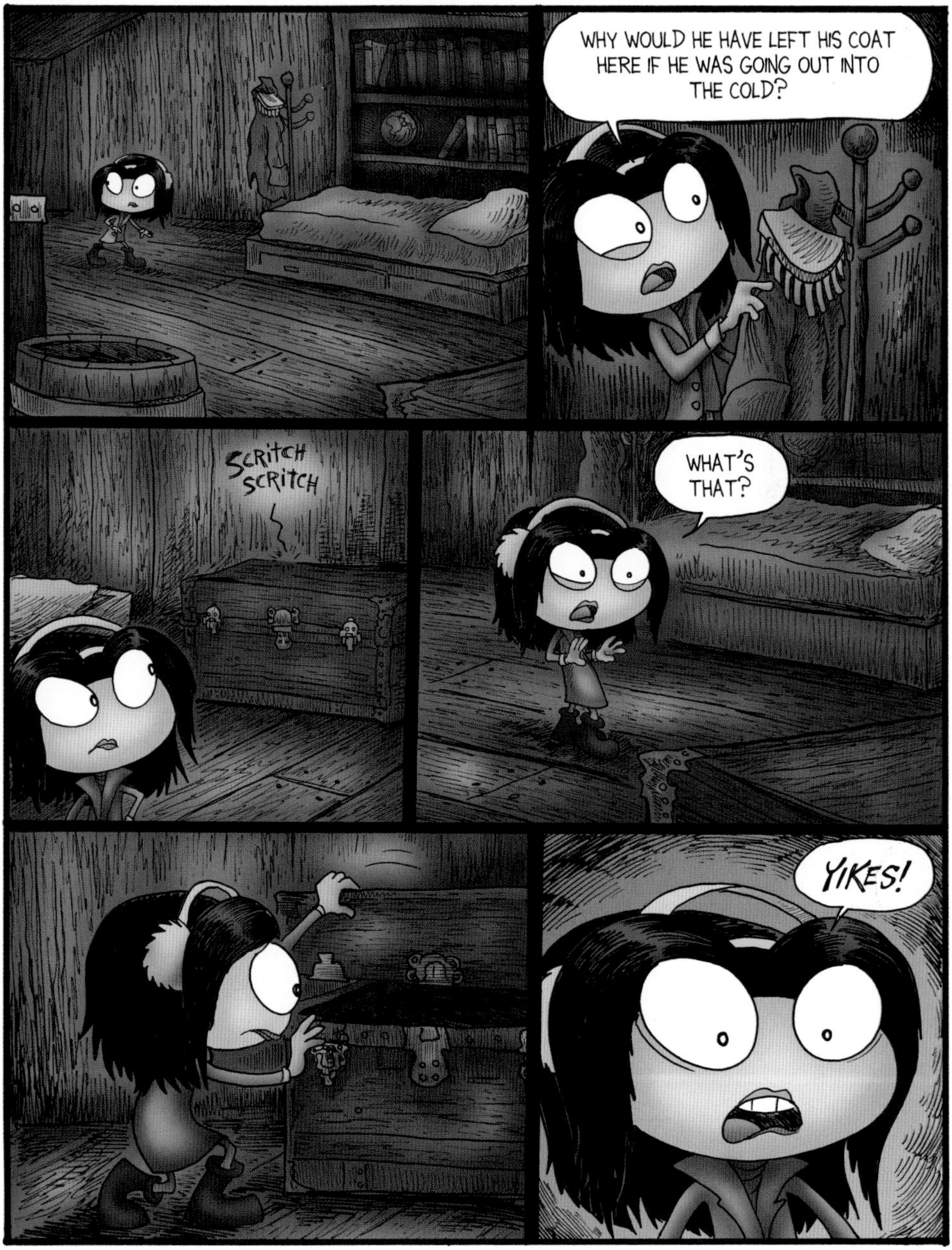
WHY WOULD HE HAVE LEFT HIS COAT HERE IF HE WAS GOING OUT INTO THE COLD?
SCRITCH SCRITCH
WHAT'S THAT?
YIKES!

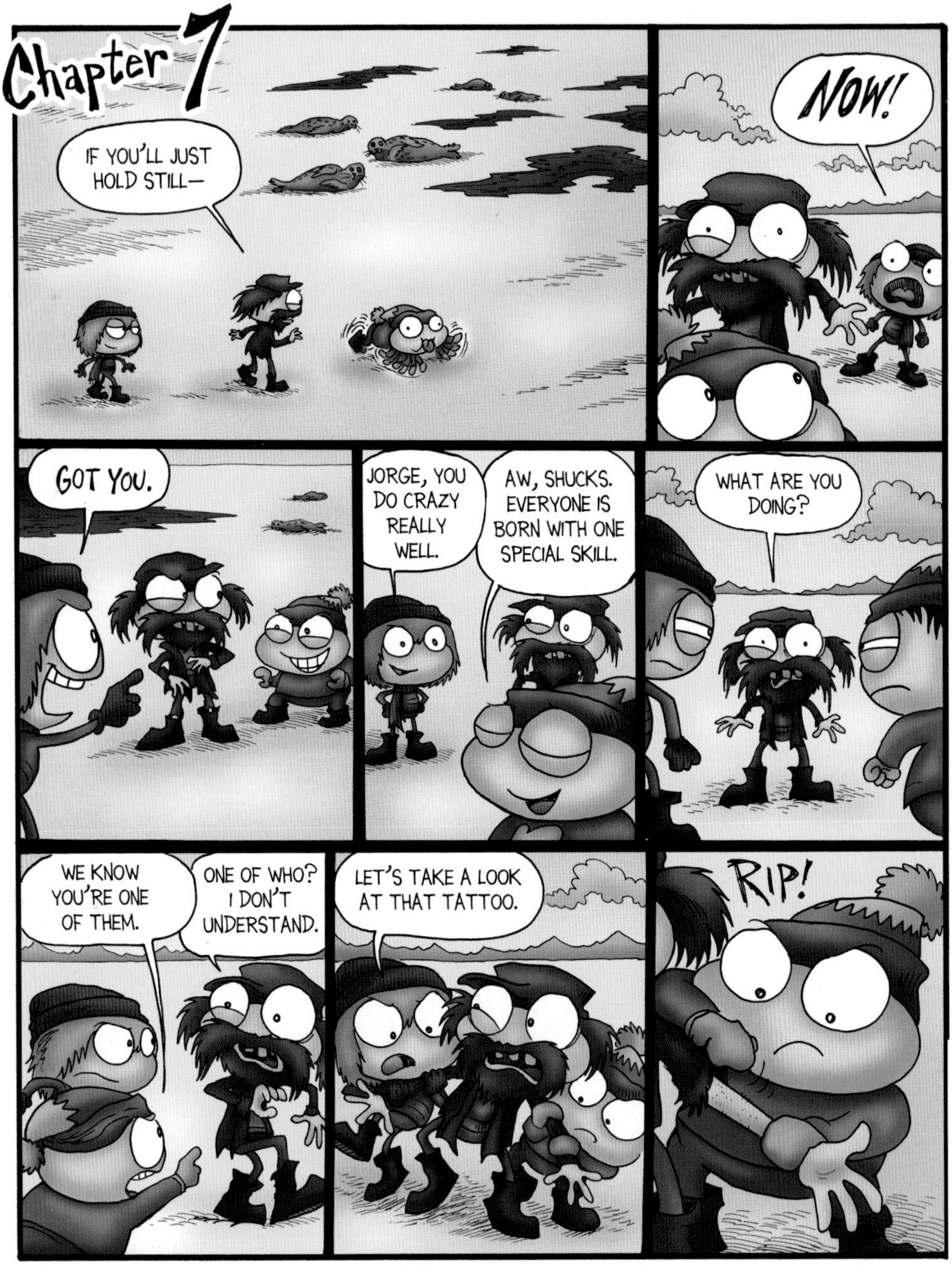
Chapter 7
IF YOU'LL JUST HOLD STILL—
NOW!
GOT YOU.
JORGE, YOU DO CRAZY REALLY WELL.
AW, SHUCKS. EVERYONE IS BORN WITH ONE SPECIAL SKILL.
WHAT ARE YOU DOING?
WE KNOW YOU'RE ONE OF THEM.
ONE OF WHO? I DON'T UNDERSTAND.
LET'S TAKE A LOOK AT THAT TATTOO.
RIP!

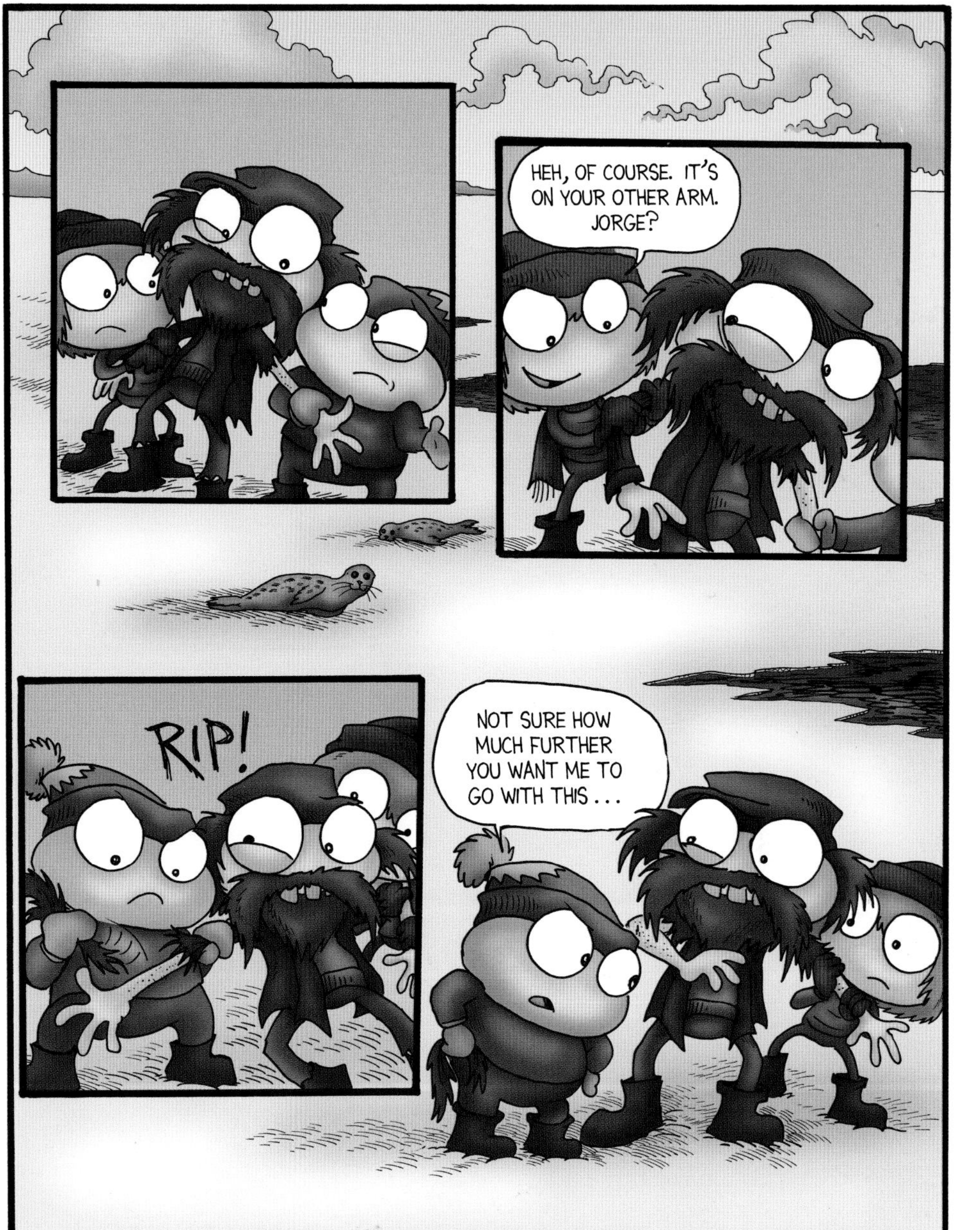
HEH, OF COURSE. IT'S ON YOUR OTHER ARM. JORGE?
RIP!
NOT SURE HOW MUCH FURTHER YOU WANT ME TO GO WITH THIS . . .

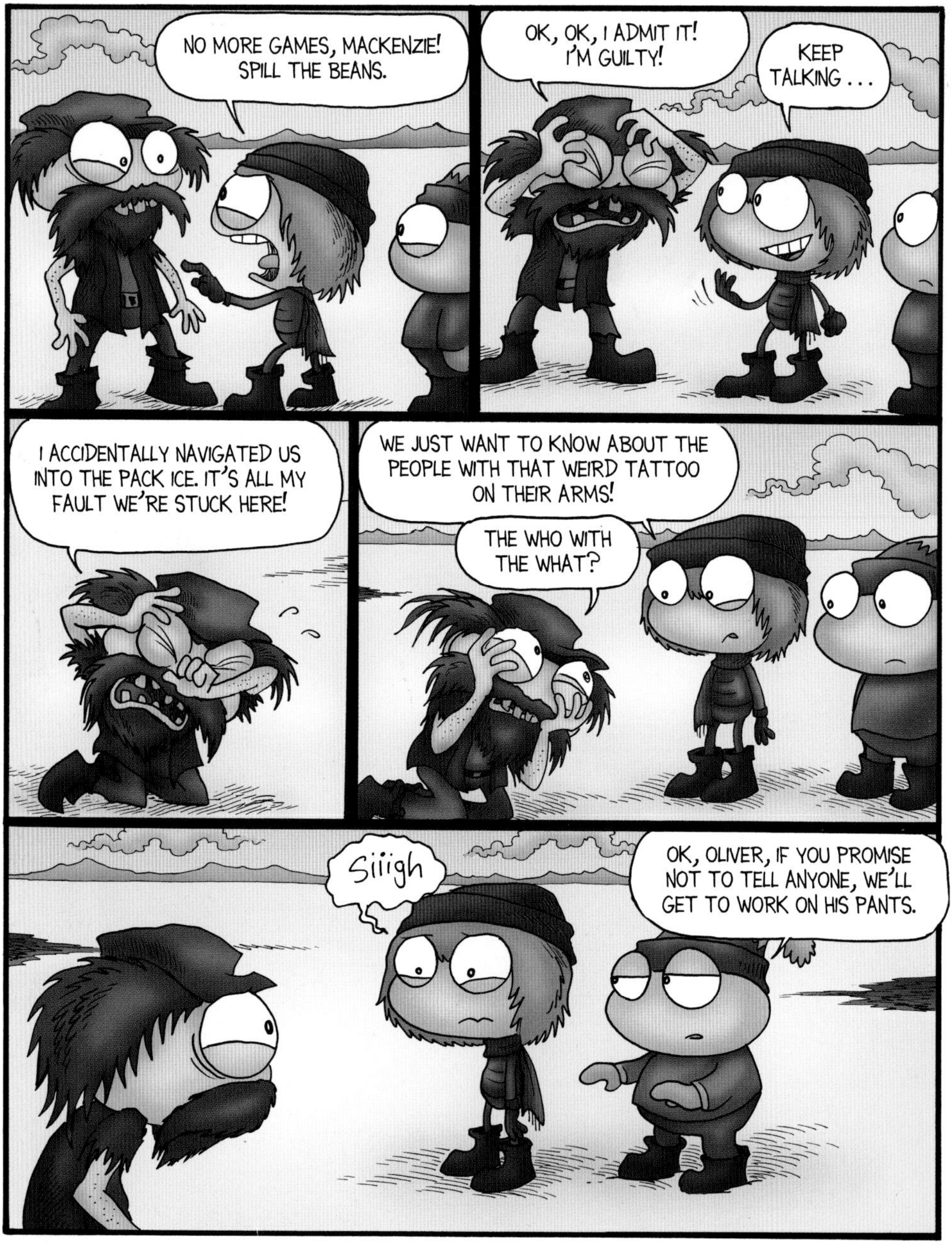
NO MORE GAMES, MACKENZIE! SPILL THE BEANS.
OK, OK, I ADMIT IT! I'M GUILTY!
KEEP TALKING . . .
I ACCIDENTALLY NAVIGATED US INTO THE PACK ICE. IT'S ALL MY FAULT WE'RE STUCK HERE!
WE JUST WANT TO KNOW ABOUT THE PEOPLE WITH THAT WEIRD TATTOO ON THEIR ARMS!
THE WHO WITH THE WHAT?
Siiigh
OK, OLIVER, IF YOU PROMISE NOT TO TELL ANYONE, WE'LL GET TO WORK ON HIS PANTS.

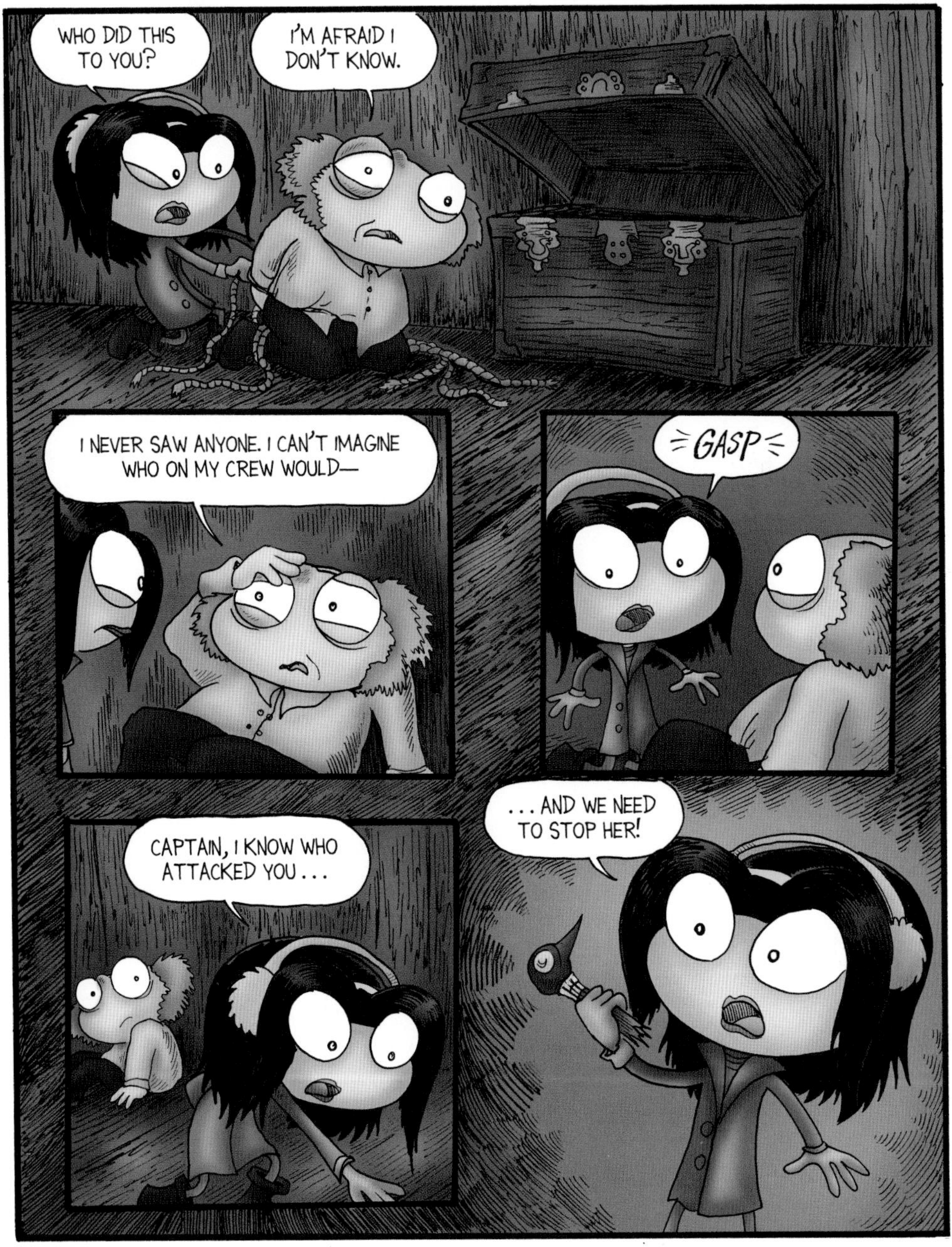
WHO DID THIS TO YOU?
I'M AFRAID I DON'T KNOW.
I NEVER SAW ANYONE. I CAN'T IMAGINE WHO ON MY CREW WOULD—
GASP
CAPTAIN, I KNOW WHO ATTACKED YOU . . .
. . . AND WE NEED TO STOP HER!

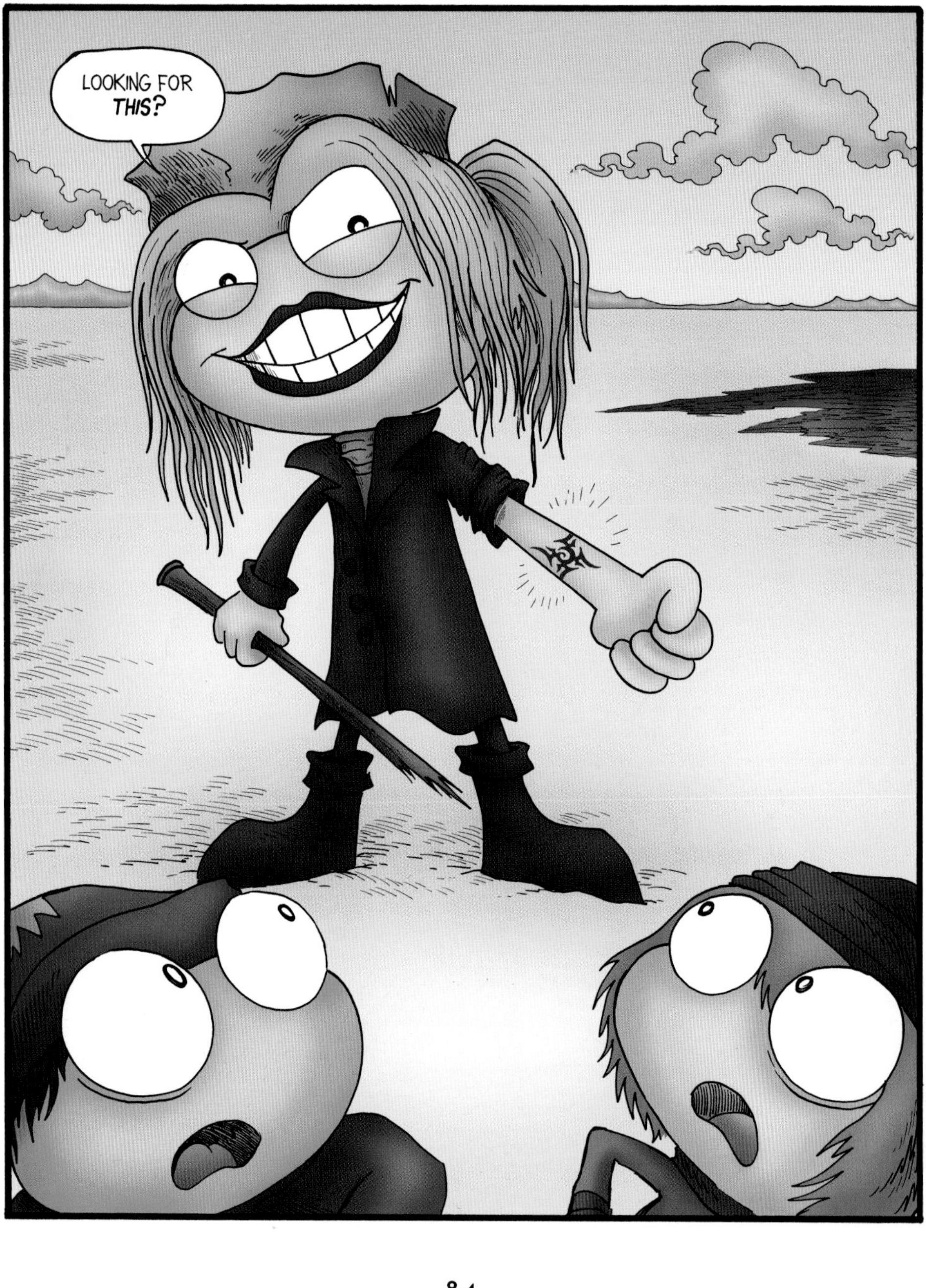
LOOKING FOR THIS?

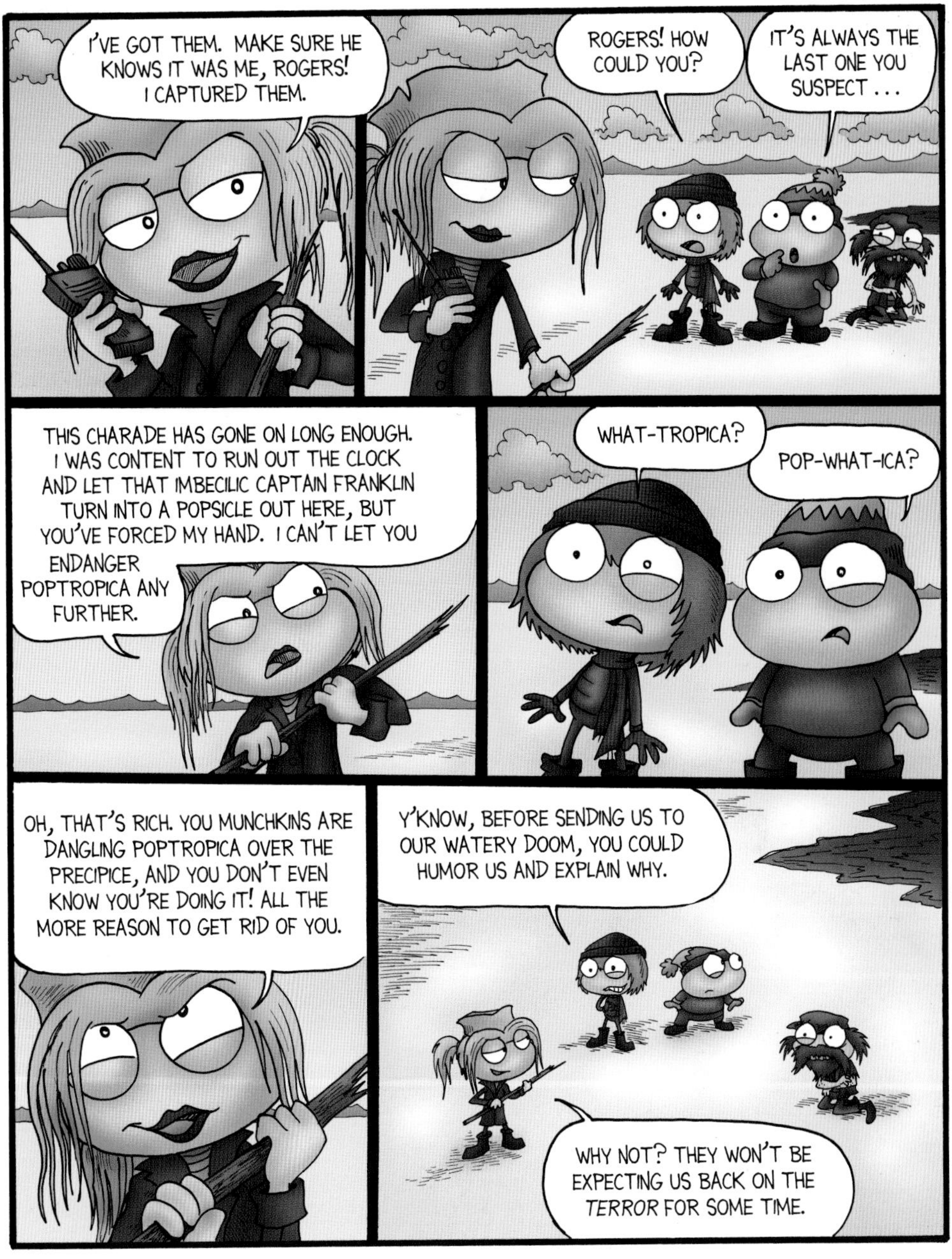
I'VE GOT THEM. MAKE SURE HE KNOWS IT WAS ME, ROGERS! I CAPTURED THEM.
ROGERS! HOW COULD YOU?
IT'S ALWAYS THE LAST ONE YOU SUSPECT . . .
THIS CHARADE HAS GONE ON LONG ENOUGH. I WAS CONTENT TO RUN OUT THE CLOCK AND LET THAT IMBECILIC CAPTAIN FRANKLIN TURN INTO A POPSICLE OUT HERE, BUT YOU'VE FORCED MY HAND. I CAN'T LET YOU ENDANGER POPTROPICA ANY FURTHER.
WHAT-TROPICA?
POP-WHAT-ICA?
OH, THAT'S RICH. YOU MUNCHKINS ARE DANGLING POPTROPICA OVER THE PRECIPICE, AND YOU DON'T EVEN KNOW YOU'RE DOING IT! ALL THE MORE REASON TO GET RID OF YOU.
Y'KNOW, BEFORE SENDING US TO OUR WATERY DOOM, YOU COULD HUMOR US AND EXPLAIN WHY.
WHY NOT? THEY WON'T BE EXPECTING US BACK ON THE *TERROR* FOR SOME TIME.

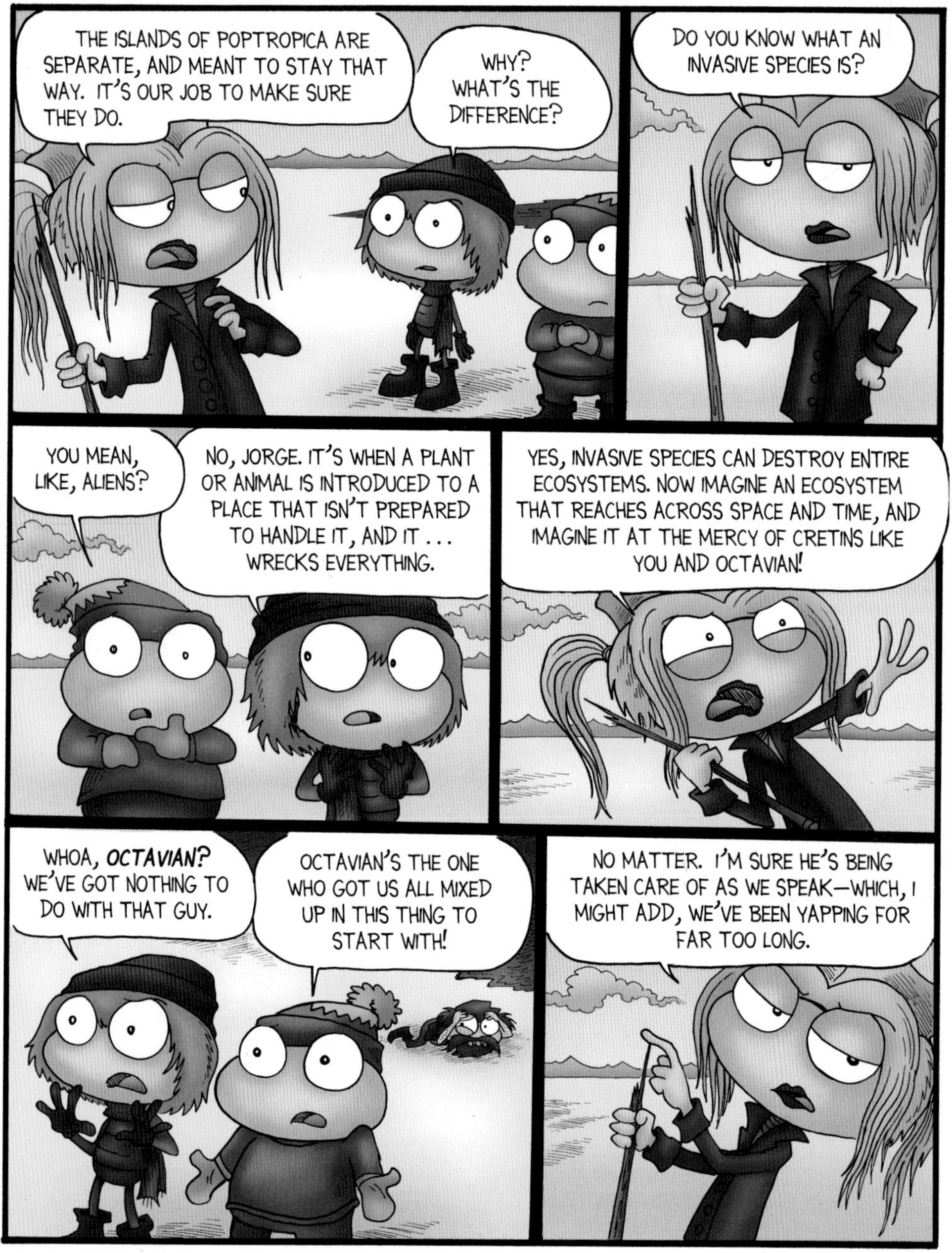
THE ISLANDS OF POPTROPICA ARE SEPARATE, AND MEANT TO STAY THAT WAY. IT'S OUR JOB TO MAKE SURE THEY DO.
WHY? WHAT'S THE DIFFERENCE?
DO YOU KNOW WHAT AN INVASIVE SPECIES IS?
YOU MEAN, LIKE, ALIENS?
NO, JORGE. IT'S WHEN A PLANT OR ANIMAL IS INTRODUCED TO A PLACE THAT ISN'T PREPARED TO HANDLE IT, AND IT . . . WRECKS EVERYTHING.
YES, INVASIVE SPECIES CAN DESTROY ENTIRE ECOSYSTEMS. NOW IMAGINE AN ECOSYSTEM THAT REACHES ACROSS SPACE AND TIME, AND IMAGINE IT AT THE MERCY OF CRETINS LIKE YOU AND OCTAVIAN!
WHOA, ***OCTAVIAN?*** WE'VE GOT NOTHING TO DO WITH THAT GUY.
OCTAVIAN'S THE ONE WHO GOT US ALL MIXED UP IN THIS THING TO START WITH!
NO MATTER. I'M SURE HE'S BEING TAKEN CARE OF AS WE SPEAK—WHICH, I MIGHT ADD, WE'VE BEEN YAPPING FOR FAR TOO LONG.

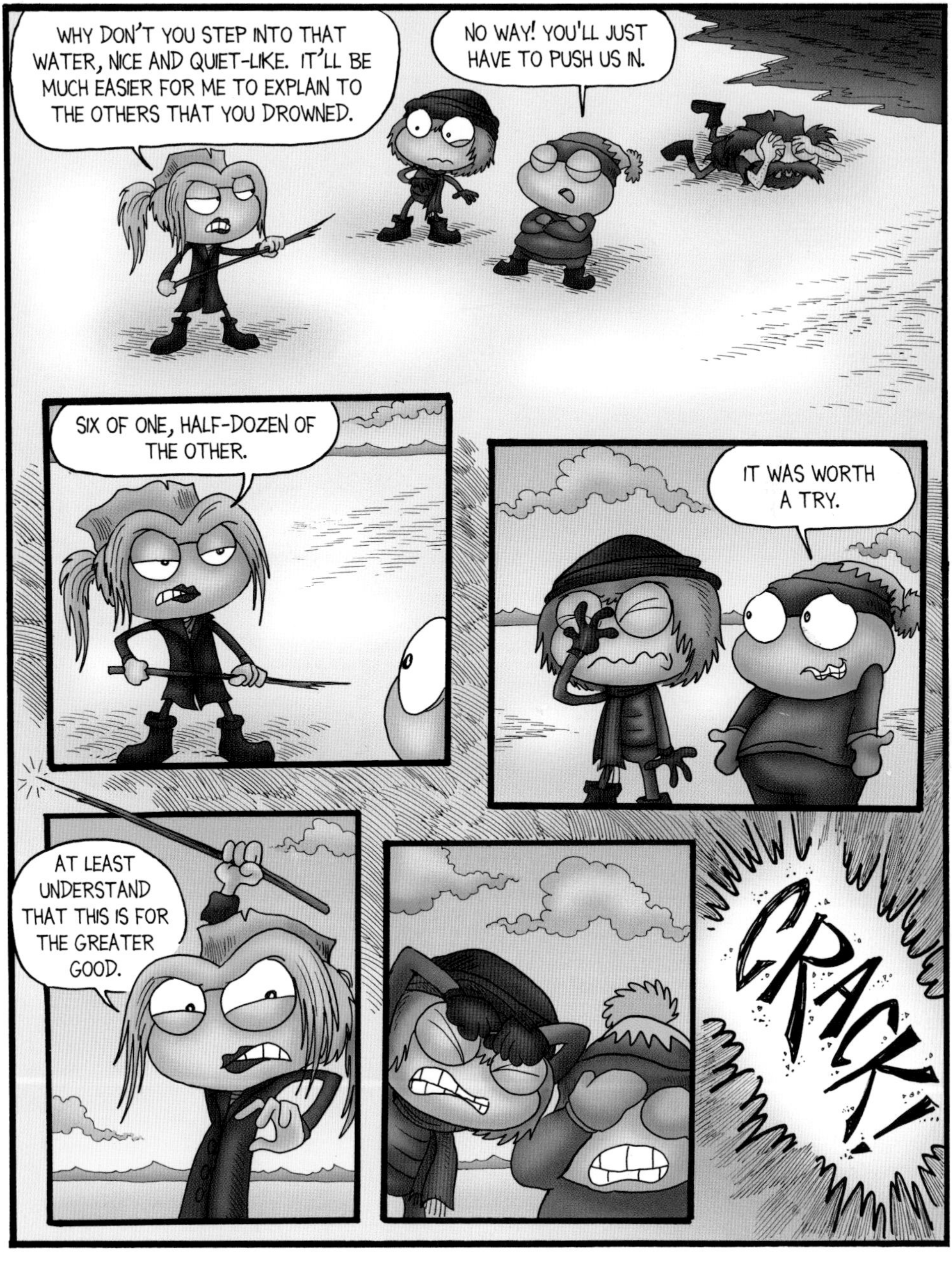
WHY DON'T YOU STEP INTO THAT WATER, NICE AND QUIET-LIKE. IT'LL BE MUCH EASIER FOR ME TO EXPLAIN TO THE OTHERS THAT YOU DROWNED.
NO WAY! YOU'LL JUST HAVE TO PUSH US IN.
SIX OF ONE, HALF-DOZEN OF THE OTHER.
IT WAS WORTH A TRY.
AT LEAST UNDERSTAND THAT THIS IS FOR THE GREATER GOOD.
CRACK!

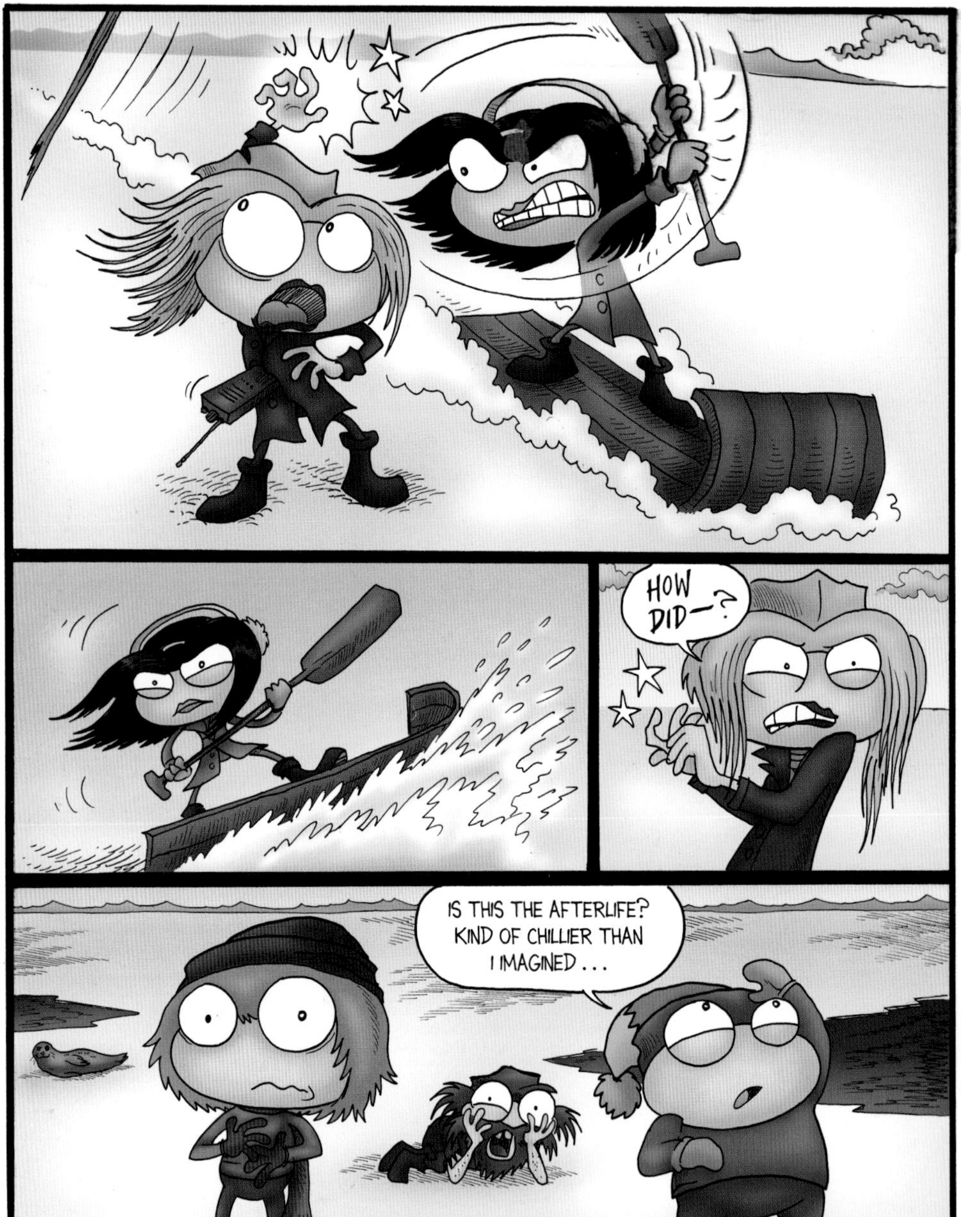
WWI
HOW DID—?
IS THIS THE AFTERLIFE? KIND OF CHILLIER THAN I IMAGINED . . .

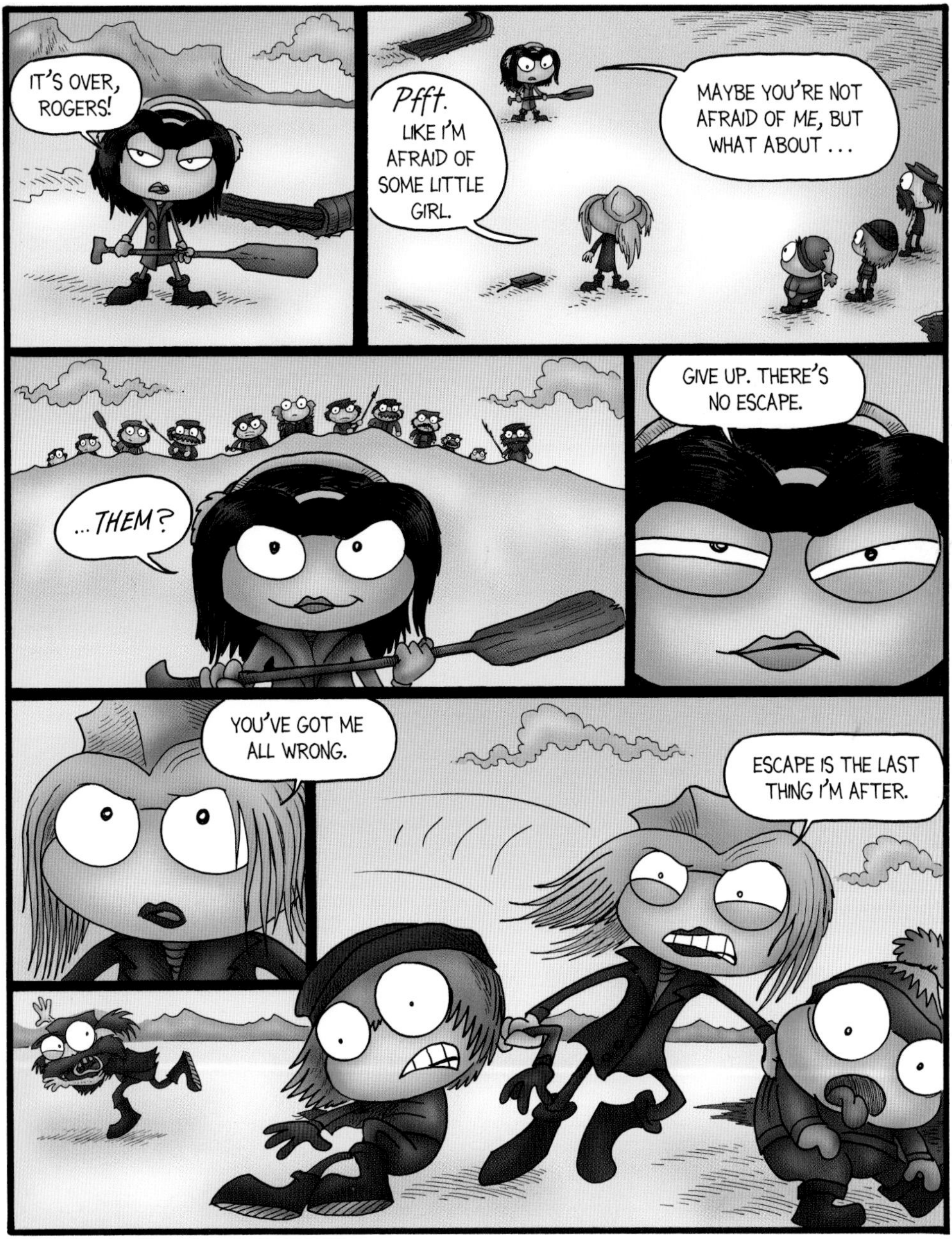
IT'S OVER, ROGERS!
Pfft. LIKE I'M AFRAID OF SOME LITTLE GIRL.
MAYBE YOU'RE NOT AFRAID OF ME, BUT WHAT ABOUT . . .
. . . THEM?
GIVE UP. THERE'S NO ESCAPE.
YOU'VE GOT ME ALL WRONG.
ESCAPE IS THE LAST THING I'M AFTER.

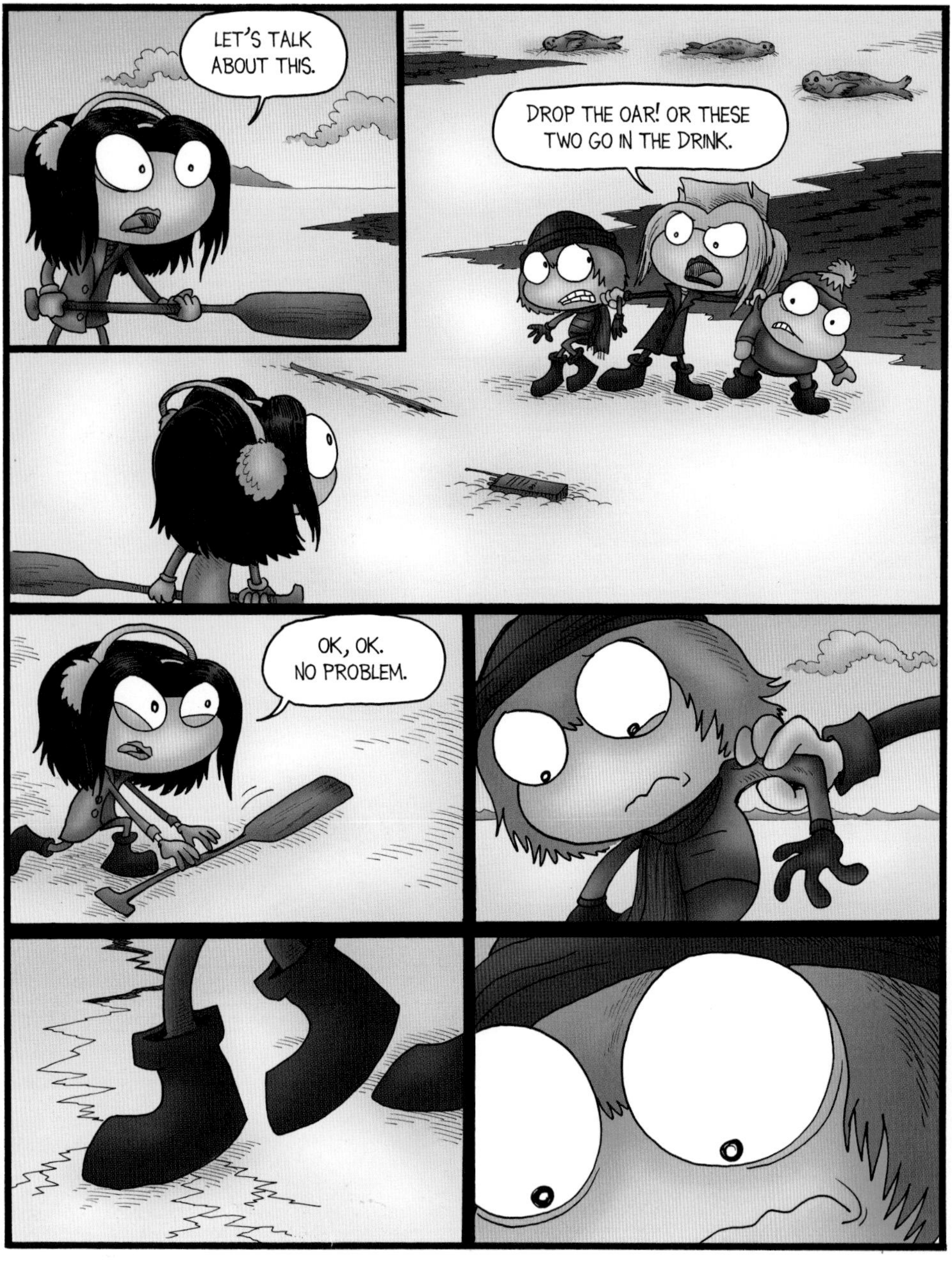
LET'S TALK ABOUT THIS.
DROP THE OAR! OR THESE TWO GO IN THE DRINK.
OK, OK. NO PROBLEM.

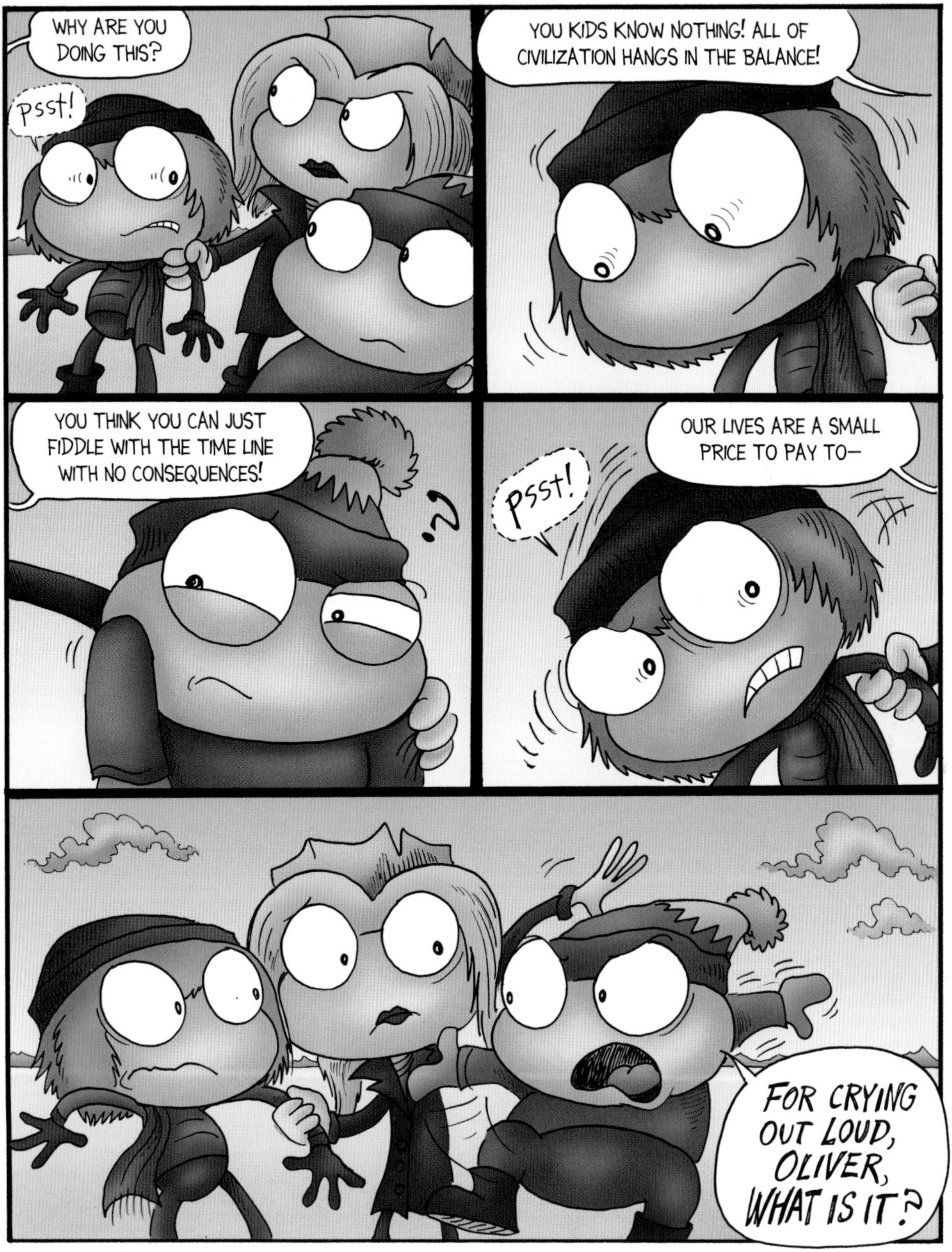
WHY ARE YOU DOING THIS?
Psst!
YOU KIDS KNOW NOTHING! ALL OF CIVILIZATION HANGS IN THE BALANCE!
YOU THINK YOU CAN JUST FIDDLE WITH THE TIME LINE WITH NO CONSEQUENCES!
?
OUR LIVES ARE A SMALL PRICE TO PAY TO—
Psst!
FOR CRYING OUT LOUD, OLIVER, WHAT IS IT?

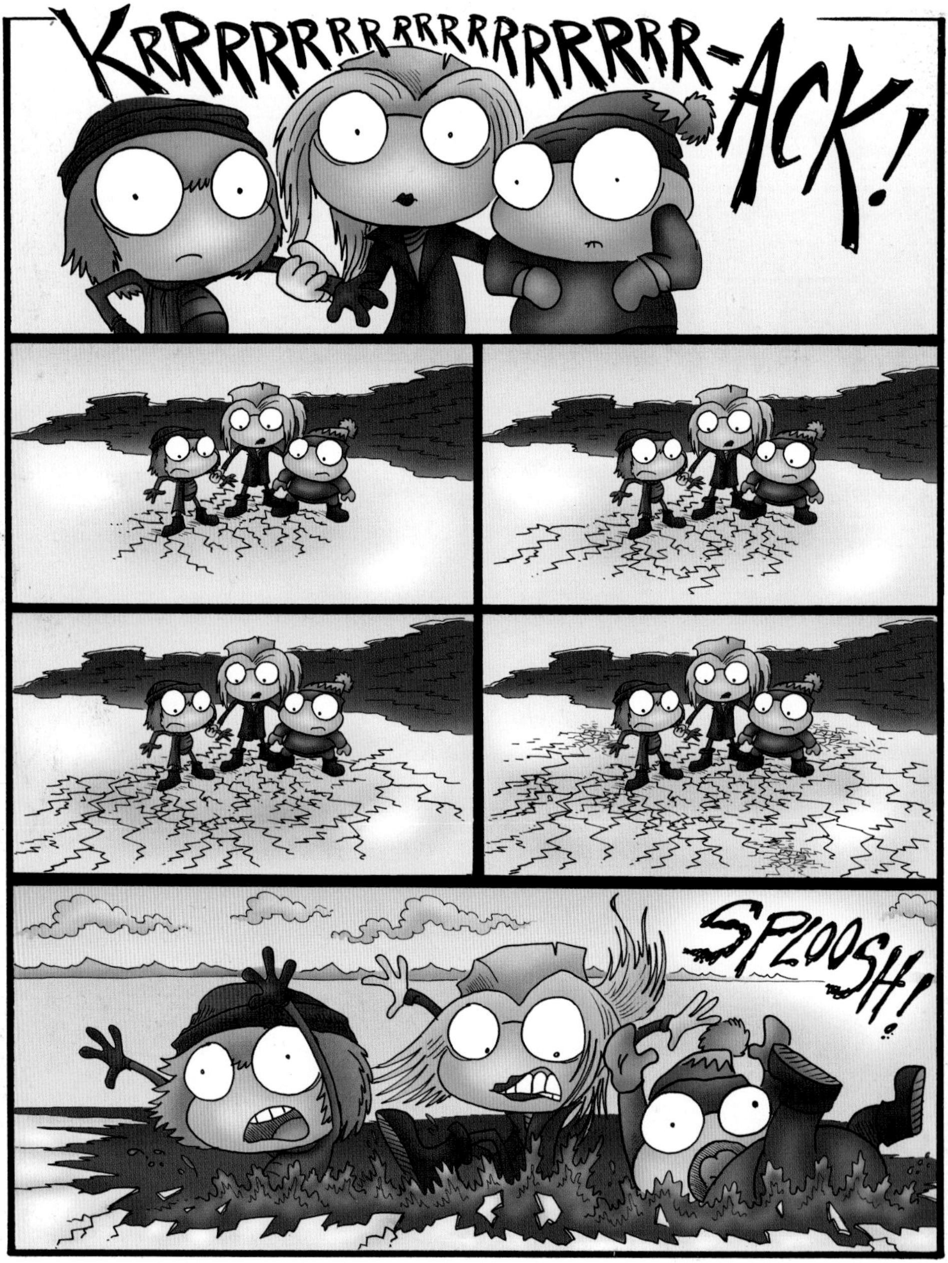
KRRRRRRRRRRRRRRRRRR-ACK!
SPLOOSH!

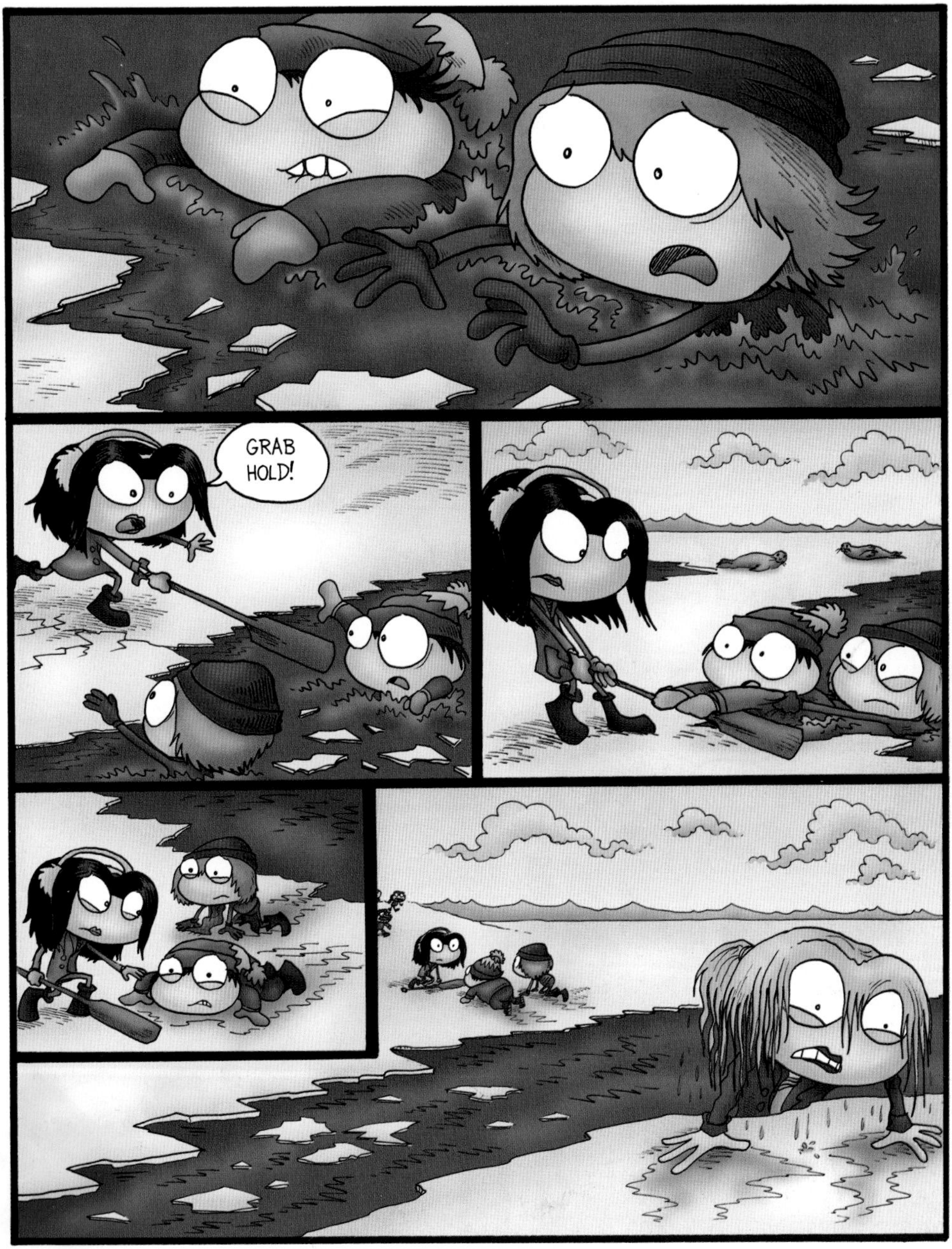
GRAB HOLD!

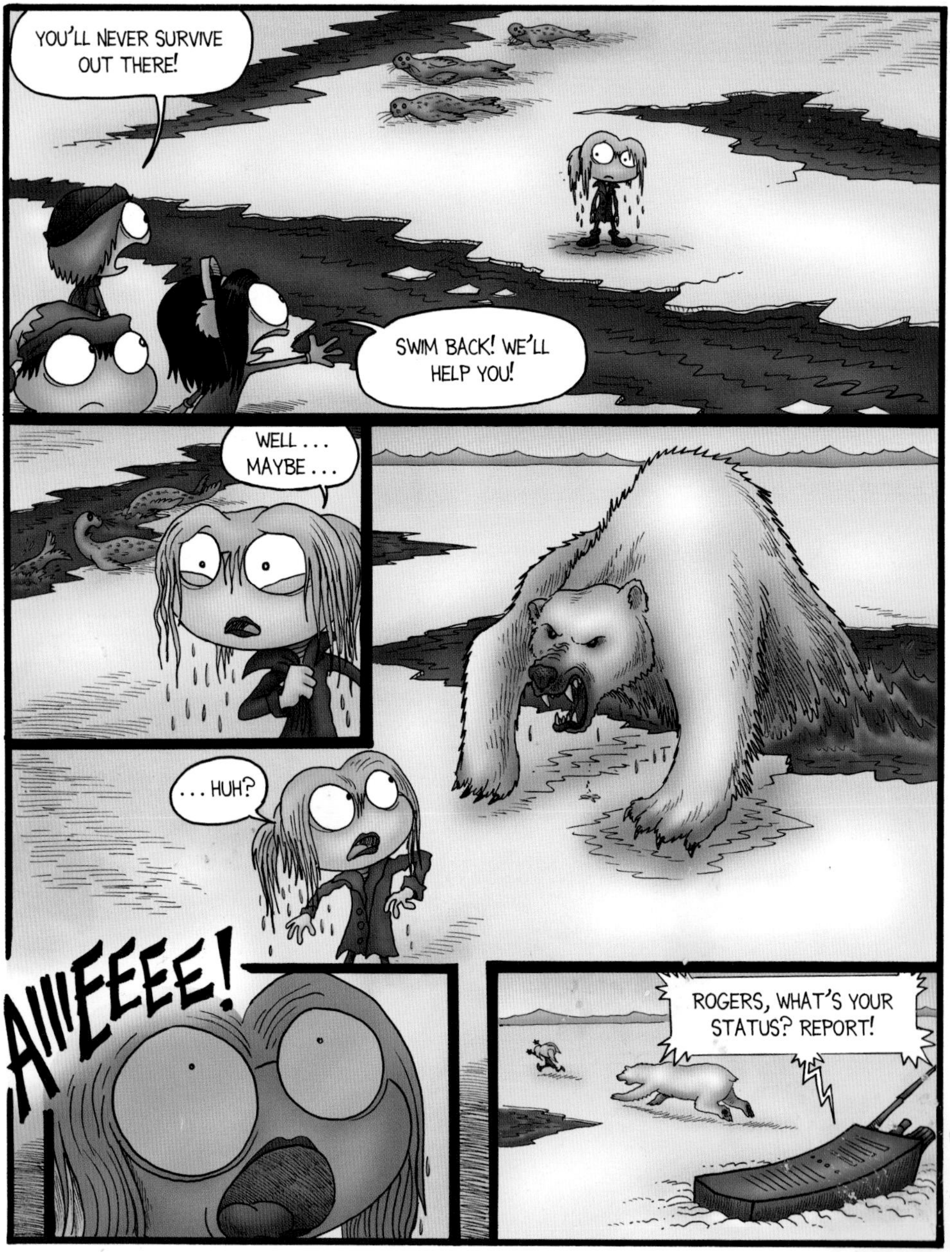

YOU'LL NEVER SURVIVE OUT THERE!
SWIM BACK! WE'LL HELP YOU!
WELL . . . MAYBE . . .
. . . HUH?
AIIIEEEE!
ROGERS, WHAT'S YOUR STATUS? REPORT!

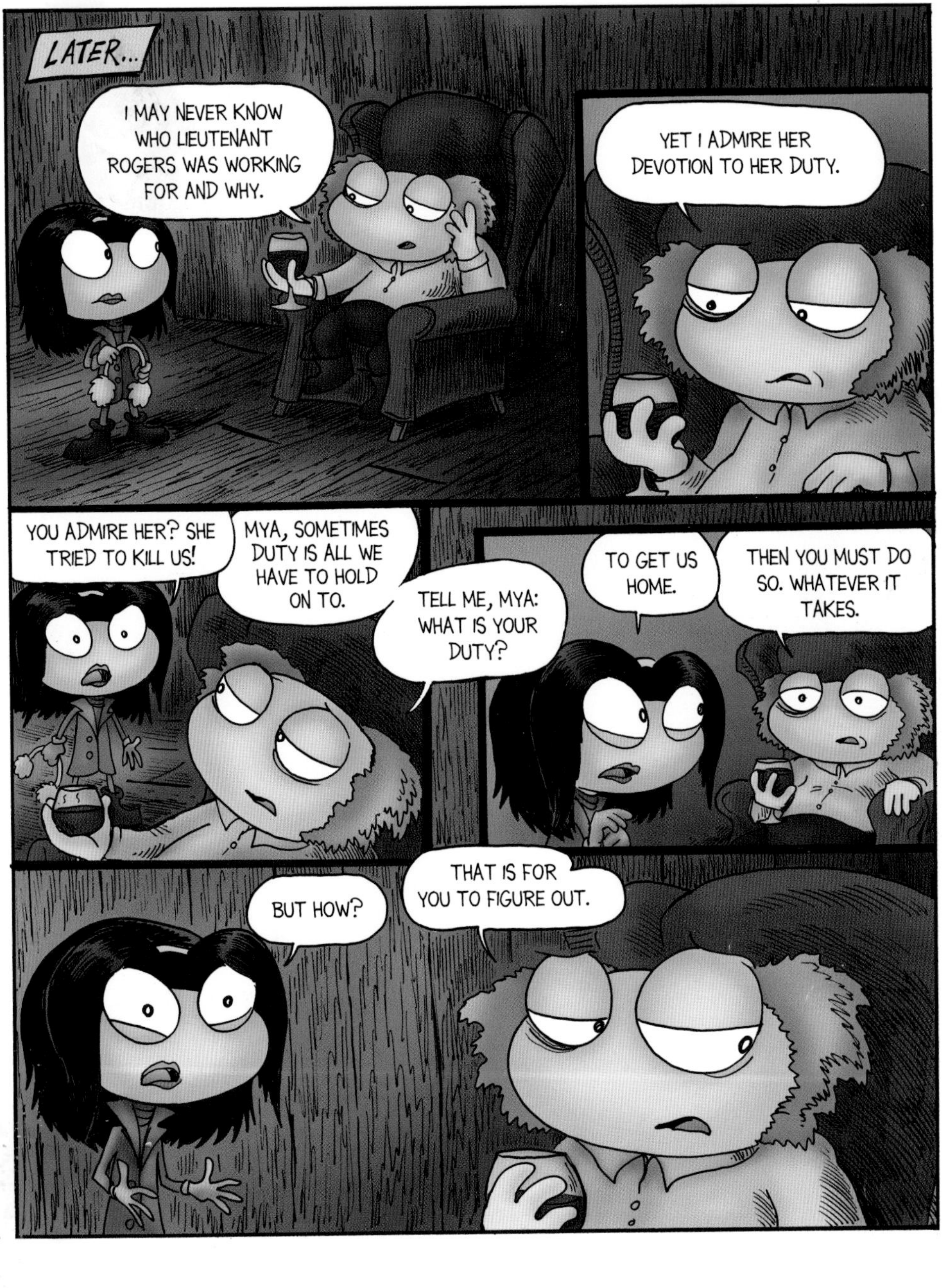
LATER...
I MAY NEVER KNOW WHO LIEUTENANT ROGERS WAS WORKING FOR AND WHY.
YET I ADMIRE HER DEVOTION TO HER DUTY.
YOU ADMIRE HER? SHE TRIED TO KILL US!
MYA, SOMETIMES DUTY IS ALL WE HAVE TO HOLD ON TO.
TELL ME, MYA: WHAT IS YOUR DUTY?
TO GET US HOME.
THEN YOU MUST DO SO. WHATEVER IT TAKES.
BUT HOW?
THAT IS FOR YOU TO FIGURE OUT.

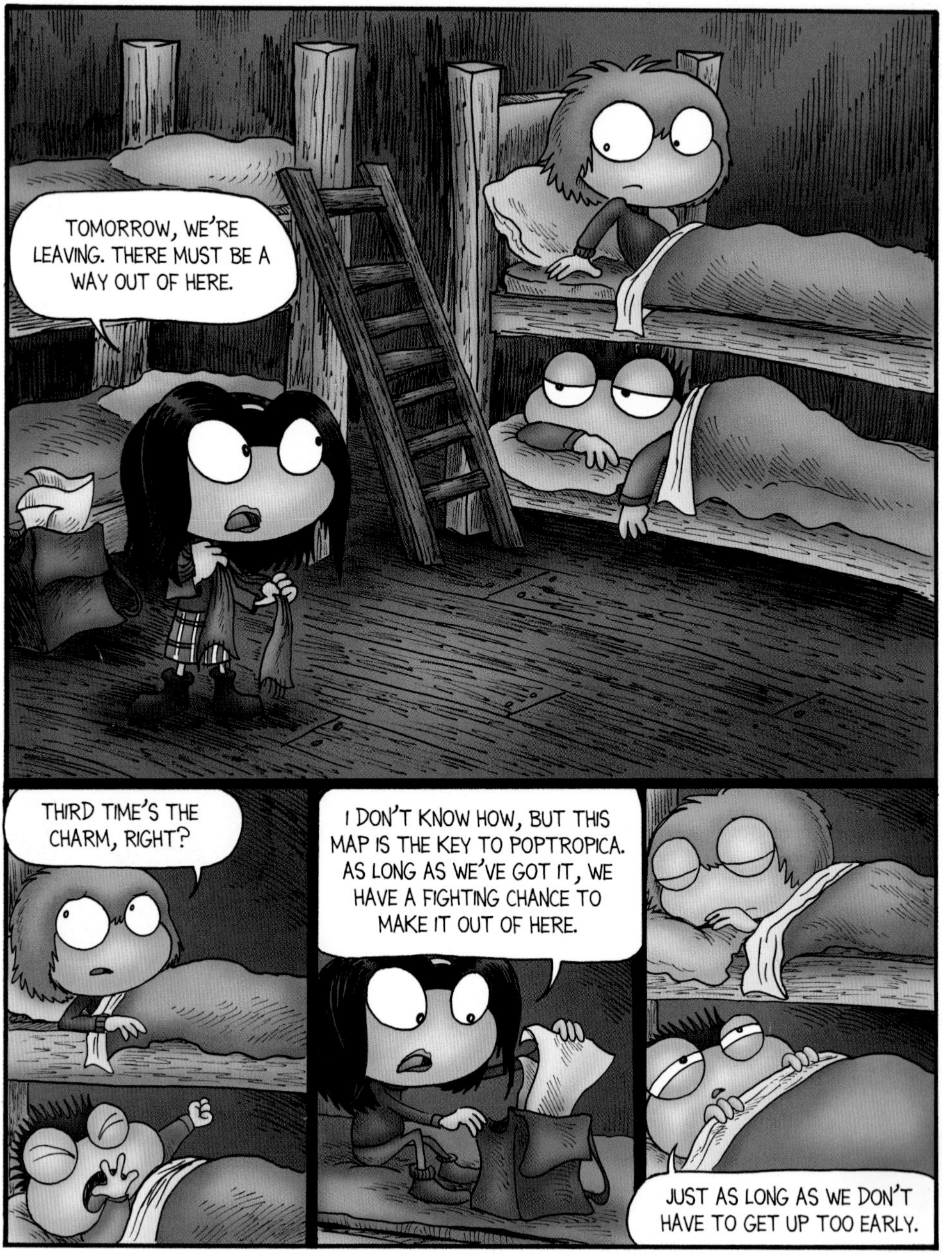
TOMORROW, WE'RE LEAVING. THERE MUST BE A WAY OUT OF HERE.
THIRD TIME'S THE CHARM, RIGHT?
I DON'T KNOW HOW, BUT THIS MAP IS THE KEY TO POPTROPICA. AS LONG AS WE'VE GOT IT, WE HAVE A FIGHTING CHANCE TO MAKE IT OUT OF HERE.
JUST AS LONG AS WE DON'T HAVE TO GET UP TOO EARLY.

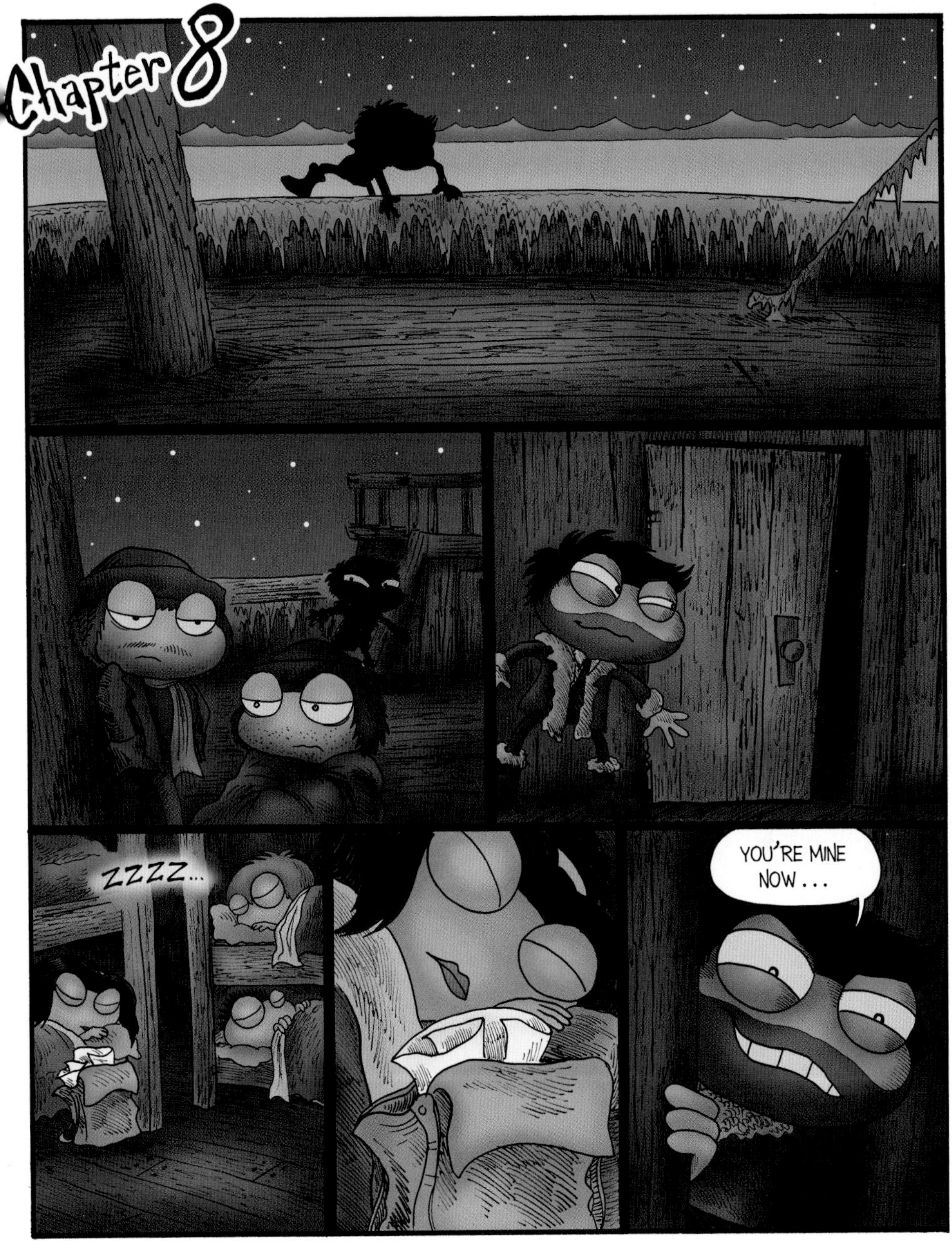
Chapter 8
ZZZZ...
YOU'RE MINE NOW . . .

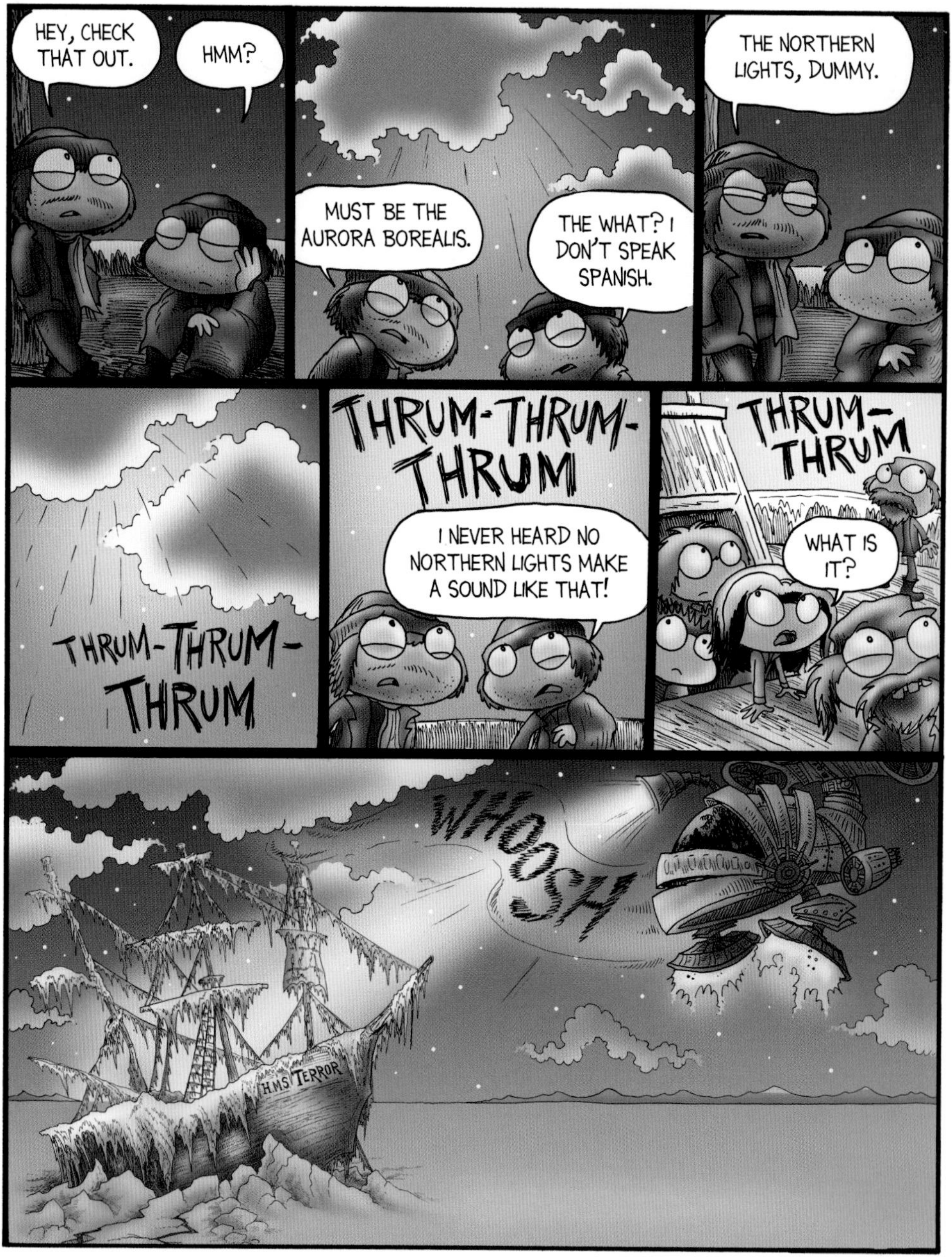
HEY, CHECK THAT OUT.
HMM?
MUST BE THE AURORA BOREALIS.
THE WHAT? I DON'T SPEAK SPANISH.
THE NORTHERN LIGHTS, DUMMY.
THRUM-THRUM-THRUM
THRUM-THRUM-THRUM
I NEVER HEARD NO NORTHERN LIGHTS MAKE A SOUND LIKE THAT!
THRUM-THRUM
WHAT IS IT?
WHOOOSH
H.M.S TERROR

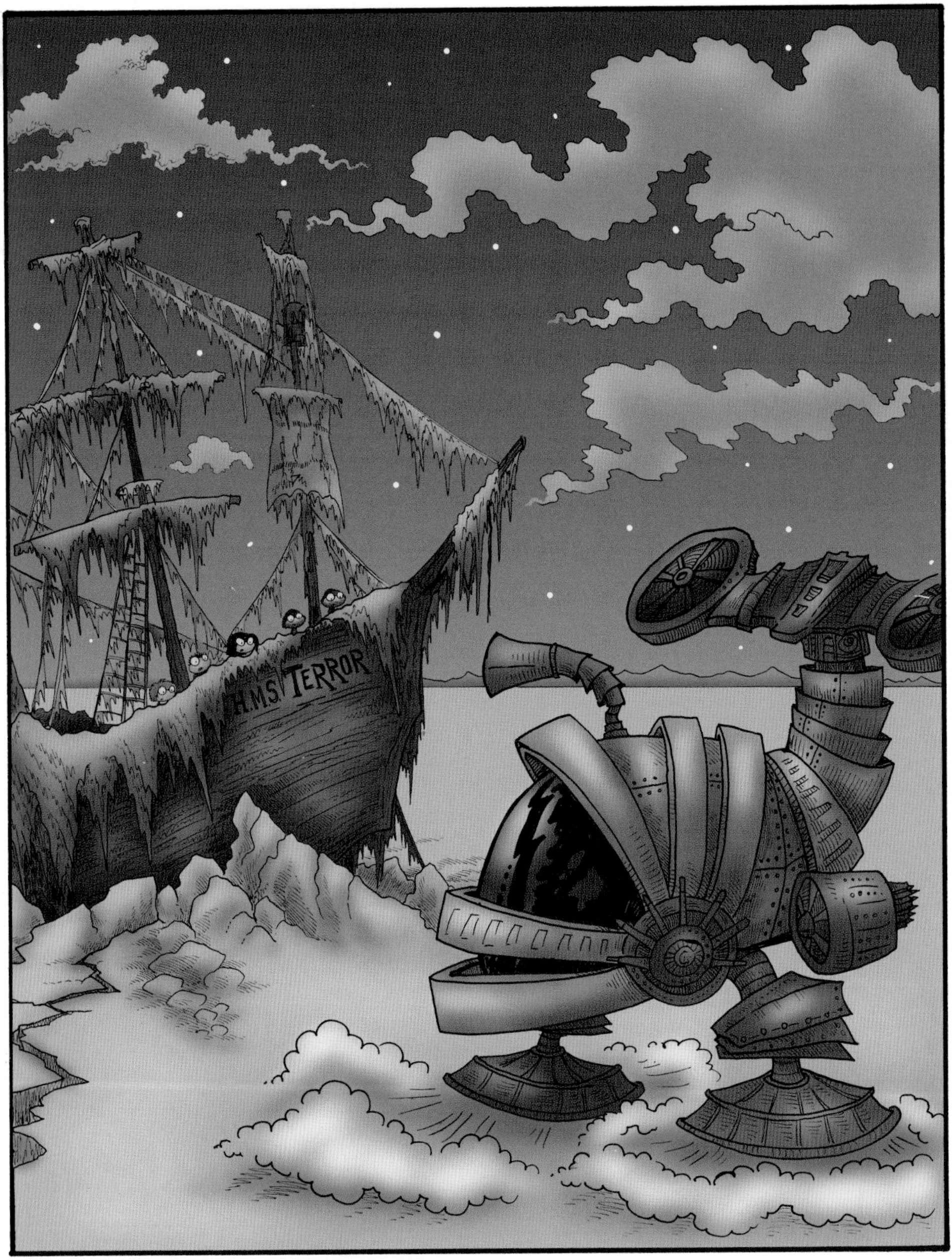
H.M.S. TERROR

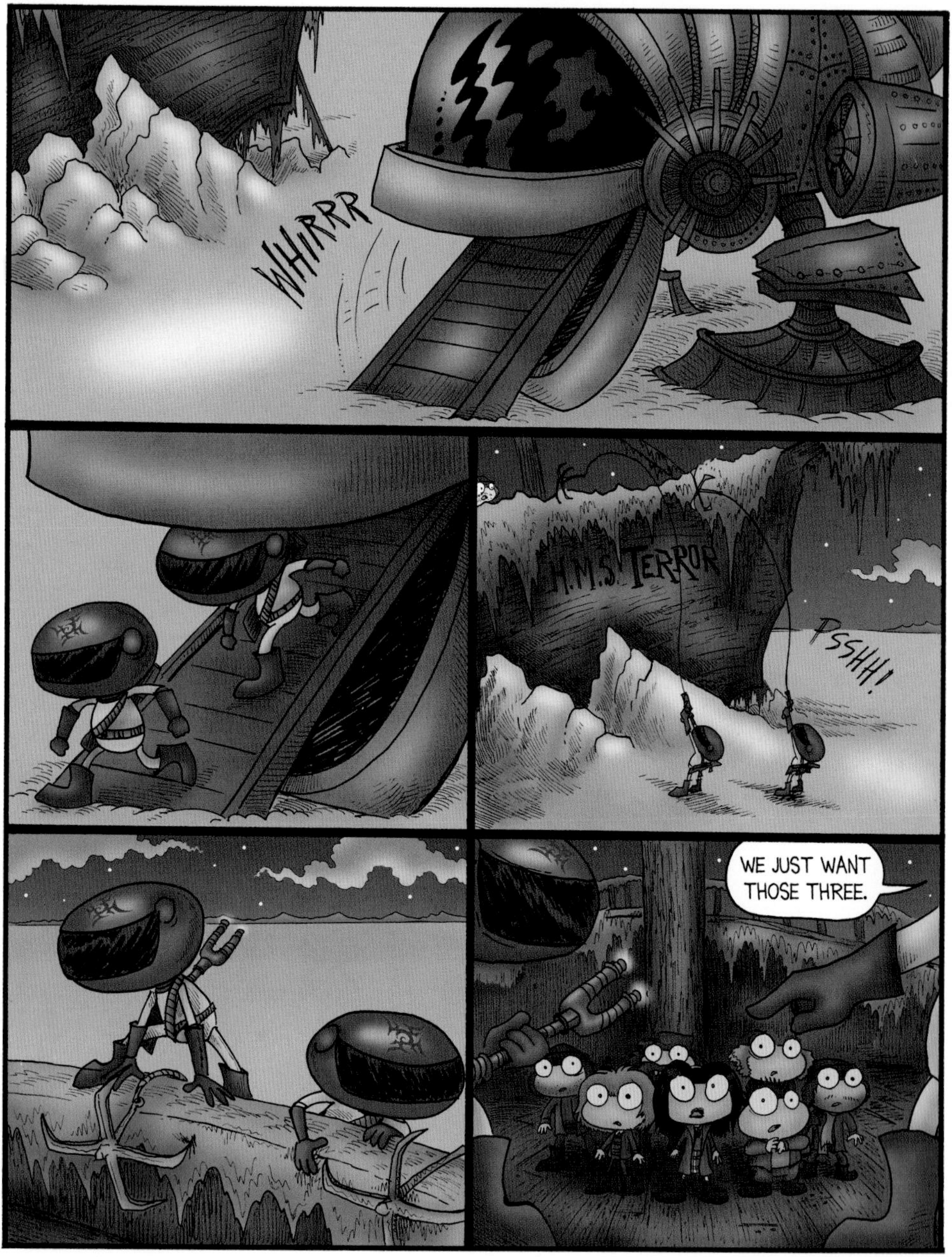
WHIRRR
H.M.S. TERROR
PSSHH!
WE JUST WANT THOSE THREE.

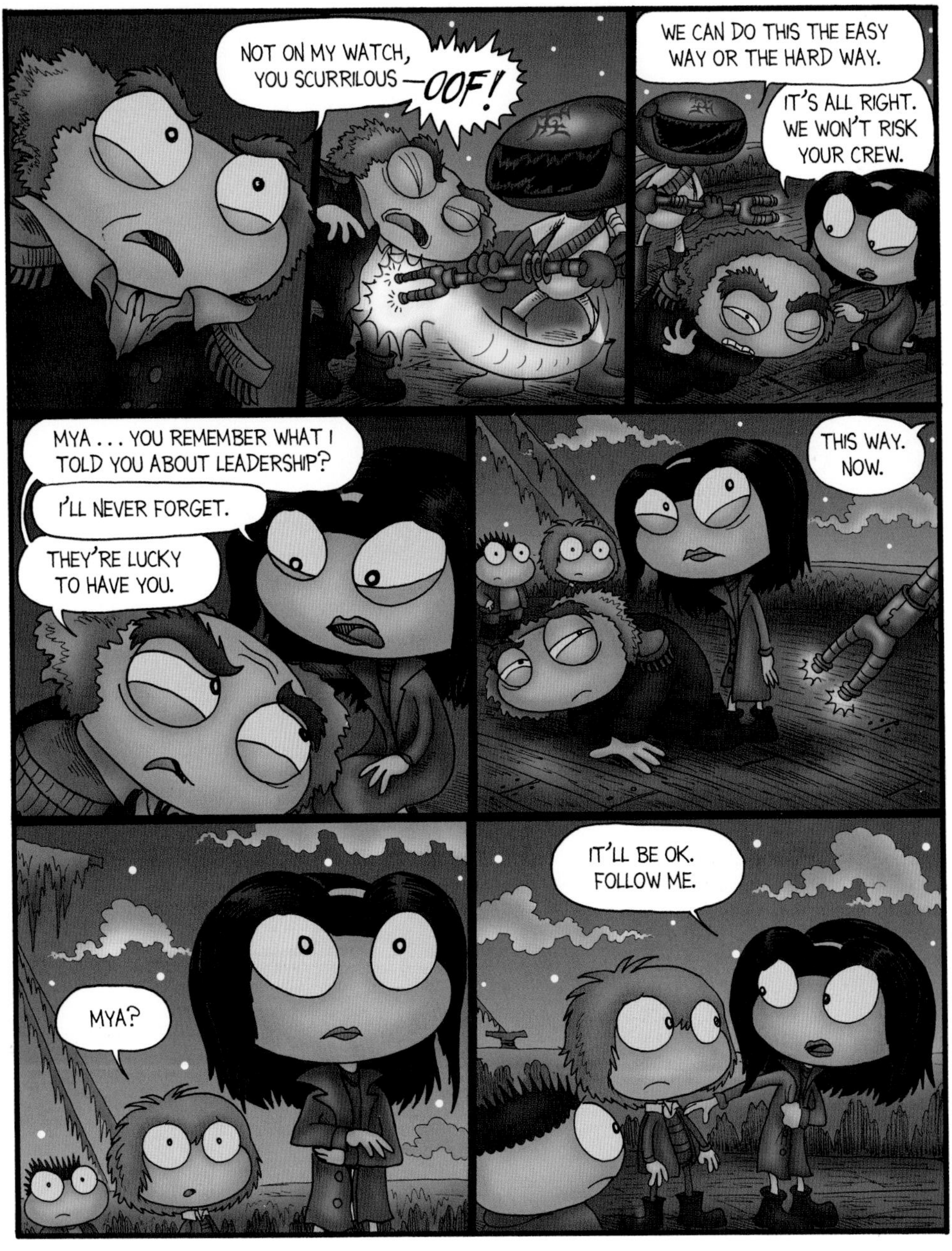
NOT ON MY WATCH, YOU SCURRILOUS —OOF!
WE CAN DO THIS THE EASY WAY OR THE HARD WAY.
IT'S ALL RIGHT. WE WON'T RISK YOUR CREW.
MYA . . . YOU REMEMBER WHAT I TOLD YOU ABOUT LEADERSHIP?
I'LL NEVER FORGET.
THEY'RE LUCKY TO HAVE YOU.
THIS WAY. NOW.
MYA?
IT'LL BE OK. FOLLOW ME.

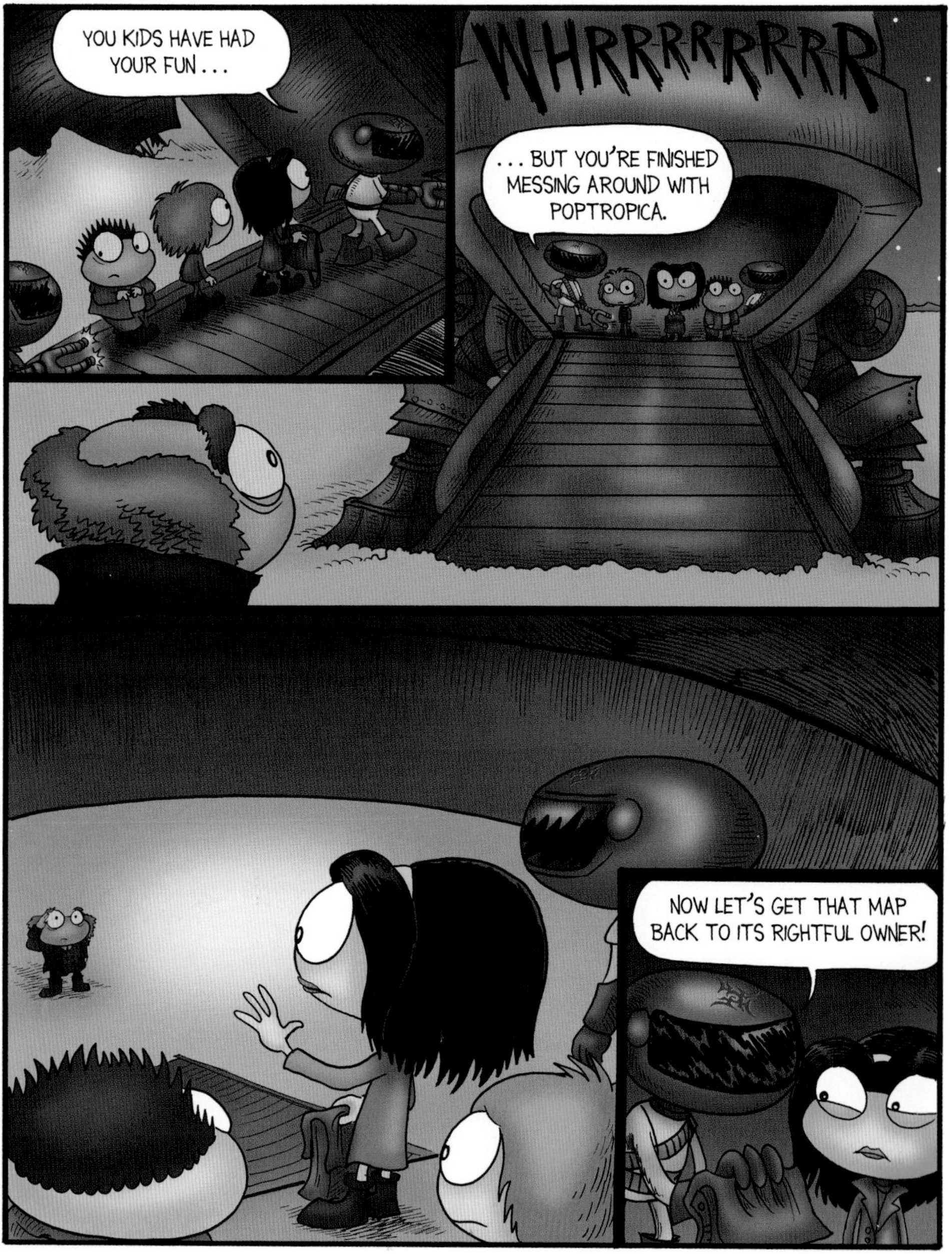
YOU KIDS HAVE HAD YOUR FUN . . .
WHRRRRRRRR
. . . BUT YOU'RE FINISHED MESSING AROUND WITH POPTROPICA.
NOW LET'S GET THAT MAP BACK TO ITS RIGHTFUL OWNER!

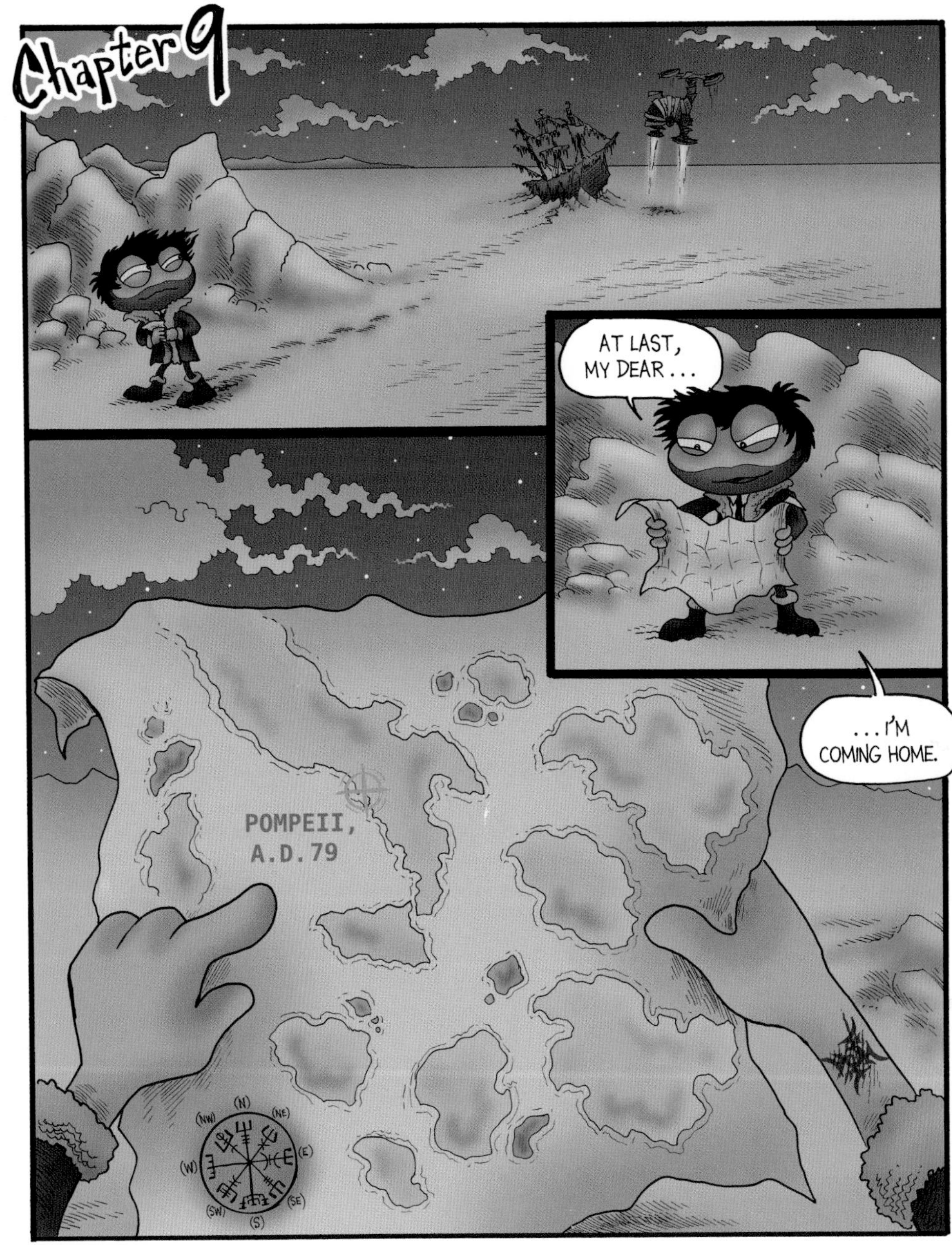
Chapter 9
AT LAST, MY DEAR . . .
. . . I'M COMING HOME.
POMPEII, A.D. 79
(N)
(NE)
(E)
(SE)
(S)
(SW)
(W)
(NW)

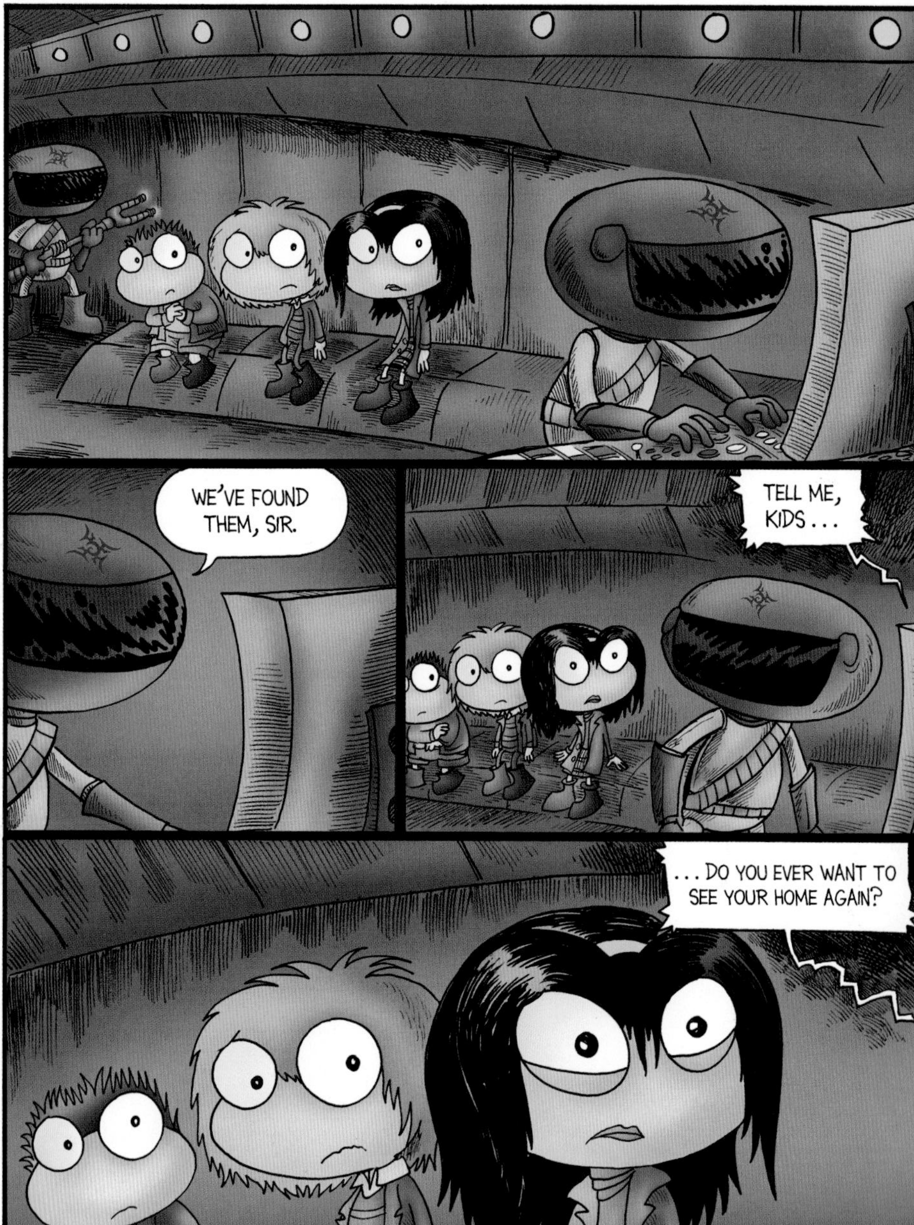
WE'VE FOUND THEM, SIR.
TELL ME, KIDS . . .
. . . DO YOU EVER WANT TO SEE YOUR HOME AGAIN?

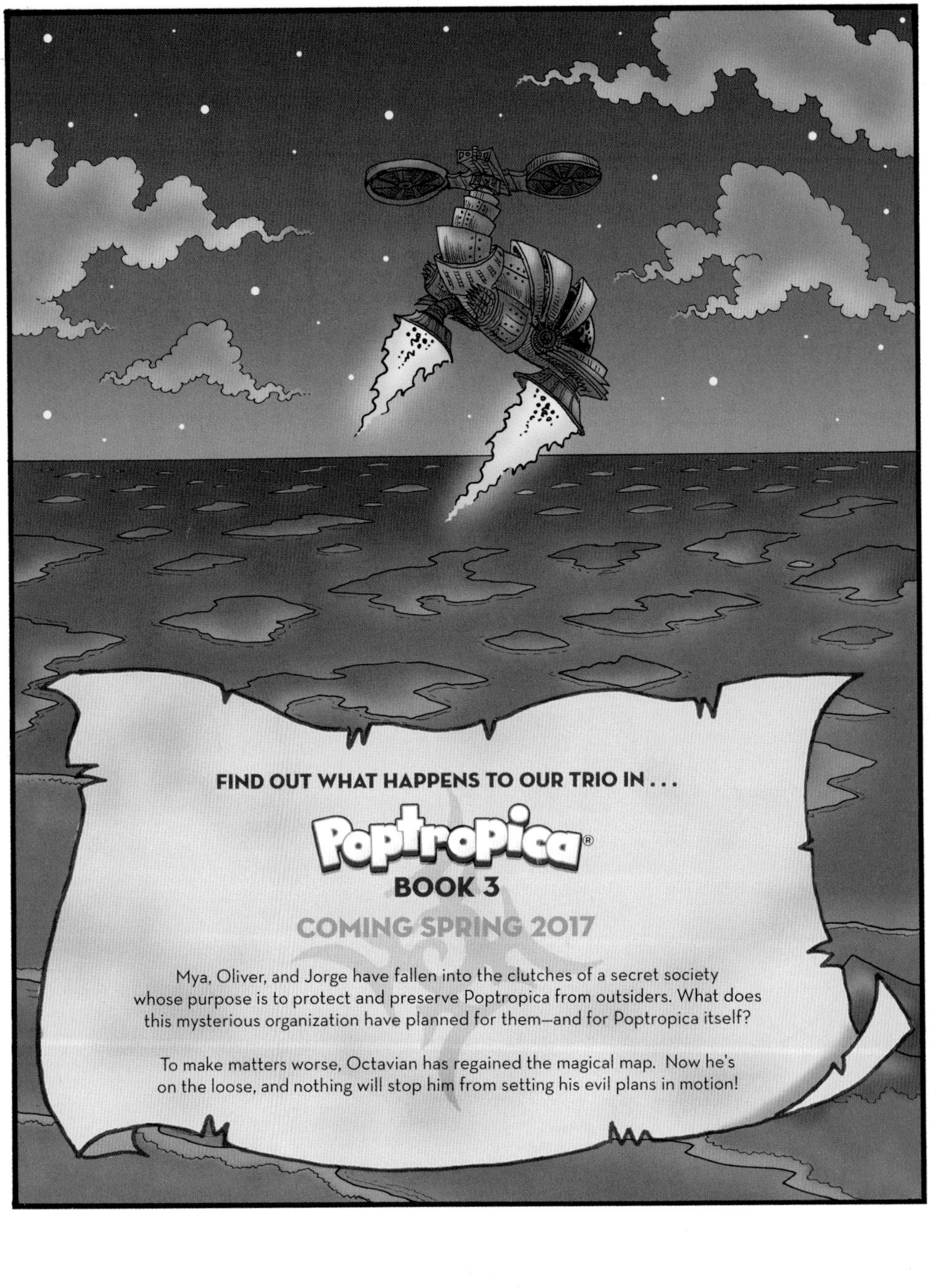
FIND OUT WHAT HAPPENS TO OUR TRIO IN . . .
Poptropica®
BOOK 3
COMING SPRING 2017
Mya, Oliver, and Jorge have fallen into the clutches of a secret society whose purpose is to protect and preserve Poptropica from outsiders. What does this mysterious organization have planned for them—and for Poptropica itself?
To make matters worse, Octavian has regained the magical map. Now he's on the loose, and nothing will stop him from setting his evil plans in motion!

THANKS TO ORLANDO DOS REIS, CHAD W. BECKERMAN,
CHARLES KOCHMAN, MICHAEL CLARK, JASON WELLS, ALISSA RUBIN,
JEFF KINNEY, AND JESS BRALLIER FOR MAKING THIS BOOK HAPPEN.
—KM

TO MRS. FINNEGAN
—MK

ABOUT THE AUTHORS

POPTROPICA is best known for its website, in which stories are shared via gaming literacy. Every month, millions of kids from around the world are entertained and informed by Poptropica's engaging quests, including those featuring Diary of a Wimpy Kid, Big Nate, Peanuts, Galactic Hot Dogs, Timmy Failure, Magic Tree House, and Charlie and the Chocolate Factory.

MITCH KRPATA is a writer and producer for the Poptropica website, and the author of the Poptropica Island Creator Kit. He has published reviews and essays in *Slate*, the *Boston Phoenix*, *Paste*, and the book *1001 Video Games You Must Play Before You Die*. Krpata lives in Massachusetts with his wife, two children, and a lazy dog.

KORY MERRITT is the co-creator of Poptropica comics. He is the illustrator of *Mystery of the Map*, and the writer/artist of *The Dreadful Fate of Jonathan York*. Merritt teaches art for kindergarten through sixth grade in Hammondsport, New York.

Library of Congress Control Number: 2016931942
ISBN: 978-1-4197-2129-8

Font designed by David Ohman and Kory Merritt • Book design by Chad W. Beckerman

Published in 2016 by Amulet Books, an imprint of ABRAMS. All rights reserved.
No portion of this book may be reproduced, stored in a retrieval system, or transmitted in any form or by any means, mechanical, electronic, photocopying, recording, or otherwise, without written permission from the publisher. Amulet Books and Amulet Paperbacks are registered trademarks of Harry N. Abrams, Inc.

Printed and bound in China
10 9 8 7 6 5 4 3 2 1

Amulet Books are available at special discounts when purchased in quantity for premiums and promotions as well as fundraising or educational use. Special editions can also be created to specification. For details, contact specialsales@abramsbooks.com or the address below.

ABRAMS The Art of Books
115 West 18th Street, New York, NY 10011
abramsbooks.com

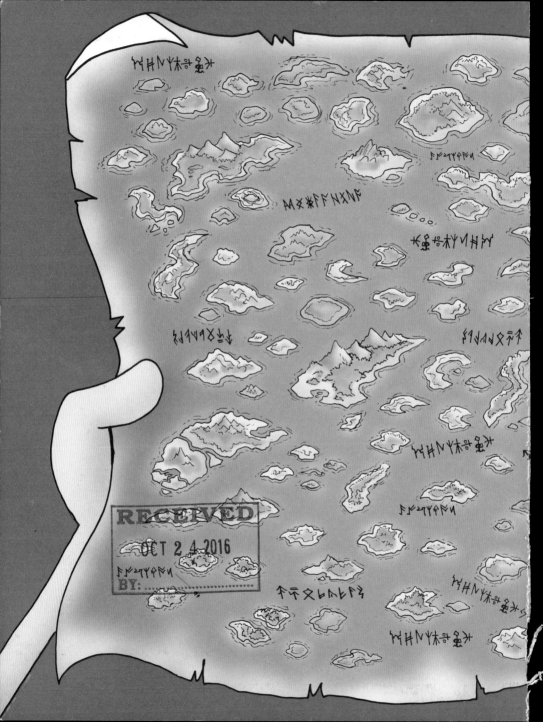